SWEET PLEASURE'S ABANDON . . .

He rolled her onto her back. He kissed her neck, her shoulders, her mouth again. Only when she was quivering with need did he move away from her.

Jamie opened her eyes and looked into his. Alec was the most frighteningly appealing man she'd ever encountered. The moonlight hadn't softened his features. He looked hard . . . and determined.

"Have you decided to stop then?" she whispered.

"Do you want me to?" he asked.

She didn't know how to answer him. Yes, she told herself, of course she wanted him to stop. A bride must have a proper wedding bed, shouldn't she? "Not yet."

She hadn't realized she'd said that until he smiled at her. "You confuse me, Alec. I don't know my own thoughts when you're touching me like this. Maybe we should stop . . ."

"Not yet . . ."

PRAISE FOR JULIE GARWOOD'S
THE LION'S LADY

Books by Julie Garwood

Gentle Warrior
Rebellious Desire
Honor's Splendor
The Lion's Lady
The Bride
Guardian Angel
The Gift
The Prize
The Secret
Castles
Saving Grace
Prince Charming
For the Roses

Published by POCKET BOOKS

JULIE GARWOOD

The Bride

POCKET BOOKS

New York   London   Toronto   Sydney   Tokyo   Singapore

An *Original* Publication of POCKET BOOKS

POCKET BOOKS, a division of Simon & Schuster Inc.
1230 Avenue of the Americas, New York, NY 10020

ISBN: 0-671-00351-8

First Pocket Books printing July 1989

20 19 18 17 16 15

POCKET and colophon are registered trademarks of Simon & Schuster Inc.

Printed in the U.S.A.

The Bride

Prologue

Scotland, 1100

The deathwatch was over.

Alec Kincaid's woman was finally being laid to rest. The weather was foul, as foul as the expressions on the faces of those few clan members gathered around the burial sight atop the stark ridge.

It was unholy ground Helena Louise Kincaid was being placed in, for the new bride of the mighty chieftain had taken her own life and was therefore doomed to a resting place outside the true Christian cemetery. The church wouldn't allow a body with a sure mortal sin to reside inside the blessed ground. A black soul was like a bad apple, the church leaders supposed, and the thought of one rotten soul staining the pure ones was too grave a possibility to ignore.

Hard rain spit down on the clansmen. The body, wrapped in the Kincaid red, black, and heather-colored plaid, was dripping wet and awkwardly weighty when settled inside the fresh pine box. Alec Kincaid saw to the task alone, allowing no other to touch his dead wife.

The old priest, Father Murdock, stood a respectable distance away from the others. He didn't look at all comfort-

1

able with the lack of proper ceremony. There weren't any prayers to cover death by suicide. And what solace could he possibly offer the mourners when one and all knew Helena was already on her way to hell? The church had decreed her sorry fate. Eternity by fire was the only penalty for suicide.

It hasn't been easy for me. I stand beside the priest, my expression as solemn as those of the other clan members. I also offer a prayer, though not for Helena's benefit. No, I give the Lord my thanks because the chore is finally finished.

Helena took the longest time dying. Three whole days of agony and suspense I had to endure, and all the while praying she wouldn't open her eyes or speak the damning truth.

Kincaid's bride put me through an ordeal, dragging out the dying time. She did it just to keep me churning inside, of course. I stopped the torment when I was finally given a chance, easily snuffing the breath out of her by holding the Kincaid plaid over her face. It didn't take me long at all, and Helena, in her weakened state, didn't put up much of a fuss.

God, it was a satisfying moment. The fear of being found out made my hands sweat, yet the thrill of it sent a burst of strength down my spine at the same time.

I got away with murder! Oh, how I wish I could boast of my cunning. I cannot say a word, of course, and I dare not let my joy show in my gaze.

I turn my attention to Alec Kincaid now. Helena's husband stands by the gaping hole in the ground. His hands are fisted at his sides and his head is bowed. I wonder if he's angry or saddened by his bride's sinful death. It's difficult to know what's going on inside his mind, for he always keeps his emotions carefully masked.

It doesn't matter to me what the Kincaid is feeling now. He'll get over her death, given the passage of time. And time is what I need, too, before I challenge him for my rightful place.

The priest suddenly coughs, a racking, aching sound that turns my attention back to him. He looks as though he wants to weep. I stare at him until he regains his composure. Then he begins to shake his head. I now know what he's thinking. The thought is there, on his face, for everyone to see.

The Kincaid woman has shamed them all.

God help me, I must not laugh.

Chapter One

England, 1102

They said he killed his first wife.

Papa said maybe she needed killing. It was a most unfortunate remark for a father to make in front of his daughters, and Baron Jamison realized his blunder as soon as the words were out of his mouth. He was, of course, immediately made sorry for blurting out his unkind comment.

Three of his four daughters had already taken to heart the foul gossip about Alec Kincaid. They didn't much care for their father's view on the atrocity, either. The baron's twins, Agnes and Alice, wept loudly and, as was their particularly irritating habit, in unison as well, while their usually sweet-tempered sister Mary marched a brisk path around the oblong table in the great hall, where their confused father sat slumped over a goblet of guilt-soothing ale. In between the twins' noisy choruses of outrage, his gentle little Mary interjected one sinful tattle after another she'd heard about the Highland warrior who would be arriving at their home in a paltry week's time.

Mary, deliberately or nay, was stirring the twins into a full

4

lather of snorting and screeching. It was enough to try the patience of the devil himself.

Papa tried to give the Scotsman his full defense. Since he'd never actually met the warrior, or heard anything but ill, unrepeatable rumors about the man's black character, he was therefore forced to make up all his favorable remarks.

And all for naught.

Aye, it was wasted effort on his part, for his daughters weren't paying the least attention to what he was saying. That shouldn't have surprised him, he realized with a grunt and a good belch; his angels never listened to his opinions.

The baron was terribly inept at soothing his daughters when they were in a state, a fact that hadn't particularly bothered him until today. Now however, he felt it most important to gain the upper hand. He didn't want to look the fool in front of his uninvited guests, be they Scots or nay, and fool he'd certainly be called if his daughters continued to ignore his instructions.

After downing a third gulp of ale, the baron summoned up a bit of gumption. He slammed his fist down on the wooden table as an attention-getter, then announced that all this talk about the Scotsman being a murderer was nonsense.

When that statement didn't get any reaction or notice, his irritation got the better of him. All right, then, he decided, if all the gossip turned true, then mayhap the Scotsman's wife had been deserving of the foul deed. It had probably just started out as a proper thrashing, he speculated, and as things had a way of doing, the beating had gotten a wee bit out of hand.

That explanation made perfectly good sense to Baron Jamison. His comments gained him an attentive audience, too, but the incredulous looks on his daughters' faces weren't the result he'd hoped to accomplish. His precious angels stared at him in horror, as if they'd just spotted a giant leech hanging off the tip of his nose. They thought him daft, he suddenly realized. The baron's weak temper exploded full measure then, and he bellowed that the sorry woman had probably sassed her lord back once too often. It was a lesson that his disrespectful daughters would do well to take to heart.

The baron had only meant to put the fear of God and father into his daughters. He knew he'd failed in the extreme when the twins started shouting again. The sound made his head ache. He cupped his hands over his ears to block out the grating noise, then closed his eyes against the hot glare Mary was giving him. The baron actually slumped lower in his chair, until his knobby knees were scraping the floor. His head was bent, his gumption gone, and in desperation, he turned to his faithful servant, Herman, and ordered him to fetch his youngest daughter.

The gray-haired servant looked relieved by the order, nodding several times before shuffling out of the room to do his lord's bidding. The baron could have sworn on the Holy Cross that he heard the servant mutter under his breath that it was high time that order was given.

A scant ten minutes elapsed before the baron's namesake walked into the middle of the chaos. Baron Jamison immediately straightened in his chair. After giving Herman a good glare to let him know he'd heard his whispered criticism, he let go of his scowl. And when he turned to watch his youngest, he let out a long sigh of relief.

His Jamie would take charge.

Baron Jamison realized he was smiling now, then admitted to himself that it just wasn't possible to stay sour when his Jamie was near.

She was such a bewitching sight, so pleasing to look upon, in fact, that a man could forget all his worries. Her presence was as commanding as her beauty, too. Jamie had been endowed with her mama's handsome looks. She had long raven-colored hair, violet eyes that reminded her papa of springtime, and skin as flawless and pure as her heart.

Although the baron boasted of loving all his daughters, in secret, Jamie was his pride and joy. It was a most amazing fact, considering he wasn't her true blood father. Jamie's mother was the baron's second wife. She had come to him when she was nearly full term with her daughter. The man who'd fathered Jamie had died in battle, a bare month after wedding and bedding his bride.

The baron had accepted the infant as his own, forbidding anyone to refer to her as his stepdaughter. From the moment he'd first held her in his arms, she had belonged to him.

Jamie was the youngest and the most magnificent of his angels. The twins, and Mary as well, were gifted with a quiet beauty, the kind that grew on a man with time and notice, but his dear little Jamie, with just one look, could fairly knock the wind out of a man. Her smile had been known to nudge a knight clear off his mount, or so her papa liked to exaggerate to his friends.

Yet there was no petty jealousy among his girls. Agnes, Alice, and Mary instinctively turned to their little sister for guidance in all matters of significance. They leaned on her almost as often as their papa did.

Jamie was now the true mistress of their home. Since the day of her mama's burial, his youngest had taken on that burden. She'd proven her value early, and the baron, liking order but having no gift for establishing it, had been most relieved to give Jamie full responsibility.

She never disappointed him. Jamie was such a sensible, untroubling daughter. She never cried, either, not since the day her mama passed on. Agnes and Alice would have done well to learn from their sister's disciplined nature, the baron thought. They tended to cry over just about everything. To his mind, their looks saved them from being completely worthless, but still he pitied the lords who would someday be saddled with his emotional daughters.

The baron worried most for his Mary. Though he never voiced the criticism, he knew she was a might more selfish than was considered fashionable. She put her own wants above those of her sisters. The bigger sin, however, was putting herself above her papa.

Aye, Mary was a worry, and a mischief-maker, too. She liked to plow up trouble just for the sheer joy of it. The baron had a nagging suspicion that Jamie was giving Mary unladylike ideas, but he never dared voice that notion, lest he be proven wrong, and fall from grace in his youngest's eyes.

Yet even though Jamie was his favorite, the baron wasn't completely oblivious to her flaws. Her temper, though seldom unleashed, could ignite a forest fire. She had a stubborn crook in her nature, too. She had inherited her mama's skill for healing, even though he'd specifically forbidden that practice. Nay, the baron wasn't pleased with that inclination, for the serfs and the house servants were constantly pulling her away from her primary duty of seeing to his comforts. Jamie was dragged out of her bed during the middle of the night quite frequently to patch up a knife wound or ease a new life into the world. The baron didn't particularly mind the nighttime calls, as he was usually sleeping quite soundly in his own bed and was therefore not inconvenienced, but he took grave exception to the daytime interruptions, especially when he had to wait for his dinner because his daughter was busy tending the injured or sick.

That thought made him sigh with regret. Then he realized the twins had quit their screeching. Jamie had already quieted the storm. Baron Jamison motioned to his steward to refill his goblet and leaned back to watch his daughter continue to weave her magic.

Agnes, Alice, and Mary had rushed over to their sister the moment she entered the room. Each was trying to tell a different version of the story.

Jamie couldn't make any sense out of their comments. "Come and sit with Papa at the table," she suggested in her husky voice. "Then we shall sort through this new problem like a family," she added with a coaxing smile.

"'Tis more than a mere problem this time," Alice wailed, mopping at the corners of her eyes. "I don't think this can be sorted out, Jamie. Truly I don't."

"Papa's done it this time," Agnes muttered. The younger twin dragged out one of the stools from under the table, sat down, and gave her father a fierce glare. "As usual, this is all his fault."

"This trickery ain't my doing," the baron whined. "So

you can quit your frowning at me, missy. I'm obeying my king's command, and that be that."

"Papa, please don't get yourself upset," Jamie cautioned. She reached over to pat her father's hand. Then she turned to Mary. "You seem to be the most in control. Agnes, quit your whimpering so I may hear what has happened. Mary, will you please explain?"

"'Tis the missive from King Henry," Mary answered. She paused to brush a lock of pale brown hair over her shoulder, then folded her hands on the tabletop. "It seems our king is most upset with Papa again."

"Upset? Mary, he's bloody furious," Alice interjected.

Mary nodded before continuing. "Papa didn't send in his taxes," she announced with a frown in her father's direction. "The king is making an example of our papa."

In unison the twins turned to add their glares.

Jamie let out a weary sigh. "Please go on, Mary," she requested. "I would hear all of this."

"Well, since King Henry has married that Scottish princess . . . What is her name, Alice?"

"Matilda."

"Yes, Matilda. Lord, how could I forget the name of our queen?"

"'Tis simple enough for me to understand how you could forget," Agnes said. "Papa's never taken us to court and we've never had a single really important visitor. We're as isolated as lepers out here in the middle of nowhere."

"Agnes, you're straying from our topic," Jamie announced. Her voice was strained with impatience. "Mary, do go on."

"Well, King Henry seems to think we must all be wed to Scots," Mary stated.

Alice shook her head. "Nay, Mary. He doesn't want all of us wed to Scots. Just one of us. And the barbarian gets to pick from the lot of us. God help me, it's so humiliating."

"Humiliating? Whoever is chosen will certainly be going to her death, Alice. If the man killed one wife, he's bound to kill another. And that, sister, is a little more than just humiliating," Mary pronounced.

"What?" Jamie gasped out, clearly appalled by such talk.

Alice ignored Jamie's outburst. "*I* heard his first wife killed herself," she interjected.

"Papa, how could you?" Mary shouted her question. She looked as if she wanted to strike her father, for her face was flushed and her hands were clenched. "You knew the king would be angry with you for not paying your taxes. Did you not think of the repercussions then?"

"Alice, will you please lower your voice? Shouting won't change this situation," Jamie said. "We all know how forgetful Papa can be. Why, he probably just forgot to send in the tax money. Isn't that the way of it, Papa?"

"A bit of the way of it, my angel," the baron hedged.

"Oh, my God. He spent the coins," Alice said with a groan.

Jamie raised her hand for silence. "Mary, finish this explanation before *I* start shouting."

"You must understand, Jamie, how difficult it is for us to be reasonable in the face of this atrocity. I shall, however, endeavor to be strong, and explain it in full to you, for I can see how puzzled you are."

Mary took her time straightening her shoulders. Jamie felt like shaking her, so thin had her patience worn. She knew it wouldn't do her cause any good, though, for Mary liked to drag out her comments, no matter what the circumstances. "And?" Jamie prodded.

"As I understand this, a barbarian from the Highlands is coming here next week. He's going to choose one of the three of us—Agnes, Alice, or me—to be his second wife. He killed his first wife, you see. You aren't included in this, Jamie. Papa said we were the only ones named in the king's letter."

"I'm certain he didn't kill his first wife," Alice said. "Cook says the woman killed herself." Alice crossed herself.

Agnes shook her head. "No. I believe the woman was murdered. Surely she wouldn't kill herself and spend eternity in hell, no matter how terrible her husband was to her."

"Could she have died by accident, do you suppose?" Alice suggested.

"The Scots are known to be clumsy," Mary said with a shrug of her shoulders.

"And you're known to believe every bit of gossip you hear," Jamie interjected in a hard voice. "Explain what you mean by 'choosing,' Mary," she added, trying to keep her expression from showing how horrified she was.

"Choose for his bride, of course. Haven't you been listening, Jamie? We have no say in the matter, and our own contracts for marriages are all set aside until the selection has been made."

"We're to be paraded in front of the monster like horses," Agnes whimpered.

"Oh, I almost forgot," Mary rushed out. "The Scottish king, Edgar, is also in favor of this marriage, Jamie. Papa said so."

"So the lord might only be doing the bidding of his king and might not want the marriage either," Alice said.

"Oh, Lord, I hadn't thought of that," Agnes blurted out. "If he doesn't want to be wed, he'll probably kill his bride before he even reaches his home, wherever in God's name that is."

"Agnes, will you calm yourself? You're screaming again," Jamie muttered. "You're going to pull your hair out of your scalp if you keep tugging on it so. Besides, you cannot know if you speak truth or fancy about the circumstances of his first wife's death."

"His name is Kincaid, Jamie, and he is a murderer. Papa said he beat his first wife to death," Agnes advised.

"I said no such thing," the baron shouted. "I merely suggested—"

"Emmett told us he threw his bride over a cliff," Mary interjected. She drummed her fingertips on the tabletop while she waited for Jamie's reaction.

"Emmett's only a groom and a lazy one at that," Jamie returned. "Why would you be listening to his stories?"

Jamie took a deep breath, hoping to calm her queasy stomach. Although she fought against it, her sisters' fear was becoming contagious. She could feel a shiver pass down her spine. She knew better than to voice her concern, though. Bedlam would erupt again.

Her trusting sisters were all staring at her with such hopeful, expectant looks on their faces. They'd just put the problem in her lap and now waited for her to come up with a solution.

Jamie didn't want to fail them. "Papa? Is there some way you can placate our king? Can you still send the taxes to him, perhaps adding a bit more to soothe his temper?"

Baron Jamison shook his head. "I'd have to collect the whole tax all over again. You know as well as I that the serfs' backs are near to broken with their own troubles. The barley crop wasn't good, either. Nay, Jamie, I cannot demand again."

Jamie nodded. She tried to hide her disappointment. She'd hoped there was still a little of the collection left, but her father's answer confirmed her fear that it was all gone.

"Emmett said Papa used up all the coins," Mary whispered.

"Emmett is just like an old woman carrying tales," Jamie countered.

"Aye," their father agreed. "He's always been one to taint the truth. Pay no attention to his rantings," he added.

"Papa? Why was I excluded?" Jamie asked. "Did the king forget you had four daughters?"

"No, no," the baron rushed out. He hastily turned his gaze from his daughter to his goblet, for he feared his youngest would see the truth in his eyes. King Henry hadn't excluded Jamie. He'd used the word "daughters" in his message. Baron Jamison, knowing he'd never be able to get along without his youngest taking care of him, had made the decision himself to exclude her. He thought his plan was most cunning. "The king named only Maudie's daughters," he announced.

"Well, that certainly doesn't make any sense to me," Agnes remarked between sniffles.

"Perhaps it's because Jamie's the youngest," Mary suggested. She shrugged, then added, "Who can know what's in our king's mind? Just be thankful, Jamie, that you weren't included in his order. Why, if you were chosen you couldn't marry your Andrew."

"That's the reason," Agnes interjected. "Baron Andrew is so powerful and well liked. He told us so. He must have swayed our king's mind. Everyone knows how smitten Andrew is with you, Jamie."

"That could be the reason," Jamie whispered. "If Andrew is as powerful as he says he is."

"I don't think Jamie really wants to marry Andrew," Mary told the twins. "You needn't frown at me, Jamie. I don't think you even like him very much."

"Papa likes him," Agnes said. She gave her father another glare before adding, "I wager it's because Andrew has promised to live here so Jamie can continue to slave for—"

"Now, Agnes, please don't start that again," Jamie begged.

"Why you think it's sinful of me to want to keep Jamie here after her marriage is beyond me," the baron muttered.

"Everything seems to be beyond you," Mary murmured.

"Watch what you say, young lady," he returned. "I'll not allow you to speak so disrespectful like in front of me."

"I know the true reason," Alice said, "and I'm going to tell Jamie. Andrew paid Papa your dowry, sister, and he—"

"What say you?" Jamie shouted. She nearly leapt out of her chair. "Alice, you're mistaken. Knights do not give a dowry. Papa, you didn't take any coins from Andrew, did you?"

Baron Jamison didn't answer his daughter. He seemed quite taken by the task of swirling his ale in his cup.

His silence was damning.

"Oh, God," Mary whispered. "Alice, do you realize what you're suggesting? If what you're telling us is true, then our father has all but sold Jamie to Baron Andrew."

"Now, Mary, don't be getting Jamie riled up," their papa advised.

"I didn't say he sold Jamie to Andrew," Alice said.

"You did so," Mary countered.

"I saw Andrew give Papa a cloth bag full of gold coins." Jamie's head was pounding. She was determined to get to the bottom of this coin exchange, no matter how long it took or how much her head hurt. Sold indeed! The very idea made her stomach turn. "Papa, you didn't really take coins for me, did you?" she asked. She couldn't keep the fear out of her tone.

"No, of course not, my angel."

"Papa? Do you know you call us your angels only when you've done something shameful?" Agnes wailed. "God's truth, I'm beginning to hate that endearment."

"I saw Andrew give Papa the coins, I tell you," Alice shouted.

"I'm just wondering how you could have known what was inside the cloth bag," Mary argued. "Do you have the sight, do you suppose?"

"He dropped the bag," Alice snapped. "Some of the coins fell out."

"It was just a little loan," their father bellowed to get their attention. "Now hush this talk about selling my baby."

Jamie's shoulders slumped with relief. "There, you see, Alice? It was just a loan Andrew was giving Papa. You had me worrying for naught. Can we return to our original problem now?"

"Papa's back to looking guilty again," Mary advised.

"Of course Papa looks guilty," Jamie said. "You needn't rub salt in his wound. I'm sure he's sorry enough as it is."

Baron Jamison smiled at his daughter for defending him. "That's my good little angel," he praised. "Now, then, Jamie, I want you to stay hidden when the Scotsmen arrive. No sense tempting them with what they can't be having."

The baron didn't realize his blunder until Alice seized on his remark. "Scotsmen, Papa? You speak of more than one. Do you mean to tell us this demon named Kincaid is bringing others with him?"

"He's probably just bringing his family to witness the marriage," Agnes suggested to her twin.

"Is that the full of it?" Jamie asked her father. She tried to concentrate on the problem at hand, but her thoughts kept returning to the gold coins. Why would her father accept a loan from Andrew?

The baron took his time answering.

"Papa, I have the feeling there's more you'd like to tell us," Jamie coaxed.

"Good God, you mean there's more?" Mary bellowed.

"Papa, what else are you keeping from us?" Alice shouted.

"Spit it out, Papa," Agnes demanded.

Jamie motioned for silence again. The urge to grab hold of her father's gray tunic and shake him into speaking nearly overwhelmed her. She could feel her temper boiling. "May I read this missive from our king?" she asked.

"We really should have learned how to read and scribble when Jamie's mama began her instructions," Agnes remarked with a weary sigh.

"Nonsense," Agnes scoffed. "No gentle lady needs such instruction. What we really should have done was learn how to speak that God-awful Gaelic language like Jamie," she announced. "You know I mean no offense, Jamie," she hastened to add when she caught her sister's frown. "'Tis the truth I wish I'd learned it with you. Beak did offer to teach all of us," she ended.

"It gave our stable master pleasure to teach me," Jamie said. "And Mama was amused. She was bedridden for such a long while before she died."

"Do you mean to tell me this monster from the Highlands cannot speak our language?" Agnes whimpered before bursting into tears.

Jamie might have been able to control her anger if Agnes hadn't started weeping. "What difference will it make, Agnes?" she blurted out. "The man's going to kill his bride, not talk to her."

"So you believe the rumor is true?" Mary gasped.

"No," Jamie answered, immediately contrite. "I was just jesting." She closed her eyes, said a quick prayer for patience, then turned to Agnes. "It was most unkind of me to get you upset, sister, and I do apologize."

"I would certainly hope so," Agnes cried.

"Papa, let Jamie look at this missive," Mary suddenly demanded.

"No," the baron blurted out. He immediately softened

his tone, lest his angels become suspicious of his true motives. "You needn't bother, Jamie. 'Tis simple to tell. There be two Scots coming week next, and two brides going home with them."

Needless to say, the baron's daughters didn't take this added news well. The twins started howling with as much indignation as sleeping babies who'd been pinched awake.

"I'm going to run away," Mary shouted.

"It would seem to me," Jamie began in a voice meant to penetrate the noise, "that we must immediately form a plan to dissuade your suitors."

Agnes stopped bellowing in mid-scream. "Plan? What are you thinking?"

"I have thought of a deceitful plan and I'm almost afraid to mention it, but your welfare is at issue and so I'll tell you that if I were the one doing the selecting, I'd certainly stay away from any contender who was . . . afflicted in some way."

A slow grin transformed Mary's face. She was always the quickest to catch Jamie's thoughts, especially when they were of a devious nature. "Or so ugly as to be painful to look upon," she said with a nod. Her brown eyes sparkled with mischief. "Agnes, you and Alice may be afflicted. I'm going to be fat and ugly."

"Afflicted?" Alice asked, clearly puzzled. "Do you understand what she means, Agnes?"

Agnes started to laugh. Her nose was red from rubbing and her cheeks were raw from her tears, yet when she smiled, she looked very pretty. "A dread disease, I do believe. We must eat berries, sister. The rash will only last a few hours, so we must time this well."

"Now I see," Alice said. "We'll make the dull-witted Scots think we always have terrible lumps on our faces."

"I shall drool," Agnes announced with a haughty nod, "and scratch until they think I'm infested with vile creatures."

The four sisters laughed over that picture. Papa took heart. He smiled at his angels. "There. Do you see, now? I told you it would work out." He hadn't said any such thing, of course, but that fact didn't bother him at all. "I shall go and have my morning lie-down while you continue with your plans." Baron Jamison couldn't leave the hall fast enough.

"These Scots might not care what you look like," Jamie advised, worrying now that she might have given her sisters false hope.

"We can only pray they're shallow," Mary returned.

"Is deceiving them a sin?" Alice asked.

"Of course," Mary answered.

"We'd best not confess to Father Charles," Agnes whispered. "He'll give us another month of penance. Besides, we're deceiving Scots, if you'll remember. God will certainly understand."

Jamie left her sisters and went to talk to the stable master. Beak, as he was affectionately called by his friends because of his large hawklike nose, was an elderly man who had long ago become Jamie's confidant. She trusted him completely. He never carried her thoughts to others. He was wise in his years, too. He'd taught her all the skills he thought she'd need. In truth, she was more of a son than daughter to him.

They disagreed only when it came to the topic of Baron Jamison. The stable master had made it quite clear that he didn't hold with the way the baron treated his youngest daughter. Since Jamie was content, she couldn't understand why Beak would feel this way. As they could not agree, they carefully avoided the issue of her father's character.

Jamie waited until Beak had sent Emmett out of the stable on an errand, then told him the full story. Beak rubbed his jaw again and again during the telling, a sure indication he was giving the matter his full attention.

"This is really all my fault," Jamie confessed.

"How do you figure that?" Beak asked.

"I should have seen to the collection of taxes," Jamie explained. "Now my dear sisters will have to pay the price for my laziness."

"Laziness, my arse," Beak muttered. "The only chores you ain't responsible for are the taxes and the keeping of the watch, my girl. You're half dead from the work you do. God forgive me for ever teaching you anything. If I hadn't shown you how to ride like the best of them and how to hunt like the best of them, you'd not be acting like the best of them. You're a fair lady, Jamie, but you've taken on the chores of a knight. 'Tis I who am to blame."

Jamie wasn't at all fooled by his forlorn expression. She laughed right in his face. "Many a time you've boasted of my abilities, Beak. You're proud of me and that's that."

"I am proud of you," Beak said with a grunt. "Still, I'll not be listening to you blame yourself for your father's sins."

"Now, Beak . . ."

"You say you ain't included in this wife-bidding?" Beak asked. "Don't you think that's a mite odd?"

"I do think it's odd, but our king must have his reasons. It isn't my place to question his decisions."

"Did you happen to look at this missive, Jamie? Did you read it?"

"No, Papa didn't want me to bother with it," Jamie answered. "Beak, what are you thinking? You've got that mean look in your eyes all of a sudden."

"I'm thinking your papa's up to something," Beak admitted. "Something shameful. I've known your papa a mite longer than you have, girl. Remember who trailed after your mama when she wed the baron. I was wise to your father's ways afore you could walk. Now I'm telling you your papa's up to something."

"Papa accepted me as his own," Jamie said. "Mama always told me it didn't matter spit to him that he wasn't my blood father. Please don't forget that kindness, Beak. Papa's a good man."

"Aye, he treated you fair by calling you daughter, but that don't change the facts none."

At that moment the groom, Emmett, came strolling back into the stables. Jamie, knowing the groom's habit of listening in on others' conversations, immediately switched to Gaelic so their talk would continue to be private. "Your loyalty is suspect," she whispered, shaking her head.

"Spit! I'm loyal to you. No one else gives a holler about

18

your future. Now, quit looking so disgruntled and tell this old man when my fellow Scotsmen will be arriving."

Jamie knew Beak was deliberately edging the conversation away from her father and was thankful. "One week's time, Beak. I must stay hidden away like a prisoner while they're here. Papa thinks it would be for the better if they don't see me, though I don't understand why. It's going to be difficult, too, what with my duties to be seen to each day. Who will do the hunting for our supper? How long do you think they'll be staying, Beak? Most likely a week, don't you suppose? I'll have to salt more pork if—"

"I hope they stay a month," Beak interrupted. "You'll get a needed rest," he predicted. "Jamie, I've said it afore and I'll be saying it again. You're digging yourself into an early grave, working from sunup to sunset. I worry about you, lass. I can still remember the young days, afore your mama took ill, God rest her soul. You were no bigger than a gnat, but a hell-raiser all the same. Remember that time I had to climb up the outside of the tower to fetch you down? You screamed my name over and over, you did. And me afeared of heights so shamefully I puked up my supper as soon as I got you down? You'd tied a flimsy rope betwixt the two towers, thinking you could walk across real nimble like."

Jamie smiled over the memory. "I remember you swatted my backside. I couldn't sit down for two days."

"But you denied to your papa that I struck you, didn't you, Jamie, guessing I'd get into trouble?"

"You would have gotten into trouble," Jamie announced.

Beak laughed. "So you got yourself another good swat from your mama. She wouldn't have punished you none if she'd known I'd already seen to your discipline."

"You saved me from sure death that time," Jamie admitted.

"I've saved you more than once and that's the truth of it."

"It was a long time ago," Jamie reminded him, her smile gentle. "I'm all grown up now. I've many responsibilities. Even Andrew understands the way of it, Beak. Why can't you?"

He wasn't about to touch that hot poker. Beak knew he'd hurt her feelings if he told her what he really thought about her Andrew. Although he'd only had the misfortune of meeting Baron Fancy Figure Andrew once, it had been quite enough for him to judge the man's spineless character. Andrew's mind was as tight as his britches. All he had time to think about was himself. God's truth, every time Beak thought about his precious Jamie saddled with such a weakling, his stomach turned sour.

"You're needing a strong man, lass. Aside from me, of course, I don't rightly know if you've ever met up with any real men. And you've still got a wee streak of wildness inside you. You're wanting to be free, whether you realize it or not."

"You're exaggerating, Beak. I'm not wild, not anymore."

"Think I haven't seen you standing on your mare's back while she races through the south meadow, Jamie? I'm sorry I ever taught you that trick. You dare the devil every once in a while, don't you?"

"Beak, you've been watching me?"

"Someone has to keep an eye on you."

Jamie let out a soft sigh, then turned the topic back to the Scotsmen. Beak let her have her way. He hoped that by listening to her talk out her worries, he was in some small measure easing her burden.

When she took her leave to return to her tasks, Beak's mind was reeling with new possibilities.

Baron Jamison was weaving a deception, all right; Beak would have staked his life on it. Well, he wasn't going to let his lord get away with it.

Beak determined to become Jamie's savior. First, however, he'd have to measure these Scots. If one turned out to be a true God-fearing, woman-caring man, then Beak vowed he'd find a way to take the lord aside and tell him Baron Jamison didn't have three daughters; he had four.

Aye, Beak would try to save Jamie from her sorry fate. God willing, he'd set her free.

* * *

THE BRIDE

The priest, Murdock, has just told us that Alec Kincaid will be coming home with an English bride. There are scowls aplenty, but they aren't because our laird has remarried. Nay, the anger is because his bride is English. Alec simply obeys the order of his king, others say in his defense. Still others wonder aloud how their laird can stomach the task.

God, I hope he falls in love with her. 'Tis too much to ask my Maker now, for Alec is as set against the English as the rest of us.

Still . . . it would make the kill so much sweeter.

Chapter Two

Alec Kincaid was in a hurry to get home. He'd honored King Edgar's request and stayed in London for nearly a month's time, studying the ways of the English court system and learning all he could about England's unpredictable king. In truth, Alec had little liking for the duty. He found the English barons a pretentious lot, their ladies dull-witted and painfully weak-spirited, and their leader, Henry, a little too soft in most of his decisions. Alec always gave a man his due, however, and therefore grudgingly admitted there had been a time or two when he'd been downright impressed with King Henry's spurts of brutality. He had given swift punishment to those foolish barons who'd been proved guilty of treason.

Although Alec hadn't complained about the duty, he was still thankful it was done. As laird over his own large clan of followers, he felt his many responsibilities pressing down on him. His domain in the rugged Highlands was probably in chaos now, what with the Campbells and the MacDonalds at it again, and God only knew what other problems he'd find waiting on his doorstep.

Now there was a further delay. Damn if he didn't have to stop along the way to get married.

Alec considered his marriage to the unknown English-woman a minor inconvenience, nothing more. He would wed the woman to please King Edgar. She would do the same by order from King Henry, of course, for that was the way of things in these advanced days, since the two leaders had formed a tenuous bond with each other.

Henry had specifically requested that Alec Kincaid be one of the lairds ordered to take an English bride. Both Alec and Edgar knew why Henry had made that special request. It was an undisputed fact that the Kincaid, though one of the youngest lairds in all of Scotland, was a power to be reckoned with. He was chieftain over approximately eight hundred fierce warriors by last year's count, but that number would be doubled if he called up his trusted allies.

The Kincaid's skill in battle was a whispered legend in England, a shouted boast in the Highlands.

Henry also knew that Alec didn't particularly like the English. He mentioned to Edgar his hope that the marriage would soften the powerful laird's attitude. Perhaps, Henry suggested, in time, harmony would be achieved.

Edgar was far more astute than Henry believed, however. He suspected Henry wanted to sway Alec's loyalty toward England.

Both Alec and his leader were highly amused by Henry's naiveté. Edgar was Henry's vassal, aye, since the day he'd knelt at the feet of the king of England and given his pledge. He'd also been raised in the English court. Still, he was king of Scotland, and his loyal clansmen came before all others . . . especially outsiders.

Henry obviously didn't understand the bond of blood ties. Both Edgar and Alec believed England's king saw only the possibility of another strong ally in his back pocket. He'd misjudged the Kincaid, though, for Alec would never turn his back on Scotland or her king, no matter what the incentives.

Daniel, Alec's friend since childhood days, and soon to be named laird over the neighboring clan Ferguson, had also been ordered to take an English bride. Daniel, too, had spent a tiring month in London. He'd found the duty as unpleasant as Alec had, and was just as anxious to get home.

Both warriors had ridden at a furious pace since dawn, pausing only twice to rest their mounts. They fully expected to spend little more than an hour or two at Jamison's holding. That would surely be time enough, they'd reasoned, to eat a full supper, choose their brides, marry them if there was a priest in residence, and then be on their way.

They didn't want to spend another night on English soil. It mattered not if their brides had other inclinations. The women were simply property, after all, and neither Daniel nor Alec considered the wants of a bride significant in the least.

They would do as they were told, and that was that.

It was Alec who won the privilege of taking first choice by tossing the caber farther afield than his friend. In truth, however, neither man had cared enough to give the feat of strength his all.

Aye, it was an errand they were completing, and a damn nuisance to be sure.

The devil and his disciple arrived at Baron Jamison's holding three days ahead of schedule.

Beak was the first to catch sight of the Scottish warlords, the first to give them those fitting names. He was sitting on the top rung of the ladder used to reach the loft, thinking to himself that it was time he had a proper snooze, for it was getting on high afternoon, after all, and he'd been working steadily in the warm spring sun without letup since his nooning meal. Still and all, Lady Mary had dragged her sister, Jamie, off to the south meadow and he really should chase after them just to make certain they weren't getting into mischief. When Jamie was nagged into putting her chores aside, the streak of wildness sometimes got the better of her nature. It was a fact that she became too uninhibited for her own good, Beak thought. Yet another reason she needed a strong man to watch over her. Why, his sweet Jamie could talk a thief out of his stealings if her mind was set on the task, and God only knew what troubles she'd talked Mary into stirring up.

Just thinking about all the possibilities sent a shiver down Beak's spine. Yes, he'd have to go after the wild pair, all right.

He let out a loud yawn and started down the ladder. He was on the second rail from the top when he spotted the two giants riding toward him.

Beak almost lost his balance. He knew his mouth gaped open just like a baby sparrow's waiting on food from his mama, but Beak couldn't seem to get it closed tight. He stopped himself from making a hasty sign of the cross, though, and was thankful the warriors couldn't possibly hear his knees knocking together when he finally managed the rest of the climb down.

He could feel his heart slamming inside his chest. Beak reminded himself he had Scottish blood running through his veins, though it came from his ancestors in the civilized Lowlands. He also tried to remember he'd never been caught judging a man solely on his appearance. Neither reminder soothed his initial reaction to the giants watching him so intently.

Beak started shivering. He excused his cowardice by telling himself he was just an ordinary man, he was, and the sight of these two warriors would give the apostles goosebumps.

The one Beak thought of as the disciple was tall and burly with wide shoulders, hair the color of rusty nails, and green-as-the-ocean eyes. The man had grim wrinkles at the corners of those chilling eyes, too.

The disciple was a big man, aye, yet seemed puny in comparison to the other.

The one Beak thought of as the devil had hair as bronze as his skin. He was a good head taller than his companion and had not a bit of softening fat on his unforgiving Herculean frame. When Beak stumbled forward to get a better look at his face, he immediately wished he hadn't made the effort.

There was a bleak coldness there, lurking in those brown eyes. That gaze could frost a summer bed of clover, Beak thought with growing despair.

So much for his foolish plan to save his Jamie. Beak decided he'd go to hell cheering like a happy man before he let either of these two barbarians near her.

"My name's Beak and I'm stable master here," he finally blurted out, hoping to give the impression there were other stablemen about so they'd think him important enough to converse with. "You're early," he added with a nervous nod. "Else the family would be lined up outside in their finery waiting to give you a proper greeting."

Beak paused for air, then waited for a reply to his remarks. His wait proved to be in vain and his eagerness quickly evaporated. He soon began to feel as important as a flea about to be swatted. It was unnerving, the way the two giants continued to stare down at him.

The stable master decided to try again. "I'll see to your mounts, milords, while you make your presence known to the household."

"We take care of our horses, old man."

It was the disciple who'd made that statement. His voice wasn't particularly pleasant, either. Beak nodded, then backed up several spaces to get out of their way. He watched the lords remove their saddles, listened as each spoke a word of praise in Gaelic to his mount. Their animals were handsome stallions, one brown, the other black, and Beak took notice that neither animal had a flaw . . . or a strap mark on its hind flanks.

A glimmer of hope was rekindled inside Beak's mind. He'd learned a long time ago that a man's true character could be discovered by the way he treated his mama and his horse. Baron Andrew's mount was riddled with deep lashings and if that wasn't proof enough that his theory was true, Beak didn't know what was.

"Have you left your soldiers waiting outside the walls, then?" Beak asked, speaking in Gaelic so they'd know he was friend, not foe.

The disciple looked pleased with his effort, for he actually smiled at the stable master. "We ride alone."

"All the way from London?" Beak asked, unable to keep the surprise out of his voice.

"Aye," the lord answered.

"With no one seeing to your backsides?"

"We don't need anyone else seeing to our protection," the lord answered. "That's an English inclination, not ours. Isn't that right, Kincaid?"

The devil didn't bother to answer.

"By what names are you called, milords?" Beak asked. It was a bold question he dared to ask, but the warriors weren't scowling at him any longer and that fact had given him courage.

The disciple turned the topic instead of answering. "You speak our language well, Beak. Are you Scottish, then?"

Beak's shoulders straightened with pride. "I am, with red hair afore it turned gray on me head."

"My name's Daniel, of the clan Ferguson. He's called Alec by those who know him well enough," he added with a nod toward the other warrior. "Alec is chieftain over the clan Kincaid."

Beak made a formal bow. "It's my humble pleasure to make your acquaintance," he announced. "I haven't spoken to a full-blooded Scotsman in so many years I've forgotten how to act," he added with a grin. "Forgot how big the Highlanders are, too. You gave me quite a start when I first spotted you, you did."

He opened the doors to two clean stalls adjacent to the entrance, saw to the feeding buckets, the water as well, and then tried to engage the two men in further conversation.

"'Tis the truth you're three days early," he said. "I'm thinking to myself the household will be in an uproar."

Neither lord commented on that remark, but Beak could tell by the way they glanced at each other that they did not particularly care if they caused any disruption.

"Who were you expecting if not us?" Lord Daniel ~ frowning over his question.

Beak was puzzled by the question. "Expecting? No one, leastwise not for three more days."

"The drawbridge was down, man, and not a single watch in sight. Surely—"

"Ah, that," Beak said with a long-drawn-out sigh. "Well, it's true the bridge is down most of the time and there never is a watch posted. You see now, Baron Jamison is a mite forgetful."

When he saw the incredulous looks on the warriors' faces, Beak thought he really should try to give his master some defense. "Being out here in the middle of nowheres like we are, we're never bothered. The baron says he doesn't have much of value to be snatched away," he said with a shrug. "And no one's ever come inside without a proper invite."

"Nothing of value?"

Alec Kincaid had finally spoken. His voice had been soft, yet surprisingly forceful at the same time. And when he turned to give Beak his full attention, the old man's knees started shaking again.

"He does have daughters, doesn't he?"

His scowl could set a fire blazing, Beak decided. He couldn't meet that gaze for long and had to stare at the tips of his boots in order to concentrate on the conversation. "He has daughters all right, more in number than he'll be wanting to admit to having, too."

"Yet he doesn't protect them?" Daniel asked. He shook his head in disbelief, then turned to Alec and said, "Have you ever heard the like?"

"Nay, I haven't."

"What kind of man is this Baron Jamison?" Daniel asked Beak.

The Kincaid answered his question. "An Englishman, Daniel."

"Ah, that does explain it, doesn't it?" Daniel remarked dryly. "Tell me this, Beak. Are the baron's daughters so unsightly there be no need for protection? Are they without virtue?"

"They're all pretty," Beak answered. "And every single one of them as pure as the day she was born. Strike me dead

28

if that ain't the truth. 'Tis their father who shirks his duty," Beak added with a scowl.

"How many daughters are there?" Daniel asked. "We never bothered to ask your king."

"You'll be seeing three," Beak muttered.

He was about to expound on his remark when both warriors turned and started for the door.

It was now or never, Beak determined. He took a deep, settling breath, then called out, "Are you both mighty lairds over your clans or is one more powerful than the other?"

Alec caught the fear in the stable master's voice. It puzzled him enough to turn back to the man. "What is the reason for such an impertinent question?"

"I mean no disrespect," Beak rushed out, "and I've good honest reasons for my question. I know I'm stepping above meself; I'm meaning to interfere. You see, someone has to look after her interests and I'm the only one who would be caring enough."

Daniel frowned over the odd explanation. It made little sense to him. "I'll become laird over my clan by right of tanistry in another year or two's time," he answered. "The Kincaid is already chieftain over his own clan. There, does that answer your question, Beak?"

"Will he have first choice in this bride-choosing then?" Beak asked Daniel.

"He will."

"And he's more powerful than you?" the stable master asked.

Daniel nodded. "For the moment," he announced with a grin. "Beak, have you never heard of the Kincaid warriors?"

"Aye, I've heard all sorts of stories."

The grimness in his tone made Daniel smile. The old man was obviously frightened of Alec. "I take it some of the stories you've heard include descriptions of Alec's methods in battle?"

"They have. I shouldn't be believing them," Beak added with a hasty glance in Alec's direction. "They were told by Englishmen, you see, and I'm sure they exaggerated the laird's . . . ruthlessness."

Daniel grinned at Alec before responding to that remark. "Oh, I doubt the stories were exaggerated in the least, Beak. Did they say he never showed mercy? Compassion?"

"Aye."

"Best believe the stories then, Beak, for they're true. Aren't they, Alec?"

"Aye, they are," Alec agreed, his tone hard.

"Beak," Daniel continued, "your questions amuse me, though I've no idea what it is you're really wanting to find out. Is there another question you'd like to put to us?"

Beak timidly nodded. He turned to stare up at Alec now. A long, silent moment passed while he tried to think of a fitting way to explain about his Jamie without being downright disloyal.

Alec could see the fear in the old man's eyes. He walked back over to stand directly in front of the stable master. "What is it you wish to say to me?"

Beak decided the Kincaid's intuition was as unsettling as his size and voice. His own voice trembled when he blurted out his question. "Have you ever mistreated a woman in all your days, Alec Kincaid?"

It was obvious the laird didn't care for that question. His expression turned as fierce as a bolt of lightning. Beak took an instinctive step back and had to steady himself by bracing his hand against the wall.

"I've been patient with you because you're Scots, old man, but if you ever put such a foul question to me again, I swear it will be your last."

Beak nodded. "I need to know, inside my heart, because I'm set on giving you a great gift and I have to know you'll recognize its value, my lord."

"He speaks in riddles," Daniel stated. He walked over to stand next to Alec. His frown, Beak noted, was almost as fierce as the Kincaid's. "You've been in England too long, old man, asking such obscene questions."

"I know I ain't making a spit of sense," Beak admitted in a forlorn tone. "Yet if I blurt out the full of it, then it would make me disloyal in my mistress's eyes. I can't have that," he added. "She'd have my hide, she would."

"You admit to being afraid of a woman?" Daniel asked.

Beak ignored the astonished look on the man's face, ignored the laughter in his voice, too. "I'm afeared of no woman. I just don't want to break my word," he explained. "The lass means the world to me. I ain't ashamed to admit I love her like a daughter."

Beak valiantly tried to meet Alec's hard stare. It was a pitiful effort, though. Oh, how he wished the other warrior were the more powerful of the two. At least the one called Daniel smiled on occasion. "Are you strong enough to protect what belongs to you?" he asked the Kincaid, wanting to get to the heart of the matter as soon as possible.

"I am."

"Baron Andrew will call forth many soldiers. He'll come after the gift I'm giving you. He's also called friend by England's King Henry," Beak added, wobbling his eyebrows to emphasize that fact.

The Kincaid didn't seem impressed with that statement. He shrugged with indifference. "It would matter not to me."

"Who is this Baron Andrew?" Daniel asked.

"An Englishman," Beak answered.

"All the better," Alec said. "If I decide to take this gift you're offering, I'll welcome a challenge from an Englishman. He'll be no threat to me."

Beak visibly relaxed. "No ifs about it," he boasted.

"Is your gift a horse perchance?" Daniel asked, shaking his head in confusion. He still didn't understand what the stable master was trying to tell Alec.

The Kincaid understood. "It isn't a horse, Daniel."

Beak grinned. The man was proving to be as astute as the best of them. "Once you see my gift, Laird Kincaid, you'll be set on having it, all right," he boasted. "Are you partial to blue eyes, milord?"

"Many have blue eyes in the Highlands, Beak," Daniel interjected.

"Well, now," Beak drawled out, "there's blue and then there's blue." He let out a loud chuckle, then cleared his throat and continued, "Now to me riddle, Laird Kincaid. Baron Jamison treats his daughters just like his horses and that's a fact. Only have a look around you and you'll get my meaning soon enough. The pretty little ladies in these three stalls are for the baron's daughters, right there for anyone to see. But if you'll walk down this long corridor and turn the bend, you'll see another stall hidden away in the far corner by the side door. It's separated from the others. That's where the baron keeps his beauty, a magnificent white pretty just waiting for a proper mating. Humor this daft old man, for I'm Scots if you'll remember, and take a good look at the horse," Beak urged, motioning the warriors forward. "It's worth your time especially, Laird Kincaid."

"He's caught my curiosity," Daniel told Alec.

Both men followed the stable master. Beak's manner changed considerably when they reached the stall. He poked a piece of straw between his front teeth, leaned against the wall with one foot casually crossed over the other, and proceeded to watch the high-strung filly put up a grand fuss when Alec reached out to stroke her. The side door was cracked open, letting the sun filter inside to cast a soft banner of light on the horse's silver mane.

The proud beauty wouldn't settle down for a good long while, but in the end, the warrior wooed her into showing a hint of her gentle nature. Beak only hoped the laird would gentle Jamie with just as much patience.

"She's a beauty, all right," Daniel remarked.

"Still half wild," Alec interjected. He actually smiled then, and Beak concluded being half wild wasn't a flaw in his mind.

"Her name's Wildfire and she's deserving of that name to be sure. The baron can't get near her. He gave her to his youngest daughter when it became evident she was the only one who could seat the horse."

Alec smiled again—a miracle, that—when the mare tried to bite his hand. "She's feisty. With a good stallion, the offspring will be sound—spirited, too."

Beak gave Alec another thorough inspection. When he met the warrior's gaze again, he was grinning. "That's exactly what I'm thinking about my gift to you."

Beak pulled away from the wall, affected an important air,

then said, "As I was telling you, Laird Kincaid, the baron treats his daughters just like his horses. Three right up front for anyone to see . . ."

He vowed he wasn't going to say another word. It was up to the Scotsman to figure the rest of the riddle.

"Beak? Are you inside?"

The interruption came from Lady Jamie. Beak was so startled he almost swallowed the piece of straw he was chewing on. "That be the youngest of the baron's daughters," he told the two warriors. "And there's the side door," he added in a soft whisper. "If you're wanting to leave now, that's the quickest way to the main house. I'd best see what my Jamie is wanting."

For his advanced years, Beak could still move with surprising speed. He rounded the corner and caught Jamie and her sister Mary in the center of the hallway.

"Were you talking to someone, Beak?" Mary asked. "I thought I heard—"

"Just having a little visit with Wildfire," Beak lied.

"Jamie said you'd be napping and we'd be able to sneak right inside and take our mounts out for another quick run," Mary confessed.

"For heaven's sake, Mary, you needn't be telling him that."

"Well, you did say—"

"Shame on you, Jamie," Beak scolded. "I never nap and you shouldn't be sneaking around anywheres." He gave her a ridiculous grin. "It ain't ladylike."

"Yes, you do nap," Jamie told him. She found his smile contagious. "You're in a fit mood today, aren't you?"

"That I am," Beak admitted. He tried to hide his eagerness, for he certainly didn't want Jamie to suspect he was up to mischief. Beak wondered if the lairds were still lingering over Wildfire. Though the warrior Kincaid couldn't see Lady Jamie, Beak knew that her voice, so soft and husky, would certainly capture his attention.

"And what are the pair of you up to this fine afternoon, I'm wondering to meself?" Beak inquired.

"We wanted to go riding," Mary said. She gave Beak a

puzzled look. "We just told you that. Are you feeling ill, Beak? Jamie, he looks flushed to me."

Jamie immediately reached up and touched Beak's forehead with the back of her hand. "He doesn't have fever," she told her sister.

"Quit your fretting over me," Beak said. "I'm fit as ever."

"Then you'll let us go riding for another hour or two?" Mary asked.

"You'll be walking and that's that," Beak announced. He folded his arms across his chest to show he meant what he'd said.

"Why can't we ride?" Mary asked.

"Because I've just bedded down the ladies," Beak said. "Your horses have been fed, pampered, and lulled to sleep."

Beak had only just finished giving that lie when he remembered the two great stallions feeding in the stalls adjacent to the front doors. He worried Jamie or Mary might take notice. The sisters usually came flying through the stables, though, and there was a good chance he could get them back outside before they took a real look around them.

"You should be getting ready for your company," Beak blurted out. He grabbed hold of Mary's right arm and Jamie's left and started dragging the two of them toward the entrance.

"Mary has convinced me not to worry about our unwanted guests on such a fine afternoon," Jamie explained. "Do quit tugging on my arm, Beak."

"We have three full days of freedom," Mary interjected. "Jamie still has plenty of time to get the household ready."

"You could try lending a hand, missy," Beak said. "It would do you good."

"Don't start nagging her, Beak. Mary would help if I asked her assistance."

Beak didn't look as if he believed that remark.

"Speaking of asking," Mary interjected, "there's something I want to ask you, Beak."

"Mary, don't bother Beak with questions now."

THE BRIDE

"I certainly *am* going to bother Beak," Mary told her sister. "I value his advice as much as you do. Besides, I want to know if you've told me the truth."

"What a sinful thing to say," Jamie replied. Her smile told Beak she really wasn't the least offended.

"Jamie told me all about these horrible Scots, Beak. I'm thinking of running away. What think you of that bold plan?"

Beak tried not to smile; Lady Mary looked so sincere. "It would depend on where you'd be running to, I suppose."

"Oh, well, I hadn't actually thought of a true destination yet . . ."

"I'm wondering why you'd want to run away, Mary," Beak said. "What sorry tales has your sister filled your head with? Do you think they're true or false?"

"Now, Beak, why would you think I'd lie to my sister?" Jamie asked, trying not to laugh.

"Because I know how your mind works, Jamie," Beak answered. "You've been at it again, haven't you? What stories have you teased your poor sister with today? I can see you got her quivering with fear. And I happen to know you don't know spit about the Scots."

"I know they've got the brains of sheep," Jamie answered. She winked at Beak when Mary wasn't noticing, then added, "Only those Scots born and raised in the Highlands, of course. The Lowland people are very intelligent, just like you, Beak."

"Don't try soothing me with pretty words," Beak countered. "It ain't going to work this time. I can see how worried Mary is. Why, she's wringing the skin right off her hands. What'd you tell her?"

"I merely mentioned that I'd heard the Scots were a lusty people."

"Well, now, Mary, that ain't so bad," Beak admitted.

"With big appetites," Mary interjected.

"And that's a sin?"

"It is," Mary answered.

"Gluttony," Jamie supplied, grinning.

35

"Jamie said they fight all the time."

"No, Mary, I said they fight most of the time. If you're going to repeat my remarks, do get them straight."

"Do they, Beak?"

"Do they what, Mary?"

"Fight all the time."

"I just said they liked to raid," Jamie announced with a delicate shrug.

Beak noticed the fine blush covering Jamie's high cheekbones. She was obviously embarrassed that her sister was telling on her.

Jamie was up to mischief, all right. She was looking just as guilty as she had the time she convinced Mary her papa had signed the order giving the convent guardianship.

She did like to jest. She was a sure sight to behold, too, dressed in Beak's favorite color, a deep royal blue. Her hair was unbound and the thick curls fell in chaotic splendor well past her slender shoulders. There were smudges of dirt on her nose and chin.

Beak wished Laird Kincaid could get a clear look at Jamie now, for her violet eyes fairly sparkled with joy.

Mary looked just as appealing. She wore pink today, but the pretty gown was bothered with splotches of dirt. Beak wondered what trouble the two sisters had gotten into, then decided he really didn't want to know.

He was pulled back to the topic of the Scotsmen when Mary blurted out, "Jamie told me the Scots take what they want when they want it. She also said they have special preferences."

"And what might those be?" Beak asked.

"Strong horses, fat sheep, and soft women," Mary said.

"Horses, sheep, and women?"

"Yes, Beak, and in that order. Jamie says they'd rather sleep next to their horses than their women. Well? Is it true? Do the women come last?"

Beak didn't answer Mary. He stared at Jamie, silently willing her with his frown to answer her sister. He thought Jamie looked a bit distressed, yet wasn't certain if she was about to burst into apology or laughter.

Laughter won out. "Honestly, Mary, I was only teasing you."

"Just look at the two of you," Beak announced. "Covered with dirt like peasant babies. Fine ladies, indeed! And you, missy," he added, pointing his finger at Jamie, "laughing like a loon. Just what were you two doing in that meadow, I'm wondering?"

"He's trying to turn the topic," Mary told her sister. "I'm going to get an apology from you, Jamie, before I move from this spot. And if I don't think you're sincere, then I'm telling Father Charles. He'll give you a penance you won't soon forget."

"It's your fault, not mine," Jamie countered. "You're as easy to lead along as a pup."

Mary turned back to Beak. "You'd think my sister would be a little more understanding of my predicament. She doesn't have to stand before the Scottish warlords and pray to God she isn't chosen. Papa's bent on hiding her away."

"Only because I wasn't named in the king's order," Jamie reminded her sister.

"I ain't so sure you weren't named," Beak interjected.

"Papa wouldn't lie," Jamie argued.

"As to that, I won't be saying you're right or wrong, Jamie," Beak said. "Mary? Jamie hasn't told you anything terrible about the Scots as far as I can tell. You're fretting over nothing, lass."

"She told me other stories, Beak," Mary said. "I was suspicious, of course, because her stories were so outrageous. I'm not that gullible, Beak, no matter what my sister thinks."

Beak turned to frown at Jamie again. "Well, milady?"

Jamie let out a soft sigh. "I'll admit I did make up some of the stories, but just as many are really true, Beak."

"How could you be knowing what's true and what's false? You shouldn't listen to gossip anyway. I taught you better than that."

"What gossip?" Mary asked.

"Scots throw cabers at one another just for the sport of it."

"Cabers?"

"Pine trees, Mary," Jamie answered.

Mary let out a loud, inelegant snort. "They don't."

"Aye, they do," Jamie countered. "And if tossing cabers at one another isn't a barbaric ritual, then I don't know what is."

"You really think I'll believe anything you tell me, don't you?"

"It's true, Mary," Beak admitted. "They do throw cabers, though not at one another."

Mary shook her head. "I can tell by the way you're grinning at me that you're teasing me, Beak. Oh, yes, you are," she added when he started to protest. "And I suppose it's true the Scots wear women's clothing?"

"What—" Beak strangled on a cough. He hoped the warriors had already left the stables, after all, and couldn't overhear this shameful talk. "I think we should stroll on outside to finish this discussion. It's too fine a day to be cooped up inside."

"It is true," Jamie told her sister, ignoring Beak's suggestion. "They do wear women's gowns. Don't they, Beak?"

"Where'd you hear that blasphemy?" Beak demanded.

"Cholie told me."

"It was Cholie?" Mary asked. "Well, if you'd bothered to mention that fact, I wouldn't have believed any of your tales. You know as well as I do that the kitchen help tips the jug of ale all day long. Cholie was probably sotted."

"Oh, spit," Jamie muttered. "She wasn't sotted."

"Oh, spit?" Mary repeated. "Honestly, Jamie, you talk just like Beak."

"They do," Beak said, trying to stop the budding argument.

"They do what?" Mary asked.

"Wear clothing that stops at their knees," Beak explained. "There, I told you so, Mary."

"Their clothing is called their plaid, Mary. Plaid," Beak repeated with a growl. "It's their sacred dress. I think they'd take exception to hearing it called a woman's gown."

"Then it's little wonder to me why they have to fight all

the time," Jamie interjected. She hadn't really believed Cholie's tale, but Beak looked so sincere she was beginning to think he was telling the truth.

"Aye," Mary agreed. "They have to defend their gowns."

"They aren't gowns."

"Now look what you've done, Jamie. You've got Beak shouting at us."

Jamie was immediately contrite. "I'm sorry, Beak, for upsetting you. My, you are nervous today. You keep looking over your shoulder. Do you think someone's going to pounce on you from behind? What in—"

"I missed me nap," Beak blurted out. "That's why I'm surly."

"You must go and have a proper rest, then," Jamie advised. "Come along, Mary. Beak's been so patient with us and I can tell he isn't feeling at all well."

She took hold of Mary's hand and started toward the door. "Good God, Mary, they actually do wear women's gowns. I didn't really believe Cholie, but now I'm convinced."

"I'm running away and that's that," Mary said, loud enough for Beak to overhear. She suddenly stopped, then whirled around. "One last question, please?" she called out.

"Yes, Mary?"

"Would you be knowing if the Scots hate fat women, Beak?"

He didn't have any answer for that absurd question. After he shrugged his shoulders, Mary turned around and chased after Jamie. Both sisters lifted the hems of their skirts and started running toward the upper bailey. Beak let out a soft chuckle as he watched the pair.

"She was given a man's name."

The stable master nearly jumped out of his tunic. He hadn't heard Alec Kincaid's approach. He turned around and came face to shoulders with the giant warrior. "'Twas her mama's way of giving her a place in this family. Baron Jamison weren't the man who fathered Jamie. He claimed her for his own, though. I'll give him that much kindness. Did you get a good look at her, then?" he added in a rush.

Alec nodded.

"You'll be taking her with you, won't you?"

The Kincaid stared at the old man a long minute before answering.

"Aye, Beak. I'll be taking her with me."

The choice had been made.

Chapter Three

Jamie didn't find out about the Scotsmen's early arrival until Merlin, the keeper of the pasture cattle, chased her down to tell her there was yet another great commotion going on up at the main house and her papa wanted her to straighten it all out for him.

Merlin failed to mention the Scotsmen in his stuttered announcement. It wasn't his fault, however, for his beautiful mistress had turned her gaze directly upon him just when he was beginning his explanation. Those violet eyes had made him quite awestruck. Then his mistress smiled, causing Merlin's heart to start fluttering like a silly little lady's maid. His mind didn't flutter, though. No, it merely emptied of all thoughts save one: Lady Jamie was giving him her undivided attention.

The stutter only worsened, of course, but it didn't really matter. Jamie couldn't immediately obey the summons anyway. There was an injury that needed her immediate attention. Poor old Silas, his eyesight as weak as his hands, was carrying on something fierce, bellowing loud enough, in fact, to cause the pigs to squeal in protest.

Silas had accidentally sliced his upper arm instead of the side of treated hide he was trying to carve into a saddle lining.

The injury was minor and didn't require searing with a hot knife, yet Jamie still had to spend a good long while soothing the old man after she'd cleaned and wrapped the injury.

He needed pampering, and that was that.

Merlin stood by cook's side during the commotion. He was a little jealous of all the attention Silas was getting from their mistress. He was also extremely anxious because he couldn't seem to remember that other bit of information he'd been ordered to relate to her.

Jamie finally finished her task and left Silas in Cholie's capable hands. She knew the two servants would share at least one jug of ale between them, but didn't think that was too sinful, considering Silas's upset and Cholie's need to give comfort the only way she knew how.

"I can only put out one fire at a time," she told Merlin when he reminded her of the fuss going on up at the main house. She smiled to soften her rebuke, then left the worried-looking cattle keeper. Jamie ran all the way up the hill, her skirts raised to her knees. Three playful greyhounds ran alongside her. Neither Jamie nor her pets slowed down until they'd rushed through the open door and entered the great hall.

She came to an abrupt halt then. The two warriors leaning casually against the mantel immediately caught her attention.

Jamie was simply too stunned to hide her initial reaction. God's truth, they were the biggest men she'd ever seen. She couldn't quit staring at them.

It was unfortunate, too, for the first words out of her mouth weren't very ladylike. "Good God!"

It was only a whispered exclamation, strangled out at that, but Jamie could tell by the way the bigger of the two giants raised his right eyebrow that he'd heard her.

She didn't dare curtsy, knowing full well she'd land on her face if she tried. And she couldn't seem to pull her gaze away from the taller of the two men, either, the one now trying to stare her to her knees.

He was the meanest-looking man she'd ever seen.

She told herself she wasn't afraid. Nay, she was too angry to be frightened. Jamie stood her ground, meeting the warrior's gaze a long minute until she could regain a little composure, then realized that as long as she continued to stare at him, she'd never be able to accomplish that feat.

Jamie finally noticed the silence that permeated the great hall. She glanced over her shoulder and saw her sisters then. The three of them were lined up like common criminals, looking as if they were about to be executed with arrows.

As soon as Agnes caught Jamie's sympathetic gaze, she started crying. Alice put her arm around her twin's shoulders, obviously intent on offering her solace. The plan failed, however, and she also burst into tears. Within a blink of the eye, the two of them had worked themselves up into hysteria.

Mary stood next to Agnes. She looked as if she, too, wanted to cry. Her hands were clasped in front of her, and after giving Jamie a "dear Lord, will you look at them" look, she turned her gaze to the floor.

Something had to be done. The twins couldn't be allowed to disgrace the family in front of the Scots.

"Agnes, Alice, cease your weeping immediately."

Both sisters mopped at the corners of their eyes and tried to control themselves.

Jamie noticed her father then. He was sitting at the table, pouring himself a drink from one of the two jugs in front of him.

It was up to her to offer a proper, civilized English greeting, she supposed. She knew what her duty was. Yet the urge to shout at the strangers that they were three whole days early, for God's sake, was very nearly overwhelming.

Duty won out. Besides, the two Scots were probably too dull-witted to realize how uncouth their behavior was.

Jamie slowly walked over to stand directly in front of the two men. She remembered the dogs at her sides when she heard them growling at the strangers, dismissed them with a quick wave of her hand, then made a curtsy befitting her status as mistress of her home. A lock of hair fell over her left eye when she bowed her head, ruining the haughty effect she was trying to achieve. Jamie tossed the hair back over her shoulder and tried to manage a smile.

"I'd like to welcome both of you to our humble home, for no one else seems capable of extending that courtesy," she began. "And I do hope you'll forgive our unreadiness to receive you, but if you'll only remember you're a good three days early, you might more easily endure our lack of preparations."

She stared at their boots while she made that speech, then ventured a quick look up when she added, "My name is—"

"Lady Jamie." The shorter of the two giants made that statement.

Jamie had been staring at the space between the two warriors and immediately turned to look at the one who'd just spoken.

He wasn't as mean-looking as the other one. Jamie came to that conclusion when he smiled at her. He had an appealing dent in the side of his cheek when he smiled, too, and his green eyes were alive with mischief.

Jamie was immediately suspicious. The man seemed to be entirely too happy for such dour circumstances, what with Alice and Agnes weeping like infants. Perhaps, she decided, he was too simple-headed to understand the disruption he was causing. He was a Scotsman, after all.

"And your name, milord?" she asked, her voice cool.

"Daniel," he answered. "He's called Alec," he drawled out with a nod toward his companion.

Daniel's smile was proving to be contagious. This one was definitely a charmer, Jamie thought. She couldn't help but smile back, either, for the man had such a ridiculous burr in his speech that she could barely understand him.

She didn't really want to talk to the other lord, but she knew she had to. Jamie kept smiling, then slowly turned to look up at the other warrior.

He'd been waiting for her to look at him. Jamie could feel her smile freeze on her face. His gaze, surely as hot as the midday sun, easily intimidated her.

He wasn't smiling.

Jamie was suddenly embarrassed and didn't know why. She'd never felt this vulnerable in all her days. She felt her cheeks grow warm and knew she'd started blushing. There was such possessiveness in his stare, a look of ownership she couldn't understand.

It suddenly dawned on her that Lord Alec wasn't looking at her the way a true lord would look at a gentle lady of breeding. No, it was an earthy lustful look he was giving her.

He was being outrageously insolent. He gave her a slow, thoroughly insulting inspection, starting at the top of her head and ending a long while later at the bottom of her gown. His gaze lingered on her mouth, her breasts and her hips.

She hated him.

He made her feel as though she were standing there without a stitch of clothing on. Jamie was infuriated with him. She wasn't about to let him get away with his behavior, either. No, she was going to give as good as she was getting. She couldn't control her blush, but she prayed she looked just as insolent as he had when she slowly gave him the same disgustingly thorough inspection.

Unfortunately, the warrior didn't seem the least bit offended by her imitation. He looked amused. She thought his eyes warmed a little and noticed his eyebrow rose again in reaction to her appraisal.

There was something there, in his gaze, that tugged at her heart. She couldn't put her finger on it, but she was beginning to think that if he hadn't been so mean-looking, she might have found him handsome. That was ridiculous,

45

of course. She'd already made up her mind to hate him. The man was too hard for her liking. He was in desperate need of a good hair trim, too. Why, the back of his reddish brown hair went way beyond the neckline of his black tunic. The hair curled a bit, reminding her of the Greek warriors she'd seen drawings of, but it certainly didn't soften his angular face or his square, unforgiving chin. His mouth looked as hard as the rest of him.

Oh, he was entirely too fierce-looking to please her. And why her heart was pounding such a wild beat was beyond her comprehension. The longer she met his gaze, the more breathless she became.

A single thought kept her from feeling like a complete fool. One of her poor sisters was going to have to marry this warlord from hell.

She started shivering.

He smiled.

Baron Jamison suddenly called out to both warriors to join him at the table for a taste of wine.

Daniel immediately moved away from the mantel and strolled over to the table. He paused on his way to wink at Mary.

Alec didn't move. Neither did Jamie. She couldn't make herself stop staring up at him.

He didn't want to stop looking at her.

"Do you have a priest in residence?"

His voice had sounded harsh. He couldn't help that, he decided, for he was still reacting to the amazingly beautiful woman standing so defiantly before him. Her eyes were the most brilliant shade of violet. She was quite magnificent, yet Alec was just as impressed with the rebellious streak he could easily see.

This one wouldn't be easily intimidated. He didn't think she'd ever cower away from him. And no other woman had ever been able to match his stare this long, this courageously.

Alec's smile widened. She was a worthy adversary, all right. He knew she was afraid of him; he had seen her tremble. Yet she valiantly tried to hide her fear from him.

She'd survive in the rugged Highlands, given care and attention, but he would have to take every precaution. She was so delicate looking. He'd have to quell the rebelliousness in her without breaking her spirit. It would be a chore, true, but Alec didn't mind. In truth, he was already looking forward to the taming.

And in the end, he would conquer and she would submit.

Jamie didn't have the faintest idea what the warrior was thinking. She finally found her voice and answered his question. "We do have a priest in residence, milord." Heaven help her, the shiver was now in her voice. "You've chosen, then?"

"I have."

"It must have been a most difficult decision for you to make."

The smile reached his eyes. "It wasn't difficult at all."

She didn't care for the arrogance in his tone or the way he was looking at her now. "I'm certain it was difficult for you," she insisted. "After all, my sisters are all very beautiful, and choosing one so quickly isn't really giving the matter your full consideration. For that reason, I would suggest you wait, perhaps return to our home in another month, after you've had time to mull this over. What think you of that idea, milord?"

He slowly shook his head.

"Then you're going to marry tomorrow?" Jamie asked.

"We'll be halfway home by then."

"You will?"

"We will."

"You plan to marry now?"

She looked horrified. Alec nodded. "I do."

"But you cannot mean—"

"We'll leave immediately after the ceremony," Alec said, his voice hard.

Lord Daniel suddenly appeared at her side. He was holding two goblets of wine. He handed one to Alec, then turned to the three sisters. "Come and join us, Mary," he called out, laughing. "We won't bite."

"I never thought you would," Mary announced. She straightened her shoulders and hurried over to stand beside Jamie.

Both Daniel and Alec drank from their goblets. They nodded to each other, then offered the cups to Jamie and Mary.

The sisters denied the offer by shaking their heads.

"Take a sip, Mary," Daniel suggested with a wink.

Alec wasn't as solicitous. "Drink this, Jamie. Now."

Perhaps it was some sort of primitive Scottish ritual, Jamie thought. As mistress of her home, she knew it was her duty to make their visitors welcome. Alec looked determined, too. She shrugged her shoulders, then took the goblet, swallowed quickly, and handed the cup back to him.

He captured her hand and wouldn't let go. His thumb brushed her palm. A frown settled on his face, and he slowly turned her hand over to look at the calluses and scars.

Mary emptied Daniel's cup. When she gave the goblet back to him, he also took hold of her hand and turned it over.

Jamie tried to pull her hand away, but it wasn't until the two men had compared Mary's smooth, unblemished skin with Jamie's flaws, that he finally let go.

It was a humiliation. She understood every damning word they said to each other in Gaelic. They didn't know she spoke their language and that fact gave Jamie a perverse spark of satisfaction.

Jamie hid her hands behind her back and waited for their next insult.

"Was sharing your drink some sort of ritual?" Mary asked. "'Tis the truth we don't know anything about the Scots."

After blurting out that statement, she turned her attention to the floor.

"Mary, you've never heard of our special preferences, then?" Daniel asked in a soft burr.

Mary's head jerked up. She had the most startled expression on her face. "Preferences, milord?"

"Certain peculiarities," Daniel qualified with a grin.

"Peculiarities?" Mary gave Jamie a wild look before turning back to Daniel. "Nay, I've not heard of these preferences."

"Ah, then, I must enlighten you," he announced.

It was obvious that Lord Daniel was vastly amused. "I don't wish to be enlightened," Mary countered.

Alec was watching Jamie. Her eyes had widened when Daniel mentioned preferences. She'd obviously caught the drift of his friend's remarks.

Alec found Jamie incredibly appealing. Just looking at her made him ache to touch her, to take her. The smile faded from his eyes when he admitted to himself how much he wanted to bed her. Odd, but it didn't matter that she was English. No, it didn't matter at all.

"Mary, sweet," Daniel began, drawing Alec's attention back to him, "surely you've heard of our list of wants. Everyone knows the Scots like strong horses, fat sheep, and soft, willing women."

He'd drew out his list just like an old woman savoring the telling of fresh gossip. Alec mimicked his friend's tone when he added, "In that order, of course."

"Of course," Daniel agreed.

Jamie turned to glare at Alec. She'd already surmised Beak had had a little talk with the giants and had mentioned Mary's fears. Jamie made a promise to blister Beak's ears the next time she saw him.

Daniel suddenly reached out to stroke Mary's cheek with the back of his hand. Mary was so surprised by the caress she forgot to move away. She was quite mesmerized by the tender look in Daniel's eyes.

"I've already got a strong horse," Daniel stated. "As for sheep, Mary, well, there are plenty grazing in the mountains back home. But a soft, willing woman, now, lass, it's a pity to admit I'm lacking one of those. It's important to me, even though it's last on my list."

"I'm not soft," Mary blurted out.

"Aye, you are," Daniel countered. "And as lovely as a spring morning," he added.

Mary's blush deepened until her face was the color of fire. "I'm neither lovely nor willing, milord," she announced. She folded her arms across her chest and concentrated on giving him a good frown. She wanted to discourage the handsome devil, yet was horribly confused by her own reaction to him. His flattery was making her light-headed. Did he really think she was lovely?

The twins started crying again. Jamie was about to give them another rebuke when it occurred to her that one or both had been chosen as brides. If that was the case, and she guessed it was, Alice and Agnes were certainly entitled to their tantrum. They could wail like wolves and it would be fine with her.

Alec simply waited for the truth to hit her. He saw the sympathetic look she was giving her sisters, wondered how long it would take her to notice they were looking at her with the identical expression.

Baron Jamison would certainly set Jamie straight, once he'd regained his composure, Alec decided. The man was still close to weeping. He'd argued something fierce when Alec had casually stated he'd chosen Jamie for his bride.

Alec had been firm with the baron. He had controlled his temper until Jamison quit sputtering and began to list all the selfish reasons he had for being against the union. None of the reasons had anything to do with Jamie's well-being. Alec's attitude hardened then. He was infuriated with the Englishman. The list of duties certainly explained the calluses on Jamie's hands. Jamison didn't want to keep his youngest by his side because of love. He wanted only a slave at his beck and call. The youngest, in Alec's opinion, was literally in bondage.

A worried-looking servant came rushing into the great

hall. He gave Baron Jamison only a brief glance before hurrying over to Jamie. After completing an awkward bow, the servant whispered, "The priest be on his way, mistress. He's dressed in his wedding vestments."

Jamie nodded to the servant. "It was good of you to quit your duties to fetch Father Charles, George. Would you like to stay for the weddings?"

The servant had a look of adoration in his eyes. "I ain't dressed for it," he whispered.

"Neither are we," Jamie whispered back.

"Go and change your gown, Mary," Daniel interjected. "I'm partial to gold. If you've a gown in that color, wear it to please me. If not, white will do well enough. I'm wedding you, Lady Mary."

Lord Daniel Ferguson caught Lady Mary before she hit the floor. He wasn't at all irritated that his intended had just fainted dead away, and he actually let out a full burst of laughter as he swept Mary up into his arms and held her against his chest.

"She's overcome with gratitude, Alec," Daniel called out to his friend.

"Aye, Daniel, I can see she is," Alec answered.

Jamie couldn't keep her anger controlled another minute. She turned to confront Alec. Her hands rested on her hips in a stance that was clearly a challenge. "Well? Which one of the twins are you going to wed?"

"Neither."

"Neither?"

She still hadn't caught on. Alec sighed. "Change your gown, Jamie, if that's your inclination. I prefer white. Now go and do my bidding. The hour grows late and we must be on our way."

He'd deliberately lengthened his speech, giving her time to react to his announcement. He thought he was being most considerate.

She thought he was demented.

Jamie was, at first, too stunned to do more than stare in horror at the warlord. When she finally gained her voice, she

51

shouted, "It will be a frigid day in heaven before I marry you, milord, a frigid day indeed."

"You've just described the Highlands in winter, lass. And you will marry me."

"Never."

Exactly one hour later, Lady Jamison was wed to Alec Kincaid.

Chapter Four

She wore black to her wedding. Her choice of attire was a purely defiant gesture meant to infuriate the Scotsman. Jamie knew her plan had failed, however, the minute she walked back into the great hall. Alec took one look at her and started laughing. The booming sound nearly felled the rafters.

Jamie didn't have any idea how much her rebellious nature pleased him, else she never would have gone to such lengths to provoke him, Alec decided. Had she known how much he detested tears, she probably would have wept. Alec didn't think she'd be as convincing as her twin sisters, though. Jamie moved like a queen. Her back was as straight as a clean lance, she bowed her head to no man, and he decided it would have cost her mightily to affect any female weakness.

She was dressed for mourning, but she still looked magnificent. Her eyes continued to captivate him. He wondered if he'd ever get used to her beauty. Lord, he certainly hoped so. He couldn't allow any interference in his primary duties.

The lass was turning out to be quite a puzzle. He knew she was English born and raised, yet she didn't appear to be the least bit cowardly. Alec wondered how that miracle had come about, then concluded her innocence and lack of fear stemmed from the fact that she'd never been tainted by King Henry's sordid court life. By the grace of God, Lady Jamie hadn't been exposed to the English inclination for debauchery.

The Kincaid had Baron Jamison to thank, he supposed, for failing to do his duty for his daughters. He wasn't about to mention his gratitude, though, and doubted Jamie's father would have heard a word anyway. The man was actually crying now. Alec was too disgusted to speak to the man. He'd never seen a grown man humiliate himself in such a foul way. It turned his stomach.

"We're all very close to our father," Jamie whispered when the baron couldn't answer the priest's question as to who was giving the brides away. The baron's face was hidden in his soggy linen cloth. "Papa's going to miss us, milord. This is most difficult for him."

She hadn't looked up at Alec when she made her whispered excuse for her father's shameful conduct, but the plea was there, in her husky voice. She was asking for his understanding, he knew, and he found her defense of her father worthy enough to make him keep his unfavorable opinion to himself.

She'd just given him another glimpse into her character, for her plea told him she was loyal to her family. He thought that was a noble quality under any circumstance, and given the character of the members of her family, Jamie's loyalty bordered on sainthood.

Jamie was too terrified to look up at her intended. She and her sister stood side by side, holding on to each other's hands for comfort. Daniel stood on Mary's right and Alec was positioned on Jamie's left. Alec's arm touched her shoulder and his thigh brushed against her. Deliberately, repeatedly.

She couldn't move away from him. Mary was squeezed up

against her side and Alec's arm blocked the possibility of a step back. Lord, how she hated being frightened. She wasn't used to such feelings. She told herself it was because he was so big. He towered over her like a huge, angry cloud. He smelled of heather and masculinity, a bit of leather, too, and under more pleasing conditions, she might have found his scent appealing. Now, of course, she detested his size, his scent, his very presence.

The priest finished his homily on the sacrament of marriage, then turned to address Jamie's sister. Mary, honest to a fault, gave Daniel a good laugh when Father Charles asked her if she'd take Daniel for her husband. Mary took a long while pondering over the question, acting as though she'd just been asked to explain the significance of the Norman Conquest, then finally blurted out her answer. "'Tis the truth I'd rather not, Father."

Jamie was nearing the point of true hysteria. She was not supposed to be marrying this warlord named Alec Kincaid. He wasn't making the situation any easier to endure, either, standing so close to her that she could feel the heat radiating from him.

While Father Charles was begging Mary to give a proper response, Jamie tried to move away from Alec. In the corner of her mind was the cowardly thought that she could just push his arm away, back up a step, and then run like lightning out of the room.

He must have read her intention, for his arm settled on her shoulders. Before she could protest, she was hauled up against his side.

She couldn't shrug herself away from him. She tried— several times, in fact—before she whispered her demand that he unhand her.

He answered her by ignoring her.

In her frustration, she turned to her sister and said, "I don't think it matters what our rathers be, Mary. If you don't agree to marry Daniel, you'll be going against your king."

"But if I say I want to take this man for my husband, then

I go against God, don't I?" Mary argued. "I wouldn't be telling the truth," she ended with a wail.

"For God's sake, Mary, answer the priest," Jamie snapped.

Mary took exception to Jamie's hostile tone. She glared at her sister before turning back to the priest. "Oh, all right. I'll take him." Turning back to Jamie, she muttered, "There, sister, are you happy now? You've forced me to lie to a man of the cloth."

"I forced you?"

The gasp in Jamie's voice wasn't due entirely to her sister's outrageous statement. Alec's hand had curved around the base of her neck. His fingers were stroking her sensitive skin.

Father Charles nodded his approval of Mary's answer.

It was now Jamie's and Alec's turn. "Your full name, milord?" the priest asked.

"Alec Kincaid."

The priest nodded. He was in a hurry to get through this marriage ordeal, for the look in his sweet Jamie's eyes had turned murderous. In his haste, Father Charles threw in the word "willingly" when he asked her if she would have Alec for her husband.

"Willingly?" Jamie asked. She took a deep breath, preparing herself for the true opinion she was going to sting the priest with, then felt Alec's fingers tighten around her throat.

The man was obviously trying to intimidate her. Jamie reached up to pull his hand away, but Alec wouldn't be budged. He simply captured her fingers and continued to apply pressure.

He wasn't being the least bit subtle. Jamie got his silent message quick enough. The arrogant man was going to strangle her to death if she provoked him any further, and being Scots, as he was, she was certain he'd carry out his threat.

Her neck was starting to sting. "I'll take him," she blurted out.

The priest sighed with relief, then rushed through the rest

of the ceremony. As soon as he gave his blessing, Mary tried to run out of the hall. Daniel caught her in two strides. He lifted her into his arms and kissed the scream right out of her, in front of Father Charles and the family. When he finished his gentle attack, Mary sagged against him. Jamie thought she looked like a wilted flower.

The twins started whimpering again, Papa began to sniffle, and Jamie wanted to die a quick death.

Alec Kincaid wasn't as forceful in his demand for a kiss to seal the vows. He merely moved to stand directly in front of his bride. His hands were settled on his hips, his muscular legs were braced apart, and his gaze was directed at the top of Jamie's bowed head.

He didn't say a word. Yet his rigid stance suggested he'd stand there all night if that was what was needed to get her to look at him. Jamie took comfort in the fact that he wasn't trying to strangle her any longer.

She could feel her heart pounding. She supposed Alec Kincaid would dare just about anything he wanted to. She gathered her courage and slowly lifted her gaze to meet his.

He really was frightening. His eyes were such a deep brown. Jamie could find very little warmth there, and after meeting his gaze for as long as she could manage without visibly cringing, she started to turn away.

Alec suddenly reached out and pulled her into his arms. His hand cupped her chin just as his mouth came down on hers. The kiss was hard, unyielding . . . and unbelievably warm.

Jamie felt as though she'd just been scorched by the sun. The kiss ended before she could even think to struggle, before she really wanted to move at all. She was temporarily speechless. She stared up at her husband a long while, wondering if the brief kiss had affected him as much as it had her.

Alec was amused by the confusion he could see in Jamie's eyes. It was apparent she hadn't been kissed much. She was blushing with embarrassment now. Her hands were clinging to each other in what looked like a death grip.

Aye, he was pleased with her, and he realized he hadn't been unaffected by the brief kiss, either. He couldn't quit looking at her. Hell, he wanted to kiss her again.

Mary's sudden bellow broke the spell.

"Now?" Mary shouted the word as though it were an obscenity. "Jamie, they mean to leave now!"

"Surely my sister misunderstood," Jamie told Alec. "You aren't really leaving now, are you?"

"We are," Alec answered. "Daniel and I have many responsibilities back home. We're leaving within the hour."

He hadn't mentioned Mary or her in his explanation. That realization captured her full attention. She almost smiled over the joyful possibility, then decided to make certain her guess was correct before getting her hopes up.

"Do you wish to share our humble dinner with us before you and Daniel leave?" she inquired.

He knew exactly what she was thinking. She'd betrayed herself when she stressed the word "you" in her question. The daft woman actually thought he was going to leave her behind. Alec felt like laughing. She looked so serious now, and so damned hopeful.

Alec shook his head.

Jamie felt as though a prison door had just been unlocked and she was once again free. She desperately tried to hide her joy, for it would have been rude by half to show such open pleasure over his leave-taking.

The marriages were to be in name only. Oh, why hadn't she realized that before? Alec and Daniel were simply doing the bidding of their overlord by marrying. Now they would go back home and resume their duties, whatever in God's name those might be, and leave their appreciative brides in England where they belonged.

It really wasn't such an unusual arrangement. Many marriages were settled in such a satisfying manner. Jamie actually felt a little foolish for not understanding sooner. She could have saved herself a good deal of worry.

Relief swept over her with a force that nearly made her knees buckle. Since she was used to making bargains with her Maker, she immediately promised God a twelve day novena for giving her this wonderful reprieve.

"Will you be returning to England for a stay in future?" she asked, trying to sound as if she thought that odious idea had an ounce of merit.

"It would take a war to bring me back."

"You needn't sound so cheerful over that possibility," Jamie countered before she thought better of it. She let him see her frown, too, and didn't care if she offended him. The man was as blunt as a cudgel. And if he wasn't going to be polite, then she wasn't going to bother with her manners either. She tossed her hair over her shoulder, turned her back on Alec, and slowly walked away from him. "'Tis already high afternoon, Kincaid," she called over her shoulder. "You'd best be on your way, for I'm sure you have a good distance to cover before the day is finished."

She almost added that it had been a pleasure to meet him, but the lie would have cost her another novena so she kept silent.

Jamie had just reached the table when her husband's hard command stopped her cold.

"Gather your things and say farewell to your family, Jamie, while Daniel and I see to the horses. Be quick about it."

"You as well, Mary," Daniel interjected in that cheerful voice of his that was beginning to drive Jamie wild.

"Why must we hurry?" Mary asked.

"Alec and I have vowed not to sleep on English soil another night. We've a good distance to cover before darkness sets in."

Jamie whirled around just in time to watch the two Scotsmen walk out of the room. Her hands gripped the table edge behind her back. "Kincaid? You're supposed to leave me here," she called out. "This is just a marriage of convenience, isn't it?"

He stopped in the center of the hallway, then turned around to face her. "Aye, wife, it is a marriage of convenience. My convenience. Do you understand me?"

59

She ignored his angry tone of voice and his harsh expression. "No, Kincaid, I don't understand."

She'd tried to sound as arrogant as he looked, yet knew her effort was ruined by the tremor in her voice.

Her bluster of anger didn't fool him. He knew she was frightened; his smile told her so. "In time I promise that you will understand. I give you my word."

She didn't want his word, but she didn't think that was going to matter very much to him. He really was a warlord from hell, after all. She wasn't up to arguing with him, either. Her eyes filled with tears just as soon as he disappeared out the doorway, and all she wanted to do was throw herself into the closest chair and have a good cry.

She was too upset to think about gathering her possessions. The twins took care of that task, allowing Jamie precious time with her father.

By the time Agnes and Alice returned to the great hall, Mary was in a fine state of nerves. She could barely stammer out her farewell before rushing out of the room.

"I'll have the rest of your things packed carefully, Jamie, and sent on to you within a week's time," Agnes vowed. "These Highlands can't be very far away."

"I'll pack your beautiful tapestries," Alice interjected. "I promise I won't forget anything. In no time at all you'll be feeling right at home."

"Alice, I already told Jamie I'd take care of that chore," Agnes muttered. "Honestly, sister, you're always trying to better me. Oh, Jamie? I put your mama's shawl in your satchel with your medicine jars."

"Thank you, sisters," Jamie said. She quickly hugged them both. "Oh, I'm going to miss you two. You're such dear sisters."

"Jamie, you're so very brave," Agnes whispered. "You look so calm, so serene. I'd be daft by now. You're married to the one who—"

"You needn't remind her," Alice muttered. "She couldn't have forgotten he killed his first wife, sister."

"We aren't absolutely sure," her twin argued.

Jamie wished the twins would stop trying to comfort her.

Their reminders about Alec Kincaid were making her more upset than ever.

Baron Jamison tugged on Jamie's skirt to get her attention. "I'll be dead in a week, I will. Who will see to my meals? Who will listen to my stories?"

"Now, Papa, Agnes and Alice will take good care of you. You're going to be just fine," she soothed. She bent over her father, kissed his forehead, and then added, "Please don't carry on so. Mary and I will come to see you and . . ."

She couldn't finish her lie, couldn't tell her father it was going to be all right. Her world had just ended; everything that was familiar and safe was being snatched away.

It was Agnes who whispered Jamie's greatest fear aloud. "We're never going to see you again, are we, Jamie? He won't let you come home, will he?"

"I promise you I'll find a way to come and see you," Jamie vowed. Her voice shook and her eyes stung with unshed tears. Dear God, this leave-taking was painful.

Baron Jamison kept muttering between his sobs that the Scots had robbed him of his precious babies and how in God's name was he ever going to get along without them? Although Jamie tried to console her father, in the end it proved to be a useless undertaking. Papa didn't want to quiet down. The more Jamie tried, the louder he wailed.

Beak came to fetch her. A small tug-of-war resulted when he tried to separate father from daughter. Baron Jamison wouldn't let go of Jamie's hand. The task was finally won when Jamie gave assistance.

"Come along, Jamie. 'Tis best not to anger your new husband. He's waiting patiently in the courtyard for you. Lord Daniel and Lady Mary have already started toward Scotland, lass. Come with me now. A new life awaits you."

Beak's soft voice helped to soothe Jamie. She took hold of his hand and walked by his side toward the entrance. When she paused to give her family one last farewell, Beak nudged her forward.

"Don't be looking back, Jamie. And quit your shivering. Start thinking about your happy future."

"It's my future that has me shivering," Jamie confessed.

"Beak, I don't know anything about this husband of mine. All the black rumors about him make me worry. I don't want to be married to him."

"What's done is done," Beak announced. "There's two ways to look at this, lass. You can go into this marriage with your eyes closed tight against your man and be miserable for the rest of your days, or you can open them real wide, accept your husband, and make the best of your life."

"I don't want to hate him."

Beak smiled. Jamie had sounded so pitifully forlorn. "Then don't hate him," he advised. "You ain't any good at hating anyway. Your heart's too tender, girl. Besides," he continued as he nudged her farther ahead, "it ain't so unordinary after all."

"What isn't so unordinary?"

"Many a bride goes to her wedding without knowing her mate."

"But those brides were English, Beak, marrying Englishmen."

"Hush, now," Beak ordered, hearing the fear in her voice. "He's a good man, this Kincaid. I took his measure, Jamie. He'll treat you right."

"How would you know that?" Jamie asked. She tried to stop and turn to face Beak but he kept nudging her forward. "There's that rumor, if you'll remember, that he killed his first wife."

"And you believe it?"

Her answer was immediate. "I don't."

"Why not?"

Jamie shrugged. "I can't explain it," she whispered. "I just think he wouldn't . . ." She let out a sigh, then added, "You'll think me daft, Beak, but his eyes . . . well, he isn't an evil man."

"I happen to know for fact it's a lie," Beak announced. "He didn't kill her. I put the question to him, Jamie, asked him right out."

"You didn't." His outrageous statement made her laugh. "Beak, he must have been furious with you."

"Spit," Beak whispered. "Your future was my concern,

62

not his anger," he boasted. "Of course, it was only after I heard he was going to choose you that I asked him anything, you understand."

"When did you have time?" Jamie asked, frowning.

"Ain't important," Beak said hurriedly. "Besides, I knew Kincaid was a good one as soon as I looked real close at his horse." He gave Jamie another gentle prod between her shoulderblades to get her moving toward her husband again. "This warrior's going to treat you with just as much care."

"Oh, for heaven's sake," Jamie muttered. "You've been a stable master too many years, old friend. There's a difference between a wife and a horse. I can see you believe this nonsense you're telling me. You're looking very pleased with yourself."

"And feeling pleased," Beak boasted. "I just got you clean outside without having to drag you none, now, didn't I?"

He knew his comment startled her, for her eyes widened and he had to nudge her again when she came to an abrupt stop.

Alec was standing in the center of the courtyard next to his mount. His expression didn't give her a guess as to what he was thinking, but Jamie didn't believe he'd been patiently waiting for her arrival, as Beak had said. No, the Kincaid didn't look like the patient sort at all.

Alec was certain she was going to cause an uproar when they reached the Highlands. He held her gaze a long minute, wondering to himself just when he was going to get accustomed to her. Her eyes were the most vivid shade of violet he'd ever seen.

There was blue and then there was blue. Beak had made that odd remark, Alec remembered. Now he understood what the stable master meant.

He couldn't allow her to captivate him this way. Her mouth was too damned appealing for his peace of mind. Yes, she was going to cause an upset all right, whether she realized it or not, Alec mused. And though he was certain none of his clansmen would dare to touch what belonged to him, their thoughts would certainly be strolling in that direction.

The woman was simply too appealing for her own good.

She was still frightened of him. Alec told himself that was a good beginning. A wife should always be a bit uncertain of her husband. Yet her fear irritated him, too. He would have ordered her to get on her mount and be quick about it if he hadn't seen the apprehension in her gaze. She reminded him of a deer just picking up the scent of danger.

It was high time he took control, he decided.

Alec gained his stallion's back in one fluid motion. The great black horse pranced a nervous sidestep into Wildfire's flanks. Jamie's horse was already in a prickly state, having been forced to stand next to a male whose scent she was unfamiliar with, and immediately tried to rear up. Alec reached over, grabbed the reins from the inattentive groom, and commanded the mare to settle down.

Wildfire immediately obeyed.

Beak heard Jamie's in-drawn breath, noticed the way she stared at the Scottish warrior, and came to the conclusion she might be in jeopardy of fainting. He put his hand on her shoulder again.

"Get your gumption back, girl. Ain't going to make you feel any better if you disgrace yourself by swooning. I taught you better, didn't I?"

The grumbled words got her immediate attention. Jamie straightened away from the stable master. "There isn't going to be any swooning," she muttered. "You insult me by suggesting I have such a weakness."

Beak hid his smile. He wasn't going to have to nudge her forward any longer. The fire was back in her eyes.

With the grace befitting royalty, Jamie lifted the hem of her gown and walked over to her mount. Beak helped her get settled on Wildfire's back, then reached up to pat her hand. "Now, give this old man your promise to get along with your husband," he ordered. "It's a sacred commandment, if you'll remember," he added with an outrageous wink.

"It is not a commandment," Jamie announced.

"It is in the Highlands."

Alec had made that statement. He had sounded as though

he meant what he said, too. Jamie gave him a disgruntled look before turning back to Beak.

The stable master was smiling at her husband. "You'll remember your promise to me, Laird Kincaid?"

Alec nodded. He tossed Wildfire's reins to Jamie, goaded his stallion forward, and left Jamie staring after him.

He wasn't going to wait for her. Jamie held Wildfire steady, determined to see just how far Alec would ride before he stopped to wait for her. When horse and rider disappeared across the drawbridge and out of sight, she came to the conclusion he wasn't going to wait at all. The man hadn't even bothered to glance back over his shoulder.

"What did you mean when you asked him to remember his promise to you?" Jamie asked almost absentmindedly while she stared at the drawbridge.

"Nothing to concern yourself with," Beak said quickly.

Jamie turned to look at him. "Out with it, Beak," she commanded.

"I just had a little talk with him, Jamie, about your . . . innocence."

"I don't understand."

"Well, now, there's going to have to be a wedding night, lass. Since I was the one who told you about the ways between a man and a woman, I thought I'd caution your husband—"

"Oh, God, you talked about that?"

"I did. He promised to be careful with you, Jamie. He'll try not to hurt you much the first time."

Jamie knew her cheeks were flaming red with embarrassment. "I'm never going to let him touch me, Beak, so your gaining his promise was all for naught."

"Now, Jamie, don't sound so stubborn. I was afeard for you. 'Tis the truth I didn't tell you much about the actual mating ways. I explained to Kincaid that you didn't understand much about—"

"I don't want to hear any more of this talk. He'll never touch me and that's that."

Beak let out a loud sigh. "You're in for a surprise, then,

me girl. The way he looks at you tells me he'll be taking you at first chance. Might as well accept that in your stubborn mind, Jamie. Just do what he tells you and you'll come out all right."

"Do what he tells me?"

"Now, lass, don't raise your voice to me. You'd best be moving on, Jamie," he urged.

Jamie shook her head. "I'll go in a minute, Beak. First I must gain your promise you'll come after me if there's trouble here."

"Trouble? What kind of trouble?"

She couldn't quite look him in the eye when she whispered her explanation. "It seems that Papa took some gold coins from Andrew. It was a loan, Beak, and not a dowry, but I'm still worried. I don't know how Papa will be able to pay Andrew back."

She dared a quick look up, to judge Beak's reaction. She needn't have bothered. His bellow of outrage nearly pushed her off her mount. "He took gold for you, Jamie? He *sold* you to Baron Andrew?"

"No, no, you misunderstand," Jamie said quickly. "It was just a loan, Beak. There isn't time to argue about this. Just give me your word you'll come for me if Papa needs help."

"Aye, lass," Beak said. His sigh sounded angry. "I give you my pledge. Any other worries I should know about?"

"I pray not."

"Then off with you. If your husband—"

"One last matter, and then I'll leave."

"You're deliberately stalling, aren't you, girl? You want to poke his temper. He'll guess the truth about you then," Beak predicted with a grin. "And after all the trouble I had telling him my lies."

"What lies?"

"Told him you were a sweet, gentle maiden, I did."

"I am a sweet, gentle maiden," Jamie countered.

Beak snorted. "As sweet as the taste of soap when your temper's riled."

"What else did you tell him?" Jamie asked, looking

suspicious. "I'd better know the full of it, Beak, so I can defend myself."

"I told him you were timid."

"You didn't!"

"Said you were weak, used to be being coddled."

"No."

"And that you liked to spend your days sewing and churchgoing."

Jamie started to laugh. "Why would you tell such stories?"

"Because I wanted to give you a little advantage," Beak explained. His words fairly tripped over one another in his haste to hurry through the explanation. "I didn't tell him you could speak Gaelic, either."

"Neither did I."

The two confidants exchanged a grin. Then Jamie asked, "You're not sorry about all the skills you taught me, are you?"

"Of course not," Beak answered. "But if your husband thinks you're puny, I figure he'll be on his guard to see to your safety, lass. He'll have more patience with you, to my way of thinking."

"I don't care what he thinks about me," Jamie returned. "My pride's pricked because you made me out to be so inferior, though."

"Most women are inferior," he countered.

"Do most women hunt for their family's supper? Do most ride their horses better than a warrior? Do most—"

"Don't turn hellion on me now," Beak pleaded. "Just keep your talents to yourself for a while, Jamie. And don't go testing him just yet. It's best not to grab a wild dog by his tail unless you want the consequences, I always say."

"You've never said that before."

"Always meant to," Beak answered. He gave another worried glance toward the drawbridge. "Get along now, Jamie."

"I've been storing this up for a long while, Beak, and I won't be rushed."

"Well?" Beak demanded in a near shout.

"I love you. I've never told you before, but I love you with all my heart. You've been a good father to me, Beak."

The bluster went out of the old man. His eyes misted with tears and his voice was strained when he whispered, "And I love you, Jamie. You've been a fine daughter to me. I've always considered you mine."

"Promise me you won't forget me."

There was a frantic edge in her voice. Beak squeezed her hand. "I won't forget."

Jamie nodded. Tears streamed down her cheeks. She brushed the wetness away, straightened her shoulders, and then nudged Wildfire into motion.

Beak stood in the center of the courtyard, watching his mistress leave. He prayed she wouldn't turn around. He didn't want her to see him in such an undisciplined state.

Heaven take mercy, he was weeping just like a man who'd lost his only child. In his heart he knew the truth: he was never going to see his baby again.

Chapter Five

Alec Kincaid was in a fine mood. He kept his smile and his pace restrained until his wife finally caught up with him. He wanted to laugh, for it was obvious to him that his naive bride had just tried to goad him into losing his temper. She took her own sweet time following after him. Jamie didn't realize what a patient man he was, especially when the matter was as insignificant as a woman. He found humor in the very idea that a mere woman would dare to challenge him at all.

As soon as he heard her approach, Alec increased his speed until both mounts were cantering. Jamie stayed right behind him, valiantly trying to ignore the dust flying up in her face. She was determined to keep up the inhuman, neck-breaking pace without uttering a word of protest. She also waited for her new husband to look back over his shoulder so he could see how well she was faring. She was going to give him a most serene expression, even if it killed her.

Alec Kincaid never bothered to look back.

Although Jamie was skilled, she wasn't used to riding in the stiff new saddle. She was more comfortable riding bareback.

Her backside and thighs were taking quite a pounding. The rocky, ill-tended north road made the beating all the more painful. Bushes barred the way and she had to dodge low-hanging branches while keeping firm control of her mount. She let her grimace show once she became convinced Alec wasn't even aware she was behind him, then began to bargain with her Maker that she'd give him twenty daily masses in a row without daydreaming once if he'd only make her demon husband slow down a little.

God wasn't in a bargaining mood. Jamie came to that conclusion when they caught up with Daniel and Mary. Alec immediately took the lead, never once breaking stride. Jamie stayed behind her husband. Mary, looking as worn out as an old boot, trailed behind, with Daniel taking up the rear.

Jamie knew it was for safety's sake they rode at such a grueling pace. She'd heard the stories about the bands of roving misfits who preyed on unsuspecting victims. She guessed that one warrior protected the women from the front in the event of a surprise attack, while the other blocked the rear for just the same reason. If bandits did try to breach the foursome, they'd have to get through Alec or Daniel in order to reach their brides.

Oh, she understood the reasons all right, but she was soon too worried about Mary to care.

They'd ridden for almost two full hours before her sister finally broke down. Jamie was immensely proud of Mary because she'd been able to last so long without complaining. Mary wasn't one to suffer discomfort of any sort.

"Jamie? I want to stop for a few minutes," Mary called out.

"Nay, lass."

Daniel shouted the denial. Jamie couldn't believe his callous attitude. She turned around just in time to see Mary's husband emphasize his denial by shaking his head.

The pained look on Mary's face upset Jamie. She had

turned to shout her own demand to Alec for a brief respite when she heard the shrill scream.

When Jamie turned around again, she found Mary's mount right behind her. Mary, however, was missing.

Everyone stopped, even Alec Kincaid.

Daniel reached his bride as Jamie and Alec had dismounted. Poor Mary was sprawled on her backside in the middle of a fat leafy bush. While Jamie dismounted, Daniel gently lifted Mary to her feet.

"Are you hurt, lass?" he asked, his voice filled with concern.

Mary brushed the hair out of her eyes before answering. "Only a little, milord," she said.

There were several leaves clinging to Mary's hair. Daniel took his time pulling them free. Jamie saw the tender way he treated Mary and decided he had a few redeeming qualities, after all.

"What the hell happened?" Alec asked from behind Jamie's back.

She jumped at the sound of his voice, then turned around to face him.

"Mary fell off her horse."

"She what?"

"She fell off her horse."

Alec looked as if he didn't believe her. "She's English, Alec, or have you forgotten?" Daniel called out.

"What does that have to do with anything?" Jamie asked. She looked from one warrior to the other, then realized they were both trying not to smile.

"She could have broken her neck," Jamie muttered.

"But she didn't," Alec answered.

"She could have," Jamie argued, infuriated by his cold attitude.

"She's all right now," Daniel stated, drawing Jamie's attention back to him. "Aren't you, Mary?"

"I'm fine," Mary said, blushing at all the attention she was getting.

"She is not fine," Jamie announced. She turned back to Alec. He'd moved indecently close to her when she wasn't

71

noticing and she almost bumped into him. Jamie took a quick step back, yet still had to tilt her head all the way back just to look into his eyes.

"Mary fell because . . ." Her voice trailed off. She'd just noticed the sprinkle of gold in his dark brown eyes. They were very appealing. She turned her gaze to his chest so she could regain her thoughts.

"Because . . . ?" Alec asked.

"Mary's too exhausted to go on, milord. She must rest. She isn't at all accustomed to riding such long distances."

"And you, English? Are you accustomed to riding such long distances?"

Jamie shrugged. "My wants aren't at issue here. Mary is more important. Surely you can see how tired she is. A few minutes won't matter much to you."

She glanced up then, took in his expression, and wondered what she'd said to cause such a fierce frown.

"Mary's a gentle lady," Jamie explained to his chest.

"And you're not?"

"Yes, of course I am," Jamie stammered. He was deliberately twisting her words around. "'Tis most unkind of you to suggest otherwise."

She glanced up at his face again just in time to catch his smile.

She suddenly realized he wasn't trying to be insulting. And he really was smiling at her, a sincere, tender smile that made her stomach feel as if it were full of sugar. She felt flooded with contentment.

She didn't know how to react.

"Are you always so serious, wife?"

The question sounded like a caress to her and had much the same effect as if he'd just brushed his hand across her heart.

God's truth, she was having an unusual reaction to this barbarian. Jamie decided she was just as exhausted as Mary was. Surely that was the reason Alec Kincaid was beginning to appeal to her. He was almost handsome now, in a raw, primitive way, of course. A lock of his hair had fallen on his forehead, giving him a rascal's appearance. That was unfortunate, a worry as well, for Jamie always did have a liking for glib-tongued carefree rascals.

Without a thought to the consequences, she reached up and brushed the errant lock back where it belonged. She didn't want him to look like a rascal; she wanted him to stay mean-looking. Then her heart would surely quit pounding so loud in her ears and she'd be able to catch her breath, wouldn't she?

Alec didn't move when she touched him, but he liked the feel of her hand on his forehead. The gentle ministration surprised him. He wanted her to touch him again. "Why did you do that?" he asked, his tone mild.

"Your hair is too long," Jamie answered, not daring to give him the truth.

"It isn't."

"You'll have to cut it."

"Why?"

"I can't trust a man whose hair is almost as long as mine," she muttered.

Her explanation sounded ridiculous to her. She blushed and frowned to cover her embarrassment.

"I asked you if you were always so serious," Alec reminded her with a grin.

"You did?"

Heaven help her, she couldn't seem to keep her mind on the conversation. It was all his fault, of course, for smiling her thoughts right out of her mind.

"I did."

Alec kept his amusement contained, for he guessed his bride would think he was laughing at her. For some reason he couldn't explain, he didn't want to harm her tender feelings. An odd reaction, he told himself, as he'd never been one to care overmuch for any woman's feelings.

He certainly cared now, he realized, even as he excused his behavior by reminding himself that she was English bred, after all, and therefore apt to be more skittish than a strong Highland lass.

Jamie was wringing her hands. Alec doubted she was aware of that telling action. It was a sign of fear, yet she contradicted the weakness by valiantly meeting his gaze now. Her high cheekbones were tinged pink with embarrassment. He knew she had to be as exhausted as her sister was. Neither woman seemed to have much stamina. The pace he'd set had been rigorous but necessary, because as long as they were on English soil, they were in danger. Yet his new bride hadn't complained or begged to stop, and that fact pleased him considerably. Gavin, Alec's second-in-command, would say she had grit. It was a high compliment for a Highlander to give a woman, and one Jamie had already earned just by standing up to him.

Gavin would have a hearty laugh if he could see his laird now, Alec decided. The smile faded from his face when he realized he was acting like a simpleton. He'd never spent this much time talking with a woman before. Yet now he was staring at his wife just like a man who'd never seen a pretty woman before. Hell, he was physically reacting to her, too; he could feel himself getting hard.

It was time to dismiss her from his thoughts.

"You're wringing your hands," he muttered as he reached out to stop that action.

"I was pretending it was your neck," Jamie said in reaction to his sudden scowl. "And, yes, milord, I am serious most of the time," she rushed on, hoping to take his mind off her insult. "When I'm leaving England, I'm very serious. I'm leaving my cherished homeland."

"'Tis the same reason I'm smiling," Alec said.

He wasn't smiling now, but Jamie decided not to mention that fact. "You're happy because you're going home?"

"Because we're going home." His voice was back to sounding like steel again.

"England is my home."

"Was," he corrected, determined to set her straight. "Scotland is your home now."

"You wish me to give my loyalty to Scotland?"

"Wish?" he asked, grinning. "I don't wish it, wife. I command it. You'll be loyal to Scotland and to me."

She was back to wringing her hands. She had raised her

voice to him when she asked her question, too, but Alec decided not to take exception to her behavior. He knew she needed time to sort the problem out in her mind. Because he was such a patient man, he decided to give her an hour or two to agree.

He thought he was being very courteous, and cautioned himself against letting such consideration become a habit.

"Let me understand this," Jamie began. "You really think I'm going—"

"It's very simple, wife. If you're loyal to Scotland, you're loyal to me. You'll see the rightness of it once you've settled in."

"Once I've what?" Her voice was suspiciously soft.

"Once you've settled in," Alec repeated.

Her throat started aching with the need to shout at this arrogant man. Then she remembered Beak's suggestion not to nudge the laird's temper until she knew what kind of reaction she was going to get.

She'd better be cautious, she decided. It was common knowledge that Scots lashed out before thinking better of it. They all beat their wives as often as the inclination came over them. "Sheep settle in, Kincaid. I'm a lady, if you haven't taken the time to notice."

"I've noticed."

The way he drew out that remark made her heart quicken. "Yes," she stammered. "Women, you see, don't settle in. It isn't at all the same."

"It is," he contradicted with a lazy grin.

"No, it isn't," she snapped. "You'll have to take my word on this."

"Are you challenging me, English?"

His voice was hard enough to frighten her, but he was determined to make her understand her place.

He waited for her to cringe . . . and apologize.

"I am challenging you," Jamie announced, nodding vigorously when he looked incredulous.

God's truth, he didn't know what to make of her now. Her voice and stance reeked with authority. She wasn't wringing her hands together, either; they were fisted at her sides. Alec knew he really shouldn't let her get away with her insolence. A wife should always agree with her husband. Jamie obviously hadn't heard of this sacred dictate, however. Why, she dared to stand up to him as though she were his equal.

That thought forced a deep chuckle. The woman was definitely daft, but she did have grit.

"I've been in England too long," he admitted, "else I'd find your arguments overbearing, wife."

"Will you quit calling me 'wife'? I have a name. Can you not call me Jamie?"

"It's a man's name."

She wanted to throttle him. "It's my name."

"We'll find another."

"We will not."

"Dare you argue with me again?"

She wished she were as big as he was. He wouldn't dare laugh at her then. Jamie took a deep breath. "You say my arguments are overbearing, yet perhaps once I've settled in, as you've so obscenely put it, you'll get rid of your confusion and see the rightness in what I'm saying."

"Since I haven't the faintest idea what it is you're saying, I doubt it," he countered.

"Now you've insulted me."

"I have?"

"You have."

He shrugged his big shoulders. "It's my right, wife."

She began a prayer for patience. "I see," she whispered hoarsely. "Then I must assume it's also my right to insult you."

"It doesn't work that way."

Jamie gave up. The man was as stubborn as she was. "Have we crossed the border yet?"

Alec shook his head. "We've only a stone's throw to go."

"Then why were you smiling?"

"In anticipation."

"Oh."

Alec started to turn his back on her, but Jamie stayed the

action with her next question. "Alec? You really dislike England, don't you?"

She hadn't been able to keep the amazement out of her voice. The very idea of anyone disliking her land was simply beyond her comprehension. Everyone loved England, even dull-witted Scotsmen who liked to throw trees at one another. Why, England was the Rome of modern times. Its grandeur couldn't be denied.

"I do dislike England most of the time. There are exceptions, though."

"Exceptions?"

He slowly nodded.

"Well? When don't you dislike England, then?"

"When I'm raiding."

"You actually admit to such a sin?" she asked, clearly appalled.

Alec's grin widened. Her blush had intensified until she looked as if the sun had burned her. His wife was so refreshingly honest in all her reactions. A deadly trait in a man, that, giving others advance warning of what he was thinking, yet most agreeable in a woman. Especially his woman.

"Well?"

Alec let out a long sigh. It was a pity, but his wife didn't seem to have any sense of humor. She couldn't tell when he was jesting with her. "Gain your mount. The sun is already setting," he told her. "You may rest when we reach safety."

"Safety?"

"Scotland."

Jamie thought about asking him if he thought safety and Scotland were one and the same, then decided not to bother. She guessed his answer would just irritate her.

She had already learned two very unpleasant things about her husband. One: he didn't like being questioned or contradicted. That was going to be a problem, Jamie knew, for she was determined to question or contradict him whenever she wanted to. She didn't care if he liked it or not. Two: when he was scowling at her, she didn't like him much at all. The second flaw was almost as worrisome as the first. Alec's mood changed like the wind. The most innocent remarks made him scowl.

"Jamie, I'm not getting back on that damn horse again."

Mary pulled on her sister's arm to get her attention. Alec heard the statement, but paid no attention to it. He turned and walked back to his mount. Jamie watched him, thinking to herself that he'd just dismissed her with as much care as one would give a piece of lint.

"That man's rude by half," she muttered.

"Jamie, aren't you listening to me?" Mary demanded. "You're going to have to insist that we rest here for the night."

Jamie's heart went out to her sister. Mary's face was streaked with dirt. She looked as exhausted as Jamie felt. Jamie had a good deal more stamina than her sister did, but she'd been up most of the night before, helping one of the servants with her sick child.

She didn't dare offer Mary any sympathy, knowing that a firm hand was needed now. Mary would start crying if Jamie gave her an ounce of compassion. That thought was quite chilling. Once Mary got started, she was worse than the twins.

"What have you done with your pride?" Jamie demanded. "It's unladylike to use a common word like 'damn' when you speak. Only serfs use such crude words, Mary."

The thunder went out of Mary's expression. "How can you lecture me now, for God's sake?" she wailed. "I want to go home. I miss my papa."

"Enough!" Jamie's command was given in a much harsher tone of voice. She patted her sister's shoulder to soften her rebuke, then whispered, "What's done is done. We're married to Scots, and that's that. Don't disgrace us by carrying on. Besides, it's only a little farther to the Highlands," she exaggerated. "Alec has promised me that we'll stop for the night just as soon as we cross the border. Surely you can last a few more minutes, sister. Let your husband see what a courageous woman you are."

Mary nodded. "What if he's too dense to notice my courage?"

"Then I'll be happy to instruct him," Jamie promised.

"Jamie, did you ever, in all your days, think we'd end up in this predicament? We're married to Scots!"

"No, Mary, I never once considered that eventuality."

"God must be very angry with us."

"Not God," Jamie qualified. "Our king."

Mary's pitiful sigh trailed behind her as she walked back to her mount. Jamie watched her sister until she'd reached Daniel's side. The Scottish lord was smiling. Jamie guessed he was amused by the sight of his bride walking like an old woman with rickety knees.

Jamie shook her head over her sister's pitiful condition until she realized she was in much the same condition. Her legs were as shaky as dried leaves. She placed the blame on the stupid saddle she was forced to put up with so Alec would think she was a lady.

It took her three attempts to climb up on Wildfire's back. She'd made her mount nervous with the distraction, too. The mare started prancing, and it took Jamie precious strength to get her calm again.

Wildfire obviously didn't like the saddle any more than Jamie did.

Daniel had assisted Mary into her saddle, but Alec hadn't shown any such gentlemanly consideration. He wasn't even watching her. She wondered what held his attention, for he was gazing intently toward the area they'd just come from, a frown of concentration on his face.

Jamie decided to ignore him as thoroughly as he was ignoring her. She turned to call a word of encouragement to her sister.

She never heard Alec approach. He was suddenly by her side. Before she could react, he'd pulled her off her mount. Then he half carried, half dragged her to the ragged boulder adjacent to the bush Mary had split down the middle when she took her fall. Alec shoved Jamie up against the rock with one hand, slapped Wildfire's flank with the other, then turned his back on her and motioned to Daniel.

"Whatever are you—"

The rest of Jamie's question was pushed from her mind when Mary was shoved up against her. Daniel positioned himself in front of his bride. His broad back kept both women pinned to the boulder behind him.

When Daniel drew his sword, Jamie understood what was happening. She took a deep breath while she watched Daniel motion to Alec and hold up three fingers.

Alec shook his head, then indicated the number was four.

Mary still didn't catch on to the threat. Jamie slapped her hand over her sister's mouth when she started to stammer a protest.

Alec walked back to the center of the small clearing. Jamie pushed Mary's hair out of her face so she could see him clearly.

He hadn't drawn his weapon yet. Then Jamie realized that Alec didn't have a sword. Good God, the man was virtually defenseless.

Jamie was sick with fear for Alec's safety. With that fear came fury. What kind of warrior journeyed through the wilderness without a weapon at his side?

A damn forgetful one, Jamie decided with a scowl. He'd probably lost his sword somewhere along the way to London and hadn't bothered to replace it.

She'd have to intervene, of course. Alec Kincaid was her husband, and no one was going to put a mark on him as long as she lived. Refusing to understand the true reason she didn't want to see him harmed, she simply told herself she didn't want to be widowed on her wedding day, and that was that.

Jamie removed the small dagger from the looped belt she wore around her waist, hoping there was still time to pass the weapon to Alec. The dagger could inflict real injury if accuracy was employed. There was also Daniel's sword, Jamie remembered. She prayed Alec's friend knew how to wield his weapon and was just about to ask him to help her husband when Alec suddenly turned around.

He was motioning to Daniel. She could see his face clearly now and immediately started to shiver. The look of fury in those cold dark eyes terrified her. She could see the raw strength in his muscular arms and thighs. Anger was there, too. It washed over her like a hot wave. Power radiated from him until it became a thick mist surrounding them all.

She'd never seen such a look before, but she recognized it all the same: he was ready to kill.

Mary started crying. "It isn't a wild boar, is it, Jamie?"

"No, Mary," Jamie whispered. She kept her gaze on her husband when she squeezed her sister's arm. "It will be all right. Our husbands will keep us safe. You'll see."

Jamie almost believed her assurance until she saw the bandits slowly advancing toward Alec. She guessed then it wasn't going to be all right at all.

Alec had moved quite a distance away from the others. Jamie thought he was deliberately trying to draw the bandits as far from the women as possible.

The thieves slowly followed him. They took their time, too, acting as if they had all the time in the world to see their kill completed. Alec was much larger than his enemies, but he was unarmed. The odds certainly didn't favor him. Two of the four bandits carried blackened clubs. The other two waved curved swords in the air. The slicing motion made the air whistle. There was dried blood crusted on the blades, indicating their earlier attacks had been successful.

Jamie thought she was going to be sick. They were such evil-looking men. They looked as if they enjoyed their sport; two were actually smiling. What teeth they had were as black as their clubs.

"Daniel, please go and help Alec," Jamie ordered, her voice weak with fear.

"There are only four of them, lass. It will be over in just a minute."

His answer infuriated her. She knew Daniel stood in front of them to offer protection, yet didn't think that was noble given the fact that his friend was about to be slaughtered.

Jamie reached over Mary's shoulder and shoved Daniel's back. "Alec doesn't have a weapon to defend himself. Give him my dagger or your sword, Daniel."

"Alec doesn't need a weapon."

He answered her in such a cheerful voice that Jamie was certain he'd lost his mind.

She stopped trying to argue with him. "Either you go and help him or I will."

"All right, lass, if you insist." Daniel shrugged Mary's hands away from his tunic and started toward the men circling Alec.

Yet when he reached the edge of the clearing, he stopped. Jamie couldn't believe what she was seeing. Daniel calmly replaced his sword in his scabbard, folded his arms across his chest, and damn if he didn't grin at Alec.

Alec grinned back.

"We're wed to half-wits," Jamie told Mary. She decided she was still more frightened than angry, as her voice actually shivered in the stillness.

A deep bellow suddenly gained her full attention. The battle cry came from Alec. The bone-chilling sound sent Mary into a fit of screaming.

The circle had tightened around Alec. He waited until the first was within striking distance, then moved so swiftly he became a blur of motion to Jamie. She watched him grab hold of one man by his throat and jaw, heard the horrid sound of bone cracking when he twisted the enemy's neck into an unnatural position.

Alec hurled the man to the ground just as two others, shouting their intentions, attacked from his left side. Alec slammed their heads together, then tossed them atop the crumpled man on the ground.

The last of the four dared to gain advantage by striking from behind. Alec whirled around, slammed his boot into the man's groin in what appeared to be the most effortless of motions, then lifted the man off the ground with one powerful blow of his fist centered beneath his jutting jaw.

The pile on the ground had grown to pyramid proportions. Daniel had been correct in his boast that it would soon be over, for less than a full minute had passed.

Alec didn't even look winded. That amazing thought had just taken root in Jamie's mind when a new sound caught her attention. She turned just as three big men came rushing toward her from the cover of the bushes on the opposite side of the boulder.

Like snakes they'd slithered through the thicket to get to the prize.

"Alec!" Jamie shouted.

"Jamie, you must protect me," Mary screamed.

Before Jamie could respond, her sister pulled her away from the boulder. Mary flattened herself against the rock, then pulled Jamie in front of her. Though Mary was almost a head taller than her younger sister, once she'd hunched her shoulders down into the crease in the rock and tucked her face between Jamie's shoulderblades, she was well insulated from attack. The boulder shielded her back, and her sister shielded her front.

Jamie didn't try to protect herself. She understood her duty. Mary came first. If need be, she'd give her life to keep her safe.

The three men were almost upon them when Jamie remembered the small dagger she held in her hand. She took aim and threw the weapon, deliberately choosing the biggest of the three. Her aim proved true. The bandit let out an ear-piercing scream and collapsed.

Daniel charged the second of the three dark-haired men and knocked the villain to the ground with a mighty blow to his midsection. Alec had a greater distance to cover. By the time he'd almost reached his prey, it was too late. Though Jamie fought like a wildcat, the bastard had her in what appeared to be a death grip. His knife was pressed against her heart.

"Stop where you be," the man shouted at Alec in a high-pitched screech. "I got nothing to lose now. If you come any closer, I'll kill her. I can snap her pretty little neck as easy as not."

Daniel had finished his fight and was slowly advancing from behind. Alec motioned for him to stop when the villain gave a fearful glance over his shoulder. He tightened his hold on Jamie's hair in reaction to this new threat, then twisted the mass around his hand as he jerked her head back.

Alec saw the wild, hunted look in the man's bleak eyes. It was obvious the bastard was terrified, for Alec could see his hands were shaking. His enemy was of medium height, with a bloated face and stomach. He was going to be a quick kill, Alec decided, once he'd released Jamie and she wasn't in jeopardy. The man was in a panic now, however. His fear made him as unpredictable as a cornered rat. The enemy might very well try to kill Jamie if provoked . . . or if he believed his situation was completely hopeless.

It was hopeless, of course. He would die. His fate had been decreed the moment he touched Jamie.

Alec kept his fury contained, waiting for his opportunity. He affected a casual stance, folded his arms across his chest, and tried his damnedest to look bored.

"I'm meaning what I say," the captor shouted. "And shut the other woman up. I can't think with her screaming like that."

Daniel immediately went over to Mary. He clamped his hand over her mouth, forcing her to be silent, yet never once spared her a sympathetic glance. His full attention was on Jamie's captor as he also waited for his chance to strike.

The fear slowly ebbed from the enemy's eyes. He snickered, obviously sensing victory was now on his side. Alec knew he had him then. The rat was getting ready to scurry out of his corner. He was feeling content, and that false confidence was going to be his destruction.

"This one be your woman?" the man bellowed at Alec.

"She is."

"You care for her?"

Alec shrugged.

"Oh, you're caring all right," the enemy shouted. He chuckled with glee then. It was a foul, grating sound. "You don't want me killing your pretty, now, do you?" He tore at Jamie's hair, hoping to cause a grimace as further proof of his power and their impotence, but when he glanced at the hellion he'd captured, he realized he'd failed.

His hostage was glaring at him. He knew he was hurting her, but she stubbornly refused to cry out.

Alec had avoided looking at his wife's face, knowing the

fear he'd see in her gaze would undermine his concentration. His rage would be uncontrollable then. Yet when the blackguard twisted Jamie's hair so forcefully, Alec instinctively looked at her.

She didn't appear to be afraid. God's truth, she looked bloody furious. Alec was so surprised by her show of courage that he almost smiled.

"Get me one of them fine horses," her captor ordered. "When I'm feeling safe and sure you ain't sniffing after me, I'll let your pretty go."

Alec shook his head. "No."

"What say you?"

"I said no," Alec answered, his voice as calm now as the soft wind. "You can have her, but you cannot have her horse."

Jamie let out a loud gasp. "Shut your mouth, bitch," her enemy muttered. He pressed his blade to her throat, glaring at Alec all the while. "I'm wanting both, damn your hide."

Alec shook his head again. "Take the woman if you want, but not the horse."

"I said I'm wanting both!" His voice sounded like the screech of a trapped bird.

"No."

"Let him have both, Alec," Daniel interjected. "You can easily replace her and her horse."

Jamie couldn't believe what she was hearing. The urge to weep was almost overwhelming. "Alec?" she whispered, her worry obvious in her tone. "You can't mean it."

"I told you to shut your mouth," the enemy ordered again. He gave her hair another vicious yank to emphasize his command.

Jamie slammed her foot down on top of his in retaliation.

"Daniel, get her horse," Alec ordered. "Now."

"Let the other woman fetch it," the captor shouted.

Daniel ignored that command and walked over to Wildfire.

Jamie couldn't believe what was happening to her. She could have sworn she heard Daniel whistling. She knew the Scots didn't like the English, but this horrendous conduct was simply untenable. She was trying desperately not to be afraid. Alec wasn't making that task easy for her. After giving her only a quick glance, he'd ignored her. God help her, he had looked downright bored—until her enemy demanded her horse, Jamie qualified. Alec hadn't looked bored then. He looked furious.

Cholie had been right, after all. The Scots did value their horses more than their women.

If she'd had anything in her stomach, she certainly would have lost it by now. The scoundrel squeezing her so indecently smelled like a forgotten chamber pot. Every time she took a breath, she wanted to gag.

"Put the horse between her man and me," Jamie's captor ordered.

Alec waited for his chance. He moved when Daniel approached, grabbed the reins out of his friend's hands, and pulled Wildfire as close to his opponent as possible.

What happened next so startled Jamie that she didn't have time to react. She suddenly found herself flying through the air like a disk. She heard her captor's scream of agony just as Daniel caught her in his arms.

Jamie turned in time to see Alec plunge the enemy's dagger into his throat.

She did gag then, twice. Daniel hastily put her down. Mary came flying across the clearing and hurled herself at Jamie. The danger was over, but Mary continued to cry hysterically.

Jamie closed her eyes and concentrated on calming her racing heartbeat. Mary was clinging to her now, squeezing the breath out of her.

Jamie was suddenly shaking like a leaf in a windstorm. Her legs felt as brittle as kindling wood.

"You may open your eyes now."

Alec gave her that order. When Jamie did as he commanded, she found her husband standing just a breath away from her.

His eyes didn't look so terribly cold now. In truth, she thought he looked close to smiling. That didn't make any sense to her. She'd just seen him kill so easily, so brutally, so casually. And now he looked as if he wanted to smile over it.

Jamie couldn't make up her mind if she wanted to run away from him or stay and throttle him.

While she stared up at her husband, she heard Daniel order Mary to come with him, then felt him pry her sister's hands away from her. She didn't have the strength to help with that chore, yet she did wonder why Daniel sounded so angry with Mary and why Alec looked so damned cheerful.

Jamie wasn't aware her hands were clenched together. Alec was. "It's finished," he told her in a soft voice.

"Finished?" she repeated. She turned to look at the man Alec had just felled, and immediately started to shake.

Alec moved to block her view. He held up her dagger, his intent to give it back to her, but stayed that action when he saw how upset she was. She acted as though the dirk had suddenly become possessed by demons.

"This belongs to you, doesn't it?" he asked, confused by the unreasonable fear in her eyes.

Jamie took a step to the side, looked down at the dead man again, staring at the gaping hole in his neck where the dagger had penetrated.

Alec again moved to block her view. "Wife?"

She started backing away from him. "I don't want the dagger anymore. Throw it away. I have another one in my satchel."

"He's dead, wife," Alec stated, trying to be reasonable. "You needn't keep looking at him, lass. He can't hurt you now."

"Aye, he's dead," she stated with a vehement nod. "You tossed me in the air, Alec, just like a . . ."

"Caber?"

She nodded again. "You killed him so easily, milord. I've never seen . . ."

When she didn't finish her statement, Alec let out a sigh. "It was good of you to notice," he said then.

She gave him an incredulous look while she continued to back away from him. "It was good of me . . . ? Do you think

I am giving you praise, husband?" She paused to take a deep breath, trying to ease the ache in her throat, then looked at the dagger he was holding. "Throw that away, if you please. I don't want to look at it."

"Does the sight of blood upset you?" he asked. He thought her behavior most confusing. The woman had been a tigress only minutes before, when she struggled with her captor, yet now was acting like a frightened child.

Alec tried once again to calm her. He tossed the dagger over his shoulder.

"Yes—I mean, no," Jamie suddenly blurted out.

"Yes and no what?" he asked.

"You asked me if the sight of blood distresses me," Jamie explained in a rush. "And I answered you."

"You did?"

She threaded her fingers through her hair, inadvertently making it more disheveled than before, then whispered, "That blood makes me sick."

She had to sigh then. She'd meant to tell him she was used to seeing blood, that she was a healer and had probably mopped up enough blood to turn a river red, but it was simply too much trouble to try to explain anything. She was still reacting to the terrible upset she'd just had, she told herself, and to her husband's incredible strength.

There was also the rather painful fact that he had been very willing to give her away. Her horse actually meant more to him than she did.

She was going to have nightmares for a month.

Alec suddenly reached out and pulled her into his arms. "If you take another step back, you'll end up on top of the heap."

Jamie took one look over her shoulder, saw the stack of bodies, and felt her knees give out on her. She would have fallen on her face if he hadn't held her up.

Yet even in her distressed state, she couldn't help noticing how very gentle he was being. A contradiction, that, given the fact that he was such a giant of a man. It didn't seem possible that someone his size could be so gentle. Yet it seemed just as unlikely that he could dispose of four armed attackers without showing the least bit of exertion. The man hadn't even worked up a proper sweat.

He smelled nice. Jamie leaned against his chest and let him hold her.

"Did you mean it, Alec?" she whispered.

"Mean what?" he asked.

She didn't explain quickly enough to suit him. He tilted her chin up so he could see her expression. "Mean what, wife?"

"When you told that horrible man he could have me but not my horse," she explained. "Did you really mean what you said?"

He would have laughed if she hadn't looked so upset. "No."

She immediately collapsed against him. "Then why did you sound as if you meant it?"

Her voice was still whisper-soft, but he heard her all the same. Alec couldn't believe she harbored such a worry. Give her up? Never! "I wanted him to think he was in control, lass."

"He was in control, Alec," Jamie argued. "He was the one with the knife."

"Ah, I see," Alec returned, a smile in his voice now. "Then the men who circled me were also in control."

"Well, no," Jamie whispered. "I mean to say, they did have weapons, but you were the one who . . . took charge."

Before he could respond to that comment, Jamie added, "Then it was all a trick, wasn't it? You lied to him."

"I lied to him."

She let out another long sigh before her shivers reminded her how frightened she'd been. She immediately shoved away from him.

Jamie was back to being bloody furious. There was fire in her eyes, Alec thought, and he didn't have the faintest idea why she was angry now. The woman was as puzzling as a maze.

Ignoring her command to let go of her, Alec draped his arm around her shoulders, hauled her up against his side, and led her over to where Daniel had collected the horses.

Jamie didn't offer a word of gratitude when he lifted her up onto Wildfire's back. She kept her gaze downcast until he handed her the reins. His hands brushed against hers, startling her. She jerked her hands away.

"Look at me."

He waited until she obeyed his command before speaking again. "You've shown me how courageous you are, wife. I'm very pleased with you."

Her eyes widened in surprise. Alec smiled. He'd just found a rather simple way to placate her: praise. Wasn't it true that all women liked to hear their husbands' expressions of approval from time to time? Alec decided to remember that fact for future use.

"You might be pleased with me, husband, but I'm certainly not pleased with you, you arrogant Scotsman."

The thunder in her voice surprised him as much as her retort.

"You don't want my approval?"

She didn't bother to answer his question, but the anger in her expression told him he'd misjudged her. She wasn't one to be swayed by praise. Alec nodded with satisfaction. "Tell me why you were so frightened."

Jamie shook her head. She stared down at her hands while he stared at her frown. "I asked you a question," he reminded her.

She shook her head. Alec held his patience. "A wife must always obey her husband's commands," he instructed.

"Is this another one of your Highland commandments?"

"It is," he answered with a grin.

"Why is it the rest of the world only needs to obey ten commandments to get to heaven, but you Scots have need for so many extra ones? Is it because you're all such sinners, do you suppose?"

"When you get your grit back, it's with a vengeance, isn't it?" he said.

"Grit?"

"Never mind."

He was smiling at her, indicating how pleased he was. She decided he was daft. "I'd like to be on my way now, Alec."

"Not until you explain why you were so frightened."

"Worried, Alec. I was worried."

"All right, worried, then," Alec agreed, letting her have her way.

"Do you want the truth?" she asked.

"The truth."

"When you were fighting . . . well, there was this moment when I thought you were looking right at me, and I did think to myself that I must never make you angry, for I couldn't defend myself against your superior strength."

Alec had to lean forward to catch all of her explanation. She sounded so forlorn. He tried not to laugh. "It's going to be difficult for me, Alec," she continued. "I know this will probably surprise you, but I think there will be times when I irritate you."

"It doesn't surprise me at all."

"Why not?" she asked, looking disgruntled.

"You're irritating me now."

"Oh."

"Jamie, I'll never hurt you."

She stared into his eyes for a long moment. "Even when your temper gets the better of you? The Scots all have fierce tempers, Alec. Surely you'll admit to that."

"I'll never lose my temper with you. I give you my word."

"But if you do?" she asked.

"I still won't hurt you."

She finally believed him. Jamie quit trying to pull her hands away from his grasp. "I've heard the Scots all beat their wives."

"I've heard the same about the English."

"Some do, others don't."

"I don't."

She nodded. "You don't?"

Alec shook his head. He was convinced she was feeling safe with him. "When we first met, I could see the apprehension in your eyes. While I believe it's good for a wife to be fearful of her husband, this unreasonable fear I saw—"

"Pray forgive my rudeness for interrupting you, but I simply must tell you it isn't at all good for a wife to be afraid of her husband. I was worried, not afraid, of course, but most women would be afraid of you. I'm made of stronger character, however."

"Why?"

"Why what?" Jamie asked, confused by the way he was grinning at her and the way her heart was reacting to his devilish smile.

"Why would most women be afraid of me?"

She had to turn her gaze away from his handsome eyes before she could give him a proper answer. "Because you happen to be a very . . . large man. 'Tis the truth you're the biggest warrior I've ever seen."

"Have you seen others?" he asked, hiding his exasperation.

She frowned over his question, then shook her head. "Actually, no, I haven't."

"So it's my size that made you . . . worried."

"You're also as strong as a legion of soldiers put together, Alec, and you just killed four men," she added. "Surely you haven't forgotten that fact."

"Only one."

"Only one what?" she asked, temporarily sidetracked by the sparkle in his eyes. She had the dark suspicion he wanted to laugh at her.

"I only killed one man," he explained. "The one who dared to touch you. Most of them aren't dead, just indisposed. Did you want me to kill all of them?"

He sounded very accommodating. "Good God, no," Jamie assured him. "But what about the man Daniel struck down when they tried to harm Mary?"

"You'll have to ask him."

"I don't want to ask him anything."

"The bastards tried to harm you, too, Jamie."

"Mary's more important."

"You actually believe this nonsense?"

"It's always been my duty to protect my sisters, Alec."

"Why haven't you asked me about the man you struck down with your dagger?" Alec asked. "Your aim was true, wife," he added, thinking to give her a little more praise. "You killed—"

"I don't wish to discuss it," she shouted, dropping Wildfire's reins.

Now what had he said? His gentle little wife looked as if she might faint. The woman was a mystery to him. Alec shook his head. Jamie seemed to have a true aversion to killing. It was another quirk in her nature, to be sure, yet at the same time, he admitted to liking that flaw.

The woman would make him soft in all his attitudes if he let her. She was going to have to get used to killing. It was the way of life in the rugged Highlands. Only the strongest survived. He was going to have to toughen her up, he decided, or she wouldn't make it through the first harsh winter.

"All right, wife," Alec stated. "We won't discuss it."

The tension went out of her shoulders. Alec noticed she was a little unsteady on her mount, so he put his arm around her waist.

"What I did, I did in self-defense," Jamie told him. "If I injured that disgusting man, God will certainly understand. Mary's life was at stake."

"Aye," Alec agreed. "You did injure him."

"On the other hand, Father Charles will never understand. If he gets wind of this business, Alec, he'll have me wearing black for the rest of my days."

"The priest who married us?" he asked, totally perplexed again.

Jamie nodded. "You worry about the strangest things," Alec remarked. "'Tis a flaw in your nature, to my way of thinking."

"Oh? Then go and give Father Charles your confession, and after, tell me I worry for naught. The man's very imaginative with his penances."

Alec started laughing. He lifted Jamie into his arms and started toward his mount.

Jamie put her arms around his neck. "What are you doing?"

"You're going to ride with me."

"Why?"

His sigh nearly parted her hair. "Are you going to question everything I do or say?"

Jamie tilted her head back so she could see his face. Alec came to an immediate stop. The sparkle in her eyes, added to her slow, sweet smile, unsettled him.

"Will it make you angry if I do?"

"Do what?"

"Question you."

"No, I'll never get angry with you."

Her smile enchanted him. "I'm wed to the most amazing man," she told him. "You never get angry or lose your temper."

"Dare you bait me, English?"

Alec's full attention was centered on her mouth. He wanted to take her lower lip between his teeth, wanted to sink his tongue inside her, to taste the sweet honey that now belonged to him. Her fingers were stroking the back of his neck, whether by intent or by accident, he couldn't discern, and her soft, full breasts were pressed against his chest.

A man could only take so much provocation, Alec told himself.

He slowly lowered his head toward her. Jamie met him halfway.

Her mouth was just as soft as he remembered, just as arousing. It was a tender, undemanding kiss, entirely too brief, and thoroughly frustrating in Alec's opinion. She wouldn't open her mouth for him and pulled away just as he was about to force his invasion.

She looked damned happy with herself, too. Alec didn't let her see how frustrated he was. For all her courage and remarkable beauty, she sure as certain didn't know how to kiss.

It would, of course, be his duty to instruct her. Alec smiled in anticipation.

"Thank you, Alec."

"Why are you thanking me?" he asked. He lifted her onto

his saddle, then settled himself behind her in one quick motion. Her backside nestled against the junction of his thighs. She moved, apparently trying to be comfortable. He grimaced in reaction. Alec wrapped his arm around her waist, lifted her high onto his lap, and held her tightly against him.

"Well?" he asked when she didn't immediately answer him.

"I'm thanking you for your consideration."

He misunderstood her comment. "'Tis obvious you haven't ridden much," he said. "I'll instruct you in the proper way when we're settled in."

Jamie didn't bother to correct him. If he wanted to believe she was uneducated, then she'd let him. He probably wouldn't believe she was really skilled anyway, or that it was the new saddle giving her trouble now. If she admitted that she liked to ride bareback, as some warriors did, he would naturally conclude she wasn't much of a lady. She would let him think what he wanted. Beak had been right, she decided, for Alec was being more patient with her. He certainly wouldn't be holding her in his lap if he knew she didn't need his help. Jamie smiled to herself and leaned back against her husband. It felt good to be pampered. In time, she promised, she would set him straight. For now, however, she'd let him take charge.

Wives were a nuisance, Alec decided, but this one . . . she smelled so feminine, felt so soft, so right in his arms. She kept trying to edge his hand away from the undersides of her breasts. He smiled over her timidity, certain that once he'd bedded her, she'd be rid of this shyness. He was suddenly eager to make camp. Tonight he would take her, make her his; tonight she would give herself to him.

For a Scot, he certainly had a most appealing scent. Jamie had to smile over that daft admission. In the space of one short day she'd gone from hating the man to almost liking him. God only knew she felt safe enough with him. If her emotions continued along this illogical course, though, she just might let him kiss her again . . . in another day or two.

And if he proved to be all she wanted in a husband, well, then, eventually, after a long, satisfying courtship, of course, she might let him bed her.

It was a blessing Alec was such a patient man. She would simply explain her reticence and he'd agree to her terms.

And that was that.

Chapter Six

They made camp an hour later, near a deep mountain-fed pool of clear water. While Daniel and Alec attended to the horses, Jamie unpacked the basket of food Agnes had thoughtfully prepared for their supper. Mary leaned against a tree trunk, watching her sister work. Jamie thought she looked quite miserable.

Jamie spread a small blanket on the ground. She sat down on one edge, folded her skirts so that not even a hint of ankle showed, and motioned for Mary to join her.

Both she and her sister were trying to ignore their husbands. Alec and Daniel had each taken a turn washing in the pool. It hadn't bothered Jamie much at all when Daniel came strolling back into camp without his tunic. Alec's bare chest was another matter altogether. When she glanced up and caught sight of him, her breath caught in her throat. His body was bronzed from the sun. The ripple of muscle in his shoulders and upper arms reminded her of his strength, and the dark gold hair covering his massive chest emphasized his raw masculinity. The hair tapered to his flat stomach, then disappeared beneath the waist of his black pants.

"I don't want Daniel to touch me."

Mary's whispered fear captured Jamie's attention. "It's only natural to be a little afraid," she whispered, trying to sound as if she knew what she was talking about.

"He kissed me."

Jamie smiled. Now she felt that she was on safe ground. She knew all about kissing. "It's his right to kiss you, Mary. Alec kissed me, too," she added. "Twice, if you count the wedding kiss. I thought it was very nice."

"Did he kiss you the way a man kisses a woman when he wants to mate with her?" Mary asked. "You know, did his tongue touch yours?"

Jamie didn't know what Mary was talking about, but she wasn't going to let her ignorance show. "You didn't like it, Mary?" she asked, avoiding a true answer.

"It was disgusting."

"Oh, Mary." Jamie sighed. "Perhaps, in time, you'll get to like the way Daniel kisses."

"I might have liked it if he hadn't been so angry with me," Mary muttered. "He just grabbed me and kissed me. I still don't know why he's upset. He keeps frowning."

"You aren't imagining this anger?"

"No. Will you speak to him, Jamie? Find out what has him so prickly."

Daniel walked over and sat down next to Mary before Jamie could answer her request. She nudged Mary, then motioned to the food. Mary caught the silent message and offered a portion of the food to her husband.

Alec separated himself from the threesome. He sat on the ground with his back against a fat tree trunk. He looked very relaxed. One leg was bent at the knee, making the sleek bulge of muscle in his thigh all the more prominent.

Jamie tried not to look as nervous as she was feeling. Alec was staring at her. She told herself she just wasn't used to being the center of anyone's attention, and surely that was the only reason she was feeling so awkward.

She motioned him over to join her. Alec shook his head, then ordered her to come to him.

Jamie decided to give in. He was her husband and she supposed it was her duty to try to get along with him. She gathered a large wedge of cheese, some crusty bread, one of the three leather pouches of ale, and finally walked over to Alec.

He accepted her offering without comment. Jamie started to go back to Mary's side, but Alec wouldn't let her leave. He pulled her down next to him, softening her fall by bracing his arm around her waist.

She couldn't help but notice how possessive his touch was. She kept her back as straight as a lance and folded her hands in her lap.

"Are you back to being afraid of me, English?"

"I was never afraid, Scot," she answered. "Only worried."

"Are you still worried?"

"No."

"Then why are you trying to ease my arm away?"

"It isn't decent to touch like this in front of others, Alec."

"It isn't?"

She ignored the amusement in his voice. "No, it isn't," she repeated. "And my name is Jamie. You've still to say it, Alec."

"It's a man's name."

"Are we back to that?"

"Aye, we are."

She refused to look at him until he finished laughing, then said, "My name certainly seems to give you vast amusement. I suppose that's all for the better, Alec, because you're in a fine mood, you see, and I wanted to tell you something you might take exception to, but once you hear me out, why, I'm certain you'll agree with my decision."

The seriousness in her tone puzzled him. "What is it you wish to ask me?"

"I would ask that you not . . . touch me. I don't know you well enough to allow such liberties."

"Allow?"

A shiver of dread passed down her spine. It was apparent from his tone of voice that he didn't care for her choice of words. "Alec? Do you want a wife who is unwilling?"

"Are you asking me or your hands?" Alec countered.

"You."

"Then look at me."

The command was given in a hard voice. She needed all her determination to do as he ordered. It would have been easier if he hadn't been sitting so close to her. He wouldn't let her scoot away from him, either, no matter how many times she tried.

She finally managed to look into his eyes for a full minute, then lowered her gaze to stare at his mouth. That error in judgment made her sigh. It didn't seem to matter where she looked. The man was hard all over. A day's growth of whiskers made him all the more fierce-looking.

Jamie had the feeling he was trying to read her thoughts when she glanced into his eyes again. It was an absurd feeling, but it was there all the same.

She was suddenly hot and cold and thoroughly confused.

"Now ask me your question again," he said.

"Do you want an unwilling wife?" she repeated, her voice a low whisper.

"I don't particularly want a wife at all."

She took immediate exception to that honesty. "Well, you've got one."

"Aye, I have, and English at that."

If her back became any straighter, Alec thought her spine might crack.

His new wife was blessed with a giant-sized temper. She looked ready to let go of that precious control of hers, too. She was clasping her hands together now in a grip that had to be painful.

"I wonder why you say the word 'English' as though it were a blasphemy."

"It is."

"It isn't."

Her blush deepened when she realized she'd just shouted at him. She glanced up to measure Alec's reaction. He was frowning, but she didn't think he realized how very angry he was making her. She was well disciplined in hiding her emotions.

"You could never care for an English wife, then?"

"Care for?"

"You know my meaning."

"Explain it."

The man was as dense as fog. "Love," Jamie snapped. Noticing that Mary and Daniel were both staring at her, she paused to give them a smile, then turned to glare at Alec. "You could never love an English wife?" she whispered.

"I doubt it."

"You doubt it?"

"You needn't shout," Alec remarked. He was thoroughly enjoying her outrage. "Does my honesty upset you?"

She had to take a deep breath before answering him. "No, your honesty doesn't upset me, but I do find your amusement most insulting, milord. We're discussing a serious topic."

"Serious by your measure, not mine."

"You don't consider marriage an important undertaking?"

"No."

"No?"

She looked appalled and furious. Alec thought it was an enchanting combination. "You're only an insignificant part of my life, wife. When you understand the way of life in the Highlands, you'll see how foolish your fears are."

"I'm insignificant and foolish? Alec, you must find me most inferior," she countered. "Yet you're ready for sainthood, aren't you? Why, you never lose your temper or get angry. Isn't that what you told me?"

"True," Alec admitted, grinning. "I did say that."

"I didn't particularly want to marry you either, Kincaid."

"I noticed."

"You did?"

She actually seemed surprised. Alec let her see his exasperation. "You wore a black gown to your wedding," he reminded her.

"I happen to like this gown," she returned, pausing to brush a bit of dust off the hem. "I might wear it every other day."

"Ah, so you could never come to care for me?" he asked.

"'Tis most doubtful."

Alec did laugh then, a low, rumbling sound that made Jamie think the earth was trembling.

"Why does my honesty make you laugh?"

"'Twas the way you gave it."

"I don't want to continue this discussion, Alec. If you've finished your meal, I'll put the food away."

"Let your sister see to that duty."

"It's my responsibility," she explained.

"Just as it was your responsibility to protect her?"

"Yes."

"Mary believes this nonsense, too, doesn't she?"

"Nonsense? Since when is doing one's duty nonsense?"

"Daniel and I heard your sister order you to guard her when the English bastards attacked. We saw her use you as her shield."

"They weren't English bastards," Jamie corrected, concentrating on that remark. He was determined not to understand about Mary and she wasn't in the mood to argue. "I'm certain the infidels came from . . ." She was about to tell him she was sure the scoundrels had crossed over the border from Scotland, then thought better of it. "They belong to no country. That is why they're called outcasts, don't you suppose?"

"I suppose," Alec allowed, letting her have her way. She was frowning enough to make him think that issue was of grave importance to her. "I thought you were the youngest daughter," he stated. "I heard your father call you his baby." He smiled after making that comment, then added, "I was mistaken?"

"No, you weren't mistaken," Jamie replied. "I am the youngest. And Papa does like to call me his baby." She blushed after making that confession.

"Yet Mary forced you to be her shield."

"Oh, no, she didn't force me," Jamie argued.

"Aye, she did."

Her voice had gone suspiciously soft. Jamie didn't retreat from his frown this time. "You can't possibly understand, Alec. You're a Scot, if you'll remember, and can't possibly know how the English do things. You'll just have to take my word on this issue. It has always been my duty to protect my older sisters. It's probably the same in every household in England."

"Your opinions displease me."

She didn't particularly care if her opinions pleased him. She shrugged to show her indifference.

"You're the baby," he continued. "For that reason, your older sister should have looked after you."

She shook her head. The man seemed determined to make her change her mind. "No, it's the other way around, milord."

Now Alec shook his head. "The strong must always protect the weak, wife; the older must always protect the younger. And that's the way it is everywhere, even in the hallowed country of England."

While he watched in fascination, Jamie's eyes turned a deep violet. She wasn't at all happy with his views. That truth was emphasized when she jabbed at his shoulder. "I am not weak."

Alec resisted the urge to take her into his arms and kiss the outrage out of her. Lord, she was really too beautiful for his peace of mind.

"No, you're not weak," he admitted.

The bluster went out of her then. "It was good of you to notice," she said.

"Yet you were afraid of me."

"Do you have to keep bringing that up? It's most unkind of you to remind me of that incident, Alec."

"Perhaps I have an unkind nature."

"You don't."

He was surprised by her quick, vehement denial. "You sound very sure of that."

"I am," Jamie admitted. "You were kind to my father when he carried on so," she reminded him. "You were

103

patient and understanding. Most men wouldn't have shown such compassion."

She thought she'd just praised him, yet his shout of laughter told her he was more amused than appreciative.

"It's bad manners to laugh when given a compliment, Alec. Damn rude, too."

"Compliment? Wife, you just insulted me when you called me compassionate. Never has that word been put to me."

"I disagree," she countered. "Just because you haven't been called compassionate before doesn't mean—"

"A wife should never disagree with her husband."

He looked sincere. It was high time, she decided, to set him straight. "A wife must give her husband her opinion," she stated, "whenever it seems needed. It's the only way a good marriage survives, Alec. You must take my word on this matter," she added before turning away from the incredulous look on his face.

"Stop trying to push my hands away. You belong to me now. I won't allow you to pull away when I touch you."

"I've already explained that I'm not ready to belong to you just yet."

"It doesn't matter if you're ready or not."

He sounded downright cheerful when he stated that truth. "Alec, I'm not going to sleep with you as wife until I've gotten to know you better. Surely you can understand my reticence."

"Oh, I understand," he said.

Jamie dared a quick look up, saw the laughter lurking in his dark eyes, and suddenly realized how much he was enjoying her embarrassment. She knew she was acting foolish. Her hands were clenched tight and she'd started trembling again.

"You're frightened. Beak explained that you . . ."

"I'm not frightened. I'm . . . worried."

He stated the obvious then. "You're blushing like a virgin."

She gave him a disgruntled look before answering. "I can't help that. I *am* a virgin."

Alec laughed in spite of himself. She sounded ashamed, as if she'd just confessed a dark sin.

"Will you please stop laughing at me? It's insulting."

"Your virginity belongs to me, Jamie. A bride shouldn't be embarrassed by her purity."

He'd finally used her name. Jamie was so pleased that she smiled.

"Alec? Would you have chosen me if I hadn't been . . . pure?"

"I would," he answered immediately.

"Really?"

"Aye, and don't make me repeat myself, Jamie."

He sounded irritated now. "You're a most unusual man, Alec. Most knights wouldn't have a woman who'd given herself to another man."

"Oh, I'd have you all right," Alec returned. "But I'd also gain the name of the man who dishonored you before marriage."

"And then?"

"I'd kill him."

Jamie believed he meant what he said. She shivered in reaction. Killing certainly didn't bother him much. "The question isn't relevant since you're a virgin, is it?"

"No, I suppose not," she admitted. "Well, Alec? Are you willing to wait until I know you better? Before you . . . that is, before we . . ."

The poor lass couldn't even get the words out. Alec suddenly wanted to ease her fear, though he didn't have the damnedest idea why. He would take her, of course, but he didn't want her cringing away from him or waiting in dread. He decided to use a little diplomacy. "Until you wear my plaid, Jamie. We'll wait until then."

She looked as though she'd just been given a reprieve from purgatory. Her reaction did chafe his good mood.

"Will you give me your word, Alec?"

"I've just given it," he stated. He suddenly hauled her up against his side, tilted her chin back until she was forced to look into his eyes. "Never ask me to repeat my word to you in future, wife."

She would have nodded agreement if he had let go of her chin. Alec slowly leaned down and kissed her. She was too stunned to resist. His mouth was hard, yet wonderfully warm, too. Once again, just as she was beginning to respond, Alec pulled away.

"I thank you for your understanding," Jamie murmured.

"Your feelings are of little significance to me. You're simply my wife, my chattel. Remember that and we'll get along well together."

"Your chattel?" Jamie all but strangled on her words. God's truth, she'd never felt this humiliated, this inferior, in all her days.

Alec reached up and gently tapped her between her shoulderblades. "Chew your food, lass, before you try to swallow it," he advised.

He knew damn good and well she hadn't eaten anything. "You're doing it on purpose, aren't you, Alec?"

"Doing what?"

"You needn't look so innocent, husband. You're trying to make me angry."

Alec nodded. That slow grin was back in evidence.

"Why?"

"To show you it's acceptable."

"I don't understand."

"No matter what you do or what you say, I will never lose my patience with you. It's my duty to keep you safe, Jamie. It's really very simple, this lesson I've just given you, and when you think about it, you'll see how I just allowed you to speak your thoughts without reacting the least unpleasantly."

"Are you telling me this entire conversation was just a lesson for your ignorant English bride?"

When Alec nodded, Jamie started laughing.

"And so, Alec, if I tell you I think you're the most insulting warrior I've ever had the misfortune to meet, you wouldn't be at all bothered?"

"I wouldn't."

"You've just given me your promise not to touch me until I wear your plaid, milord, and now I'll give you a promise.

You'll rue the day you ever boasted of never losing your patience with me, husband. I give you my word."

Before Alec could answer her challenge, she slapped his hand away and moved away from him. "I'm going to have a bath. That horrible man touched me," she told him. "And I'm going to scrub until I feel clean again. Do you have any other insults you'd like to throw my way before I leave?"

Alec shook his head. The low-hanging branches on the tree he was leaning against actually swayed with his movement. Jamie realized that his size didn't intimidate her any longer. She didn't understand why her reaction to him had changed, but the fear was gone.

He hadn't killed his first wife. That sudden thought popped into her mind all at once and was immediately followed by another startling one.

She trusted him. Completely.

"None at the moment."

"None what?"

His wife had trouble holding on to her thoughts, Alec decided. "I don't have any other insults to give you," he explained dryly.

She nodded, then turned to walk away from him. "Jamie, I would warn you," he called out. "The water's cold."

"I don't need any warnings," she called over her shoulder in a tone as sassy as her walk. "We English are made of tougher stuff than you Scots think."

It wasn't until Jamie had gathered clean clothes, soap, and her brush and was standing on the shore of the lake that she completely let her guard down.

"Simply his chattel?" she muttered to herself as she stripped out of her black chemise and bliaut. "He wants me to feel as insignificant as his dog."

She continued to mutter to herself, thankful she was all alone. Daniel had taken Mary to the other side of the camp. Jamie hoped Mary was behaving herself. She didn't think she had the patience to intervene in her sister's behalf if Daniel crushed her tender feelings.

"It's a blessing my feelings aren't so tender," she told herself. "The sun will have to fall to the ground before I wear his colors. He'll have to woo me as any decent man would before he touches me."

A sudden frown crossed her face. Well, hell, the man didn't even like her.

Now what was the matter with her? Damn if her eyes didn't fill up with tears. That didn't make a spit of sense to her. She didn't want Alec to touch her yet, but she wanted him to want to touch her.

It was too confusing to understand. Jamie was so occupied trying to forget all the hurtful things Alec had said to her that she forgot to test the water. She grabbed her soap and jumped into the center of the pond she'd already judged to be approximately shoulder deep.

Alec heard the splash of water. A scant second later, his gentle little bride's bellow of outrage followed. He let out a sigh, then got to his feet. He suspected she'd need his assistance in just a few more minutes.

The frigidness all but knocked the wind out of her. Jamie felt as if she'd just jumped into a vat of wet snow. She knew she'd shouted a very unladylike word, worried that Alec might have heard her, then decided it was too late to take the word back and if he felt like adding "bawdy" to "insignificant," she certainly didn't care.

She was shivering uncontrollably by the time she'd finished washing her hair with the rose-scented soap. She hurried through the rest of her bath, tossed the lump of soap on the grassy slope, and tried to climb out.

The cramp caught her off guard. She'd nearly gained the shore when the arch in her right foot twisted into an excruciating knot. The pain doubled her over. She grabbed hold of her foot while underwater, then shot up for a gulp of air.

"Alec!"

He was there before she could scream his name a second time. Jamie had just gone under the water again when she felt his strong arms around her waist.

She couldn't let go of her foot long enough to help him. Alec didn't need her assistance, though, a fact that didn't settle in her mind until he had her out of the water and on his lap. She was still doubled over and shaking like a wet dog while she fought the knot in her foot.

Jamie didn't realize she was whimpering. Alec pushed her hands away from her foot, then slowly forced the knot out of her arch with the palm of his hand.

He was being incredibly gentle with her. Jamie buried her head against the side of his neck so he wouldn't see how close she was to crying. She didn't think she could stand for him to see her weakness now.

She didn't want him to stop holding her, either. He smelled so good, so masculine. His skin warmed her shivers away, too.

"It's better now?"

His voice was whisper-soft against her ear. Jamie nodded, yet still didn't pull away from him.

His other hand was resting on her silky thigh. She had magnificent long legs. Alec could see how flawless her skin was, could feel her soft breasts through the thin material of her chemise. Her nipples were hard. His loins followed suit. He told himself not to think about it, but his body refused to obey the order from his mind. God, she was soft all over. Alec was fully aroused now. His physical reaction had happened so quickly that his discipline all but deserted him.

"It's better now," Jamie whispered. Her voice betrayed her shyness. "I must thank you again. I would have drowned if you hadn't saved me."

"I have the feeling it's going to happen again and again."

The teasing lilt in his thick Scottish burr made her smile. "My drowning?" she asked, knowing full well that wasn't what he meant at all.

"Nay," Alec countered. "My saving you."

Jamie edged away just enough so she could see his expression. She had to push a lock of wet hair off her face to get a proper look. "Perhaps I'll save you once or twice," she announced, mimicking his burr.

She could see he was pleased with her effort. Jamie brazenly cuddled up against his warm chest again. "Alec, I must borrow some of your heat. It's bloody cold tonight, isn't it?"

"It's unusually mild by my measure," he contradicted. He paused to grin over the soft sigh she gave him, then added, "Do you always bathe with your clothes on?"

His voice felt like a caress against the top of her head. "No, but someone might have come along," she explained. "I was being modest."

Alec thought the wet fabric was just as provocative as her bare skin. He gritted his teeth against the urge to show her just how provocative he thought she was, then said, "You're turning blue. You'd better get out of your wet clothes."

He had to ease her out of his arms after making that suggestion. Jamie didn't seem inclined to let go of him until he suggested he see the task done for her.

She moved with lightning speed then. Jamie turned her back on Alec, rushed over to the stack of clothes she'd placed on the ground, and quickly wrapped a thin blanket around herself. "I'd like a few minutes privacy, if you please."

He must have anticipated her request, for when she turned around, he'd already left. The leaves of the arched branches still swayed from his silent retreat back to their camp.

She stripped out of her wet garment, patted her skin dry as best she could, then put on a fresh chemise. She couldn't get the silk ribbon tied, though. Her fingers had become too numb to grasp the sliver-thin pink threads together. The white chemise dipped low, exposing a fair amount of her generous bosom. She didn't care if she looked wanton. Gooseflesh covered her skin. Every time she moved, locks of her wet hair rained water down her back, like daggers of ice scraping her skin raw.

Her teeth were chattering by the time she finished brushing her hair into some semblance of order. She tossed the brush aside, then wrapped the damp blanket around her again. Tucking the material under her arms, she clasped the edges together over her chest and rushed back to camp.

She was in too much of a hurry to bother putting her shoes on. All she could think about was the roaring fire Alec had surely started by now, and she kept telling herself she'd be as warm as a freshly baked biscuit in just a few minutes.

The last rays of sunlight slanted through the branches. Jamie stumbled to an abrupt stop when she reached the clearing. There was no fire waiting to warm her.

Alec wasn't waiting either.

He was sound asleep. Jamie would have screamed at him if she'd had the strength. She feared her best effort would have been a pitiful wail, though, so she didn't say anything.

He looked damned comfortable. And warm. He was wrapped in his plaid. His back rested against the same tree trunk he'd sought out earlier. His eyes were closed, his breathing deep and even.

She didn't know what she was supposed to do. Tears of frustration trailed down her cheeks. She glanced around, looking for a spot that would protect her against the rising wind, then decided it really didn't matter where she slept. The linen cloth she'd wrapped around herself was too wet now to offer any protection.

What did it matter where she slept? She'd freeze to death before morning light.

Jamie took her time walking over to him. She timidly nudged his leg with her toes.

"Alec?"

He'd been patiently waiting for her to come to him. He slowly opened his eyes and looked at her.

He decided he wouldn't make her ask. She was shaking almost violently. There were tears in her eyes and he knew she was close to losing her control.

Without showing a hint of expression, Alec held out the edges of his plaid and opened his arms to her.

Jamie didn't hesitate. She dropped her blanket and fell into his arms. She landed with an unladylike thud against his chest, heard him grunt in reaction, and shivered her apology against the crook of his neck.

Alec wrapped his plaid around her. Her knees were

wedged between his thighs. With one hand he held her tightly against him, and with the other he forced her legs down until she was stretched out on top of him.

Her pelvis was flat against the junction of his thighs. Alec draped one leg over both of hers, trying to absorb the chill with his heat.

She smelled as if she'd just bathed in wildflowers. Her skin was as smooth as the petals of a rose.

It only took a few minutes for Jamie to get warm again. She let out a long sigh of contentment. His wonderful heat was making her light-headed.

He really wasn't such a bad sort, after all. He was a Scot, aye, and a giant as well, but he was her giant she supposed, and she knew he wouldn't let anything happen to her. He would always keep her safe.

She smiled against his chest. She just might let him kiss her tomorrow. She had to sigh then, for that thought was such an unladylike one, and she'd only known her husband for one short day. Aye, it was shameful thinking on her part.

Still, Jamie decided she had better revise her opinion of Alec Kincaid. If she really put her mind to it, she was sure she'd be able to find a few more redeeming qualities.

She was just drifting off to sleep when Alec spoke to her. "Jamie?"

"Yes, Alec?" she whispered against his ear.

"You're wearing my plaid."

Chapter Seven

The man was a pig.

Alec Kincaid had no redeeming qualities. His sense of humor was simply beyond her understanding. After making that outrageous remark about wearing his ugly plaid, he had the audacity to laugh. His chest rumbled so with his amusement that Jamie felt as though she were in the center of an earthquake.

He knew she thought he was jesting with her. She wouldn't have glared up at him if she'd known what he was really contemplating. Her innocence and his promise kept her mind free of any fear, though. Alec wanted her, aye, but he didn't want her afraid. He wanted her willing. And hot.

Jamie stacked her hands on his chest, rested her chin on top, then stared into his eyes. "Your sense of humor is as warped as a saddle left out in the rain too long."

She waited for his reply. Alec didn't respond to her barb. He just continued to stare at her mouth. Jamie soon became self-conscious. She instinctively wet her lips. Alec's expression hardened in reaction. Jamie didn't know what to make of that.

"I won't let you bait me so easily once I know how your mind works," she told him.

"That day will never come," he predicted.

"Why are you staring at me like that?"

"Like what?"

"Like you want to kiss me again," she said. "Am I good at kissing, then?"

"No," he answered.

The tenderness in his voice took the sting out of his insult.

"Well, why not, do you suppose?"

A slow grin, heartbreakingly sensual, transformed his face. Jamie was warmed by it. This one could certainly be a charmer if he ever put his mind to it, she decided. Fortunately, the man was too dull to realize his own special magic.

Jamie drummed her fingertips on his chest while she waited for his answer. When he continued to keep silent, she came to the conclusion that he didn't like kissing her at all. That realization hurt. "I'm not any good at it, am I?"

"Good at what?" he asked, his voice deceptively mild.

"At kissing," she snapped. "Will you please pay attention to what I'm saying?"

"No, baby, you aren't any good at it," he answered. "Yet."

"Don't call me baby," Jamie whispered. "It isn't proper," she added. "Besides, you don't say it the same way Papa did."

Alec laughed. "Hell, I hope not."

Jamie smiled in spite of her irritation. Alec's voice was so appealing. That burr of his could thrill the breath right out of her.

"You didn't answer my question," she blurted out as he started to massage the backs of her thighs. His thumbs had slid up under the hem of her chemise. Jamie pretended not to notice. It felt so very wonderful.

"I did answer you."

"I don't remember."

"I said no."

"No? You weren't jesting with me?"

"No."

"Alec, if I'm not any good at kissing, it's your fault, not mine. Maybe you aren't any good, either. What think you of that possibility?"

"I think you've lost your mind." Alec smiled over the outrage that statement caused.

"I refuse to feel inferior about this," Jamie said. "You're the only man I've ever kissed, and the responsibility therefore belongs to you."

"Didn't the man you were pledged to ever kiss you? I know he came to see you on several occasions."

"You know about Andrew?"

Alec shrugged. He began to stroke her smooth buttocks. He was trying desperately not to think about how good she was going to taste. He was going to have to go slowly. He knew it would be more honorable to wait until they'd reached the Highlands before bedding her. The ride there was going to be difficult for her under the best of circumstances. And if he made love to her now, she'd be too tender to keep up the grueling pace.

Yes, it would be more honorable to wait. Alec wasn't going to, though. He would slow their pace tomorrow as a concession, and that was all. His desire was fierce. And if she wiggled her backside just one more time, he wasn't even going to go slow.

"Alec? What do you know about Andrew?" she asked again.

"What is there to know?"

"Nothing."

"Answer me."

His voice turned as hard as the look in his eyes. "Andrew never kissed me," she said. "We were pledged when we were very young. I've known him for the longest time. I care for Andrew, of course. It's my duty to care for him."

"Cared for," Alec corrected. "You cared for this man."

"Well, yes," Jamie agreed, hoping to soothe his frown

away. "He's a good friend of the family, and since I was pledged to him, I was supposed to care for him, wasn't I, Alec?"

He didn't answer her. The scowl left his face, though, and he relaxed his hold on her. He was inordinately pleased with her. She hadn't given her heart to the Englishman. She didn't love him. Alec grinned. He didn't know why it mattered to him, but it did matter . . . fiercely.

"Andrew was always very proper," Jamie continued. "When he came to pay his respects, we were never left unchaperoned. I do believe that's the reason he never kissed me."

Jamie had been very sincere in her explanation. She expected a sincere reply.

Alec laughed.

"Just what's so amusing to you now? The fact that Andrew never kissed me or that we were never left alone?"

"If he'd been a Scot, I promise you he would have found a way," Alec answered. "You'd probably have one or two of his bairns by now."

"Andrew is considerate."

"Not considerate," Alec contradicted. "Stupid."

"He's a noble Englishman," Jamie countered. "He understands a woman's tender feelings, Alec. Why, he constantly gives me compliments. He is—"

"Was."

"Why do you insist on speaking as though the man were dead?" she asked.

"Because he isn't a part of your life now. You will not mention his name to me again, wife."

He didn't have to sound so irritated with her. Alec eased himself away from the tree, then stretched out on the ground. Jamie started to roll to his side, but Alec held her steady with his hands cupping her backside.

It was indecent, the way he was holding her, but it felt too good to ask him to let go.

The sun was completely gone now, yet the moon was bright enough for her to see her husband's face. He looked relaxed, at peace, and almost asleep. For that reason she didn't take exception when his hands eased up under her chemise again. She thought he probably wasn't even aware of what he was doing.

God, it felt sinful. Jamie moved her hands to his shoulders and rested the side of her face against his warm chest. His golden hair tickled her nose. "Alec?" she whispered. "I really would like to know what it feels like."

His hands stopped their gentle massage. Jamie felt him tense under her.

"What exactly are you wanting to feel, Jamie?"

"When a man kisses a woman with the intent of bedding her. It's a different sort of kiss from the one you gave me."

She sounded as if she were instructing him. Alec had to shake his head. This conversation was ridiculous. And thoroughly arousing.

"Aye, it is," he finally acknowledged.

"Daniel uses his tongue when he kisses."

"What?"

"You needn't raise your voice to me, Alec."

"How would you know Daniel—"

"Mary told me. She said it was disgusting."

"You won't think it is." Alec growled that prediction.

"I won't?" She sounded out of breath again. "How do you know that?"

"Because you've wanted me to touch you since the moment we met."

"I haven't."

"Because I can feel the passion inside you. Because your body reacts whenever I look at you. Because—"

"You're embarrassing me."

"No, I'm making you hot."

"You're not."

"I am."

"You may not speak to me this way," she ordered.

"I'll speak to you any damn way I want to," Alec answered. "I want you, Jamie."

His voice didn't leave room for argument. Before Jamie could catch her breath, he'd cupped the sides of her face and claimed her mouth.

She deliberately kept her mouth as tightly shut as a locked door.

His hand moved to her chin; then she felt pressure when he forced her mouth open for him. As soon as she gave in to his silent demand, he thrust his tongue inside her mouth, deeply, swiftly, completely. Jamie was so startled she tried to pull back. Alec wouldn't let her move. His mouth slanted over hers, sealing her whimper of protest. He wasn't gentle now. His mouth was hot, hungry, his tongue thorough and wild as he learned the taste of her and forced her to learn the taste of him.

Jamie's last coherent thought was that Alec Kincaid certainly knew how to kiss.

She was a quick learner. Her tongue became as wild as his, as undisciplined. She tried to struggle when he gripped her thighs. He spread his own, then trapped her between his heavy legs. She felt his hard arousal, tried to move away, but Alec coaxed her into submission again by stoking the fire in her. His tongue slid in and out, again and again, until her whole body was straining for more of him.

God, she was sweet. Holding her like this made him shake with desire. The sexy little whimpers she made in the back of her throat were driving him wild.

Jamie didn't offer true resistance until he pulled her hands away from his shoulders and slowly edged the straps of her chemise down her arms. She tore her mouth free then, thinking to roll away from him, but by the time her body responded to her mind's command, her chemise was already down to her waist.

Her breasts were flattened against his chest, her nipples hardened by the erotic touch of his crisp hair and hot skin against her sensitive skin.

"I want you to stop now," she moaned.

Alec didn't pay any attention to her weak protest. His mouth moved to the side of her neck. His tongue flicked over her ear. Jamie tilted her head to one side, giving him better access. She gasped when he took her tender earlobe between his teeth. His ragged breathing was hot, sweet, incredibly exciting. He whispered dark, seductive promises that made her tremble with a need she'd never felt before.

"Alec?" She said his name in a ragged moan when he tugged her chemise down over her hips. "I don't have anything on under this garment."

"I know, lass."

"Shouldn't you stop now?"

"Not yet, Jamie," he whispered, his voice as soft as velvet.

He rolled her onto her back. He kissed her neck, her shoulders, her mouth, again. Only when she was quivering with need did he move away from her. Jamie realized she was completely naked then. She turned to watch Alec. The shadows darkened his powerful form. She could hear the rustle of clothing, knew he was stripping out of the rest of his garments, and in that moment of separation, she became desperately afraid.

God help her, she wanted to run. Alec caught hold of her before she had even rolled over. His hands grabbed hers, stretching her arms high above her head in one fluid motion before he completely blanketed her with his body.

The contact of his hot skin against hers made her gasp. Alec made a low groaning sound before claiming her mouth again. The kiss was openly carnal. He meant to have her surrender. When she arched up against him, he knew her passionate nature was overcoming her timidity. He let go of her hands at the same time he thrust his tongue inside her mouth, then let out a grunt of satisfaction when her fingers dug into his shoulderblades.

His chest rubbed against her soft breasts while he stroked her. Jamie kept trying to edge away from the junction of his thighs, but when she felt his hardness against her belly, she quit her struggles. A warm, tingling ache suddenly claimed her full attention.

Alec massaged her breasts, cupping the undersides with loving care. His thumbs rubbed her distended nipples. His ragged sigh told her how much he liked touching her so intimately. Jamie was honest enough with herself to admit she liked the chaos his touch evoked.

When his mouth replaced his hand on her breast, when he took the nipple inside and began to suckle, she thought she would go out of her mind. The sensation was so overwhelming that she squeezed her eyes shut and let the wonderful feelings wash over her. She arched against him with need and her legs moved impatiently against his.

Alec took a deep breath to try to calm his need and braced himself on his elbows so he could look down into her face.

She felt the change in him immediately. Jamie opened her eyes and looked into his. She reached up to stroke his jaw. His whiskers tickled her fingers, but she didn't smile. Alec was the most frighteningly appealing man she'd ever encountered. The moonlight hadn't softened his features. He looked hard . . . and determined.

"Have you decided to stop, then?" she whispered.

"Do you want me to?" he asked.

She didn't know how to answer him. Yes, she told herself, of course she wanted him to stop. A bride should have a proper wedding bed, shouldn't she? "Not yet."

She hadn't realized she'd said that until he smiled at her. "You confuse me, Alec. I don't know my own thoughts when you're touching me like this. Maybe we should stop . . ."

"Not yet." Sweat dotted his forehead. His jaw was clenched, his breathing labored.

He didn't have any intention of stopping. Her eyes widened when that realization hit her. Alec must have read her mind . . . and her fear, for he suddenly pushed her legs apart with his thigh. The action was rough, demanding.

While he held her stare, his right hand moved down between them, low on her stomach. His fingers slid into the junction of her thighs. Jamie reached down and tried to pull his hand away. "No, Alec. You mustn't."

He wouldn't be deterred. His fingers stroked the tender folds. When he felt the wetness there, he almost lost his control. "You're hot for me, Jamie," he whispered. "God, you're so sweet, so soft . . ."

His finger slowly penetrated her, then stretched up inside. "You're so tight."

Her mind wanted him to stop but her body didn't have

any reservations at all. She raised her hips to keep him inside her when he started to pull away.

"Now are you going to stop?" she asked in a voice that betrayed her.

"Not yet," Alec repeated, smiling over the confusion he heard in her voice. He took hold of her hand, then pressed it against his hardness. Her reaction was instantaneous. Her whole body shivered and bucked against him. "Hold me," he instructed. "Like this." He forced her fingers to close around his shaft, then thrust his fingers inside her again to rid her of her fear.

He pulled her hand away when he couldn't stand the sweet torture any longer. His mouth branded hers and his tongue thrust deep inside to the back of her throat. Jamie was soon as wild, as out of control as Alec was. He knew just where to touch, how much pressure to exert, how to make her melt in his arms.

He became rougher in his quest. "We aren't going to stop, are we, Alec?"

"Nay, love, we aren't."

He withdrew his fingers, then thrust them demandingly into her tight sheath again.

She cried out in pain. "Don't do that, Alec. It hurts."

"Hush, love," he whispered. "I'll make it easier for you."

She didn't understand what he was telling her. His mouth claimed hers for another long, hot kiss then and she decided he really was going to stop when his hand moved away from her most private place.

Alec kissed a slow trail down her neck, her chest, her stomach. When he moved lower, into the soft triangle of black curls shielding her virginity, she cried out again and tried to push him away from her.

He wouldn't be deterred, though. The taste of her was intoxicating. His tongue teased the sensitive nub of flesh, then pressed high into the soft, slick opening.

She became lost to the splendor he forced on her. She clung to him now, demanding more. The muscles in her thighs tensed against him in anticipation. She welcomed the rush of blazing ecstasy consuming her.

As soon as Alec felt the first tremors of release, he moved. He spread her thighs wide and eased into her. He paused when he reached her maidenhood, then drove forward with one powerful surge.

Jamie cried out in pain. Alec immediately stilled his movements. He was fully embedded inside her now, his possession complete. He tried to hold on to his discipline, wanting to give her time to adjust to his invasion. "Don't move just yet," he ordered, his voice a grating sound against her ear. "God, Jamie. You're so tight."

She couldn't have moved if she'd wanted to. His weight held her in place. He cupped her face, then slowly licked the salty tears from her flushed cheeks. Her eyes were dark blue with passion, her rosy lips swollen from his demanding kisses.

"Does it still hurt, Jamie?"

He sounded as though he'd just run a great distance uphill. But the worry was there, too, in his tone of voice and his intense expression. Jamie nodded, then whispered, "It will pass, this pain, won't it, Alec? Am I supposed to be this tight?"

"Oh, yes," Alec groaned.

When he started to move, to begin the ritual as old as time itself, Jamie thought he was finished. She wrapped her legs around his thighs to keep him deep inside her. "Don't stop, Alec. Not yet."

"Not yet," he promised.

Neither one of them was capable of speaking again. Alec did withdraw from her, then thrust deep inside once more. She raised her hips to meet him halfway. She wanted all of him to squeeze tight. Passion, like wildfire, raged between them. Alec buried his face against her neck as he slammed into her again and again.

He wanted to be gentle.

She wouldn't let him.

She didn't know her nails dug into his shoulderblades. Alec didn't mind. When the climax was almost upon her, when she thought she was surely going to die from the incredible pressure building inside her, she clung to her husband and cried out his name.

"Come with me, love," Alec whispered. "Come with me. Now."

She didn't know where Alec was taking her, only knew she was safe in his arms. She gave herself over to the blissful surrender and found that surrender was also fulfillment.

He'd known all along where they were going, yet never before had he been so out of control or felt such overwhelming passion. He wanted to show her the stars. He was the experienced one, she the innocent. He knew where to touch, where to stroke, when to push, when to retreat. And yet, when he finally reached his own release, he realized his gentle little bride had taken him far beyond the stars.

She'd taken him to heaven.

She slept like the dead. Morning sun was full upon the meadow when she stretched herself awake. Jamie let out a low groan as soon as she moved. She was horribly tender. Her eyes flew open. The memory of what had happened last night made her cheeks burn with embarrassment.

God help her, she was never going to be able to look him in the eye again. She had behaved like a complete wanton. She did tell him to stop, she reminded herself, but the man was bent on having his way. She was going to stay under his plaid for the rest of the day, she decided, when she admitted she'd also insisted, rather vehemently, that he not stop.

Still, he did seem to like what they were doing. Jamie pushed the blanket away from her face then. She saw Alec immediately. He was standing on the other side of the clearing, between their mounts. The horses, she noticed, had already been saddled in readiness for the day's ride.

Wildfire was acting like a lovesick female. She kept nudging Alec's hand for another pat of affection.

Jamie suddenly wanted a pat of affection, too. She thought she might have pleased him last night. Unfortunately, she'd fallen asleep before he had a chance to tell her so.

She was going to have to bluster through her embarrassment. Since he wasn't paying her any attention, she stood up, unwrapped his plaid, and quickly put her chemise back on. She knew her attire was immodest, but she was determined not to show any shyness in front of him. He would take it as weakness, she guessed.

Alec didn't even glance her way. She gathered her clothes and walked to the pond with as much dignity as her sore thighs would allow. She washed and dressed in a pale blue gown, then braided her hair. Her mood was vastly improved when she walked back to camp. It was a new day, after all, and certainly a new beginning.

Besides, she'd done her duty as his wife. She had let him bed her.

Did she think he was made of iron? Alec asked himself that question as soon as his wife walked away from him.

No other woman had ever enticed him this way. He'd never known such fierce desire before. Bed them and forget them, that had always been his attitude in the past. She was different, though. God help him, she was beginning to matter to him. She wasn't the forgetting kind, either. White-hot desire had claimed him the minute she stood up and faced him. Her hair was in wild, curly disarray. He remembered the silky feel of it when he'd held the strands up for the wind to dry. Jamie had slept through his ministrations. He hadn't been able to quit stroking her skin after he'd made love to her. She'd slept through that, too.

He hadn't slept at all. Her hips had cushioned his hardness. Every time she moved, he wanted to take her again. The only reason he held back was that she wouldn't be able to walk for a week if he did all the things he wanted to do to her. It was too soon for her. She needed time for the soreness to ease. He'd made the decision not to touch her again until they reached his home. And he was already regretting it.

He wasn't made of iron. His innocent little wife didn't understand that yet. She wouldn't have stood there so scantily clad if she'd had any idea of what was going on inside his mind. Perhaps she did know, he considered.

Could she be trying to get him to make love to her again without actually asking him outright? Alec debated that possibility a long minute, then decided she was simply too naive to realize how easily she could arouse him.

He would, of course, enlighten her as soon as they reached his home.

"Alec? Thank you for loaning me your plaid."

He turned at the sound of her voice and found her staring at his boots.

"It's yours to keep, Jamie."

"A wedding present?"

She wouldn't look at him. Though her head was bent, he could still see how red her cheeks were. Her embarrassment was terribly obvious. And vastly amusing. Hell, the woman had been a wildcat in his arms. He had the marks to prove it. Now she acted as if the wrong word might send her into a swoon.

"You may call it such," he announced with a shrug. He took her satchel and turned to secure it on Wildfire's back.

"I've eleven shillings, Alec."

She waited for him to turn back to her. He didn't respond to her announcement. Jamie wasn't deterred. "Do you have a priest in your Highlands?"

That question did get his notice. He half turned to look at her. She immediately lowered her gaze. She was getting a bit more courage back, for she now stared at his chest instead of his boots. "We do have a priest," he answered. "Why do you ask?"

"I want to use one of my shillings to buy you an indulgence," Jamie announced. She tucked the plaid under her arm and folded her hands together.

"A what?"

"An indulgence," Jamie explained. "It's my wedding gift to you."

"I see," he replied, trying not to laugh. He wanted to ask her if she thought his soul was in need of aid, but the seriousness in her tone made him once again consider her tender feelings.

He was going to have to get over this ridiculous affliction, he told himself. Her feelings shouldn't matter to him at all.

"Does that please you?" she asked, hoping for a kind word in reply.

He shrugged his answer.

"I thought it would be an appropriate gift because you accidentally killed a man yesterday. The indulgence will halve your time in purgatory. That's what Father Charles says."

"It wasn't accidental, Jamie, and you killed one man yourself."

"I didn't."

"Aye, you did."

"You needn't sound so cheerful about it," Jamie muttered. "And if I did kill the man, well, he needed killing, so I don't have to buy an indulgence for myself."

"So it's only my soul that concerns you?"

Jamie nodded. He didn't know whether to be insulted or amused. He had to shake his head when he thought about all the coins Father Murdock was going to be collecting in future if his wife continued to buy him an indulgence every time he killed a man. The priest would end up richer than England's king by year's end.

Alec certainly wasn't the appreciative sort, Jamie decided. He still hadn't offered her a word of gratitude. "Do you have a blacksmith as well?"

He nodded, then waited for her next remark. God only knew what was going on inside her mind now. Odd, but he found himself eager to hear what she was thinking. Another affliction, he told himself. He'd have to work on that flaw as well.

"Then I'll use my remaining shillings to buy you a second wedding gift," she said.

She saw she'd captured his full attention when she glanced up to see his reaction. "I've thought of just the gift for you. I know you'll be pleased."

"And what might that be?" he asked, finding her enthusiasm as captivating as her smile. He didn't have the heart to tell her no one used shillings as payment for anything in the Highlands. He knew she'd find out soon enough.

"A sword."

She thought he looked quite stunned by her gift. She nodded to let him know she meant what she promised, then turned her gaze to the ground again.

He couldn't believe he'd heard her correctly. "A what?"

"A sword, Alec. It's a good gift, isn't it? Every warrior should carry one at his side. I noticed you were lacking in such equipment when the outcasts attacked us. I considered that highly unusual, for it did seem to me that all warriors would have need of such a handy weapon. Then I considered the fact that you're a Scotsman, after all, and mayhap your training didn't include . . . Alec, why are you looking at me like that?"

He couldn't answer her.

"Does my gift please you?" she asked.

She sounded worried now. Alec managed a brisk nod. It was the best he could do.

Jamie smiled with relief. "I knew you'd be pleased," she told him.

He nodded again, then had to turn away from her.

For the first time in his life, Alec Kincaid was speechless.

Jamie didn't seem to notice. "Daniel carries a sword. I noticed that right away. Perhaps, since the two of you are such good friends, he might take time to instruct you in the proper use of the weapon. I'm told it can be most effective in battle."

Alec's forehead dropped to the saddle. Jamie couldn't see his face because he was turned away from her, but his shoulders were shaking.

He was obviously overcome with gratitude.

Jamie was feeling proud of herself. She had just offered him a branch of friendship and he had accepted it. Their situation would certainly improve now.

In time he just might forget she was English and begin to like her.

She walked away from her husband, for she wished to

spend a few minutes with Mary before they started out on their journey again. Now that she had figured out how to get along with her husband, she thought she'd share her expertise with her sister. She certainly wasn't going to mention last night, though. No, Mary would have to find out all about that part of marriage from her own husband. Perhaps, Jamie considered, Mary had already found out.

Jamie felt as if she'd just discovered the secrets of the world. Kindness begat kindness. One didn't bite the hand that was patting one, now, did one?

"Jamie? Come here."

His command was a little too brisk for her liking, but she held her smile and walked back to Alec's side. She stared at his chest, waiting to hear what he had to say.

Alec tilted her chin up. "Are you all right, wife? Will you be able to ride today?"

She didn't understand what he was asking. "I'm fine, Alec, really."

"You're not too sore?" Alec persisted.

The immediate blush told him she now understood what he was asking. "You aren't supposed to mention that," she whispered.

He couldn't resist. "Mention what?"

Though it didn't seem possible to him, her blush intensified. "My—my being sore," she stammered out.

"Jamie, I know I hurt you last night."

He didn't sound overly contrite to her. God's truth, he sounded downright arrogant. "Yes, you did hurt me," she muttered. "And, yes, I am sore. Are there any other intimate questions you wish to put to me?"

He squeezed her jaw, forcing her to look up at him again. And then he lowered his head and brushed his mouth against hers. It was such a tender kiss that Jamie was all but undone. Her eyes filled with tears. Now he'd give her the praise she so desperately needed to hear.

"If I think of any I'll let you know," he announced before he let go of her.

"Think of any what?"

A rock could hold fleas longer than she could hold on to a thought. "Any other intimate questions," he said.

She stood where she was while Alec swung up into his saddle. "Come now, Jamie. 'Tis time to ride."

"But what about Daniel and Mary? Shouldn't we wait for them?"

"They left over two hours ago," Alec answered.

"They left without us?" she asked, her voice incredulous.

"They did."

"Why didn't you wake me?"

Alec held his grin. His wife looked thoroughly disgruntled. Wisps of curly hair had already separated from her braid. The strands floated around her face and down the nape of her slender neck.

She looked lovely.

"You needed your sleep," Alec told her, his voice suddenly gruff.

"They didn't even say good-bye," Jamie said. "It was a rudeness, don't you suppose, Alec?" She walked over to Wildfire's side, paused to give her horse a whispered word of praise and a good pat, then gained the saddle. She grimaced against the ache that motion caused. "Are we going to try to catch up with them?"

Alec shook his head. "They've left the north road by now."

Jamie couldn't hide her disappointment. "How long must we travel before we reach your home?"

"Three more days."

"Three?"

She looked disgruntled again. "Three if we set a brisk pace, wife."

"In the opposite direction from my sister?"

Before he could answer her, she whispered, "I'm never going to see my sister again, am I?"

"Don't look so upset, Jamie. Mary's home is just an hour's ride from us. You may see her as often as you like."

His explanation didn't make sense to her. "We go for three days in the opposite direction, you tell me, yet Mary will end up only an hour's ride away when we finally reach your home? I don't understand, Alec. You do remember where you live, don't you?"

"There are clans friendly to Daniel and he must therefore pass through their lands, just as there are clans friendly to me, Jamie. I must also stop to give greeting as laird over the clan Kincaid."

"Why couldn't the four of us—"

"There are also clans who would give their collective hide to see me dead."

She could certainly understand that, she decided. If Alec acted as impatient with the clans as he was now acting with her, he would certainly collect a lot of enemies. "And Daniel is friend to some of your enemies?" she asked.

Alec nodded. "Then why do you call Daniel your friend? Your enemies should also be his if he's loyal to you."

He gave up. He knew she still didn't understand. "Do we have many enemies, Alec?"

"We?"

"I'm your wife now, I would remind you," she answered. "For that reason, your enemies are now mine, aren't they?"

"Aye, they are," he announced.

"Why are you smiling? Do you like having so many enemies?"

"I'm smiling because I've just realized you have the makings of a true Scot," he answered. "This pleases me."

She gave him a magnificent smile. Alec immediately guessed she was up to mischief. He'd already noticed that when her eyes sparkled the way they were now, she was about to give him a clever retort.

He wasn't disappointed. "I'll never be a Scot, Alec. But you, sir, well you have the makings of a true English baron. This pleases me."

He didn't know why he laughed, for she'd just insulted him mightily, but he did laugh all the same. He shook his head over her comment and his reaction. "Remember this conversation, Jamie. One day soon, you'll see the error in all your opinions."

"All my opinions, Alec?" She frowned at him, then added, "I think I'm beginning to understand why we have so many enemies."

She ended their conversation by nudging Wildfire into a full gallop, deliberately taking the lead away from him.

She ignored him when he called out to her, determined to make him stay behind her today. Let him choke on the dust from the lead horse.

Alec was suddenly at her side. He took hold of Wildfire's reins. He never said a word to her, just turned her mount around and tossed the reins back to her.

"Well?" she asked.

"You were going the wrong way," Alec told her, his exasperation obvious. "Unless of course you were thinking of going back to England."

"I wasn't."

"Then your sense of direction is yet another—"

"A simple mistake, Alec," Jamie argued. "I have a fine sense of direction."

"Have you been many places to test this theory?"

"No. And while you're scowling at me, I have another question to put to you. Were you pleased with me last night?"

He looked as if he wanted to laugh. Jamie thought she'd kill him if he did.

"Well? Was I any good at it? And don't you dare ask me to explain my question. You know very well what I'm talking about."

She would die if he told her she wasn't any good. Her hands were squeezing the reins tightly, making indentations in her palms, so horribly nervous had she suddenly become, and she was furious with herself for asking.

"You'll get better."

He knew exactly what to say to her to get her temper riled. She thought there might be fire in her eyes when she looked up at him.

Alec was smiling at her. The tenderness in his eyes told her he knew how important her question was to her. "I'll get better?" she strangled out. "Why you—"

"We'll practice, Jamie, once we get home, every single night, until you get it right."

That promise given, he nudged his stallion forward. Jamie didn't know what to make of his outrageous remark. She thought he'd just insulted her, but the way he was looking at her when he said they were going to practice did make her think he was looking forward to it.

No matter how she looked at it, she always came up with the same conclusion: Alec Kincaid had about as much compassion as a goat.

Still, she guessed she should give him his due. He had acted with true kindness when he allowed her to sleep well past dawn. She'd needed the additional rest, and though she blamed Alec for draining all the strength out of her the night before, she still admitted he'd shown a little mercy.

Perhaps he wasn't completely hopeless, after all.

Jamie changed her mind about her husband by late afternoon. They'd ridden through the woods most of the morning, pausing only once to refresh themselves by a rippling river. Alec barely spoke a civil word to her. He seemed preoccupied with his own thoughts. Jamie tried, several times in fact, to engage him in conversation, but Alec ignored her questions with a rudeness she found disconcerting. He stood on the grassy bank, his hands clasped behind his back. Jamie guessed he was impatient to continue their journey.

"Are you waiting for the horses to have their rest or for me?" she called out when she couldn't stand the silence a moment longer.

"The horses are ready," he answered.

He hadn't even bothered to look at her when he spoke. She briefly considered pushing him into the river to get his full attention, then decided against it. If he didn't drown, he would surely be spitting mad, and she had enough to worry about with her own aches and pains. Listening to him rant and rave would only make her day all the more sour.

Jamie settled herself on Wildfire's back before calling out to Alec again. "I'm ready now. Thank you for stopping."

"You asked."

His voice was so filled with surprise she was taken aback. "I must always ask?"

"Of course."

Well, hell, he could have mentioned that odd little rule hours sooner. "And you'll always honor my requests, Alec?"

He swung up into his saddle before answering her. "If it's possible."

Their horses were so close together that Alec's leg brushed against hers.

"Then why didn't you stop when I asked you to last night?" she blurted out.

He grabbed hold of the back of her neck and pulled her toward him. Jamie clung to the saddle, trying to keep her balance.

He waited for her to look up at him, then easily captured her gaze. "You didn't want me to." He grinned at her.

"That is the most arrogant—"

He kissed her just to silence her. He meant only to remind her just who was the laird and who was the chattel, but her lips went all soft under his, reminding him just how good she really was. He swept the inside of her mouth with his tongue before pulling away from her. She looked totally bemused. Her hand rested on his cheek, her touch as light as a butterfly. He doubted she even realized she was still caressing him.

"I said I'd honor your requests whenever possible, Jamie. It wasn't possible for me to stop last night."

"It wasn't?"

The woman was going to make him daft if she continued to ask him to repeat his every word. Alec let her see his exasperation. "You may take the lead this time," he announced, thinking to snap her back to the present.

Jamie nodded. She guided Wildfire around Alec's mount and was just ducking under a fat branch barring her way when Alec appeared at her side. The minute he took hold of her reins, she realized her error.

He didn't mention her pitiful sense of direction, and neither did she.

They stopped at sunset in the center of a wide meadow.

Alec reached out to pull on Wildfire's reins. When their mounts were side by side, he still didn't let go of the reins. His face was impassive now and he stared straight ahead.

"Is there danger, Alec?"

She hadn't been able to keep her worry out of her voice.

Alec shook his head. Would he be sitting in the middle of such an open expanse if there was danger? Her question seemed absurd until he remembered she had no knowledge of the ways of fighting men.

Jamie thought she'd stretch her legs a bit but when she started to dismount, Alec stayed her action by placing his hand on her thigh. His grip wasn't at all gentle.

She caught his silent message quickly enough, but his behavior didn't make any sense to her. She folded her hands on the cantle of her saddle, patiently waiting for Alec to explain what he was doing.

A faint whistle sounded from the forest a fair distance away from them. The trees suddenly seemed to come alive when men wearing brown and yellow plaid began to walk toward them.

Jamie didn't realize she was clutching Alec's leg until his hand covered hers. "They're allies, Jamie."

She immediately let go of him, straightened her back, and refolded her hands in her lap. "I guessed as much," she whispered.

It was a lie, made blacker still when she added, "Even from this distance I can see them smiling."

"An eagle couldn't see their faces from this distance," he answered dryly.

"We English have perfect eyesight."

Alec finally turned to look at her. "Are you jesting with me, wife?"

"You decide, husband."

"Aye, you are," Alec answered. "I've already learned all about the English sense of humor."

"And what have you learned?"

"You don't have any."

"That isn't true," Jamie argued. "Why, I have the most

134

wonderful sense of humor." After making that emphatic statement, she turned her face away from him.

"Jamie?"

"Aye, Alec?"

"When they reach us, keep your gaze directed on me. Do not look at anyone else. Do you understand?"

"You don't want me to look at any of them?"

"That's correct."

"Why?"

"Don't question my motives, wife."

His voice had become as brisk as the rising wind. "Should I speak to them?"

"No."

"They'll think me rude."

"They'll think you subservient."

"I'm not."

"You will be."

Jamie felt her face heat up. She frowned at Alec, but it was wasted effort for he was staring straight ahead again, ignoring her. "Perhaps, Alec, I should get off my horse and kneel at your feet. Then your allies will surely see how very subservient your wife is."

She didn't care that her voice shook with anger. "Well, milord?"

"The suggestion has merit," he answered.

He didn't sound as if he was jesting with her. Jamie was too astonished by his outrageous comment to think of a clever comeback.

She wasn't about to let her displeasure show in front of strangers, though, no matter how upset she was with her husband. Oh, she'd play the obedient wife, all right, until she and Alec were alone again. Then she was going to blister his ears.

When the allies finally reached them, Jamie kept her gaze directed on her husband's hard profile. It took all her concentration to keep her expression devoid of any true emotion. Serenity was simply too much to ask for.

Alec never even looked her way. The conversation was in Gaelic. Jamie understood most of the words, even though the dialect was a little different from the Lowland Gaelic that Beak had taught her.

Alec didn't know she was fluent in his language, and his ignorance gave her a perverse satisfaction. She decided then and there she was never going to enlighten him.

She listened to him refuse the allies' offer of drink, food, and shelter as well. His hard, unyielding manner was that of a mighty warlord now, and when they'd finished with their offers and he'd finished with his refusals, they reported to him the latest happenings among the clans.

Jamie knew they were staring at her. She tried to keep her expression tranquil. In true desperation she offered her Maker a month of daily masses and one litany if he'd only help her through this humiliating ordeal.

Alec was ashamed of her. That sudden realization made her want to weep. Her self-pity lasted only a minute or two. Then she became furious. How dare he be ashamed of her? She knew she wasn't as pretty as most, but she wasn't horribly disfigured, either. Once her papa had even called her beautiful. Of course, it was his duty to give her such praise; she was his baby after all, and his opinion was certainly colored. Still, she'd never noticed people turning their faces away from her so they wouldn't lose their supper.

When Alec reached over and took hold of Wildfire's reins, Jamie was pulled back to the conversation. She heard one of his allies ask who she was.

"My wife."

There hadn't been a tinge of pride in his voice. God's truth, he could have been referring to his dog. No, she qualified; his dog probably meant more to him.

He hadn't gagged over the words either, Jamie decided, trying to find something redeeming in his attitude.

Alec was about to nudge his mount forward through the throng of warriors when another ally called out. "By what name is she called, Kincaid?"

He took a long time answering. Alec slowly scanned his audience. The look on his face chilled Jamie. His expression could have been carved in stone.

And then he answered at last. His voice, as cold as sleet, lashed out like a battle cry.

"Mine."

Chapter Eight

She was beginning to think he wasn't human. Alec never seemed to get hungry or thirsty or tired. The only time he stopped to rest was when Jamie asked him to, and God only knew how she hated asking him for anything.

An Englishman certainly would have seen to his wife's comforts. Alec had difficulty remembering he had a wife. Jamie felt as wanted as a thorn in his side.

She was exhausted, guessed she probably looked as worn out as an old hag, too, then told herself it didn't matter what she looked like. Alec had made his position perfectly clear when he refused to introduce her to his allies. She didn't appeal to him at all.

Well, he wasn't any prize, either, she decided. His hair was almost as long as hers, for God's sake, and if that wasn't a primitive inclination, she didn't know what was.

Her feelings about her husband might not have been so black if his attitude had been a little more pleasant. The mountain air had obviously affected his mind, for the higher they climbed, the more distant and cold his manner became.

He had more flaws than Satan. The man couldn't even count. He'd specifically told her it would take them three days to reach his holding, yet here they were, camped for their fifth night, and still not another Kincaid plaid in sight.

Was his sense of direction as poor as his ability to count? Jamie decided she was too tired to worry about that possibility. As soon as Alec turned his attention to the horses, Jamie walked to the lake to gain a few moments' privacy. She stripped down to her chemise, washed as best she could in the frigid water Alec called a loch, then stretched out on the grassy slope. She was bone-weary. She thought to just close her eyes for a few minutes before getting dressed again. In truth, the bitterness in the air didn't even bother her.

A thick mist rolled into the glen. Alec gave Jamie as much time as he thought she needed to see to her bath, but when the haze covered his bare feet, he called out to her, commanding that she come to him.

His summons went unanswered. Alec's heart started pounding. He wasn't worried that his enemies had caught her unaware. No, they were on Kincaid land now, in a protected area none but his own would dare to breach. Still, she hadn't answered him. Alec broke through the lush green foliage and came to an abrupt stop. His breath caught in his throat at the sight he came upon.

She looked like a beautiful goddess. She was sound asleep. The fog floated around her, giving her a mystical appearance. The streamers of sunlight only added to that fantasy, for her skin was a true golden color. She was sleeping on her side. The white chemise she wore rode high on her hip, revealing her long legs.

He stood there a long while, drinking his fill. Desire swelled up inside him until it became almost painful. She was simply magnificent to him. He remembered what it felt like to have those legs wrapped around him, remembered the feel of her when he thrust inside.

His wife. A fierce surge of possessiveness shook him. He knew he wouldn't last another night without making love to her again. His promise to wait until they'd reached his holding wasn't going to last. This time, however, he was determined to go slowly. He would be a tender, undemanding lover. And he'd be gentle . . . even if it killed him.

Alec stood there watching her sleep until the sun was completely gone. She started to roll down the slope then. He rushed over to her and caught her in his arms just in the nick of time.

What a trusting nature she had. He knew she'd awakened, yet she didn't open her eyes. When he lifted her up against his bare chest, she put her arms around his neck, nuzzled up against him, and let out a soft sigh.

He carried her back to their camp, wrapped his plaid around both of them, and stretched out on the ground. Jamie was completely covered from the brisk mountain air, covered from head to toe by the blanket and her husband.

Her mouth was just a few inches away from his own.

"Alec?" she asked, her voice a sleepy whisper.

"Yes?"

"Are you angry with me?"

"No."

"You're certain?"

She wished she could see his face. His hold was like iron, though, and she could barely move at all.

"I'm certain."

"I'm so tired tonight. It was a hard day's ride, wasn't it?"

He hadn't thought so, but he decided to agree anyway. "Aye, it was."

"Alec? I'd like to ask you something." Jamie scooted upward, then let out a loud groan when his hands moved to her backside and he forced her against him. His thighs were harder than the ground.

He knew she didn't have any idea what her little motions were doing to him. Alec closed his eyes in reaction. She was too tired and obviously too sore to be attacked by her husband. He would have to wait, he told himself. It was the only decent thing to do.

It was going to be his most difficult challenge.

"Alec, please move your hands. You're hurting me."

"Go to sleep, wife. You need your rest." His voice sounded ragged.

She arched against him. Alec gritted his teeth.

"My backside is sore."

He could hear the blush in her soft confession. Her gasp wasn't soft, though; it was loud and full of outrage when he began to rub the stiffness out of her muscles. He ignored both her struggles and her groans.

"Your education has been sorely neglected," Alec told her. "'Tis the truth you're the most unskilled woman I've ever known. What think you of that, wife?"

"I think you believe I'm about to cry, husband," Jamie answered. "I know my voice trembled when I told you I was sore. And you're a man who hates a weeping woman, aren't you? Oh, don't be denying it, husband. I saw the way you watched my sisters when they were carrying on so. You looked most ill at ease."

"Yes, it's true," Alec admitted.

"And so, to prevent my weeping all over you, you insult me to prick my temper. You've guessed I have a temper and you'd rather have me shouting at you than crying."

"You're learning my ways, Jamie."

"I told you I would," Jamie boasted. "But you've still to learn mine."

"I have no need to—"

"Oh, yes, you do," she argued. "You confuse inexperienced with unskilled, Alec. What if I told you I could shoot an arrow better than any of your warriors? Or that I could probably outride them—bareback, of course. Or that I could—"

"I'd say you were jesting with me. You can barely hold on to the saddle, wife."

"You've already made up your mind about me, then?"

He ignored that question and asked one of his own. "What is it you wanted to ask me? Something has you worried, doesn't it?"

"I'm not worrying."

"Tell me."

He wasn't going to let her change her mind. "I merely wondered if you were going to give me similar instructions when we reach your holding and your men."

"What instructions?" he interrupted. He didn't have any idea what she was talking about.

"I know you're ashamed of me, Alec, but I don't think I shall be able to keep silent all the time. I'm used to speaking quite freely, and I really don't—"

"You think I'm ashamed of you?"

He actually sounded surprised. Jamie turned in his arms. She pushed the blanket aside and looked into his face. Even in the moonlight, she could see his astonishment.

She wasn't believing it for a minute. "You needn't pretend ignorance with me, Alec Kincaid. I know the truth. A woman would have to be daft not to know why you wouldn't let me speak to your allies. You think I'm ugly. And English."

"You *are* English," he reminded her.

"And pleased that I am, husband. Do you know how shallow a man is to judge a woman solely by her appearance?"

His laughter stopped her lecture. "Your rudeness is worse than my appearance," she muttered.

"And you, wife, are the most opinionated woman I've ever encountered."

"'Tis nothing compared to your sins," Jamie answered. "You're as riddled as an old shield."

"You aren't ugly."

Alec could tell by the way she continued to frown up at him that she didn't believe him. "When did you come to this conclusion?"

"I've already explained," Jamie answered. "'Twas when you wouldn't let me take my gaze off you, when you didn't introduce me to your friends, when you wouldn't let me speak a thought of my own. That's when I came to my conclusion. Make no mistake, Alec," she rushed on when he seemed about to laugh again, "I don't care if you think I'm pretty or not."

He captured her chin and held it steady. "If you'd stared

at one man longer than another, by chance or want, he would have concluded you were fair for the taking. The Kerrys can't be trusted, at least not by my measure. They would have challenged me for you. 'Tis simple enough to understand, even for you, English. Some would perhaps have thought your violet eyes were magical; others might have wanted to touch your hair to see if it felt as silky as it looks. All certainly would have wanted to touch you."

"They would?"

Her eyes had widened in amazement during his explanation. Alec realized she had absolutely no understanding of her own appeal.

"I think you exaggerate, Alec. Those men wouldn't have wanted to touch me."

She was pleading for a compliment. He decided to give it to her. "They would. I didn't want to chance a fight because I know how the sight of blood distresses you."

Jamie was stunned by his casually spoken explanation. Had he just complimented her? Were her eyes magical to him?

"What has you frowning now?"

"I was wondering if you . . . that is . . ." She let out a sigh, nudged his hand away from her chin, and rested her face against his warm shoulder again. "Then you don't think I'm ugly."

"I don't."

"I never thought you did," she admitted, a smile in her voice. "'Tis good to know you don't find me unappealing."

"I didn't say that."

Jamie decided he was jesting with her again. "I never said *you* weren't ugly," she said. "Perhaps I think you are."

He laughed again, a rich, full sound that made her smile all the more. Was it possible she was actually beginning to get used to him?

Alec brushed her hair away from her forehead. "Your face was burned by the sun today. Your nose is as red as fire. I don't find you at all appealing."

"You don't?" She looked startled.

Alec let her see his exasperation. "I was jesting."

"I knew you were," she said, smiling again.

She yawned, reminding him of how exhausted she was. "Go to sleep, Jamie."

The tender way he was stroking her back took the bark out of his command. When he started to rub the stiffness out of her shoulders, she closed her eyes and let out a loud, lusty sigh. The palm of her hand rested on his chest. She could feel his heart beating under her fingertips. Almost absentmindedly, she began to stroke a circle around the nipple hidden beneath his chest hair. She liked the feel of him. His wonderful scent reminded her of the outdoors. It was so clean, so earthy.

Alec suddenly grabbed hold of her hand and flattened it against his chest. She guessed he was ticklish.

He guessed she was trying to drive him out of his mind. "Stop that," he ordered, his voice as gritty as sand.

Jamie didn't remember falling asleep, but she remembered waking up, all right. She was having the most delicious dream. She was sleeping on a bed of wildflowers, completely unclothed. She was letting the sun warm her skin into a fever. The erotic heat made her forget to breathe. That familiar pressure was beginning to build up inside her, and that excruciating ache between her thighs was demanding to be appeased.

Her moan of desire woke her up. It hadn't been a dream at all. Her mind had been playing tricks on her. Alec was the sun, fueling the fever in her blood. She wasn't surrounded by wildflowers, either; she was stretched out on Alec's soft plaid. She had lost her chemise, though. She wondered how that could have happened, then put the negligent worry aside. Alec kept insisting on her attention. He was nuzzling the side of her neck. He rested between her parted thighs.

He was making love to her. Her sleepy confusion suddenly vanished. She was wide awake now. She couldn't see him, the darkness was too heavy, but his ragged breathing, added to the sweet music of the insistent wind, pushed most of her resistance away. She didn't want it to hurt again, thought to tell him just that, but his mouth moved to her breast just as his hand slid into the soft curls between her thighs. She didn't care then if it hurt or not.

His fingers were magical. He knew just where to touch her to make her wild, wet. She tensed against him when his fingers pushed aside the soft, slick folds and moved up inside her. The blissful agony made her cry out for release.

She pulled on his hair to get him to stop. Her mind was quickly changed when his thumb began to stroke the sensitive nub and his fingers thrust back inside her.

Her nails sank into his shoulders again. He grunted in reaction. Jamie was desperate to touch him, to give him the kind of pleasure he was giving her. She tried to move away, but Alec wouldn't let her.

They kissed, a hot, open-mouthed, ravenous kiss. He gave her his tongue. She sucked on it.

"You're so wet," he told her.

"I can't help it," she whispered on a half-groan.

His hands spread her thighs wide, and he slowly began to penetrate her. "I don't want you to help it."

"You don't?" she asked, trying to pull him inside her. He was making her daft, easing so slowly inside. She knew she was going to die, but she wanted him filling her, burning her, first.

"It means you're hot for me," he murmured. "Don't move like that. Let me . . ."

"This isn't the time for jests, Alec!"

He would have laughed if he'd had the strength. "I'm trying to be gentle," he told her. "But you're so tight, I . . ."

She arched against him. Alec forgot all about being gentle then. He pulled her legs high about his waist, twisted her hair around his hands to keep her from moving away from him, and drove inside her with one powerful surge.

He was so out of control he didn't know if he was hurting her or not. He couldn't stop. His mouth trapped any protests she might have tried to make, and when he knew he couldn't hold back any longer, when he felt his seed about to pour into her, he reached down between their bodies and stroked her into joining him.

Her legs were surprisingly strong. She squeezed him between her thighs, inside, forcing his immediate release.

He collapsed on top of her. It took him long minutes before he could regain enough strength to look at her. His first thought, when he could catch hold of one, was that he'd misused her. "Jamie? Did I hurt you? Was I too rough with you?" he whispered.

She didn't answer. Alec leaned up on his elbows to look down on her, his worry obvious in his gaze.

She was sound asleep. Alec didn't know what to make of that. He realized his fingers were tangled in her hair, and slowly, with patience he found surprising, he separated the curls. He took his time smoothing her hair away from her cheeks.

He knew he'd satisfied her. Lady Kincaid was in deep slumber, aye, but she'd fallen asleep with a smile on her face.

The next day proved to be the most difficult for Jamie. It was such beautiful, untamed land they journeyed over, with lochs the wind nudged ripples into, and open moorland expanses covered with grass the color of bright emeralds. There were stark ridges, too. Some of the hilly terrain was thick with green foliage called wild leek, which gave off a most peculiar stench when trodden upon. The grandeur of the Highlands made Jamie think she was slowly climbing up to heaven.

By noon the scenery had lost its appeal. There was a noticeable bite in the air that gained in intensity with each passing hour. Jamie hugged her winter cloak. She was so sleepy she almost fell off her mount. Alec was suddenly by her side. He lifted her onto his stallion. Jamie didn't resist, even when he jerked her cloak away and tossed it to the ground. He wrapped his heavy plaid around her and held her against him.

She let out a loud yawn, then asked, "Why did you throw my cape away, Alec?"

"You'll wear my colors to keep warm, Jamie."

He couldn't resist brushing his mouth against the top of her head. He was beginning to think his wife was the most

146

amazing creature. She could fall asleep within the blink of an eye.

He liked the feel of her against him, her womanly scent as well, and in the back of his mind was the realization that she trusted him completely. He liked that most of all.

He hadn't mentioned last night's passionate lovemaking to her. Her blush in the morning light had told him she didn't want him to bring that topic up.

Her shyness amused him.

His wife wasn't very strong, though. She didn't know her own body's limitations, either. Alec had recognized her exhaustion immediately. For that reason, he'd set a much slower pace.

She was sleeping soundly; he had to nudge her awake several times before getting any kind of response. "Jamie, wake up. We're home," he repeated for the third time.

"We're home?" she asked, sounding confused.

Alec patiently dodged her elbows while she rubbed the sleep from her eyes. "Do you always have such trouble waking after a nap?" he asked.

"I don't know," Jamie answered. "I've never taken a nap before."

She missed his frown when she turned to look around. "The only thing I'm seeing are trees, Alec. Did you wake me just to jest with me?"

In answer, Alec tilted her chin and pointed. "There, wife. Above the next ridge. You can see the smoke from my hearth."

She did see the stream of smoke curling up into the clouds, and a glimpse of his tower when he nudged his mount farther up the steep slope.

The wall surrounding his castle finally came into view. Lord, it was gigantic. A section looked as though it had been built into the side of the mountain. It was made of brown stone, an innovative break from English tradition, for most of the barons' holdings were built of wood. His wall was much taller, too. Why the top looked as if it reached the clouds. The structure was new, incomplete, too, as there was a wide breach adjacent to the drawbridge.

The trees had all been clipped away to make a wide margin around the wall. There wasn't a blade of grass along the rocky slope to soften the starkness.

The moat, with water as black as parchment ink, curved around the structure. The wooden drawbridge was down, but they headed through the opening in the wall instead.

His castle was much more grand than her papa's humble home. Alec was a rich man, she decided. The main dwelling boasted not one but two turrets, and everyone knew how costly just one was to build.

Jamie certainly hadn't expected anything this magnificent. She thought all Scots lived in stone cottages with thatched roofs and earthen floors, like the serfs in England. She realized now she'd made a prejudicial assumption. There were cottages, however—at least fifty of them, she guessed, peeking through the branches of the trees as high up the hillside as the eye could see. Jamie assumed the huts belonged to the Kincaid clansmen and their families.

"Alec, your home is grand," she told him. "When your wall is finished, your lower bailey will enclose half of Scotland, don't you suppose?"

He smiled over the astonishment in her voice. "Do you live alone, then? There isn't a single soldier in evidence."

"My men will be waiting for me atop the hill," Alec answered. "In the courtyard."

"The women as well?"

"A few," he answered. "Most of the women and children have gone to Gillebrid's holding for the spring festival. Half my number of soldiers are with them."

"And that's the reason it's so quiet?" She turned, smiled up at Alec, and then asked, "How many serve under your command?"

Jamie forgot her question as soon as she'd asked it. His smile had captured her full attention. "You're happy to be home again, aren't you?" she said.

Her eagerness pleased him. "There are five, perhaps six hundred men now, when they're all called together, and yes, English, I'm happy to be home."

Jamie let him see her exasperation. "Five or six hundred? Oh, Alec, you do like to jest with me."

"'Tis the truth, Jamie. There are many Kincaid clansmen."

She could tell he believed what he was telling her. "By a Scotsman's method of counting. I believe you think you have that many men."

"What do you mean by that?"

"I'm merely suggesting you need help counting, Alec. After all, you did tell me it would take us three days to get to your home, and it took us several added days."

"I slowed the pace because of your condition," Alec explained.

"What condition?"

"You were tender, or have you forgotten that fact?"

She immediately blushed, telling him she hadn't forgotten at all.

"And you're clearly exhausted."

"I'm not," Jamie replied. "It isn't important," she rushed on when he started frowning. She was about to meet his relatives and wanted to keep him in a cheerful mood. "If you tell me there are seven hundred men under your direction, then I'll believe you."

His smile told her she'd placated him. Yet she couldn't resist pricking his arrogance just a little. "Isn't it strange, though, Alec, that I don't see any men? Could all six hundred be waiting in your courtyard?"

He laughed over the exasperation she tried to hide from him. And then he let out a shrill whistle.

His call was immediately answered. They came from the top of the wall, the cottages, the stables, from the trees and forest surrounding them, these fierce-looking fighting men, until they covered the ground.

He hadn't exaggerated. If anything, she thought he'd understated their number. While she stared at the soldiers, Alec nodded his approval, then raised his hand into the air. When he made a fist, a resounding cheer split the air.

Jamie was so jarred by the noise that she grabbed hold of

Alec's other hand where it rested possessively around her waist. She couldn't stop staring at the men, even though she knew it was rude. She'd come to the land of giants, she decided, as most of the soldiers seemed to be as tall as the pine trees she'd heard they liked to throw.

Their size was most impressive, their watchful gazes unnerving, aye, but it was their state of dress that stunned her speechless.

Cholie hadn't been sotted. She'd known what she was talking about. The Scots did wear women's gowns. Half-naked women's gowns, she qualified. Jamie shook her head. No, they weren't gowns; they were blankets, the Gaelic word for their plaid.

All wore the same plaid. Alec's colors they were. The men had them wrapped around their waists and belted in place; and the plaids barely reached their knees.

Some of the men wore saffron-yellow shirts; others went without. Most were barefoot.

"Would you like to count their number?" Alec asked. He nudged his mount forward, then said, "I would guess around two hundred are here now, wife. But if you'd like to—"

"I'd say five hundred," Jamie whispered.

"Now you exaggerate."

Jamie glanced up at Alec and tried to find her voice. A wall of soldiers lined the path they climbed, and she therefore kept her voice low when she said, "You have your own legion, Alec, if this be only half your number."

"Nay. A legion is three thousand, sometimes as many as six thousand men. My number is not so high, Jamie, unless I call up my allies, of course."

"Of course."

"You needn't be afraid."

"I'm not afraid. Why would you think I was afraid?"

"You're shaking."

"I'm not," she denied. "They're all staring at us."

"They're curious."

"We didn't catch them unprepared, did we, Alec?" Her voice sounded terribly forlorn.

"What are you talking about?"

She was staring at his chin. He nudged her chin up, saw her wild blush, and became all the more bewildered. "My warriors are always prepared."

"They don't look prepared."

He suddenly understood why she sounded so embarrassed. "We don't call them gowns."

Her eyes widened in astonishment. "Did Beak tell you—"

"I was there."

"Where?"

"In the stable."

"You weren't!"

"I was."

"Oh, God."

Jamie frantically tried to remember the conversation she'd had with the stable master. "What else did you overhear?" she asked.

"That Scots have minds of sheep, that we throw pine trees at one another, that we—"

"I was just jesting with my sister when I told her . . . and I thought Cholie was sotted when she told me . . . Alec, do they always dress so indecently? With their knees showing?"

It was sinful for him to laugh right in her face. "You'll get used to our habits once you settle in," he promised.

"You don't dress like your soldiers, do you?"

She sounded appalled. "I do."

"No, you don't." Jamie sighed when she realized she'd just contradicted him again. He did seem to take offense whenever she corrected him. "I mean to say, you're wearing proper breeches now and for that reason I did assume—"

"I've been in England, Jamie. 'Tis the reason I wear such cumbersome garb."

Jamie glanced around her again, then returned her attention to her husband.

"How do they keep their britches rolled up above the hem of their plaids?" she asked.

"They don't."

"Then what . . ." From the devilish look in his eyes,

Jamie decided she didn't want to know. "Never mind," she blurted out. "I've changed my mind. I don't want to know what they wear underneath."

"Oh, but I want to tell you."

He was smiling just like a rascal. Jamie had to sigh over his ungentlemanly remarks and her own unladylike reaction. Lord, he was becoming more handsome by the minute. Her heart started fluttering like a butterfly's wings.

"You may tell me later, then," she whispered. "Late at night, Alec, when it's dark and you can't see my embarrassment. Do they wear chain mail when they go into battle?" She added that question to get him to forget about the soldiers' lack of undergarments.

"We never wear armor," Alec explained. "Most of us just wear the plaid. The seasoned warriors prefer the old ways, though."

"What is the old way?" she asked.

"They don't wear anything."

She was certain now he was jesting with her. The picture of naked warriors riding their mounts into war made her laugh with delight. "So they just throw off their blankets and—"

"Aye, they do."

"Alec, you must think me naive indeed to believe that fool's story. Do quit your jesting, please. You're being rude by half ignoring your men for so long."

After making that pronouncement, she turned her back on him, leaned against his chest, and forced a serene expression for the soldiers they passed on their way up the hill.

It took a mighty effort, what with the shameful thoughts Alec had just put into her head.

"You must learn not to give orders, wife."

He dropped his chin to rest on the top of her head as he whispered that order. It was a gentle rebuke. A shiver of pleasure rippled through her stomach. "I would like to do the right thing, husband, and so should you. Rudeness is never acceptable by anyone's measure, even a Scotsman's."

A shout echoed through the trees when they reached the second clearing. Alec jerked on Wildfire's reins as soon as she started fussing, then dismounted. He left Jamie on his stallion and led both horses toward the throng of waiting soldiers.

My, but she was nervous. She folded her hands together so his men wouldn't see how much they shook.

A blond man about Alec's size separated himself from the others and walked over to give greeting to his laird. The man's good looks made her think he was related to Alec. She assumed, too, that he was Alec's second-in-command and a friend as well, for he actually embraced his leader and slapped him mightily on the back.

The loud whack would have felled her to the ground, but Alec didn't even shrug. The burr in the soldier's voice was so thick Jamie couldn't catch every word. She heard enough, though, to blush in reaction. The two giants were taking turns insulting each other. It was yet another odd habit, she supposed.

The talk turned serious then. She could tell it wasn't good news the man was giving her husband. Alec's voice had taken on a hard edge, and a scowl had settled on his face. He looked furious. The soldier looked worried.

He didn't pay any attention to Jamie until they'd reached the inner courtyard. Then he tossed Wildfire's reins toward the men circling them and turned to lift Jamie to the ground.

He didn't even glance at her. Jamie stood at his side while he continued his conversation with the soldier.

Alec's men seemed to be divided in their curiosity. Half the number stared intently at her; their scowls suggested they didn't like what they were seeing. The other half circled Wildfire. They were smiling. And just what was she to think about that?

Wildfire didn't like the attention she was getting any more than Jamie did. The nervous horse reared up, snorted her displeasure, and rudely tried to trample the men trying to catch hold of her reins.

Jamie instinctively reacted. Like a mother whose child

was being naughty, she immediately sought to stop the budding temper tantrum.

She moved too quickly for Alec to catch hold of her. Without a thought to her audience, Jamie skirted her way around her husband and his stallion, nudged two big soldiers apart, and rushed forward to soothe her baby.

She stopped when she was just a few feet away from her pet. Jamie didn't have to say a harsh word. She simply held out her hand and waited.

Wildfire immediately ceased her tantrum. The wild look left her eyes. While the warriors watched in open fascination, the proud white beauty trotted forward to receive a touch from her mistress.

Alec suddenly appeared at Jamie's side. He put his arm around her shoulders and pulled her up against his side.

"She's usually very docile," Jamie told her husband. "But she's tired, Alec, and hungry, too. Perhaps I should take her—"

"Donald will see to that task."

She didn't want to argue with him in front of his men. Alec took Wildfire's reins, spoke in rapid Gaelic as he gave instructions to the young man who'd just rushed over to him.

Donald was a mite young to be stable master in Jamie's opinion. Yet as soon as he announced that Wildfire was a fine horse indeed, Jamie decided to trust his capabilities. He obviously knew good horseflesh when he saw it. He had a gentle voice, too, at great odds with his flaming red hair and complexion, and an easy smile that made her want to smile back.

Wildfire hated him. The fussy horse tried to push her way between Jamie and Alec. Donald proved determined, however. When Alec added a harsh command, the stable master was able to gain complete control. He led Wildfire across the yard. Jamie watched, feeling like an anxious mother being separated from her baby.

"She'll settle in."

Alec's remark irritated her. So she and her mare were the same in his eyes, were they? He'd said the same thing to her. Horse and wife. "She might," Jamie answered, stressing the word "she."

They started walking toward the steps leading to his castle doors. Alec still hadn't introduced her to his men. She wondered about that oversight a long minute, then decided he was waiting for the right moment to do it properly.

They reached the top of the steps before he finally paused. He turned around, forcing her to follow with his arm still anchored around her shoulders.

He let go of her then, accepted a plaid from one of his soldiers, and draped it over Jamie's right shoulder. As soon as that action was accomplished, silence filled the courtyard. The soldiers placed their hands over their hearts. Their heads were bowed.

The moment had arrived. Jamie stood as straight as a lance, her hands at her sides, waiting to hear the wonderful speech Alec would give his men. He'd have to give her praise now, she told herself, whether he wanted to or not.

Jamie told herself to remember every single word so she could pull the speech out of her memory and savor it whenever Alec irritated her.

It was a short speech, over and done with, in fact, before she realized it. Alec's voice rang out over the crowd when he shouted, "My wife."

My wife? That was it? He had nothing else to say? When he continued to keep silent, she guessed he was finished. And since he'd spoken in Gaelic, and she'd already decided against letting him know she understood his language, she couldn't very well let him see how irritated she was over his abruptness.

When Alec gave the signal, his men drew their swords. Another great shout echoed throughout the courtyard.

Jamie edged closer to Alec, then bowed her head and made a curtsy to his soldiers.

Their renewed cheers startled her. Alec thought she might

be a little intimidated. She looked overwhelmed by all the attention.

"What did you say to them, Alec?" she whispered, knowing full well what he'd said. As soon as he answered her, she thought to tell him that he really should expound upon his introduction.

She never got the chance to enlighten him, however.

"I told them you were English," Alec lied. He threw his arm around her shoulders again and, as was his disturbing habit, literally hauled her up against his side. God's truth, he treated her just like a satchel.

"And that, of course, is the reason they're cheering," Jamie countered. "Because I'm English."

"Nay, wife. 'Tis the reason they're screaming."

He was outrageous. Jamie shook her head.

"What think you of my men?" he asked, his tone serious now.

She didn't look at him when she gave her answer. "I'm thinking they all have swords, Kincaid, and you don't. That's what I'm thinking."

The woman had grit, all right. Alec grinned in response to her barb.

The soldiers were openly staring at her. Alec knew they'd have to look their fill. It would take them time to get used to her appearance. In truth, he was still having difficulty with that task.

The soldier Jamie had guessed was Alec's second-in-command rushed up the steps at his leader's beckoning. He stopped in front of Jamie, waiting for an introduction.

"This is Gavin, wife. He's in command whenever I'm away from home."

When Gavin looked into her eyes, she smiled her greeting. Her smile began to falter though, the longer he continued to stare at her. She wondered if he was waiting for her to say something, or if there was some formality she'd yet to complete.

He was a very attractive man. He reminded her of Mary's new husband, Daniel, for when he did finally smile at her, his green eyes sparkled with amusement. "I'm honored to meet you, Lady Kincaid."

Gavin didn't take his gaze away from her when he spoke to Alec. "You've chosen well, Alec. I'm wondering how you ever talked Daniel—"

"A toss of the caber settled the issue of first choice," Alec announced. "My wife was pick of the litter."

"Pick of the litter?" Jamie turned to frown at her husband. "Are you jesting with me in front of your friend, Alec, or do you really believe what you say?"

"I am jesting," Alec answered.

"He's always jesting," Jamie told Gavin, her roundabout way of apologizing for her husband's outrageous remarks.

Gavin was astonished. In all his years, he'd never known Alec to jest about anything. He wasn't about to contradict the new Lady Kincaid, however.

He turned just in time to see Alec wink at his wife. "She's exhausted, Gavin," Alec said, drawing his soldier's full attention. "A good supper and a long night's rest are just what she needs."

"She needs to see your home first," Jamie announced. Her voice echoed her exasperation. "For she is most curious."

Both Alec and Gavin grinned over the subtle way Jamie had just censured them for speaking as though she weren't there. Jamie smiled, too, for she was pleased with the way she'd just bested them. "May I also have a bath, Alec?"

"I'll see to that task at once, milady," Gavin called out before Alec could answer.

He followed behind his new mistress like a puppy. Alec watched Gavin staring at his wife. He was amused by the way his friend tried to hide his reaction to Jamie. Gavin couldn't seem to take his gaze off her.

"Thank you, Gavin," Jamie replied. "You needn't be so formal with me, though. Please call me Jamie. 'Tis my given name."

When Alec's friend didn't respond to her suggestion,

Jamie turned around to look at him. Gavin was frowning over her request. "It isn't acceptable?" she asked.

"Did you say your name was Jane?"

"No, it's Jamie," she instructed.

She nodded when Gavin continued to look confused.

The soldier turned to Alec and blurted out, "But that's a man's name."

Chapter Nine

"You put him up to it, didn't you, Alec?"

He didn't bother to answer that absurd question. Jamie did have a man's name, and Alec had far more important matters to see to than to stand in his doorway debating this issue with her.

Both he and Gavin left her frowning after them as they walked down the three steps into the great hall. In truth, he had to give Gavin a good shove to get him started.

Jamie looked around with curiosity. A stone wall as tall as a church steeple was on her right. The stones were cool to the touch, smooth as polished gems, and without a single speck of dust blunting the golden brown color. A wooden staircase led to the second level, where it angled into a balcony that stretched all the way across one side of the building. Jamie counted three doors on the upper level and assumed they were sleeping chambers for Alec and his relatives.

There certainly wasn't much privacy offered by the construction. Anyone in the great hall or the entrance could see who was coming and who was going from the rooms above, so open was the area.

The great hall was large enough for giants. It was stark in appearance, yet immaculate as well. Straight ahead of her was a massive stone fireplace. A blazing fire barely warmed the air in the gigantic room.

The hall was the biggest she'd ever seen. Of course, she'd only seen her papa's hall, and she guessed that didn't really signify; her papa's chamber would have been lost in this hall. The room was as broad as a meadow and was equally divided by a long center pathway of rushes leading to the hearth. A table with at least twenty stools lining its sides took up only a small portion on the left side. Another table of identical dimensions was situated on the right. Just a few feet beyond that table was a tall wooden screen. Jamie assumed the square partition closeted the buttery.

Alec and Gavin were seated at the table in front of the screen. Since neither warrior was paying her any attention, she strolled over to the screen, looked behind it, and was surprised to find a bed there, built on a tall platform. Several pegs cluttered the wall behind the huge bed, and from the size of the garments hanging there, she thought this might be where Alec slept. She prayed she was wrong.

A soldier walked past her and placed her satchel on the foot of the platform. Jamie knew her guess had been accurate then. The soldier gave her a startled look and a gruff reply when she thanked him for bringing her baggage, then motioned her out of the way when another big man carried a circular wooden tub behind the screen and placed it in the far corner.

She was going to have the quietest bath she'd ever had, and that was that. Jamie felt herself blush just thinking about her lack of privacy. The screen would hide her nakedness, aye, yet anyone who happened to walk into the hall would hear the noise and surely guess what she was doing.

Jamie went back to her husband, determined to find out where the kitchen was located so she could order their supper. She reached his side and stood there several long minutes, but Alec still didn't acknowledge her. Gavin was giving his accounting to his laird and had his full attention. Jamie sat down on the stool adjacent to her husband, folded her hands in her lap, and patiently waited for him to finish.

It would have been rude for her to interrupt. Jamie knew it was her duty not to complain either. She was wife of an important laird, after all, and if she had to sit there until morning light before she gained his attention, then sit there she would.

She soon became too sleepy to think about eating. She was just about to get up from the table when two women came rushing into the hall.

Their gowns were made from the Kincaid colors, and from their bearing, Jamie knew they weren't servants. Both women had dark blond hair, brown eyes, and sincere smiles as well, until they turned their attention to her.

Their smiles immediately vanished. The taller of the two actually glared at Jamie.

Jamie glared back. She was too exhausted to put up with such nonsense. Tomorrow, she decided, would be soon enough to try to win the woman's friendship. For now she was going to give as good as she was getting.

A soldier, with features showing a marked resemblance to both women, came into the hall next. He stopped directly behind the two women, placed his hands on their shoulders, and stared at Jamie. His hair was black, almost as black as the scowl he was giving her.

This one had already made up his mind to hate her, Jamie supposed. She assumed it was because she was English. She was an outsider here; it would take time for Alec's clan to accept her. God only knew it was going to take her time to get used to them.

Alec didn't notice the intrusion until Jamie nudged him with her foot. He gave her a frown for interrupting him, then saw the threesome waiting near the entrance. Alec broke into a wide smile immediately. Both women smiled back. The taller of the two rushed forward.

"Come and join us," Alec called out. "Marcus?" he added when the scowling soldier had walked over to his side, "I'll hear your accounting after supper. Did you bring Elizabeth back with you?"

"I did," Marcus answered in a clipped voice.

"Where is she?"

"She wanted to wait in her cottage for word of Angus."

Alec nodded. He remembered his wife when Marcus turned his gaze to her. "This is my wife," he announced with a shrug in his voice.

"Her name is Jamie." Alec turned to his wife and said, "This is Marcus. And this is Edith," he added with a nod toward the woman standing beside the brooding warrior. "Marcus and Edith are brother and sister and first cousins of Helena."

She could have guessed they were sister and brother. Their scowls were quite alike. She was too busy trying to follow Alec's explanation to bother about their rudeness, though. Where was Helena? And who was this Elizabeth that Marcus had just mentioned?

Alec interrupted her puzzling by motioning to the last of the threesome. "Last but certainly not least is my Annie," he announced. His tone was filled with affection. "Come closer, child," he called out. "You must meet your new mistress."

When Annie hurried across the room, Jamie realized she was actually a grown woman. Annie appeared to be just a year or two younger than Jamie. Yet there was a childlike expression on her lovely face. She radiated wide-eyed innocence, too.

Annie made an awkward curtsy to Jamie, then smiled sweetly. Her voice was that of a very little girl when she said, "Do I have to like her, Alec?"

"You do," Alec answered.

"Why?"

"Because it will please me."

"Then I shall like her," Annie answered. "Even though she's English." Her smile widened when she added, "I've missed you, milord."

Before Alec had a chance to respond to that remark,

Annie hurried down to the far end of the table and took her place between Marcus and Edith.

Jamie continued to watch Annie a long moment. She understood what was wrong with the girl. She was one of those special people who stayed childlike all their lives. Jamie's heart went out to Annie and to Alec as well, for he'd shown such kindness.

"Is Annie Marcus's sister, too?" Jamie asked.

"No, she's Helena's sister."

"Who is Helena?"

"She was my wife."

Alec turned his attention back to Gavin before Jamie could ask another question. A group of servants came bustling into the hall, drawing her attention. Jamie's stomach immediately started grumbling when she spotted the platters of food the stout women carried.

Trenchers made of hollowed out stale bread covered the table. A large platter of mutton was placed directly in front of Jamie. She tried not to gag, but the sight and smell made her stomach turn. Jamie detested mutton with a passion, ever since she'd taken ill after eating a portion of tainted mutton when she was just a little girl. She hadn't touched it since.

Wedges of cheese, some yellow, others orange with red streaks, fat tarts overflowing with dark purple berries, and crusty rounds of brown freckled bread were added to the fare. Jugs of ale and pitchers of water completed the supper.

Alec ignored all the commotion until the servants had left the hall. When a group of soldiers walked inside, he acknowledged each man with a curt nod, then went back to questioning Gavin.

He was beginning to get irritated with his second-in-command. While Gavin gave quick, efficient answers to all his questions, he certainly wasn't giving his laird his full attention; he kept staring across the table at Jamie.

Alec's voice turned hard in reaction to the unintentional insult. Jamie looked at her husband. "This news displeases you?" she asked when she caught his attention.

"Angus is missing."

"Angus?"

"A soldier under my command," Alec explained. "He's equal in rank to Gavin, though his duties are of a different nature."

"He is your friend as well?"

Alec tore a piece of bread in half and offered Jamie one portion before he answered her. "Yes, he has been a good friend as well."

"Who is Elizabeth?" Jamie asked. "I heard you ask Marcus if he'd—"

"She's Angus's wife."

"Oh, the poor woman," Jamie responded, her voice filled with sympathy. "She must be terribly worried. Couldn't Angus just be late in returning home?"

Alec shook his head. He couldn't understand why Jamie was so concerned. She didn't even know the man. Still, her sympathy pleased him. "He isn't late," he announced. "Tardiness would be an insult to me, wife. No, something has happened to him."

"He's dead or he'd be here," Gavin interjected with a shrug.

"Yes," Alec agreed.

The other soldiers had been intently listening to their conversation. Jamie noticed that, along with the fact that they must all know her language as well as Alec did. They all agreed with Gavin's comment, too.

"You cannot know if this man is dead," she announced. Their cold attitude was most barbaric. "'Tis unkind of you to speak this way about your friend."

"Why?" Gavin asked, frowning.

Jamie ignored his question and asked one of her own. "Why aren't you out looking for him?"

"There are soldiers searching the hills now," Alec answered.

"We'll probably find his body come morning," Gavin predicted.

"Gavin, surely you don't mean to sound so uncaring,

now, do you?" Jamie asked. "You should believe your friend is safe."

"I should?"

"You all should," Jamie announced, looking down the length of the table to include everyone in her statement. "One must always have hope."

Alec hid his smile. His wife hadn't been inside his home for more than an hour and she was already giving orders. "It would be a false hope," he answered. "And you needn't sound so outraged, wife."

He directed the soldiers to join in the conversation. Everyone began talking at once, each giving his own opinion as to what had happened to Angus. While their speculations as to how he was waylaid differed, their conclusion was unanimous: Angus was dead.

Jamie kept silent throughout the remainder of the meal while she listened to each give his own guess. It was soon apparent the missing man was important to them. Still, they harbored no hope.

Neither Edith nor Annie had a comment to make. They kept their gazes directed on their dinner.

Alec touched Jamie's arm. When she looked up at him, he offered her a portion of mutton.

"No, thank you."

"You'll eat this."

"I'll not."

He raised one eyebrow in disbelief. She'd actually argued with him in front of his men. It was unthinkable.

Jamie thought he looked quite astonished. She assumed he didn't like being contradicted. "I don't want any mutton, but thank you so much for offering."

"You will eat this," Alec ordered. "You're weak. You need to build up your strength."

"I'm strong enough now," Jamie whispered. "Alec, I can't eat mutton. It won't stay in my stomach. Even the smell makes me sick. The rest of this meal is very nice, though. I couldn't eat another bite."

"Then go and have your bath," he instructed. He

frowned, noticing again the fatigue in her eyes. "Darkness will be here soon, and with it a chill that will settle in your bones if you're not in bed."

"And will it settle in your bones, too?" she asked.

"Nay," he answered with a grin. "We Scots are made of tougher stuff."

She laughed. The musical sound drew everyone's attention. "You turn my own words back on me," she remarked.

He didn't answer that comment.

"Where do I sleep, Alec?"

"With me."

His tone didn't leave room for her to argue. "But where?" she persisted. "Do we sleep behind the screen, Alec, or in one of the rooms above the stairs?"

She turned to motion to the balcony and suddenly froze. God's truth, she couldn't believe what she was seeing. Her eyes widened in astonishment.

Jamie stood up and faced the entrance. There were weapons everywhere. They filled the walls from top to bottom on both sides of the yawning entrance. The fact that her husband had a bloody arsenal wasn't what held Jamie so mesmerized, though. No, it was the sword hanging in the center of the far wall.

It was magnificent, this Herculean sword, with clusters of gleaming red and green gems imbedded in the handle. They looked like fat grapes. She stared at the sword a long minute before she looked over at the other weapons. Then she took her time counting. There were five swords in all, hanging among the maces, clubs, lances, and other weapons she couldn't name.

Yes, there were five swords; she counted again just to be sure.

And every damn one of them belonged to him. Oh, how he must have laughed at her when she offered to spend her hard-saved shillings to have a sword made for him. She'd made a fool of herself, she had, but Alec's shame was worse. He'd let her.

She was too embarrassed by her own naiveté to look at her husband. She continued to stare at the wall when she said,

"Gavin? Those weapons all belong to my husband, don't they?"

"They do," Gavin answered. He looked over at Alec to judge his reaction to Lady Kincaid's change in behavior. Surely Alec had noticed how her voice trembled, and surely he could see how she blushed. Gavin thought it odd indeed. His mistress had been very docile, almost timid, during their supper. Why, she'd barely spoken a word.

Alec was watching his wife, but a slow grin settled on his face when she finally turned to him.

Her hands were clenched on her hips. She had the courage to scowl at her husband, too. Gavin was amazed by the transformation in the woman. He'd judged her to be shy, yet when her eyes turned such a deep, angry violet, he changed his mind. Lady Kincaid didn't look timid now. She looked ready to do battle.

Alec seemed to be the man she wanted to do battle with. Didn't she know what a fierce temper Alec possessed? Gavin decided she apparently didn't know, else she wouldn't challenge him so boldly.

"Gavin? In England, what belongs to a husband also belongs to his wife. Is it the same here?"

She hadn't taken her gaze away from her husband when she questioned his soldier. "It's the same," Gavin answered. "Why do you ask, milady? Is there something in particular you want?"

"There is."

"What, then?" Gavin asked.

"The sword."

"A sword, milady?" Gavin asked.

"No, Gavin, not a sword," Jamie explained. "The sword. The one in the middle of that wall over there. I want that sword."

A collective gasp filled the hall. Gavin's mouth dropped open. He looked down the table, knew then that the entire conversation had been overheard by all the others. They looked as stunned as he felt. "But that's the laird's very own sword," Gavin stammered out. "Surely—"

Alec's laughter stopped his explanation. "A wife couldn't

even lift that sword," he said. "No, a mere woman would never have enough strength, especially one who can't eat mutton."

Jamie didn't answer that challenge for a long minute. "Are there daggers she could lift with her puny strength?" she asked at last, smiling ever so sweetly at her husband.

"Of course."

"Then perhaps—"

"A dirk could easily be knocked out of such puny hands, Jamie."

She nodded agreement. Alec was a little disappointed because he'd won their game of sparring so easily. Jamie bowed to him and started toward the screen. Alec watched the gentle sway of her hips until he saw that his men were also noticing. He cleared his throat to get their attention, then let them see his displeasure.

Jamie was almost out of sight when she called back over her shoulder, "Unless, of course, you were sleeping, Alec. Then my puny little hands would be strong enough, don't you suppose? Good night, husband. I pray you have pleasant dreams."

Alec's laughter followed her behind the screen.

"Did I misunderstand?" Gavin asked. "Or did your wife just threaten to murder you?"

"You didn't misunderstand."

"Yet you laugh?"

"Quit your frown," Alec instructed. "I'm safe enough. My wife wouldn't try to harm me. It isn't in her nature."

"It isn't? She's English, Alec."

"You'll understand when you get to know her better."

"She's very beautiful," Gavin said. He grinned. "I couldn't help noticing."

"I noticed you noticing," Alec muttered.

"Yes . . . well, it's going to take a long while before I get used to her," Gavin admitted, embarrassed that his laird had caught him staring at his wife. "The men would give their lives to keep her safe, Alec, but I don't honestly know if they'll ever give her their loyalty. 'Tis because she's English, of course."

"I haven't forgotten that fact," Alec answered. "Every time she opens her mouth, her accent reminds me. Perhaps, in time, Jamie will be able to earn the men's trust. I won't demand it."

"I thought she was timid, but now I'm not so certain."

"She's about as timid as I am," Alec said. "The woman has few fears. She likes to speak her mind. 'Tis another of her numerous flaws. But she's too gentle for her own good, Gavin."

"I see."

"What the hell are you smiling about?" Alec snapped.

"Nothing, milord."

"Listen to me," Alec continued. "I want you to guard Jamie whenever I'm away. She's not to be out of your sight, Gavin."

"You expect trouble?"

"I don't," Alec answered. "Just do as I command without questioning me."

"Of course."

"I want her adjustment to be as smooth as possible. She isn't at all strong."

"You've mentioned that," Gavin remarked before he thought better of it.

Alec gave him a good scowl to let him know he didn't appreciate his comment. "Even the sight of blood distresses the woman."

"So does the sight of mutton."

The two men shared a laugh. It didn't last long. As soon as Alec glanced down the table, he quit laughing altogether. All his soldiers were staring intently at the screen. They might not trust their laird's wife, but they sure as hell were captivated by her.

Jamie didn't have any idea what an uproar she'd caused. She patiently waited while the servants filled the tub with steaming hot water, visiting with a gray-haired, soft-spoken woman by name of Frieda, until the chore was done.

Frieda was about to leave the area when Jamie asked where the kitchen was located.

"To hell and gone," Frieda whispered. "Oh, Lord, I dinna mean to say that, mistress."

Jamie held her laughter. The poor woman looked mortified. She didn't want to add to her embarrassment. "I'll not tell anyone," she promised. "Do you mean, then, that the kitchen is in a separate building?"

Frieda nodded so vigorously that the bun of hair atop her head wobbled. "Some winters is so poor we got to wade through the snow up to our knees. It gets a might cold, lass."

"Tomorrow will you show me where this building is?"

"Why are you wanting to see it?"

"Now that I'm mistress, I might make a few changes here and there," Jamie explained. "It does sound as though the kitchen needs to be moved closer to the main building, now, doesn't it?"

"Do you mean it, lass?" Frieda asked, her enthusiasm obvious. She frowned then and whispered, "I wouldn't be boasting of making changes, though, leastways not in front of Edith. She likes to think of herself as mistress. She's a bossy bit of goods, that one."

Jamie smiled. "That, too, will have to be changed, won't it?"

She could tell from the beaming smile on the elderly woman's face that she'd made an ally for life.

"You'd best see to your bath before the water turns cold," Frieda advised before taking her leave.

Jamie thought about Frieda's remarks while she stripped out of her clothes. She eased into the tub without making a sound. She didn't want to make any noise because Alec and his soldiers were just a shout away, but by the time she'd washed her hair and given herself a good scrubbing, she was too tired to care if they heard her or not. She put on a clean sleeping gown, tied the pretty pink ribbons together from waist to neck, and climbed into the huge bed.

It took another half-hour or so to get her hair brushed and partially dried. Alec's sword kept intruding into her thoughts. It was downright humiliating the way he'd let her go on and on about a knight needing a trusty sword. Yet she was smiling about it now. She couldn't stay angry with Alec.

She actually let out a soft chuckle when she remembered suggesting to him that Daniel give him training. Alec probably thought she was the one with brains of sheep. He certainly didn't think she was any better than an ignorant country mouse.

Her last thought before drifting off to sleep was a most revealing one: she wished Alec would come to bed. Heaven help her, she was falling in love with the barbaric Scotsman.

I see the way Alec keeps glancing over at the screen. The English bitch has him wanting her already. Was his love for Helena so shallow he can replace her so easily?

He doesn't remember the lesson. Perhaps he has already given his heart to his bride. God, I hope so. Her death will be all the more painful then.

I won't wait to kill her.

Chapter Ten

The whispers awakened Jamie. She was disoriented at first. The candles were burning still, casting shadows that danced along the screen. Jamie stared at the dark reflections a long minute before she remembered where she was.

The whispers brushed through the air again. She strained to catch a word or two, and when she'd managed that feat, she was wide awake and trembling with fear. Oh, she understood the words now. It was the holy sacrament of extreme unction she was listening to, the sacred rite for a departing soul.

They must have found Angus. Jamie made a hasty sign of the cross, put on her robe, and went to offer her own prayers. She knew she was considered an outsider, but she was Alec's wife all the same. Wasn't it her duty to stand by her husband when he said his farewell to his friend?

Alec didn't hear her approach. Jamie stood behind his back, watching while the priest read the holy rite.

The body had been placed on the table opposite the one in front of the screen. The old priest, dressed in requiem vestments of black with purple trim, stood at one end of the table. He had gray hair, a complexion to match, and spoke in a voice graveled with sadness.

Alec stood at the opposite end of the long table. Soldiers of varying rank filled the spaces between. Anna, Edith, and another woman Jamie guessed was Elizabeth, stood near the hearth.

Jamie's heart went out to the grieving woman. She could see the tears streaming down Elizabeth's face. The woman didn't make a sound, though, a fact that made Jamie admire her all the more. Under similar circumstances, she'd probably be wailing uncontrollably.

She peeked around her husband to get a better look at the man they were mourning.

At first she thought he was dead. Jamie was used to seeing injuries of every sort, and for that reason she barely blanched over the horrible sight before her. There was blood everywhere, or so it appeared to her at first notice. Jamie couldn't tell how much was bluster, though, and how much was real damage. A large curved gash took up a fair portion of the warrior's chest. His lower left arm was broken, too, near the wrist, but it looked like a clean break to her.

He was a battle-scarred man with rugged features and dark brown hair. A large welt had made his brow swell up, giving him a grotesque appearance. Jamie stared at the bump a long while, wondering if that was the blow that had caused his death.

The dead man suddenly grimaced. It was an ever-so-slight movement she would have missed if she hadn't been watching him so intently.

A spark of hope was ignited in her mind. She concentrated on the way the warrior was breathing. It was a mite shallow, she decided, yet true as a rooster's. A good sign, that, for there was usually a rattle shivering through the air when death came stalking his prey.

The truth still took her by surprise. Angus wasn't dying . . . yet.

The priest was taking forever to finish his prayers. Jamie didn't want to wait. The man they were mourning would surely catch a fever and die before morning unless she could take care of his injuries.

Jamie reached up to tap Alec's shoulder. He immediately turned around, then moved to block her view of the wounded soldier. He didn't look overly happy to see her.

"It's Angus?" she whispered.

Alec nodded. "Go back to bed, Jamie."

"He isn't dead."

"He's dying."

"No, I don't think he is, Alec."

"Go to bed."

"But Alec—"

"Now."

The harshness in his command worried her. Jamie turned around and slowly walked back to her bed. She was already listing the items she would need to help Angus.

When she returned to her husband, her arms were filled with her precious medicine jars. She had tucked a long needle and sturdy thread into one pocket of her robe. Three white stockings dangled from her other pocket. Jamie was determined to do what she could to save the warrior, with or without her husband's cooperation. She only hoped Alec wouldn't make too much of a fuss before he gave in.

He was going to have to give in, though, and that was that.

The priest gave the final blessing and knelt down. Alec motioned to his men, turned, and very nearly knocked Jamie to the floor. He instinctively reached out to steady her.

He was bloody furious with her. The look on his face said as much. So did his hard grip on her shoulders. Jamie took a deep breath, then blurted out, "In England we have a rather quaint custom, Alec. We don't mourn a man until he's dead, and we don't call for our priest until we're sure he's dying."

She'd certainly gained his full attention with that statement. "Alec, you cannot know for certain that Angus is dying. Let me see to his injuries. If God is determined to have him now, nothing I do will make any difference."

She shrugged his hands away while she waited for his

answer. It was a long time in coming. Alec was looking at her as though she'd just lost her mind. Jamie tried to move to his side, but he blocked her view once again. "There's blood."

"I saw it."

"Blood makes you sick."

"Alec, where do you get your ideas?"

He didn't answer that challenge. "It will not make me sick."

"If you get ill, I'll be very displeased with you."

And if his voice turned any harsher, it would probably cause lightning to strike, Jamie thought. "I'm going to take care of him, husband, with or without your permission. Now get out of my way."

He didn't budge, but his eyes had widened over her sharp command. Jamie thought he might be considering strangling her. She decided then that ordering him about wasn't the right approach. "Alec, did I tell you how to fight those bandits who attacked us on our way here?"

He thought that question was too ridiculous to answer. Jamie answered for him. "No, of course I didn't. I don't know anything about fighting, husband, but I do know a bloody lot about healing. I'm going to help Angus and that's that. Now please move out of my way. Your friend is in terrible pain."

It was her last remark that gained his cooperation. "How can you know he's in pain?"

"I saw him grimace."

"You're certain?"

"Very certain."

The fierceness in her tone amazed him. Before his eyes she was turning into a tigress. "Do what you can."

Jamie let out a weary sigh as she hurried to the table. She placed her jars near one corner, then bent over Angus to study his injuries.

The warriors all returned to the table. They looked outraged. Alec thought he might have a rebellion on his hands. He folded his arms across his chest and slowly scanned his audience, for one and all had turned to look at him now. They were obviously waiting to see what he was going to do about his wife's disrespectful interference.

Jamie didn't pay any attention to the soldiers. She gently prodded the edges of the welt on Angus's forehead. She studied his chest wound next.

"'Tis just as I suspected," she said.

"The damage?" Alec asked.

Jamie shook her head. There was a smile in her voice when she said, "It's mostly bluster."

"Bluster?"

"Meaning it looks worse than it really is," Jamie explained.

"He isn't dying?"

The priest asked that question. The old man struggled to his feet, wheezing from the effort. He stared at Jamie with a frown as fierce as any she'd ever seen.

"He has a good chance, Father," Jamie said. She heard a woman cry out and guessed it was Elizabeth.

"I would like to help you," the priest announced.

"I would appreciate your help," she replied. She heard the soldiers grumbling under their breath behind her. She ignored them and turned back to her husband. "You were leaving with your men, I noticed, but if it wasn't an important errand, I could use your assistance."

"We were going to build a box," Alec explained.

"A box?"

"A burial box," the priest interjected.

Jamie looked incredulous. She felt like putting her hands over Angus's ears so he wouldn't hear this discouraging talk. "For heaven's sake, you'd put Angus in the ground before he quit breathing?"

"No, we'd wait," Alec answered. "You really think you can save him, don't you?"

"What can I do to help?" Gavin asked before Jamie could answer her husband.

"I need more light, linen strips, a goblet of warm water, bowls with more water, and two slats of wood, Gavin, about this size and length," she instructed, showing him with her hands the desired dimensions.

If they thought her requests didn't make any sense, they didn't mention it to her.

"His arm is broken, lass. Do you think to cut it off?" the priest asked.

A soldier behind Jamie's back muttered, "Angus would rather die than have his arm removed."

"We aren't going to cut his arm off," Jamie announced in exasperation. "We're going to straighten it."

"You can do this?" the priest asked.

"I can."

The circle of men tightened around the table. Gavin nudged his way next to his mistress. "Here's the goblet of water you wanted. The bowls are behind you."

Jamie opened one of the medicine jars, pinched a sprinkle of brown powder between her thumb and forefinger, and mixed it with the water in the goblet. When the liquid had turned murky, she handed it to Gavin. "Please hold this for just a moment."

"What is it, mistress?" Gavin asked, sniffing the potion.

"A sleeping drink for Angus. It will also ease his pain."

"He's already sleeping."

Jamie didn't recognize the voice, knew another soldier had called out that comment. His tone had been filled with anger.

"Aye, he's sleeping," another muttered. "Anyone can see he is."

"He is not sleeping," Jamie countered, trying to hold her patience. She knew she'd have to gain their confidence if she was going to get their help.

"Then why ain't he talking to us or looking at us?"

"He's in too much pain," Jamie answered. "Alec, would you hold his head up so he can drink more easily?"

Alec was the only one who didn't argue with her. He moved closer to the table and lifted Angus's head. Jamie leaned over his friend, cupped his face in her hands, and spoke to him. "Angus, open your eyes and look at me."

She had to repeat her demand three times, bellowing the last, before the warrior finally complied.

A surprised murmur rushed around the table. The doubting Thomases had just been convinced.

"Angus, you must drink this," Jamie ordered. "It will take your pain away." She didn't let up on her prodding until the warrior had swallowed a large portion.

Then she sighed with satisfaction. "It will only take a minute or two before the potion does its work."

After making that statement, Jamie glanced up.

Alec was smiling at her.

"He could still catch fever and die," she whispered, fearing she'd given him too much hope and not enough caution.

"He wouldn't dare."

"He wouldn't?"

"Not after the way you screamed at him," Alec replied.

Jamie felt herself blush. "I had to raise my voice," she explained. "'Twas the only way I could get him to respond."

"I think he's sleeping now," Gavin interjected.

"We shall see," Jamie announced. She once again leaned over Angus and cupped his face in her hands.

"Is the pain leaving you yet?" she asked.

The warrior slowly opened his eyes. Jamie could see the medicine was beginning to work, for his brown eyes were glazed.

His face had taken on a tranquil expression, too. "Have I gone to heaven?" Angus asked, his voice a scratchy whisper. "Are you my angel?"

Jamie smiled. "No, Angus. You're still in the Highlands."

A look of horror crossed the warrior's face. "Good God Almighty, I ain't in heaven. I'm in hell. It be a cruel trick the devil plays. You look like an angel, but you sound . . . English."

He'd roared the last of his statement and immediately started struggling. Jamie leaned so close to his right ear she was almost kissing him, then whispered in Gaelic, "Rest easy, friend. You're safe in Scots' hands, you are," she lied. "Picture your next battle with the English if it will make you feel any better, but hush your talk now. Let the potion woo you to sleep."

The soft burr she'd deliberately put in her voice sounded awful to her. Angus was too drowsy to notice, though. He quit his struggles and closed his eyes again.

He fell asleep with a smile on his face.

Jamie thought he might be counting the number of English soldiers he was going to kill.

"What did you say to him, milady?" a soldier asked over her shoulder.

"I told him he was too stubborn to die just yet," Jamie replied with a dainty shrug.

Gavin was disconcerted. "But how would you be knowing if Angus was stubborn or not?"

"He's a Scotsman, isn't he?"

Gavin looked over at Alec to see if they were supposed to be amused or insulted by Lady Kincaid's comment. Alec was smiling. Gavin decided his mistress must have meant to jest with him. A frown marred his brow, and he began to wonder how long it was going to take him to understand this unusual Englishwoman. Her sweet voice was as deceptive as her appearance. She was such a delicate-looking little thing. Why, the top of her head barely reached her husband's shoulder. That husky voice of hers could coax him into complying with each and every request she gave if he didn't stay on his guard.

"I would also like to help you."

The tearful voice belonged to Elizabeth. She stood across the table, facing Jamie. The fair-haired woman still looked frightened, but determined, too, and when Jamie smiled at her, she gave a hesitant smile back. "Angus is my husband. I'll do whatever you tell me to do."

"I'm thankful for your help," Jamie told her. "Dampen this cloth and press it to your husband's brow," she directed.

Jamie pulled three stockings out of her pocket and slipped one of them over the wood slat Gavin had provided. Before she was finished, one of the soldiers had covered the second slat for her.

Her hands were shaking now, for the task she most

dreaded couldn't be delayed any longer. It was time to straighten Angus's arm.

"In England, it has become fashionable to use a sleeping sponge to put a man to sleep, but I don't hold with that form of treatment," she rambled. "I pray Angus will sleep through this."

"Would he sleep better if you'd used the sponge?" a soldier asked.

"Oh, yes," Jamie answered. "But he might not wake up. Most don't. The disadvantage does outweigh the merit, don't you think?"

The soldiers immediately blurted out their agreement.

"Alec? You're going to have to do this for me. I don't have the strength," she said. "Gavin, I'll need long strips of linen ready to bind the slats together."

Jamie worked the third stocking over Angus's swollen hand, paused to cut five holes in the toe of the sock, then eased his fingers and thumb through the openings. Each time she touched his arm, she gave Angus a quick, worried glance to see if he'd awakened.

"Alec, take hold of his hand. Gavin, you hold his upper arm," she directed. "Pull, but ever so slowly please, until I can straighten the bone. Elizabeth, you must turn your back now. I don't want you watching this."

Jamie took a deep, settling breath, then murmured, "God, I do hate this part of my duties. Do it now."

It took three attempts before she was satisfied that the broken ends of the bone were in the correct position. She slid the first slat under the arm, then put the second on top. Her hands shook. Alec held the slats in place while Jamie wound the strips of linen around and around the wood. When she was finished, Angus's arm was firmly locked in place.

"There, the worst is finished," she said with a deep sigh of relief.

"But his chest, milady," the priest reminded her. He let out a loud, painful-sounding cough, then added, "It's got a gaping hole in it."

"It looks worse than it truly is," Jamie answered.

A collective sigh made her smile. When she requested additional light, she was almost blinded by the number of candles the soldiers held up for her.

Jamie asked for another goblet of warm water. She opened yet another one of her jars, sprinkled a fair amount of orange powder into the liquid, and then surprised the priest by handing it to him. "Drink this. It will cure your cough," she told him. "I can tell it pains you."

The priest was speechless. Her consideration astonished him. He took a fair gulp, then grimaced. "Drink every bit of it, Father," Jamie ordered.

Like a child, he balked for a minute, then did as she ordered.

Jamie turned her attention to Angus's chest injury. She worked well into the night. The wound was crusted with dirt and dried blood. Jamie was meticulous in her task, for she knew from past experience, and from her mother's instructions, the terrible damage a single fleck of dirt could do if left inside the wound. She didn't understand the reason behind this truth but believed it to be fact all the same. Since the wound was ragged, she used needle and thread to sew the edges together.

Alec had ordered a bed carried into the great hall. He knew Jamie would wish to have her patient nearby, and Angus's cottage was a good distance away.

Angus's wife hadn't spoken another word during the long night. She hadn't moved from her position across from Jamie and watched her every move.

Jamie barely paid her any attention. She'd been bent over the warrior for such a long time that when she finally straightened away from the table, pain rushed up her spine, startling a gasp out of her. She stumbled backwards. Before she could regain her balance, she felt at least a dozen hands on her back bracing her.

"Elizabeth, please help me bandage your husband's chest," she asked, thinking to include the worried-looking woman.

Elizabeth was eager to assist. As soon as the task was done, Alec carried his friend over to the bed. Jamie and Elizabeth followed behind.

"He'll be spitting mad with pain when he wakes up," Jamie predicted. "You're going to have a bear on your hands, Elizabeth."

"But he will wake up."

There was a smile in Elizabeth's voice. "Aye, he will wake up," Jamie confirmed.

She let Elizabeth tuck the covers around her husband's shoulders before she asked, "Where did Edith and Annie go?"

"Back to their cottage to sleep," Elizabeth answered. She brushed her hand across Angus's brow in a gentle, loving action that told how very much she cared for her husband. "I'm to wake them when Angus . . . when he dies."

Jamie gave Alec a perplexed look.

Father Murdock started snoring, drawing everyone's attention. The old priest was sprawled in a chair he'd pulled up next to the table. "Oh, dear," Jamie said. "I forgot to tell him the potion would make him sleepy."

"He can sleep there," Alec announced. He turned to Angus's wife and said, "Elizabeth, go and get some rest. Gavin and I will take turns sitting with your husband until you return."

From the crestfallen look on Elizabeth's face, Jamie could tell she didn't want to leave her husband. Yet she immediately nodded and started for the door. Jamie assumed that obedience to her laird overrode all other considerations.

"Alec, if you were ill, I certainly wouldn't leave your side. Why can't Elizabeth sleep here? She could rest in a chair or perhaps use one of the rooms above the stairs, don't you suppose?"

Elizabeth whirled around. "I would be most comfortable," she interjected.

Alec looked from one woman to the other, then nodded. "Go and gather your things," he said. "You'll sleep in one of the rooms upstairs, Elizabeth. You must remember your condition. Angus will be angry if he wakes up and finds you exhausted."

Elizabeth made a formal curtsy. "Thank you, milord," she said.

"Marcus? Take Elizabeth to her cottage to get her things," Alec called out.

Jamie stood next to the bed, watching Angus. Elizabeth walked over to her side, hesitated, then reached out to touch her hand. "I would thank you, mistress," she whispered.

"You won't have to wake Edith and Annie," Jamie replied.

Elizabeth smiled. "No, I won't have to wake them." She started to turn away, then changed her mind. "My son will carry his father's name when he arrives."

"When does this blessed event take place?" Jamie asked.

"In six months' time. And if it's a girl . . ."

"Yes?"

"I shall name her after you, milady."

Jamie would have laughed if she'd had the strength. She was so exhausted, though, she could only manage a smile. "Did you hear her promise, Alec? Elizabeth doesn't seem to think Jamie is a man's name. What think you of that."

Elizabeth smiled at Alec, received his nod, and then said, "Jamie? I thought your name was Jane, milady."

Alec laughed for his wife. Elizabeth squeezed Jamie's hand to let her know she was jesting, then left the hall with Marcus.

"Does that man ever smile?" Jamie asked Alec when they were once again alone.

"Who?"

"Marcus."

"Nay, he doesn't, Jamie."

"He dislikes me immensely."

"Aye, he does."

Jamie gave Alec a disgruntled look over his easy compliance, then mixed another potion that was known to chase fever away. She was walking back to the bed when she suddenly realized she hadn't looked at the lower half of

Angus's body to see if there were other injuries needing her attention.

She decided to let Alec do the looking while she kept her eyes closed.

"There aren't any other injuries," Alec announced after he'd done as Jamie asked.

Her relief was short-lived. When she opened her eyes, Alec was standing just a foot or so away, smiling down at her. "You're blushing, wife. Answer me this question," he commanded in a soft, teasing voice. "If there had been injury, what would you have done?"

"Repaired it if possible," Jamie answered. "And probably blushed all the while. You must remember, Alec, I'm a mere woman."

She waited for him to contradict her.

"Aye, you are that."

The way he was looking at her made her blush intensify. Whatever was the matter with him? He acted as though he wanted to say something more to her, yet couldn't make up his mind.

"Am I back to looking ugly, husband? I know I must look a mess."

"You were never ugly," Alec answered. He brushed a lock of her hair back over her shoulder. The tender action sent a shiver down her arms. "But you do look a mess."

She didn't know how to take that remark. He was smiling at her, so she guessed he hadn't just insulted her. Or had he? The man did have an odd sense of what was amusing.

The longer he continued to stare at her, the more nervous she became. "Here, make Angus drink this." She thrust the goblet into his hands.

"For the last several hours you've snapped out orders like a commander on a field of battle, Jamie. Now you act shy with me. What has caused this change?"

"You," Jamie replied. "You make me shy when you stare at me like that."

"'Tis good to know."

"No, it certainly is not good to know," Jamie muttered.

She snatched the goblet out of his hands, hurried over to Angus's side, and nagged her patient into drinking the full portion.

"I want you to wear my plaid," Alec said.

"What?"

"I want you to wear my colors, wife."

"Why?"

"Because you belong to me now," Alec patiently explained.

"I'll wear your plaid when my heart wants to belong to you, Kincaid, and not a minute sooner. What think you of that?"

"I could order you to—"

"But you won't."

Alec smiled. His gentle little wife was beginning to understand him, after all. But he was also learning just how her mind worked. The foolish woman didn't realize her heart had already softened toward him. Still, he wanted her to admit it. "Did you mean what you said to Elizabeth? Would you have stayed by my side if I'd been wounded?"

"Of course."

She didn't even look over her shoulder when she added, "You can rid yourself of that cocky smile, husband. Any wife would stay by her husband. It's her duty."

"And you would always do your duty."

"I would."

"I will give you two weeks to make up your mind, Jamie, but you will eventually wear my plaid."

While he watched Jamie, the truth nudged a rather contradictory admission from him. He actually wanted her to care for him. He wanted her to love him. He was, however, quite determined not to love her. His reason was simple: a warrior did not love his wife; he owned her. There was good reason for this, of course: love complicated a relationship. It could also undermine the duties of a laird. No, he could never love Jamie. But he'd be damned if she didn't start to love him soon.

"Two weeks."

She didn't need that reminder. "You are very arrogant, husband."

"'Tis good of you to notice."

Alec left the hall before she could stifle her laughter enough to bait him again. His soldiers would be waiting in the courtyard and the bailey below, wishing to hear how their friend was doing. Several hundred men were keeping Angus's deathwatch. They wouldn't take to their pallets until they'd come inside to see their friend. It was their right, and Alec wouldn't deny them.

Angus was just waking up from his drug-induced sleep when Jamie was closing her eyes. She knelt on the floor, her feet tucked under the hem of her robe. Her long hair was spread like a blanket across her back. Angus groaned when he tried to move his throbbing arm. He wanted to rub the sting away, yet when he tried to move his other hand, he felt someone take hold of him.

He opened his eyes and immediately saw the woman. Her head rested next to his thigh. Her eyes were closed. He didn't know how he knew, but he was certain her eyes were violet, clear, enchanting violet.

Angus thought she was asleep, yet when he tried to pull his hand away from her grasp, she wouldn't let him.

The soldiers began to file into the hall then, drawing his attention. His friends were all smiling at him. Angus tried to return their greeting. He was in pain, aye, but their smiles told him he was not dying. Perhaps, he thought, the last rites he'd overheard were for someone else.

Alec, with Gavin at his side, stood near the entrance, waiting. Alec stared at his wife, but Gavin watched the men.

It was a magical moment, by Gavin's reckoning. The soldiers looked stunned by the sight they witnessed. One and all knew Lady Kincaid had saved their friend from certain death. Angus's weak smile confirmed the miracle.

The hall could only hold a third of their number, yet when the first man knelt down and bowed his head, the others followed his lead, until even the soldiers outside were kneeling.

It was a united show of loyalty, Alec knew, but it wasn't for Angus that the soldiers knelt. No, Angus was their equal. They wouldn't kneel before him. The soldiers were now giving Lady Kincaid their loyalty, their complete trust.

And his wife slept through their silent pledge.

"I boasted it would take her a long time to earn their trust," Gavin told Alec. "I was wrong. It has taken her less than one day."

Marcus, with his sister Edith, walked into the hall just as the last of the soldiers filed past. They waited by Gavin's side, until Elizabeth, holding on to Annie's hand, caught up with them.

"Do you see, Annie? I told you Angus was better. Look how he's smiling." Elizabeth whispered her happy news, then dropped Annie's hand to rush forward to her husband's side.

"Lady Kincaid saved Angus," Gavin told Marcus. "'Tis a time for joy, my friend, not anger. Why do you frown so?"

"Angus would have made it with or without Lady Kincaid's assistance. It was God's decision, not hers."

The harshness in his tone turned Alec's attention to him. "You do not accept my wife, Marcus?" he asked, his voice deceptively mild.

The warrior immediately shook his head. "I accept her because she's your wife, Alec, and I would protect her with my life," he added. "But she won't win my loyalty so easily."

Anna and Edith stood by Marcus's side, mimicking his frown as they listened to the conversation. Alec looked at each one, then spoke again. "All of you will make her welcome. Do you understand me?"

The women immediately nodded their compliance. Marcus took a bit longer to agree. "Have you forgotten our Helena so soon, Alec?"

"It's been almost three years," Gavin interjected.

"I haven't forgotten," Alec announced.

"Then why—"

"I married to please my king, Marcus, and you damn well know it. Before you turn your back on my wife, remember this, all of you. Jamie also married by command from her king. She didn't want this marriage any more than I did. Honor her for doing her duty."

"She really didn't wish to marry you?" Annie asked. Her brown eyes mirrored her surprise.

Alec shook his head. "The only reason I discuss such matters with you, Annie, is because of your sister, Helena. Jamie was pledged to another man. Why would she want to marry me?"

"The English dislike us as much as we dislike them," Gavin interjected.

"Your wife doesn't know how fortunate she is," Annie shyly interjected.

Alec smiled at the sincerity in Annie's voice. He left the three staring after him as he walked over to his sleeping wife and gently lifted her into his arms. He held her close against his chest.

Gavin followed behind, thinking to take over the watch by Angus's side.

"I wonder, Alec, how long it's going to take your wife to accept us?" he remarked.

"Little time at all," Alec predicted. He started toward his bed, then called over his shoulder, "She'll settle in, Gavin. You'll see."

Chapter Eleven

S he started three wars the first week.

Jamie's intentions were quite honorable. She'd decided to make the best of her situation, accepting the fact that she was married to a laird now. She would do her duty as his wife and take care of him and his household. No matter how difficult the adjustment might be for Alec, she wouldn't shirk her obligations.

In the back of her mind was a glimmer of hope that while she was busy tending to her new duties, she would also start making a few necessary changes. Why, if she really put her mind to it, she might even be able to civilize these Highlanders.

The wars, coming one atop the other, actually crept up on Jamie. She wasn't about to take the blame for instigating any of the conflicts. No, the blame belonged to the Scots, their ridiculous customs, their stubborn nature, and most especially, their unbending pride. Was it her fault none of these barbarians ever made a bit of sense?

Jamie slept past the nooning meal the day after she

patched up Angus. She thought she deserved the long rest until she remembered it was Sunday and she'd missed mass. It was a duty to attend the service, and the realization that no one had bothered to wake her up irritated her. Now she was going to have to use one of her shillings to buy an indulgence.

She dressed in a cream-colored chemise and a ruby-colored bliaut, then draped a braided belt around her waist ever so loosely so it would rest on her hips, as was the fashion these days. She might not have gone to court, but she kept up with the newest styles, even though it was a bother. Still, she didn't want the Scots thinking she was just an ignorant country girl. She was their laird's wife now and must always look fashionable. She brushed her hair, gave her cheeks a good pinch for color, and went to see how her patient was doing. If all was well with Angus, she would find the priest and put the matter of her sin in his hands.

She dreaded the coming penance.

Luck was on her side, however. Not only was Angus sleeping peacefully, but the priest was also in the hall. He was taking his turn sitting beside the warrior.

The priest started to stand when he saw Jamie approaching. "Pray stay seated, Father," Jamie requested with a smile.

"We've not been properly introduced," the priest announced. "I'm Father Murdock, Lady Kincaid."

It was still difficult to understand him. The priest's voice was as thin as his hair. The soft burr in his speech only added to the problem. He sounded in dire need of a good cough. Jamie resisted her urge to cough for him.

"Has the pain in your chest let up, Father?" she asked.

"It has, milady, it surely has," Father Murdock answered. "I haven't slept so well in many a night. That potion you gave me turned the trick."

"I'd like to make a salve for you to rub on your chest," Jamie said. "We'll have that cough gone by week's end."

"Thank you, lass, for taking the time to help this old man."

"I must warn you, Father, the stench in this paste will make your friends keep well away from you."

Father Murdock smiled. "I shall not mind."

"Has Angus been resting well?"

"He's sleeping now, but earlier Gavin had to restrain him. Angus was trying to tear the bandages off his bad arm. Elizabeth was so distressed she wanted to awaken you. Gavin ordered her to bed."

Jamie frowned over this news while she studied the warrior's swollen fingers. The color was good enough to please her. She put her hand on his brow next. "The fever didn't catch hold of him," she announced. "Your prayers have saved him, Father."

"Nay, lass," the priest contradicted. "You are the one who saved him. God must have decided to let Angus stay with us, and in his wisdom he sent you here to tend to him."

His praise embarrassed her. "Well, he sent you a sinner," she blurted out, wanting to get the dreaded business over. "I missed mass this morning," she explained after she'd pressed a shilling in his hand. "Please accept this coin for an indulgence."

"But mistress—"

"Now, Father, before you decide upon my penance, I would like to explain my reasons. I wouldn't have missed mass if Alec had wakened me," she said. Her hands settled on her hips and she tossed her hair back over her shoulder in a gesture Father Murdock found enchanting. A frown worried her brow. "Come to think of it, this really should be Alec's sin, too. What think you of that?"

The priest didn't answer her soon enough. "Do you know," she continued, "the more I reflect on this problem, the more I become convinced Alec should be the one giving you his coin. Why, this is really his sin."

Father Murdock was having difficulty following her train of thought. He felt as though a whirlwind had just filled the room. A whirlwind with the sun shining through. The priest wanted to laugh with sheer joy. The gloom that had hovered over Alec's home since Helena's death would leave now. He was sure of it. He'd seen the way his laird watched his wife all during the night while she worked on Angus. He'd looked just as surprised as the rest of them . . . and just as pleased.

"Father?" Jamie asked. "What think you of my worry?"

"Neither one of you has sinned."

"We haven't?"

Father Murdock smiled over the surprise his statement had caused. Lady Kincaid looked flabbergasted. "You're very devout, aren't you, Lady Kincaid?"

It would have been a sin to let the priest think that. "Oh, heavens no," she said hurriedly. "I cannot let you believe such a lie. It's just that our priest back home . . . well, he is most devout, and I must tell you his penances are usually bloody awful. I think boredom led him to be strict. He made Agnes cut her hair once. She cried for a week."

"Agnes?"

"One of my dear sisters," Jamie explained.

"It must have been a terrible sin," Father Murdock remarked.

"She fell asleep during one of his sermons," Jamie confessed.

The priest tried not to laugh. "We're not so rigorous here," he advised. "I promise I will never make you cut your hair, Lady Kincaid."

"What a shame you didn't live with us then," Jamie interjected. "Agnes's hair hasn't curled since she was forced to cut it."

"How many are there in your family?" the priest asked.

"There were five of us, all girls, but the eldest, Eleanor, died when I was just seven, so I don't remember her very well. The twins, Agnes and Alice, came next, then Mary, and I'm the baby. Papa raised us mostly by himself," she added with a gentle smile.

"A sound family it seems to me," the priest remarked with a nod. "Are your sisters as pretty as you are?"

"Oh, much prettier," Jamie stated. "Mama was fat with me when she married Papa. He'd lost his wife, you see, and Mama had lost her husband right after she'd married him. It made no matter to Papa though. I became his baby as soon as he wed Mama."

"A good man," Father Murdock commented.

"Yes," Jamie agreed with a sigh. "Just mentioning my family makes me miss them."

"Then we won't speak of this any longer," Father Murdock advised. "Take this coin back, please, and put it to better use."

"I'd rather you kept the shilling. My husband's soul could surely use some attention. He's a laird, after all, and has had to kill men in battle. Do not misunderstand me, Father, for Alec would never, ever take a life without a good reason. Though I don't know him as well as you do, I do believe he wouldn't go looking for trouble. In my heart I know this is true. You must take my word on this matter, Father."

Alec walked into the hall just in time to overhear his wife's defense of his character.

"I agree with you, lass," the priest answered. He glanced up and saw the exasperated look on his laird's face. He had trouble restraining his chuckle.

"Well, now," Jamie said, her sigh of relief evident. "I'm pleased you agree. Though it's shameful of me to admit, I do get tired of having to think about my soul all the time. Father Charles made us confess every thought. 'Tis the truth there were times I made up a few just to appease the man. He's a most conscientious priest and we did lead a very sedate life. Nothing sinful ever happened."

Father Murdock thought the priest sounded like a fanatic. "We're much more relaxed here, Lady Kincaid."

"I'm pleased to hear this," Jamie returned. "Now that I'm married, I must also take care of my husband's soul, and if that isn't enough to turn my hair gray, I don't know what is. Father, I do believe we shall become good friends. You must begin by calling me Jamie, don't you suppose?"

"What I suppose, Jamie, is that you have a gentle heart. You're just the breath of fresh air this cold old castle is needing."

"Aye, Father, she does have a gentle heart," Alec interjected. "She'll have to try to overcome that flaw."

"Having a gentle heart isn't a flaw."

Jamie was thankful she'd made that emphatic statement while still looking at the priest, for once she turned around to confront her husband, she wasn't able to speak at all. She gasped instead.

Alec was half naked.

Alec was dressed like a barbarian. He wore a white shirt but that was the only civilized garment covering his huge body. The shirt was partially covered by the end of his plaid draped over his shoulder. The rest of his plaid was wrapped around his waist. It was folded into wide pleats, held in place by a narrow roped belt, and fell only to mid-thigh. Black boots, that were gray in the worn places, covered only a part of his muscular legs.

His knees were as bare as a baby's arse.

Alec thought she looked ready to faint. He hid his irritation while he patiently waited for her to get accustomed to his attire, then said, "How's Angus doing?"

"I beg your pardon?"

She was still staring at his knees. "Angus," Alec repeated a bit more forcefully.

"Oh, yes, Angus, of course," she answered, nodding several times.

When she didn't say another word, Alec commanded, "You'll look at my face when I speak to you, wife."

Jamie was startled by the harshness in his rebuke. She quickly did as he had ordered.

Alec was sure her blush could start a fire. "How long do you think it's going to take you to get used to seeing me dressed this way?" he asked, his exasperation obvious.

She recovered quickly. "What way?" she asked, smiling innocently.

A wry grin softened his mouth. "Will I always have to repeat myself to you?"

She shrugged her answer. "Was there something you wanted to speak to me about?" she asked.

He decided to embarrass her again. "Wife, you've seen me without any clothes on, yet now you act—"

She rushed over and clapped her hand over his mouth. "I've felt you naked, husband. I've not seen you naked. There is a difference," she added. She dropped her hand when she realized what she'd just done, then backed up a space. "Remember your manners in front of the priest, Alec."

He rolled his eyes heavenward. She thought he was praying for patience. "Now tell me what it is you wished to say to me."

"I want to speak to Angus," Alec answered. He started toward the bed, but Jamie stepped directly into his path, blocking his way. Her hands were settled on her hips again.

"He's sleeping now, Alec. You may speak to him later."

He couldn't believe what he'd just heard. "Wake him."

"Your roar probably just did," she muttered.

He took a deep breath. "Wake him," he ordered again. In a softer tone of voice, he added, "And, Jamie?"

"Yes?"

"Don't ever tell me what I may or may not do."

"Why?"

"Why?"

Before she could find the courage to answer him she had to remind herself that her husband had promised never to lose his temper with her. The look on his face was chilling. "Why must I never tell you what you may or may not do?"

She knew he didn't like her question. His jaw was clenched now. The muscles in his cheeks flexed once, then again. She wondered if her husband had always had this nervous affliction or if it was of recent origin.

"'Tis the way it's done here," Father Murdock blurted out.

The priest wheezed his way out of his chair and rushed over to stand next to Lady Kincaid. His worry was well founded. He'd known Alec Kincaid for long years, recognized that look in his eyes all too well, and sought to intervene in Jamie's behalf before Alec's temper exploded. In time, Jamie would surely learn the perils of questioning such a powerful man. Until then, the priest decided he would have to watch out for her. "The lass has only been here a short time, Alec. Surely she doesn't mean to challenge you."

Alec nodded. Jamie shook her head. "I do so mean to challenge him, Father, though I don't wish to sound insolent. I would simply like him to explain why I can't tell him what to do. He tells me often enough."

She had the audacity to look disgruntled with him. "I'm your husband and your laird, wife. Are those two reasons sufficient for you?"

The muscle in his jaw flexed again. Jamie was fascinated by it. She wondered what potion she could give him to rid him of that affliction, then decided that since he was glaring at her, she wouldn't bother.

"Well?" Alec demanded, taking a threatening step toward her.

She didn't retreat an inch. God's truth, she took a step toward him. Alec was amazed. He'd been known to send grown men running for safety, but this slip of a woman was boldly trying to stand up to him.

Hell, he admitted with a growl, she *was* standing up to him.

The priest once again tried to intervene. "Lady Kincaid, dare you incite him to anger?"

"Alec won't lose his temper with me," Jamie announced, her gaze directed on her husband. "Alec is a very patient man." Because she was looking at Alec, she missed the priest's astonished expression.

"He gave me his word, Father. He would never break it."

God, how she was baiting him. Alec couldn't make up his mind if he wanted to strangle her or kiss her. "Do you make me regret my promise to you, wife?"

She shook her head. "I don't. Your attitude does give me concern, though. How are we ever going to get along if you don't learn to bend? Alec, I'm your wife. Doesn't my position allow for telling you—"

"It does not," Alec announced, his voice as hard as rock. "And if there's any bending to be done around here, you'll be the one doing it. Do I make myself clear?"

The look on his face suggested she not argue with him. Jamie ignored it. "A wife may not even give her opinion?"

"She may not." Alec let out a long sigh before continuing. "I can see you don't understand the way we do things here, Jamie, and for that reason I'll excuse your insolent behavior today. But in future—"

"I wasn't being insolent," Jamie countered. "I just want to get this straight in my inferior mind. Tell me this, please," she added. "What are my duties as your wife? I would like to begin as soon as possible."

"You don't have any duties."

She reacted as though he'd just struck her. Alec saw the flash of true anger in her eyes when she took a step away from him. He didn't know what to make of such an odd reaction. Didn't she know how considerate he was being?

He guessed she didn't know when she gave him yet another insolent remark.

"Every wife has duties, even those with opinions."

"You don't."

"By Scotland's law or by yours?"

"Mine," he answered. "You'll rid yourself of those calluses on your palms, Jamie. You will not be a slave here."

She let out an outraged gasp. "Are you suggesting I was a slave back home?"

"You were a slave."

"I wasn't," she returned in a near shout. "Am I so unimportant to you that you won't let me find my place here, Alec?"

He didn't answer her, for in truth he didn't know what in God's name she was ranting about.

Angus was awakened by a hard command from his laird, then questioned in rapid Gaelic. The injured warrior's mind was surprisingly clear. Though his voice was weak, he was able to answer Alec's questions in a concise manner. When his laird finished his inquisition, Angus managed a smile and asked if he might go along on the hunt.

Alec denied the offer with a grin. Jamie heard him tell the soldier that as soon as he was feeling better, he'd have him moved to his own cottage, where his wife could look after him.

He started to leave the hall without speaking to his wife again, but Jamie chased after him. "Alec?"

"What is it?" he snapped, turning around to confront her again.

"In England it's proper conduct for a husband to give his wife a morning kiss," she lied. She'd made up that dictate but felt certain he didn't know that.

"We're not in England."

"It's proper everywhere," she muttered.

"It's proper here when the wife wears her husband's plaid."

"So that's the way of it, is it?"

"My hearing is quite sound, wife. You needn't raise your voice to me."

Alec kept his expression hard. It was a difficult effort. Her disappointment was obvious. She wanted him to touch her. Alec decided he had just acquired the edge he needed over her. He didn't feel the least bit remorseful using their physical attraction to each other to his own advantage and was actually disappointed with himself for not having thought of it sooner. She'd be wearing his plaid by the end of the week, he estimated, especially if he refused to touch her in the meantime.

"Alec, where may I keep my coins safe?" she asked.

"There's a box on the mantel behind you," he answered. "Put your shillings with the other coins if you want."

"May I borrow some of your coins if I have need?" she asked.

"I don't care," he told her over his shoulder.

She frowned at Alec's back, irritated because he hadn't even bothered to say good-bye, then wondered what he was up to when he reached up and claimed his sword from the wall.

"Do you know where he's going, Father?" she asked after Alec had left the hall.

"Hunting," Father Murdock answered as he resumed his seat next to Angus.

"But not for game for our supper?"

"Nay, lass. He hunts the men who did this to Angus. When he finds them, they won't come away so fortunate."

Jamie knew such retaliation was considered honorable by a warrior's standards. Still, she didn't like it. Not at all. Violence only gave birth to more of the same, didn't it? It was yet another topic she and her husband were never going to agree on.

Jamie let out a resigned sigh. "I shall go and fetch some more coins for you," she told the priest. "God only knows how many indulgences that man's going to need by day's end."

Father Murdock held his smile. He wondered if Alec realized how well he'd chosen. "There are going to be fires aplenty blazing in our mountains," he told Angus, ignoring the fact that the warrior appeared to be sleeping again.

"'Tis the truth you speak," Angus whispered.

"Did you listen to the way Alec and his bride shouted at each other? If your eyes had been open, you would have seen the sparks."

"I heard."

"What think you of your savior, Angus?"

"She'll make him crazed."

"It's time."

Angus nodded. "Aye, it's time. The Kincaid has had enough pain."

"He doesn't know what to make of her. I can tell by the way he watches her."

"Is she going to give you a coin every time Alec irritates her?"

"I believe so."

Father Murdock let out a rich chuckle as he slapped his knee. "She's going to have a time of it fitting into our way of life. Yet it's going to be a joy for this old man to watch."

Jamie returned to the priest, handed him two more coins, and asked him why he was smiling.

"I was thinking of all the changes you're going to have to

make, lass," the priest admitted. "I know it won't be easy on you, but in time you'll come to love this clan as much as I do."

"Have you considered, Father, that it just might be the clan making all these changes?" Jamie asked, her eyes alight with mischief.

The priest thought she was jesting with him. "I fear you've set yourself an impossible goal," he told her with a snort of enjoyment.

"How impossible, do you suppose?" she asked. "As impossible as eating a giant bear all by myself?"

"Aye, just as impossible."

"I could do it."

"How?" the priest asked, falling nicely into her trap.

"One bite at a time."

Father Murdock slapped his knee again and let out a whoop of laughter, which was followed by a fit of coughing. Jamie hurried to her bedroom area, mixed the foul-smelling salve she'd promised him, and went back to his side. "You must wait an hour or two for this to settle before you rub it on your chest, Father."

The priest accepted her offering with a frown. "It smells like the dead, lass."

"The smell isn't important, Father. I promise it will help your cough."

"I believe you, Jamie."

"Father? Do you think Alec would mind if I had a look upstairs?"

"Of course not, lass. This is your home now."

"Are the rooms occupied?"

The priest shook his head.

"Then I should be able to move my things up to one of the rooms, shouldn't I?"

"You're wanting to move your . . . Lass, Alec won't like you leaving him."

"It's Alec I'm thinking about," Jamie countered. "There isn't any privacy down here, Father. I'm sure he'll be much more comfortable in one of the rooms upstairs. You'll put the question to him for me, won't you?"

He couldn't refuse her request. Lady Jamie had the most enchanting smile. "I'll ask," he promised.

Father Murdock was content to sit by Angus's side and rest. He was almost asleep when the screech of metal scraping against stone drew his attention. He turned toward the noise and saw Lady Jamie struggling with a large chest. She was pushing the piece of furniture out of the first bedroom at the top of the stairs.

The priest hurried across the hall and up the steps. "What are you trying to do, Jamie?" he asked.

"I thought I'd use the front bedroom, Father," Jamie answered. "It has a nice, wide window."

"But why are you moving this chest?"

"It takes up too much room," Jamie interrupted. "Don't strain yourself, Father. I'm strong enough to move this by myself."

The priest ignored her boast and put his back to the chore of getting the trunk into the second room. "You should have emptied it before you moved it," he stated as an after-thought.

Jamie shook her head. "It wouldn't have been right to look inside. It isn't my property, and everyone's entitled to his privacy."

"The chest belonged to Helena," Father Murdock announced. "I suppose you could call it yours now, Jamie."

Before she could respond to that announcement, the priest turned and started out the door. "I'd best get back down to Angus. I'm supposed to be watching out for him until Gavin brings Elizabeth back."

"Thank you for your help," Jamie called after him.

The lass was taking forever, Father Murdock decided almost an hour later. He kept looking up at the bedroom, wondering what she was up to. When Elizabeth came back into the great hall, Father Murdock decided to see what had Jamie so occupied.

She was still in the second bedroom. Two candles had been lit, giving the room a soft glow. Lady Jamie was kneeling in front of the chest. She was just closing the lid when Father Murdock walked inside.

"Did you find anything useful?" the priest asked.

He didn't realize she was crying until she turned to look up at him. "What is it, lass? What's upset you?"

"I'm being foolish," Jamie whispered. "She's dead now and I didn't even know her, Father, yet I'm crying as though she were my very own sister. Will you tell me about Helena?"

"Alec should tell you," Father Murdock said.

"Please, Father," Jamie begged. "I want to know what happened. I'm sure Alec didn't kill her."

"Good Lord, no," the priest agreed. "Where did you hear that talk?"

"In England."

"Helena killed herself, Jamie. She jumped off the ridge above the pasture."

"It couldn't have been an accident? She didn't fall?"

"No, it wasn't an accident. She was seen."

Jamie shook her head. "I don't understand, Father. Was she very unhappy here?"

The priest bowed his head. "She must have been terribly unhappy, Jamie, but she hid her feelings well. We didn't watch out for her the way we should have, I now realize. Both Annie and Edith think she planned to kill herself from the moment she was wed to Alec."

"Does Alec believe this?" Jamie asked.

"I would guess so."

"Her death must have hurt him terribly."

Father Murdock didn't comment on that statement, but he believed she was right. The fact that Alec wouldn't discuss Helena was proof the topic was too tender still.

"Father, why would a woman who is contemplating suicide bother to bring all her cherished possessions to her husband's home? She even packed baby clothes," Jamie continued. "And beautiful linens too. Don't you think that's odd for someone—"

"She wasn't thinking clearly," Father Murdock countered.

Jamie shook her head. "No, Father. I don't think she killed herself. I'm sure it was an accident."

"You have a tender heart, lass, and if it makes you feel better to believe that's how Helena died, then I'll agree with you."

He helped Jamie to her feet. She blew out the candles and walked by the priest's side back down the stairs. "I'll pray for her soul every night, Father," she promised.

A servant came rushing into the hall, spotted Jamie, and called out, "Your sister's here, milady."

Jamie clasped Father Murdock's hand. "It must be Mary calling on me," she explained to the priest. "Will you excuse me, please?"

She was halfway out the door before Father Murdock nodded permission. "I'll bring Mary inside to meet you," she called over her shoulder.

Jamie hurried on outside, a smile of greeting on her face. The minute she caught sight of her sister, however, her smile evaporated. Mary was in tears. Jamie glanced around to see where Daniel was, then realized her sister was all alone.

"How did you ever find your way here, Mary?" she asked after giving her sister a proper hug.

"You're the one who gets lost all the time, Jamie, not me," Mary told her.

"I never get lost," Jamie countered. "Hush your weeping now." She noticed several Kincaid soldiers watching them. "Come, we'll take a nice walk so we may speak in private. You must tell me what has you so upset."

Jamie tugged her sister along the path down to the lower bailey. "Three of Daniel's men showed me the way here," Mary explained when she'd regained her composure. "I lied to them, Jamie. I told them I had Daniel's permission to come calling."

"Oh, Mary, you shouldn't have done that," Jamie said. "Why didn't you just tell Daniel you wanted to see me?"

"You can't tell that man anything," Mary muttered. She lifted the hem of her yellow bliaut and mopped the corners of her eyes. "I hate him, Jamie. I've run away."

"No, you cannot mean what you say."

"Don't sound so horrified, sister. I hate him, I tell you.

He's cruel and mean. When I tell you what happened, I swear you'll hate him, too."

They reached the gap in the wall. Jamie and her sister sat down on the low stone ledge. "All right, Mary, tell me what happened," Jamie instructed. "We're quite alone here."

"It's such an embarrassment," Mary warned. "But you're the only one I dare talk about this to, sister."

"Yes?" Jamie prodded.

"Daniel didn't demand that I give myself to him."

The sentence fell between them. Jamie kept waiting for Mary to say more, and Mary kept waiting for Jamie's reaction.

"Did he give you a reason?"

"He did," Mary answered. "And at first I thought he was being most considerate. He said he would give me time to get to know him."

"That was very considerate of him," Jamie admitted. She frowned, wondering why Alec hadn't shown such compassion with her. Then she remembered Alec didn't have any compassion to show anyone.

Mary burst into fresh tears. "I thought so, as I've told you. Then he told me he was most unhappy with me because I made you protect me when those men attacked us. He actually thought *I* should have shielded *you.*"

"Why?"

"Because you're the baby."

"Didn't you explain that I was far better trained than you in the skills—"

"I tried to explain but he wouldn't listen to me. And then he insulted me again. I admit I said some rather mean things to him. Still . . ."

"What did he say?"

"He said I was probably just as cold as a fish, Jamie, that all the Englishwomen are."

"Oh, Mary, it was an unkind thing to say to a new bride."

"That isn't the worse of it, Jamie," Mary mumbled. "When we reached his home, there was a fat, ugly woman waiting for him. She threw herself in Daniel's arms right away. He didn't fight off her advances, either. They kissed each other in front of me. What think you of that?"

"You're right, sister."

"I'm right?"

"You've made me hate him."

"I told you I could," Mary announced. "Well? What am I going to do, I ask you? I'll never find my way back to Papa, and I'm certain Daniel's men won't believe me if I tell them I have their laird's permission to go back to England."

"No, I doubt they'll believe that lie," Jamie agreed.

"I want Papa!"

"I know you do, Mary. I also miss him. Sometimes I want to go home, too."

"Does Alec think you're as cold as a fish?"

Jamie shrugged. "He hasn't said so."

"Does Alec have a leman?"

"What?"

"Does Alec have a mistress?" Mary repeated.

"I don't know," Jamie answered. "Perhaps he does have another woman," she whispered. "Oh, God, Mary, I hadn't thought of that possibility."

"Could I live here with you, Jamie?"

"Are you certain you want to do this?"

Her sister nodded. "Mary, do you know, when we first met our husbands, I thought Daniel was the kinder of the two. He smiled and seemed to have such a cheerful disposition."

"I noticed that, too," Mary said. "Jamie, what if he's right? What if I *am* as cold as a fish? There are women who can't respond to a man's touch. I think Aunt Ruth was like that. Remember how mean she was to her husband?"

"She was mean to everyone," Jamie interjected.

"I know this is embarrassing for you, but I was wondering . . ."

"Yes, Mary?"

"Are all men like Daniel, or is Alec more . . . Oh, I don't know what it is I'm asking. I'm terrified of letting Daniel touch me now, and it's all his fault."

Jamie didn't know how to help Mary, but she was determined to try. "Mary, I must catch Alec before he leaves on his hunt," she blurted out.

"Do you need his permission for me to stay?" Mary asked, her fear obvious. "What if he says no?"

"I don't need his permission," Jamie boasted, trying to make that lie sound true. "It's another matter I must speak to him about. Go and wait in the hall, Mary. Introduce yourself to our priest. His name is Father Murdock. Now, don't frown, sister. You'll like him. He isn't at all like our Father Charles. I'll join you just as soon as I've spoken to Alec. Then we'll finish this discussion, I promise."

Jamie watched her sister leave before she started down the hill. She thought she'd look to the road below to see if Alec and his men had already left.

Her exit as soon as she stepped outside the wall was blocked by a line of soldiers. They filled the wooden planks of the pathway across the moat. She thought they'd dropped out of the sky. They were certainly more formidable than the wall. And damn if she didn't have to look up at every single one of them.

"Why are you blocking my way?" she asked a red-bearded man directly in front of her.

"By order, mistress," the soldier announced.

"Whose order?"

"The Kincaid's."

"I see," Jamie replied, trying to keep her irritation out of her voice. "And has my husband left his fortress yet?"

"Nay," the soldier answered. A smile softened the corners of his eyes. "He's standing right behind you."

She didn't believe him until she turned around and came face to chest with Alec. "You move like a shadow," she muttered when she'd regained her composure.

"Where did you think you were going?" Alec asked.

"I was looking for you. Why did you order your men to block my way?"

"For your safety, of course."

"I'm to be a prisoner while you're gone, then?"

"If you choose to look at it that way," Alec answered.

"Alec, I would like to go riding in the afternoons. If I give you my promise not to run away. Surely—"

"Jamie, I never thought you'd run away," Alec countered, his exasperation most evident.

"Then why?"

"You'd get lost."

"I never get lost."

"Aye, you do."

"If I promise not to get lost?"

He let her see how foolish he thought that question was. Gavin approached his laird, holding the reins of Alec's stallion. Before Jamie could explain her need to talk to him about Mary, he had mounted his steed.

She blocked his path. "Mary's here."

"I saw her."

"I must talk to you about my sister before you leave. It's a very important matter, Alec, else I wouldn't bother you."

"I'm listening, wife. Ask me what you will."

"Oh, no, it must be in private," Jamie explained hurriedly.

"Why?"

Jamie frowned. The obstinate man certainly wasn't making this easy for her. She walked over to his side, touched his leg with her finger, and then said, "Kincaid, I'm asking to speak to you in private. You did tell me you'd give me all I asked for if it was possible. This certainly seems possible enough to me."

She stared at the ground while he made up his mind. She knew she'd won when she heard him sigh, yet still let out a surprised yelp when he reached down and effortlessly lifted her onto his horse. Jamie only had enough time to grab hold of his waist before the stallion was in full gallop. Alec didn't stop until they were well away from the men and the wall.

Jamie took her time smoothing her skirts. They were surrounded by trees. She gave the area a thorough look just to make certain they were all alone. Then she turned her attention to her hands.

Alec's patience was nearly gone when his wife suddenly blurted out, "Why didn't you wait to bed me?"

He hadn't been prepared for that question.

"Alec, Daniel is waiting out of consideration for Mary's feelings. He wants her to get to know him better first. What think you of that?"

"I think he doesn't particularly want to bed her, else he would have by now; that's what I think.

"And I took you because I wanted to," he continued. "You wanted me to, didn't you?"

"Yes," Jamie admitted. "I mean, no, not at first anyway. Look, Alec, it is Mary's problem we have to discuss, not mine."

He ignored her embarrassment. "You liked it."

She gave him the truth, knowing full well his arrogance would get completely out of hand. "I did."

"Look at me."

"I would rather not."

"I would rather you did."

He slowly lifted her chin, forcing her to gaze at his face. Alec saw how she blushed. He couldn't resist leaning down and kissing her wrinkled brow. "Now what has you worried?"

"Did you like it?" she asked.

"You couldn't tell?"

"Daniel says all Englishwomen are as cold as fish," she said with a nod, lest he think she was jesting.

Alec laughed.

"This isn't amusing," she said sternly. "And you've yet to answer my question."

"What question?" he teased.

"Am I as cold as a fish?"

"No."

She sighed with relief. "A wife does need to hear these things, Alec."

"Do you want me to bed you now?"

"In daylight? Heavens no!"

"I'm going to make love to you now if you don't move your hands away," he said hoarsely.

She realized she was gripping his bare thigh with her hands. She immediately let go of him. "Then it wouldn't matter if I was wearing your plaid or not, as you suggested earlier to me?"

"I didn't suggest it; I stated it as a fact. You will wear my plaid before I touch you again. Now, are you finished with your questions?"

"Are you getting angry?"

"No."

"You sound angry."

"Quit challenging me."

"Do you have another woman?"

Alec decided then and there he was never going to understand how her mind worked. She came up with the most absurd worries. "Would it matter to you if I did?" he asked.

She nodded. "Would it matter to you if I took up with another man?"

"Took up with?"

"You know what I mean."

"I wouldn't allow it, Jamie."

"Well, neither would I."

"You speak as though we're equals, wife."

She knew she'd angered him. She wanted to brush the frown away from his brow. "You still haven't answered my question, Alec."

"No, I don't have another woman."

She smiled. "You aren't cold," he told her. "And you insult me by asking such a question."

"How do I insult you?"

"Because it's my duty to make you hot. And you were hot, Jamie, weren't you?"

His arrogance actually comforted her, though she had absolutely no idea why. "Perhaps," she whispered, staring at his mouth. "And then again, perhaps not, husband. I seemed to have forgotten."

He decided to remind her. He captured her face with his hands and lowered his mouth to hers. Jamie closed her eyes in anticipation.

His mouth settled on hers possessively, and his tongue thrust in and out in a sexual ritual that made her heart feel as if it might shatter. She tried to pull away when she felt her own surrender, but Alec wouldn't let her retreat. His mouth slanted over hers again and again, hungrily, thoroughly, and she soon forgot all about stopping.

He made her burn for more. Jamie imitated his action, timidly at first, then boldly, until their tongues were rubbing against each other in the most erotic, arousing way. When she moaned and instinctively tried to get closer to him, he knew it was time to stop. He'd take her now if he didn't gain control over his own raging emotions.

Hell, he was probably hotter than she was. With a growl of frustration, he pulled away from her. He had to pry her hands away from his shoulders. Jamie immediately buried her face in the crook of his neck. Her breathing was ragged, as if she'd just run a long distance, all uphill, and she noticed his breathing was sounding almost as uneven. The realization made her think the kiss had affected him almost as much as it had affected her.

Her hope was destroyed when he said, "If you're finished with your foolish questions, I'd like to get back to more important matters."

How dare he sound so bored after sharing such a wonderful intimacy with her? "You needn't act as though I'm nothing but a bother to you, Alec."

"You are that," he returned with a sigh. He nudged his horse forward just as Jamie shoved away from him. He immediately slammed her back up against his chest. The woman needed to learn her position in his household. He was her master, her laird, and she'd better start accepting that fact soon.

"You don't know your own strength," she muttered.

"Nay, wife. You're the one who doesn't understand my strength yet."

She shivered over the harshness in his voice. "Are you—"

"Don't you dare ask me if I'm angry with you," he roared.

She guessed she had her answer. The man was angry, and that was that. God's truth, her ears were going to ring for a week. "You needn't shout at me," she said. "And I was only going to ask if Mary could—"

"Don't bother me with your sister's problems," he ordered. He softened his voice when he added, "Your family is always welcome to visit."

A visit wasn't exactly what she had in mind, but she decided she'd bothered him enough for one day.

"Your moods are most difficult to judge," she remarked when they'd returned to the wall and Alec had assisted her to the ground.

"Alec?"

"What now?"

"I think I'll use every day of the two weeks you've given me before I wear your plaid. Perhaps you'll use that time to learn to . . . to care for me just a little."

Alec leaned down, gripped her chin with his hand, and said, "Care for you? Hell, woman, right this minute I don't even like you."

He'd spoken in anger and frustration because he believed she'd dared to taunt him. Yet the hurt look in her eyes made him regret his outburst. She hadn't been goading him at all, he realized. And she looked as if she wanted to cry.

Jamie suddenly pulled away from him and let him see how angry she was. She reminded him of a wildcat now. And she didn't look as if she was going to cry, either. Alec was vastly amused. And relieved.

"I don't particularly like you either, Kincaid."

He had the bad manners to smile at her. "You're too bloody arrogant," she added. "No, I don't like you at all."

Alec motioned to his men, then glanced down at his wife again. "You lie."

"I never lie."

"Aye, you do, Jamie, and not well at all."

She turned away from her husband and started up the hill. Alec watched her, thinking to himself how pretty she was going to look wearing his plaid. She suddenly whirled around and called out to him, "Alec? You will be careful, won't you?"

He responded to the fear in her voice. He nodded, giving her what he thought she wanted, yet couldn't resist adding,

"I thought you didn't particularly like me, English. Have you changed your mind so soon?"

"I haven't."

"Then why—"

"Look, Kincaid, this isn't the time for a lengthy discussion," Jamie told him. She hurried back to his side so their conversation wouldn't be overheard by his soldiers. "You have your hunting to do," she said. "And I have Mary to get comfortable. I'm asking you to be careful, Alec." Her hand touched his leg and she began to pat him. Alec doubted she was even aware of that action. Her worried gaze was directed at his face. "Do it just to annoy me."

"Do you know that you call me Kincaid whenever you're angry?"

She pinched him. "I never get angry," she announced. "Even when you won't give me duties," she added with a nod. "Would it be all right if I rearrange the kitchens while you're away? It will give me something to do, Alec, and I'll ask others to do the actual work. I'll just direct them."

He didn't have the heart to deny her. "You won't lift a finger?"

"I won't."

He nodded. Before she could waylay him again, he told her to let go of his leg, else he'd drag her with him.

She didn't look as if she believed that threat.

He had to sigh over her attitude. Then he put her out of his mind and turned his attention to more important considerations. It was only later in the day, when Gavin caught up with him, that he recalled Jamie's remark about helping her sister get comfortable.

He'd thought she meant for a long day's visit.

She'd obviously meant forever.

Aye, he understood well enough when Gavin announced that Lady Kincaid had given her sister sanctuary.

The Fergusons had declared war.

Alec knew Daniel had to be fighting angry. He sent Gavin back home to keep an eye on his wife, placed another trusted soldier in charge of continuing the hunt, and then headed for Ferguson land.

He was able to intercept Daniel near the border separating their lands. Alec rode alone—a deliberate choice, that—but Daniel had a small army with him. All were armed for battle.

Alec forced his stallion to a halt and waited for Daniel to make the first move.

It wasn't long in coming. Daniel drew his sword, threw it into the air so the tip of the blade would imbed itself in the ground directly in front of Alec's stallion.

The action was a symbol that war had been declared. Now Daniel waited for Alec to repeat the ritual. Daniel's expression was impassive, yet quickly changed to a look of real astonishment when Alec shook his head, refusing to throw his weapon.

"You dare refuse to do battle?" Daniel bellowed. He was so angry the veins stood out on the sides of his neck.

"Damn right I do," Alec bellowed back.

"You can't."

"I just did."

Now it was Daniel's turn to shake his head. "What game are you playing, Alec?" he demanded to know, though he no longer sounded as if he were spitting hot embers out of his mouth.

"I'll not fight a war I don't want to win," Alec stated.

"You don't want to win?"

"I don't."

"Why the hell not?"

"Daniel, do you honestly believe I want two English-women in my household?"

That question took some of Daniel's anger away. "But—"

"If I won, I'd have Mary living with Jamie for the rest of my days. You ask too much of me, friend."

"You didn't agree to give my wife sanctuary?" Daniel asked. A hint of a smile mellowed his expression.

"I did not," Alec returned in exasperation.

"Your wife dared to protect Mary from me, Alec. From *me*. And my wife let her. Hid behind her back like a child."

"They're English, Daniel. Your error was in forgetting that fact."

"'Tis the truth," Daniel admitted with a sigh. "I did forget. I don't wish my wife to act the coward, though. It's shameful the way she makes her little sister—"

"She isn't a coward, Daniel," Alec interjected. "She's been trained to act that way. Jamie had all her sisters believing she would protect them."

Daniel grinned. "They're both daft."

"Aye, they are," Alec agreed. "We've been friends too long to let women force a breach between us. I've come to you in good faith, Daniel, to ask . . . nay, to demand you return to my holding and collect your wife."

"Have I just been given a command?" Daniel asked, grinning.

"You have."

"And if I still ache for a fight?"

"Then I will accommodate you," Alec drawled. "But the rules will have to be changed."

Daniel was intrigued by the laughter in Alec's voice. "How?"

"Winner takes both brides."

Daniel threw back his head and shouted with laughter. Alec had helped him save face in front of his men. He'd allowed him to back down without looking like a loser. "You wouldn't give up your prize, Alec, but it warms my heart to know you aren't having such an easy time with your wife, either."

"She'll settle in."

"I have my doubts about Mary."

"A firm hand is all that's needed, Daniel."

Daniel dismissed his soldiers before answering Alec's comment. "A firm hand and a gag, Alec. The woman hasn't quit complaining since we reached my home. Do you know, she actually took exception to the fact I have a mistress?"

Alec smiled. "They're funny that way," he said.

"Perhaps I'll let her stay with Jamie . . ."

"There would be war then, Daniel. Mary belongs to you."

"You should have seen the pair of them, Alec." He withdrew his sword from the ground, replaced it in his sheath before adding, "Your wife was protecting Mary, all the while hurling insults at me. She called me a pig."

"You've been called worse."

"Aye, but only by men, and they didn't live long enough to boast of it."

"My wife has a temper," Alec admitted, smiling.

"I wish some of it would rub off on Mary. The woman acts like a frightened rabbit."

"I was in the midst of tracking down Angus's attackers when I was informed of this problem," Alec said, turning the topic.

"We heard what happened," Daniel answered. "What say I ride with you on this hunt? I understand the mountain barons were responsible?" Daniel asked, referring to the band of men who'd been cast out of their clans and had formed a unit of their own. They were called barons because it was a title the English valued, and therefore the most offensive name the Highlanders could come up with. It was fitting as well, for like the English, these mountain men were also blackguards who fought without honor or conscience.

"You're welcome to come along, Daniel, but first you must take Mary home. You can catch up with us near the Peak."

Neither Alec nor Daniel spoke again until they'd reached Alec's home. Jamie was standing next to her sister in the center of the courtyard. She smiled when she saw her husband until she got a good look at his face. Her smile faded away then.

"Oh, God, Daniel looks as if he wants to kill me," Mary whispered, moving closer to her sister's side.

"Smile, Mary, it will confuse him," Jamie instructed.

Alec dismounted and slowly advanced toward his wife. He certainly wasn't smiling. God's truth, his expression could have curdled milk. Jamie took a deep breath. "Have you finished your hunt, Alec?"

He ignored her question. "Did you give Lady Ferguson sanctuary?"

"Sanctuary?" Jamie repeated. "I hadn't quite thought of it in that light, husband."

"Answer me."

The anger in his tone burned her like a hot iron. Jamie's temper ignited. How dare he criticize her in front of their guests? "Mary asked me if she could stay here, and I gave her permission," she said. "If you want to call it sanctuary, then by all means do so. I would protect Mary."

"Protect her from her own husband?" Alec asked, looking incredulous.

"When the husband happens to be an unfeeling clout, aye," Jamie answered. She paused to frown up at Daniel, then turned back to her husband. "He has abused her tender feelings, Alec. What would you have had me do?"

"I'd have you mind your own affairs," Alec snapped.

"He was cruel to her."

"Aye, he was," Mary shouted, catching her sister's fever. "If it isn't convenient for me to stay here, then I'll find my way back to England."

"I just might lead the way," Jamie muttered. She folded her hands together and waited for Alec to respond to that threat.

"You'd end up in Normandy," Alec predicted.

Before Jamie could answer, Alec turned to Mary. He glared at her until she left his wife's side; then he hauled Jamie into his arms. His grip was like steel. Jamie didn't resist, knowing how futile that would be. Besides, she'd just spotted Father Murdock standing on the steps, watching them.

She certainly didn't want a man of the cloth to think she was unladylike.

"I'm not going home with you, Daniel," Mary shouted.

That challenge didn't go unanswered. Daniel moved with astonishing speed for such a big man. Before Mary could let out a full scream, she found herself face down over her husband's lap in the saddle.

Jamie desperately tried to maintain her dignity through this monstrous situation. Poor Mary was draped over the saddle like a sack of barley. It was a humiliation, aye, but Jamie still wished Mary wouldn't carry on so. Her bellows of outrage were drawing even more attention to her sorry plight.

"I can't stand idle while he shames her this way," Jamie whispered.

"Oh, yes you can," Alec stated.

"Alec, do something."

"I'm not going to interfere and neither are you," he answered. "Mary's getting off lightly, Jamie. Daniel's temper is almost as fierce as my own. Your sister has disgraced her husband."

Jamie watched Daniel and Mary until they'd disappeared across the planks.

"He won't really hurt her, will he, Alec?"

Her fear was very evident. Alec thought it unreasonable. "He won't beat her, if that's what you're worrying about," he answered. "Mary's his problem now."

"She forgot her horse."

"She won't be needing it."

Jamie was staring up at Alec's mouth, remembering what it felt like to be kissed by him. It was such a foolish thought, especially now, what with Mary's problem still to be solved, but she couldn't seem to help herself.

"Perhaps I shall take her horse over to her tomorrow," Jamie said, wondering how she could get him to kiss her again.

He let go of her and started to walk away. She didn't want him to leave just yet. "Alec? You said Daniel's temper was almost as quick as your own, yet you told me you didn't have a temper. 'Tis an odd contradiction, don't you think?"

"You misunderstood," Alec answered. "I told you I wouldn't lose my temper with you."

He started down the hill. Jamie picked up her skirts and chased after him. "When *do* you lose your temper, then?"

He couldn't resist the temptation. His wife was so incredibly easy to bait. He didn't turn around because he didn't want her to see his smile. "When it's something that matters to me. Something important."

Her gasp made his smile widen.

"Jamie?"

"What is it?" She sounded as if she wanted to throttle him.

"Don't inconvenience me again."

It was the last insult she was going to take from him. "Look, Kincaid, it isn't necessary to harp on the fact that you find me so vastly inferior. I understand your meaning clearly," she announced. "If I were to run away, you wouldn't even come after me, would you?"

He didn't answer her.

"Well, of course you wouldn't come after me. I'm too insignificant to bother with?"

"No, I wouldn't come after you."

Jamie had to lower her gaze to the ground lest he turn around and see how much his words had hurt her.

Why did she care if he came after her or not? The man was a Scottish barbarian, she reminded herself.

"I'd send someone after you." He finally turned around and caught her in his arms. "But since you aren't going anywhere, the question isn't important, is it?"

"I'm beginning to dislike you immensely, Alec Kincaid."

"You really should do something about your temper, English." He brushed his hand across her cheek. "Try to stay out of trouble while I'm gone."

It was as much of a good-bye as she was going to get, she supposed, when he mounted his steed and left her staring after him.

Her hand touched her cheek where Alec had stroked her.

Then she straightened her shoulders and jerked her hand away.

She almost hated him. Almost.

She remembered he'd given her permission to rearrange his kitchens. It was only a little chore, she realized, but it was still a beginning. He would come to depend on her eventually, when he saw how much nicer his home was going to be.

Jamie straightened her shoulders and started up the hill. She'd best get started right away.

She smiled with new enthusiasm. Alec had given her a duty.

Chapter Twelve

Word of Lady Kincaid's remarkable healing ability swept through the Highlands as swiftly as a storm. The tale of Angus's recovery wasn't exaggerated, however, for the truth was thought to be impressive enough not to need flowering around the borders. The recounting always began the same way, too, with the announcement that the Kincaid warrior had just been given the last rites, he had, and was only a breath away from death. That beginning always gained just the amount of astonishment each storyteller wanted.

The members of the clans attending the annual spring festival at Gillebrid's holding heard the news a short half-day after they'd been told Angus was dead. Lydia Louise, Angus's younger sister and only relative, save for his wife, Elizabeth, was in quite a state. She wept first with true anguish over her brother's untimely death, then wept with acute relief over his miraculous recovery. By long day's end, the confused woman had to be given a sizable dose of heavy wine and forcefully put to bed.

None of the McPherson clan attended the festival. The old chieftain's only child, a son of just three wee months, was doing so poorly the clan was convinced he was dying. The bairn, given a stubborn streak he'd inherited from his father, had suddenly taken an extreme dislike to his mama's milk. The violent vomiting after each feeding had soon made him too weak to suckle at all.

Laird McPherson had gone off to find solace in his peaceful woods. His grief was nearly uncontrollable. He wept like a child, for he fully expected to bury his namesake when he returned to his home.

It was a fact the Fergusons were united with the McPhersons against the hated fishermen, the McCoys. That feud had existed for so many years no one could recollect the beginning. The Kincaids, on the other hand, were allies with the McCoys, ever since a McCoy warrior fished a drowning Kincaid lass out of the river, and the Kincaids were therefore forced, for honor's sake, to stand beside the McCoys against the McPhersons.

Yet when word reached Lady Cecily McPherson of Lady Kincaid's healing skills, she ignored all the laws of the Highlands.

Cecily McPherson would have bargained with the devil to save her child. Without telling anyone her plan, she took the infant to the Ferguson holding and begged Lady Ferguson's assistance. Mary was most sympathetic to the poor woman's plight. Since Daniel was still away on the hunt for Angus's attackers, she didn't have to bother gaining his permission. She immediately took the little one to Jamie.

All the Kincaid soldiers knew whom the child belonged to, of course, as everyone in the mountains knew everyone else's business. None mentioned to their mistress the fact that she was taking care of their enemy's son, though. They guessed it wouldn't matter to her. Lady Kincaid was English, after all, and therefore ignorant of the feuds existing in their land. She was a woman, too, and the mothering instinct would probably mean more to her than war. Just as important, she was too gentle to understand a feud, and

221

from the way she'd demanded to take over Angus's care in the face of Alec's resistance, she'd proven to be a mite too stubborn to understand.

Gavin knew what would happen if the bairn died on Kincaid land, however. After giving the pitiful infant one quick glance, he was convinced war was inevitable. He commanded his troops to prepare for battle, sent two messengers to track Alec down, and then patiently waited for the McPhersons to attack.

The babe was fat and sassy four days later when the entire McPherson army came to demand the body for burial.

Gavin only allowed entrance to the laird and two others. With Marcus at his side, he waited on the steps of the castle.

Jamie had just put the baby to sleep on Alec's bed when she heard the shouts coming from the courtyard. She rushed outside to see what all the commotion was about, but came to a quick stop on the top step when she saw the three fierce-looking soldiers on horseback. She immediately knew they weren't Kincaid soldiers, as their dark plaid wasn't at all the same.

"I'll not leave without my dead," the burly man in the middle bellowed. "And when I come back, there'll be blood spattering your walls. Kincaid blood."

"Has someone died, Gavin?" Jamie asked.

The second-in-command answered her without turning around. Jamie thought he didn't want to take his gaze off the strangers. She certainly couldn't fault Gavin, for the strangers did look the type to strike a man down when his back was turned. "Laird McPherson has come to reclaim his son."

The anger in Gavin's voice startled Jamie. She caught the tension in the air, then realized the three strangers were all glaring at her. She straightened her shoulders in reaction to their rudeness.

"Is she the Kincaid's woman?" the man in the middle bellowed.

"She is," Gavin answered.

"Then she's the one who stole my son away."

Did the laird have to shout every word? Jamie couldn't

believe this was the father of such a sweet-tempered babe. The chieftain was an old man, with bushy brows that hid most of his dark eyes. She guessed he smelled as rank as he looked, too.

Marcus turned around to look at Jamie. His face didn't show a hint of what he was thinking. "Go and get the bairn," he ordered.

"Be quick about it, woman."

Jamie had just started back into the castle when the laird shouted that order. She stopped, then slowly turned around to face him again.

"I'll take my time," she said.

"I want my dead."

Her hearing was never going to be the same. The belligerent man was roaring like a wounded bear. Jamie tried to contain her temper. She told herself the man thought his son was dead, after all, and grief was robbing him of his manners.

Not a word was exchanged until Jamie came back outside. She carried the sleeping infant in her arms. The laird's son was completely covered by a thick woolen blanket to protect him from the biting wind.

The old laird's face showed no outward reaction. Jamie walked over to his side and pulled the cover away from the baby's face.

"Give him to me."

"You will quit your shouting this minute," she ordered in a low voice. "If you wake this child after all the trouble I had lulling him to sleep, there'll be hell to pay and you'll be the one paying it. Do I make myself clear?"

"Wake him up?"

"I just told you not to shout," Jamie reminded him in a near shout of her own. She immediately regretted her outburst, for the infant opened his eyes and began to fidget in her arms. She paused to smile down at the child, then glared up at his father.

She missed the look of astonishment that crossed the laird's face when his little one moved.

"Now see what you've done? Your shouts have upset the

223

baby," Jamie muttered. She moved the infant up against her shoulder and began to pat his back. The baby immediately let out a loud belch. "That's a good boy," she crooned after placing a quick kiss on the top of his bald head.

Her expression hardened when she turned back to the laird. "Why God blessed you with such a dear child I'll never understand. This little one has just had his noon feeding and if you get him riled, he's bound to throw up."

The chieftain didn't respond to her comments. Jamie reluctantly handed the infant to his father. She noticed the man's hands shook when he took hold of his baby. "I have instructions to give you before you leave," she told him.

The old warrior didn't say a word for a long while. He squinted down at his son while he tried to regain his control. He couldn't show any joy now, for to do so would certainly soften his position in front of the Kincaids, yet it was a nearly impossible feat that made his eyes bulge. The bairn let out another lusty belch in the sudden stillness, then smiled sweetly over his feat, as if he knew of his father's struggles and was deliberately testing his endurance.

"He ain't dead."

"You'll scream him to death if you keep up your shouts," Jamie announced. "Now pray give me your attention, sir. You will tell your wife to feed your son only goat's milk."

"I will not."

Jamie reacted as though she'd just been hit by lightning. Before the laird could react, she snatched the baby out of his arms, settled him back against her bosom, and began to pace alongside the laird's horse. "Then you can just go home without your son, McPherson. I won't let you kill him with your ignorance. Come back when he's old enough to fend for himself."

The laird's beady eyes widened in astonishment. He glanced over to Gavin, then back to Lady Kincaid. "Give him to me."

"You'll give me your promise to feed him only goat's milk first."

"He'll be getting his mama's milk, woman."

"He doesn't like his mama's milk."

"Have you just insulted my wife?"

Jamie wished she had the strength to beat some sense into the old man. "I'm telling you what you have to do to keep this baby alive," she shouted. "He cannot stand another bout of sickness." She moved closer to the laird, until she was just an inch or so away from his knee, then said, "Promise me."

His abrupt nod pleased her. She handed the baby back to his father, then started toward Gavin and Marcus. "You're the most ungrateful man I've ever met," she muttered.

"Ungrateful?"

He was back to bellowing. Jamie whirled around, her hands on her hips, and gave the warrior a look meant to burn. "Aye, ungrateful," she shouted back. "You should be expressing your appreciation, McPherson, not shouting at me."

The laird's eyes turned to slits again. Jamie knew his pride was somehow injured, but she didn't have the faintest idea why. "I'll have your apology for taking my son out of my home," the man bellowed. "It's war we're speaking of if I don't get what I want."

"What you need is a good kick in your backside, you old goat," Jamie shouted back. "And that's what you're going to get if you don't show some respect around me."

"You took my bairn."

She couldn't believe the man's stupidity. His horse was just as obnoxious as his master was, too. As soon as the old man let up on the reins, the animal tried to take a bite out of Jamie's shoulder. McPherson didn't seem to want to control his mount any more than he did his temper.

"You'll apologize," he roared.

Jamie slapped his horse away before answering that challenge. "How dare you ask for my apology? I didn't take your son away and you know it. You can sit there until you rot, but you aren't getting an apology from me."

The baby started to wail, disrupting Jamie's concentration. "Oh, take your son home to his mama," she ordered. "And don't you dare come back on Kincaid land until you've learned some manners."

The chieftain looked as if he was itching to strike her. He deliberately let up on his reins, just to be contrary. The horse immediately tried to get a taste of Jamie's shoulder again. She hit the horse, harder.

McPherson let out a roar in reaction. "She hit me horse," he shouted. "You seen it, men. The Kincaid woman hit me horse. 'Tis one thing to insult a man's wife, but to strike his horse—"

"Oh, for God's sake," Jamie interrupted. "Leave now or I'll hit *you.*"

When the soldier on the left of the laird reached for his sword, Jamie pulled her dagger from the sheath in her belt. She turned to the soldier, took aim, and said, "You'll take your hand away from your weapon or you'll find my dagger in your throat before you draw your next breath. And when I cause an injury," she challenged, "I don't repair it."

The soldier hesitated for the briefest of seconds, then did as she commanded. Jamie nodded. "Now get off my land," she ordered as she replaced her dagger.

She was suddenly exhausted. She hadn't lost her temper this thoroughly in a good long while. She was a little ashamed of her behavior, too, and was immensely thankful only Gavin and Marcus were there to witness her unleashed temper.

It was all McPherson's fault, of course. The man probably lived in a cave. He certainly had the manners of a wild animal. He could provoke a saint into screaming.

Retreat seemed the logical choice now. Jamie turned around, her intent to walk back inside the castle without sparing a single glance over her shoulder. She was going to dismiss the McPhersons as rudely as possible.

She came to a staggering halt when she saw the line of Kincaid soldiers behind her. All were armed and ready for battle. While Jamie noticed this fact quickly enough, that wasn't what really started her head to pounding. No, it was Alec Kincaid standing in the center of his soldiers who captured her full attention and gave her such a headache.

Well, hell, he'd probably seen the whole thing.

Jamie was mortified. She suddenly wished she could just turn around and walk back to England.

She really wasn't certain who was the bigger threat now. The look on Alec's face could scare the wool off sheep. Laird McPherson looked like a saint in comparison.

Alec's arms were folded across his chest. His legs were braced apart—a bad sign, that—and his expression was as rigid as the rest of him. It was the same position she'd seen the day the outcasts attacked. She'd thought he looked bored then.

She knew better now.

He was still the safer bet, she decided. If he was going to kill her, he'd probably do it in privacy, she supposed with a sinking flutter in her stomach. She wasn't important enough in his mind to make a scene over. Nay, he probably wouldn't get around to it until next week.

He didn't say a word to her when she walked over to his side. He simply pushed her behind his back and then took a step forward. The wall of men immediately surrounded her.

The shield of warriors blocked her view, even when she stood on tiptoe and tried to see over Marcus's shoulder.

Angry words flew like arrows between the two mighty chieftains. Jamie was stunned when she realized Alec was actually defending her. He'd taken deep offense over the fact that one of the McPhersons had dared to touch his sword in Lady Kincaid's presence. Oh, Alec was furious, all right. Bloody furious.

He had a blazing temper, and Jamie was racing through a prayer of thanksgiving to her Maker that it wasn't directed at her.

Then she heard the hateful word "war" bellowed again. McPherson called for a battle and Alec couldn't have been more emphatic in his agreement.

Good God, what had she done?

Alec was never going to believe this wasn't all her fault. If she'd held on to her temper, perhaps she could have averted this war.

The soldiers didn't move away from her until the

McPhersons were well on their way down the path. Jamie decided it would be best for her to leave before her husband turned his attention to her. She certainly wasn't running away, she told herself. No, she just needed a little time to sort this confusing matter out. With any luck, it might only take her a day or two.

She turned her back on Marcus and started up the stairs. Just when she thought she'd escaped Alec's notice, he grabbed hold of her arm. He wasn't at all gentle when he forced her around to face him. Since Marcus and Gavin were watching, she decided to smile. Alec's scowl, however, changed her inclination.

"Would you care to explain?" he asked. His voice was as mild as a lion's yawn.

"Nay," Jamie answered. "I would rather not."

He didn't like her answer. The muscle in his jaw was at it again, flexing like an insistent tic. The grip on her arm intensified until the freckles turned pink.

She was determined to meet his glare so he would know she wasn't afraid of the mean look in his eyes, but she didn't even last through the first real blink.

"The babe was sick," she told him.

"And?"

"I took care of him."

"How did a McPherson bairn get here?"

"I was wondering that very thing," she said.

"Answer me."

He hadn't raised his voice, yet Jamie knew he was furious. She decided to appease him without actually giving him a direct answer. "Alec, I was simply trying to do the right thing. Even if I'd known that dear child belonged to such a sour old man, I still would have taken care of him. The babe was suffering so. Would you have me turn my back on him?"

"I would have you answer my question," he reminded her.

"You'll blame Mary."

"Mary was involved in this?" Alec demanded. He shook his head, then said, "I shouldn't be surprised."

"Mary brought the baby to me. McPherson's wife gave her son to Mary, begging for my help."

Alec finally let go of her arm. Jamie resisted the urge to rub the sting away. "Now you're bent on being angry with Mary for interfering, aren't you, Alec?"

He didn't bother to answer her. Gavin gave her a sympathetic look, then asked Alec, "Did Daniel know about this?"

"He couldn't have," Alec answered. "He was hunting with me. If he went directly home, he's probably finding out now. God willing, he'll keep her under lock and key."

"Mary has a good heart," Jamie interjected. "Surely Daniel won't be angry with her for helping a sick child."

"You may go back inside now," Alec announced, ignoring her defense of her sister.

His cold attitude upset her. God only knew she should be used to his contrary ways by now. He'd been away from home for four long days and nights, but she certainly hadn't missed him.

"I'm not ready to go back inside," Jamie returned, startling Gavin and Marcus. Alec didn't look surprised, though. He looked resigned. "I have a question to ask you first."

Alec let out a sigh of impatience. "Marcus, send some men to follow the McPhersons to the border," he ordered before giving Jamie his attention again. "Well? What is this question?"

"I was wondering if your hunt went well."

"It did."

"Then you found the men who hurt Angus?"

"Aye."

"And?"

"And what?"

"Did you have to kill anyone?"

He thought that had to be the most ridiculous question ever put to him. She whispered it and then gave Gavin a worried glance. Alec didn't know what to make of his wife. She looked irritated with him. The woman was simply too illogical to bother with.

But very appealing. He'd only been away four short days and nights, but it seemed much, much longer to him now. That admission made his mood black. She was still dressed in her English garb—he'd noticed that sin right away—and he was beginning to realize she was just as stubborn as he was. Mayhap even more so. "Six, seven," he announced in a hard voice. "Would you like to know how I killed them?"

She took a step back, forgetting she was standing on the stairs. Alec grabbed her shoulders to keep her from falling. "I assume, then, that you don't want to know?"

She shrugged his hands away. "No, I don't want to know how you killed them, you impossible man, but I do want the true number. Was it six or seven?"

"How in God's name would I know?" he asked, clearly exasperated. "I was in the thick of battle, Jamie. I didn't take time to count."

"Well, you should have," Jamie muttered. "In future, I would ask you do keep count. It's the least you could do."

"Why?"

"Because I only have eight shillings left, that's why."

He didn't know what she was talking about. That didn't surprise him, though; he never knew what she was talking about. The color had left her face, reminding him of how much she disliked battles. He guessed she didn't want him killing anyone. That was such an amusing thought that he couldn't help but smile. Hell, he'd probably killed twice that number. The fight had been fierce. He wasn't about to share that information with Jamie, though.

"You're smiling, Alec. Does that mean you were jesting with me?"

"I was," he lied, thinking to ease her frown away.

She gave him a look that suggested she didn't believe him. Then she picked up her skirts and hurried back inside.

"Alec," Gavin said, "what did she think would happen when you caught up with our enemies?"

"I haven't the faintest idea."

Gavin held his grin. "By the way," he said, turning the topic, "Franklin rode ahead to say the clan's on their way home from Gillebrid's holding. They should be here by tomorrow afternoon at the latest. Some of Harold's clan is tagging along. They mean to pay their respects."

"The hell they do," Alec barked. "They mean to look at my wife."

"Yes," Gavin replied with a chuckle. "Her beauty is already becoming legend. There's also the fact that she saved Angus. Anyone with an ache or a pain will be camping on our doorstep."

"How is Angus doing?"

"Docile now."

"What does that mean?"

"He wanted to get back to his duties. Your wife caught him just as he was leaving his cottage. Elizabeth had gone to enlist her aid." Gavin let out a rich laugh before continuing. "I could hear Angus shouting all the way to the castle doors. When I got there—"

"He raised his voice to Jamie?"

"He had good reason," Gavin explained when he saw how angry Alec was getting. "She'd taken his sword away from him."

Alec raised an eyebrow in reaction to that statement. "He did have reason, then," he admitted with a grin. "What happened next?"

"She never raised her voice to him, but she had him back in bed in minutes."

Alec started toward the stables, his hands clasped behind his back. Gavin walked at his side. "I don't trust any of Harold's men, especially his bastard sons," he said, turning the topic back to their coming visitors.

"The twins?"

"Justin will be a problem," Alec stated. "He's used to taking what he wants."

"You think he'd actually go after another man's wife?"

"He would. The man's fathered more bastard children than England's king."

"With his handsome looks, the women do fall at his feet. It's odd that Philip, though identical in appearance, is so opposite in nature. He's too timid to try anything."

"I don't trust Philip, either," Alec muttered.

Gavin smiled. "You speak like a man who cares for his wife, Alec."

"She's my property," Alec countered. "No one's going to insult her but me."

"She isn't having an easy time of it," Gavin remarked. "The task you gave her has helped, of course, but Edith is making it difficult still. She countermands every order Jamie gives. Annie isn't much better. She won't even speak to Jamie."

Alec didn't answer that remark, for he'd just noticed Jamie rushing down the steps. "Where do you think you're going?" he shouted.

"To visit the blacksmith," Jamie called back. She turned the corner and was soon out of sight.

Alec shook his head. "The daft woman's gone in the wrong direction."

Gavin chuckled. "Alec, she begs me to give her more duties. I can't let her do the heavy work, moving the stones, but I want to give her something—"

"What are you talking about?" Alec asked. "Moving what stones?"

Gavin gave his laird a puzzled look. "The kitchens," he reminded him.

When Alec continued to frown, Gavin explained, "You did give her permission to move the kitchens, didn't you?"

Alec shrugged. "I might have," he admitted. "In a weak moment. Still, it couldn't take her more than an hour to rearrange whatever in God's name she wants rearranged."

"Rearrange?" Gavin repeated in astonishment. God help him, he started laughing.

"What the hell's so amusing, Gavin?" Alec demanded. "Did my wife tell you—"

"Nay, she's doing exactly what you gave her permission to do," Gavin said, nearly choking. "You'll see soon enough, Alec. It might be a pleasant surprise," he added hastily when Alec seemed about to lose his patience. "I wouldn't want to spoil it."

Father Murdock came rushing toward his laird, drawing

his full attention. The priest's black cassock was flapping in the wind. "Alec? If it's convenient, I'd like to have a word with you."

Both Alec and Gavin immediately tried to get downwind of the priest. The foul odor radiating from the man made their eyes water. Out of respect, Alec didn't mention his fragrant condition. Gavin, however, wasn't as diplomatic. "Good God, Father Murdock, what have you done to yourself? You smell like pig swill."

The priest wasn't insulted. He laughed and nodded his head. "I do smell foul, my boy, but I'm feeling better than I have in years. Jamie gave me a special paste to put on my chest. She mixed me another potion, too. My cough is near to gone now."

He took a step forward. Alec stood his ground, but Gavin took a hasty step back. "Now, then, enough about my health and on to my important question," he said, addressing Alec with his gaze. "Your wife has given me all her shillings," he stated as he opened his hands to show the coins. "She wished to buy indulgences. I didn't have the heart to tell her we don't use coins here."

Alec shook his head. "She worries overmuch about her soul. 'Tis an English inclination if I'm not mistaken."

The priest grinned. "Her soul doesn't concern her at all, Alec."

"Then why?"

"It's your soul that has her worried."

Gavin covered his laughter with a loud cough. "I count seven shillings," he told Alec.

"Eight," Father Murdock corrected. "One, she said, just as a precaution against a faulty memory. I didn't understand what she meant by that remark."

"The woman's daft."

"She's caring," Father Murdock argued. "Now tell me what to do with these coins."

"Put them in the box atop the mantel," Alec suggested with a shrug.

"As you wish," the priest agreed. "Now, while we're on

the topic of your dear little wife, I was wondering if you'd give her permission to use one of the empty rooms above the stairs. She asked me to put the question to you, Alec."

"I see no harm in granting this request," Alec answered. "What does she want the room for?"

"Her bedroom."

"Like hell."

"Now, son, no need to get lathered up," Father Murdock soothed. He could see his laird's mood was spoiling as fast as fish left out in the sun too long. He blurted out his next question. "May she go riding on the hillside—staying on Kincaid land, of course? It will give her something to do. I can tell she misses you something fierce when you're away."

The last comment softened Alec's expression. "Of course she misses me," he boasted. "All right, Father Murdock. Tell her she may ride if she has an escort."

"You can't be thinking she'd run away, Alec? She misses her home, but I—"

"Father, the woman can't find her way out of a room with only one door. No, I don't think she'll try to go back to England, but she will certainly get lost. She has no sense of direction."

"Yes," the priest agreed with a sparkle in his eyes. "She's as flawed as a clear blue sky."

"You contradict yourself," Gavin interjected. "A blue sky isn't flawed."

"To a blind man it is," Murdock answered, staring intently up at Alec. "If your wife is so inferior, I will be happy to see about gaining an annulment."

"You will not."

Alec hadn't meant to sound so forceful in his denial of the priest's ludicrous suggestion. Father Murdock had deliberately implied that an annulment could be quite easily obtained. Alec knew he'd fallen into the old man's trap, for he'd just admitted how much he cared about Jamie. "I grow weary of women's talk," he muttered. "Gavin? Do you think you can keep my wife from starting another war while I see to other matters?"

"She asked about Helena."

234

The priest's quiet statement fell between them. Alec slowly turned to face Father Murdock again.

"And?" he asked, his voice devoid of all emotion.

"Did you know she'd been told that you killed Helena?"

Alec shook his head. "When did she hear this foul gossip?" Gavin demanded.

"Before Alec arrived at her home," Father Murdock answered.

"Did she ask you if it was true?" Gavin asked when he realized Alec wasn't going to question the priest.

"No, she didn't ask me if it was true," Father Murdock answered. He gave Gavin a frown of displeasure. "In fact, she told me she never believed that gossip. She doesn't think Helena killed herself, either. She believes it was an accident. She has a tender heart, Gavin, and she has complete faith in her husband."

Alec nodded. "No, she wouldn't believe gossip," he stated. His voice was filled with pride. "Jamie's such a gentle, caring woman."

"Aye, she is," Gavin returned.

"Of course, she can be a might stubborn, too," Father Murdock admitted. "She keeps nagging me to give her some duties. I believe she wants to become part of this family, Alec. She's falling in love with you, son. Treat her heart kindly."

Alec wasn't at all convinced the priest's words about Jamie falling in love with him were true, but he grinned over the possibility.

"Now you'll be sure to praise her efforts with the kitchen, won't you, Alec?" the priest said. "What think you of the new addition? It's coming along quite nicely, now that the men have quit their grumbling."

"What are you talking about?" Alec asked.

Murdock gave Gavin a quick look, then turned back to Alec. "The kitchen, Alec. Surely you haven't forgotten you gave Jamie permission to move the building."

"I what?" Alec roared.

The priest took a hasty step back to get away from Alec's wrath. "She said she had your permission to rearrange the kitchen, Alec. The sweet little lass wouldn't lie. Could you have forgotten . . ."

He quit trying to defend his mistress when Alec started for the doors of his castle. "Gavin, he looked very . . . surprised."

"Surprised? He was that," Gavin returned. "You better keep close to Jamie until his thunder quiets down. He should just about be noticing the gaping hole in the back—"

Alec's bellow of outrage filled the courtyard. "He's seen it," Father Murdock whispered. "Oh, Lord save us, here comes Jamie."

The priest picked up the hem of his cassock and started running toward his mistress. "Wait, lass," he shouted.

Jamie heard the priest's frantic call. She turned around immediately, a worried expression on her face. "Father, you shouldn't be running until your chest is better," she called out.

The priest climbed the steps and grabbed her arm. "Alec just saw the hole in the back wall."

She gave him a gentle smile. "He was bound to notice, Father."

It was clear to him that the sweet lass didn't understand her jeopardy. "You'd best come along with me to the chapel until Alec hears all the soldiers' explanations. He'll calm down in an hour or two. Then you can—"

"Have more faith in your laird," Jamie countered. "He'll see the rightness in the change, once it's finished. I'm sure of it, Father. Besides, he won't yell at me. I have his promise. Please don't worry. I'll go inside and explain it all to Alec. I'm certainly not afraid."

"'Tis your lack of fear that has me most afeared," the old man admitted. He knew Alec wouldn't touch her in anger. Still, he could destroy her delicate feelings with his shouts. Father Murdock made a hasty sign of the cross after Jamie patted his hand and walked inside. He was too weak in his knees to go after her.

Jamie braced herself against her husband's irritation and hurried on into the hall. She came to an abrupt stop when she saw what was going on. Alec was sitting at the head of the table. A soldier stood at his side, giving his accounting.

Alec didn't look overly upset. His elbow rested on the tabletop and his forehead rested in his hand. He looked more weary than angry.

All the soldiers who'd worked on dismantling the kitchen building were there, too.

Well, hell, they were standing in line, obviously waiting their turn to tell on her. Jamie gave them a good frown to let them know what she thought of their disloyalty, then walked toward her husband.

When he finally glanced up, Jamie froze. He was furious. The tic was back in his clenched jaw. His eyes were blazing with anger. The wind didn't aid her cause much either. The whistling sound coming through the large hole reminded Alec of what she'd done.

He stared at her for a long silent moment. "I would like to explain," she said.

"Leave this room immediately, wife."

He hadn't raised his voice to her, but his rude command stung just the same.

"Alec, you promised me you wouldn't forget your temper," she reminded him. Heaven help her, she was suddenly quite terrified by the look in his eyes.

He did yell at her then. "Get out before I . . . now, wife."

Jamie nodded. She rushed over to the mantel, grabbed a coin from the box, and then walked out of the hall with as much dignity as she could muster under such humiliating circumstances.

Edith and Annie were standing near the entrance. They snickered when she passed them.

Jamie didn't start crying until she reached the stables. She ordered Donald to ready Wildfire. The stable master didn't argue with her command, and once he'd helped her mount her horse, he asked if he should prepare Alec's steed.

She shook her head, then started for the gate.

Father Murdock was standing in the courtyard, waiting for her to pass him.

Jamie leaned down and handed him her coin. "He lied to me," she whispered. "This is for an indulgence for his soul."

Murdock grabbed hold of the stirrup. "Where are you going, lass?" he asked, pretending not to notice her tears. "You have me worrying."

"Out."

"Out?"

"His order, Father, and I am ever dutiful. Which way is England?"

The priest was too stunned to point the direction. Jamie guessed it was downhill. "Thank you for being kind to me," she said.

She left the priest staring after her with his mouth hanging open in disbelief.

Jamie knew he'd eventually go and tell on her, then decided it didn't matter. Alec wouldn't come after her. She wasn't significant enough. He'd be happy to be rid of her.

She thought she'd have trouble at the drawbridge, yet after she'd explained that she was doing their laird's bidding, the soldiers immediately let her pass.

She let Wildfire race with the wind then. Jamie simply held on, openly weeping. She didn't know where they were headed or how long they continued at the neck-breaking pace. In truth, she didn't care about anything but having her cry. When the horse finally stopped in the shelter of the trees, Jamie decided it was time to regain a bit of control.

She saw the boy then. He wasn't a Kincaid, she realized, as his plaid was of a different color. Jamie didn't make a sound. She hoped the boy wouldn't notice her, for she didn't want anyone to see her in such a disgraceful condition, not even a child.

The boy was too preoccupied to look behind him. He was staring intently at the bushes to his right. Jamie wondered what held him so entranced.

He suddenly cried out and started to back away just as a giant boar let out a vile-sounding snort and charged forward.

Jamie instinctively reacted. She slapped Wildfire's flank, sending her into a full gallop. The mare flew down the slope.

Jamie clutched the reins and Wildfire's mane in her left hand and leaned to the right side.

The child saw her coming. He started running toward her, his hands outstretched. Jamie prayed she had the strength to lift the boy. God proved merciful. With the child's eager assistance and his death grip on her right arm, she was able to haul him up high enough for him to swing one leg over Wildfire's back.

They both held on for dear life. The boar gave up his chase a few minutes later, but Wildfire was still prickly with fear. The horse suddenly turned. Jamie and the boy went tumbling to the ground.

She landed on her side. He landed on top of her. He quickly rolled to the side, then stood and tried to help her.

He was tugging on her right arm. She grimaced against the pain. "Are you hurt?" the child asked, his fear obvious in his thick Gaelic burr.

"Just bruised," Jamie answered in Gaelic. She slowly regained her feet, then noticed her bliaut was torn at the shoulder seam.

They were standing in the center of a narrow clearing. Jamie was shaking from head to toe. "We've had a close call, we have," she announced. "Lord, I was scared. Were you?" she asked when the boy looked up at her.

The child nodded.

They both smiled then. "We gave him what-for, didn't we?"

"Aye, we did give him what-for," she said, thinking to herself what an adorable child he was. He had long red hair. It curled around his cherubic face. His nose was painted with large freckles. "I'm Lady Kincaid," she continued. "And your name?"

"I shouldn't be telling," the boy whispered. "I'm not supposed to be on Kincaid land."

"Did you get lost?"

He shook his head. "You'll tell."

"No, I won't tell. What are you doing here, then?"

The child lifted his shoulders in a shrug. "I like to go hunting. My name's Lindsay."

"And what is your clan's name?"

"Lindsay," he repeated. "You speak Gaelic, but you sound different. You aren't wearing the Kincaid plaid, either."

"I'm English."

His eyes widened.

"I'm Alec Kincaid's wife, Lindsay," she explained. "How old are you?"

"Nine, this summer."

"Your mother will be looking for you, I would think."

"My father will be doing the looking. He'll be getting worried," he added. "I better go home now."

Jamie nodded. She didn't smile, for the child's expression had turned very serious.

"You saved my life," the boy said. "Father must repay."

"No," Jamie countered. "He doesn't have to repay. You have to promise me you won't go hunting on your own again. Will you give me your word?"

When he nodded, she smiled. "Do you want me to follow you home?"

"They'd keep you if you did. We're feuding with the Kincaids," he explained very matter-of-factly.

"Be careful, then," she cautioned. "Hurry. I think I hear someone coming."

The child disappeared behind the line of trees before Jamie had taken a step toward Wildfire.

She was standing all alone in the center of the clearing when Alec and his stallion broke through the branches. He was so relieved to see her that he stopped his mount and sat there, staring down at her, while he calmed his ragged breathing.

Alec couldn't tell if she was upset or not. Her head was bowed. He knew he'd terrified her. The look on her face when he'd shouted at her had shown how frightened she was.

He hoped to heaven she'd gotten over her fear, though . . . and her tears. He'd noticed those, too, when she walked past him with her coin in her hand.

Hell, he'd probably have to apologize. He wasn't any good at it, he knew, but he'd still have to give it a try, he decided. He would force himself to be calm . . . and reasonable.

Then he noticed the leaves in her hair and the tear in her gown. "What the hell happened?" he shouted. "Did someone . . ."

He was off his stallion and racing toward her before she could answer. Jamie took a quick step back. "Nothing happened to me," she announced.

"Don't lie to me." He grabbed her in his arms and pulled her up against his chest.

"You lied to me."

"I didn't," he answered, calming once again.

"You lost your temper with me."

"You had the men tear out the back wall of my home," he countered.

"You said I could rearrange your kitchens," Jamie whispered. "In the winter, Frieda and Hessie and all the other servants have to wade through the snow to get your supper. I was trying to do the right thing, Alec. It made sense to add the building onto the back of the house. You wouldn't let me explain, though."

Alec closed his eyes and prayed for patience. He couldn't seem to quit hugging her long enough to lecture her. "I did forget my temper," he admitted. "And I'm furious with you."

"Because of the hole in your wall?"

"No," he told her. "Because you were afraid of me. Did you think I'd hurt you?"

"No," she answered. She put her arms around his waist and relaxed against him. "You embarrassed me. A husband shouldn't yell at his wife."

"I will try in future to remember this dictate," he promised. "Jamie, there will be times when I will forget again."

"I'll have to get used to it, I suppose," she said. "Your shout could fell a pine tree. But you're mostly bluster, aren't you, Alec?"

Alec rested his chin on the top of her head while he

decided whether or not to let her get away with that small insult. "Father Murdock said you were going back to England. Was that your intent?"

"You told me to get out," she reminded him.

A smile eased his frown away. "I meant for you to leave the hall, Jamie, not Scotland."

"I just wanted to leave for a while, husband. 'Tis the truth I'm not settling in very well."

She sounded terribly forlorn. "I know you'll find this difficult to believe, but back home people actually liked me. They did! I'm not at all used to being thought of as inferior, Alec. That does take some adjustment. Your soldiers were waiting to tell on me, weren't they? They don't like me any better than you do."

Jamie suddenly burst into tears. "Oh, I'm being pitiful, aren't I? Why did you bother to come after me?"

"Jamie, the soldiers were waiting to have their chance to defend you," he announced. His voice was a gruff, affectionate whisper. "They're as loyal to you as they are to me, wife."

He let her pull away so she could see his nod. It was his undoing, however, for once he saw the tears streaming down her cheeks, his discipline all but deserted him. "I came after you because you belong to me. Don't ever try to leave me again, Jamie, or you'll truly see my anger. Love, quit your tears now. I didn't mean to . . ."

His voice shook too much to continue. Alec leaned down and kissed her brow. Jamie mopped at the corners of her eyes with the backs of her hands. Her arm started throbbing from her bruising, reminding her of her mishap. "I fell off my horse," she admitted.

"I know."

Now he sounded forlorn. Jamie smiled. "I'm really very skilled, Alec, but the boar frightened Wildfire and . . ."

She quit trying to explain when she saw his frown. "Never mind," she said. "Alec? When a husband and wife have had a disagreement, they usually kiss after they've made up."

"The wife is wearing her husband's plaid, though," Alec

pointed out. "Still, I wouldn't break my word if she wasn't wearing anything at all."

She didn't understand his meaning until he'd pulled her torn bliaut over her head and tossed it on the ground.

"You cannot mean to—to—" she stammered. She took a step back.

"Oh, I mean to, all right." He took a step forward.

She let out a scream of laughter when he lunged for her, then turned and ran into the cover of the trees. "You're daft, Alec," she called over her shoulder. "'Tis the middle of the day."

He grabbed her from behind and pulled her up against him. "There are children about," she pointed out.

Alec nuzzled the side of her throat. "You want a proper kiss, don't you?"

"This isn't at all proper," she answered. Her breath caught in her throat then and a shiver raced across her shoulders. Alec was nibbling on her earlobe while he whispered in great detail all the erotic things he was going to do to her.

She went limp against him. Alec leaned back against a thick tree, bracing her between his thighs. He took his time undressing her, ignoring her feeble protests and when he'd completed that task, he pulled her up against his hardness. His hands cupped her breasts while his thumbs lazily stroked her nipples.

He knew he had her surrender when she let out a soft moan. "Now I'm going to show you how inferior you are to me," he whispered.

"You are?" she asked on a gasp. His hand had just moved between her thighs.

He grunted with pleasure when he felt her heat. She was already wet and hot for him. "I'm going to kiss every inch of your inferior body," he promised.

He turned her around finally. Their open mouths met in a ravenous kiss. She wrapped her arms around his neck, rubbed her breasts against his plaid. Alec tore his mouth away, then discarded his own clothing in quick time. He turned her until she was leaning against the tree, facing him, and lowered his head to the valley between her breasts. His tongue drove her wild. His hands massaged her breasts, and then he finally moved to take one nipple into his mouth. The pressure was excruciatingly wonderful. She cried out in pleasure, clinging to his shoulders now for support. Alec gave her other breast the same blissful attention, then trailed hot kisses down her stomach.

He made her forget to breathe. He knelt down in front of her, cupped her smooth buttocks with his hands, and roughly pulled her up against his open mouth.

She wasn't capable of thinking. His tongue stroked the passion in her, pressing, in, out, again and again, until she was whimpering for release from the sweet torture. She was begging him not to stop when he stood up to face her. Jamie tried to capture his mouth for a long, hot kiss, but he pulled back. He suddenly grabbed hold of her hair, twisted it around his fist and jerked her forward. "Don't ever try to leave me again."

He didn't give her time to answer. His open mouth claimed hers. His tongue thrust inside. She melted against him. He lifted her high, spreading her thighs in one powerful motion. She wrapped her legs around him. "Alec," she demanded in a near shout when he hesitated.

"Promise me." His voice grated against her ear.

The agony in his voice drove through her sexual haze. "I promise," she whispered.

He groaned his approval, then thrust inside her with one forceful surge. He whispered love words against her ear as he withdrew and then drove back into her.

Jamie clung to him, chanting her own love words, and when she knew she was about to find her release, she cried out his name.

Their surrender was absolute, their passion appeased. He stayed inside her a long while. Even after his breathing had slowed and his heart had quit hammering he still didn't move. He didn't want to lose the scent of their lovemaking, didn't want to quit holding her.

For the first time in his life, he was content. He understood what that meant, yet instinctively rebelled against admitting the full truth. It was too soon, he told himself. Far too soon. It would weaken him, make him vulnerable. . . . He wasn't ready.

Jamie felt Alec tense against her. He eased her back down to the ground, then turned away from her to gather their clothes. She caught only a glimpse of his dark expression. "Alec?" she whispered. "I didn't please you just now?"

He immediately responded to the worry in her voice. "You pleased me very much, wife." His voice was rough with emotion.

Jamie didn't ask him any more questions until they were both dressed. "Why are you frowning so? If I truly made you happy—"

"I'm frowning because you told me you were feeling inferior. I never, ever want you to think such ridiculous thoughts in future, wife. Where in God's name you ever came up with such an ignorant idea—"

"You called me inferior," she reminded him, thoroughly puzzled now.

He had the audacity to look surprised. Jamie's eyes widened in reaction. "You called me insignificant, too. Don't you remember, Alec?"

He shrugged. He went to collect their mounts, but he was smiling now instead of scowling. His gentle wife had sounded so incensed.

"You can't even keep track of your own opinions?"

"Not opinions," he called over his shoulder. "Insults, love."

"You admit insulting me then?" she shouted, chasing after him.

"Of course."

He let out a shout of laughter when her unladylike expletive filled the air.

She was more horrified by her shameful blasphemy than he was. She apologized profusely.

He laughed right in her face.

Jamie didn't know what to make of him now. She turned her back on her husband and walked over to Wildfire. Alec

Kincaid was the most impossible man in the world, she decided. Didn't he realize how much she wanted to hear him say that he cared for her?

Jamie gained Wildfire's back and picked up the reins. She suddenly remembered Alec's hard demand that she never try to leave him again.

He did care. She whirled around to look at her husband, thinking to shout that very thought. His arrogant grin changed her mind. He didn't realize he cared, she guessed, and he'd probably just get angry with her if she dared instruct him in his true feelings.

Jamie let out a lusty laugh. He'd have to settle in first. Then he'd see the rightness in loving her.

She nudged Wildfire before he could question her further. Alec grabbed her reins, then shook his head.

She gave him a resigned look.

"Listen carefully, love. Up," he said, pointing behind him, "is Kincaid land. Down is England. Got that?"

She bit her lower lip so she wouldn't smile. "I've got it," she finally agreed when he continued to stare at her.

He let out a long sigh, then pulled Wildfire along as he changed directions. "No, you haven't, love," he muttered.

Jamie did smile then. Lord, she felt good. She didn't even care if Alec lost his temper with her in future. She certainly didn't mind his insults, guessing now it was his way of protecting his own feelings. No, she didn't mind his contrary ways at all.

The reason was simple to understand.

He'd just called her his love.

Chapter Thirteen

Alec was scowling when they returned to the stables. Jamie was smiling. Gavin stood next to the priest on the steps of the castle, watching the pair.

"She's giving him fits," Gavin remarked.

"I heard she threatened to put her dagger in one of the McPhersons," Father Murdock said.

"She did," Gavin answered. "She's courageous, bluffing the old laird and his men the way she did."

"Why do you think it was a bluff?"

"Well, of course, it was a bluff. She couldn't possibly know how to throw a dagger."

"You're very like your laird, Gavin, for you've taken on all his judgments. He's already drawn his own conclusions about Lady Jamie. I'd keep my mind a bit more open if I were you. If she says she could put her blade in someone, then I think I'd believe she was capable. She'd have to be protecting someone else, though. Aye, she's much more skilled than you and Alec credit her. Mark my words, boy."

"Alec complains she's too gentle," Gavin countered.

"She's strong, too," Father Murdock answered. "She isn't going to settle in as peacefully as Alec believes, either. The sparks are just beginning to fly."

Both Gavin and Father Murdock turned to watch Alec assist his wife to the ground. Alec held Jamie much longer than the task required, and from the way the two were staring at each other, neither the priest nor the soldier wished to interfere. The two men turned and strolled away, both of them grinning like simpletons.

Alec knew he should get back to more important duties. Still, he couldn't resist brushing his mouth across hers just one more time. He might have kissed her again if Donald hadn't intruded. Alec handed the soldier Wildfire's reins. Jamie bowed and started to turn away. "Where are you going now?" Alec asked, just to keep her close another minute or two.

"To change my torn gown," Jamie answered. "First I must go and fetch some candles, though."

Alec thought he might walk along with her, but Donald changed his mind. "Alec? If I might have a word with you?"

"What is it?" Alec asked. He pulled his stallion toward the interior of the stables.

"It's milady's mare," Donald began. "I hate to burden you with such a paltry problem, but I'm at a loss as to how to control the stubborn animal. She isn't eating. She's going to break a leg sure as certain trying to get out of her stall. She's already torn three slats apart."

"Then put her in another stall," Alec suggested.

"I've already tried that," Donald answered.

Alec could hear Wildfire butting against the wooden slats. He led his stallion over to the damaged stall. Jamie's horse eased her tantrum as soon as Alec reached out to stroke her. "She's calm now," he remarked, smiling.

"'Tis because your black is near her," Donald answered. "When she can see him or smell his scent, she settles down. She's used to him. I was wondering, milord, if we might try putting the two of them together."

"He'd kill her."

"I don't think so," Donald rushed out. "And she'll take ill if she doesn't start eating."

Alec decided to test Donald's suggestion immediately. If the stallion tried to harm Wildfire, he could intervene before real damage was caused.

As soon as the big black entered Wildfire's stall, he went to her feed box and began to eat, completely ignoring the mare. Wildfire blustered over the invasion of her territory, but the stallion quickly established his superiority by letting out an ear-piercing snort that made Alec grin. The horse flared his nostrils, then lashed out with a solid kick to her backside. Wildfire was duly intimidated. There wasn't room enough for her to rear up. She gave it several good tries anyway. The stallion let her have her way, and in the end, she quit her blustering and joined him at the feed box. She only tried to nudge the stallion away from her food once.

"My stallion is just as possessive as I am," Alec remarked.

"Milord?" Donald asked, obviously confused by that comment.

"Never mind," Alec said. He was smiling, for he was thinking of Jamie. Then he remembered Father Murdock's comment that Jamie wanted a bedroom of her own. "Like hell," he muttered. The horse had more sense than her mistress, he decided.

Alec wasn't going to let the matter rest. He was going to have a quick talk with her. The only bed she was going to be sleeping in was his bed. He'd soften his lecture, of course, because he didn't want her to cry again. But he was going to stand firm in his decision. And that, as she liked to say, was that.

Jamie didn't have any idea of the worry she was causing her husband. She'd only just realized she'd taken the wrong direction. After having a pleasant conversation with the blacksmith, she decided to meet the occupants of the other cottages nestled together near the back wall.

"They all be at their nooning meal," the blacksmith announced.

"Could I have a look inside each hut, do you suppose, Henry?" she asked.

"Of course, mistress," the bald man agreed. "They'll be honored when I tell them you were interested enough."

Jamie took her time climbing the steep hill. She paused to pick some sweet-smelling wildflowers growing near the wall, then continued on. She thought she heard a sound behind her and turned to greet whoever was approaching.

There wasn't anyone there, however, and she concluded the wind was playing tricks on her.

Jamie looked inside the cutter's cottage, walked on to the last hut, the tannery, and was just peeking inside when she was given a mighty shove from behind. She was so startled by the sudden attack, she fell forward to her knees. The door slammed shut on her soft gasp of disbelief.

There weren't any windows in the hut. It was as dark as night inside. She whispered an unladylike expletive as she began to feel around the earthen floor for the flowers she'd dropped.

Jamie assumed the wind had pushed the door forward and she just hadn't gotten out of the way in time.

She gave up trying to find the flowers in the dark, stood up, and brushed the dirt off her skirt.

Alec would certainly think she was as awkward as a new foal if he could see her now, she thought to herself.

She still hadn't caught the danger. Jamie didn't begin to worry until she smelled the smoke. She tried to get the door open. It wouldn't budge.

She did panic then. She pounded on the door with all her might, shouting for Alec. The little square hut was turning into an inferno. In less than a minute, the entire roof was in flames.

Her screams soon turned into weak coughs. A piece of timber fell next to her feet. Jamie moved away from the beam, amazed that such an easy feat could be so difficult. She stared in fascination at the long-stemmed pink rose she was holding until the heat began to curl the edges of the soft petals.

The flames were licking their way toward her. The hut became filled with smoke, and it was simply too difficult to stand.

Jamie collapsed to the ground, gasping for clean air. The earthen floor felt wonderfully cool against her face.

She refused to believe she was going to die. Alec would get there in time. He'd save her. He had promised to protect her.

Oh, God, please make him hurry. Don't let him be left alone again. He needs me. He still needs to tell me he loves me, she thought.

And just where in bloody hell was he?

Jamie was suddenly furious. After he saved her, she was going to give him a good lecture on the merits of being prompt.

Lord, she was losing her mind. The burst of anger had drained the remainder of her strength. Jamie closed her eyes and began to pray.

Alec's anguished roar reached her through the haze of smoke. Jamie managed a weak smile. "Thank you," she whispered to her Maker.

Alec had just started up the hill when he heard the shouts. He'd seen the flames atop the tannery hut then. He quit breathing and started running. By the time he caught up with Gavin, he was in a rage. He *knew* she was inside. He knew.

He and Gavin reached the hut at the same moment. They both saw the beam of wood propped against the door. Gavin kicked the wood out of the way just as Alec ripped the door off its hinges and threw it to the ground.

Terror gave him added strength. And when he saw Jamie, he was so consumed with fury, he nearly felled the walls with his tormented bellow.

He had her in his arms and outside the hut before the walls collapsed. Alec knelt on the ground, protecting her in his arms, afraid to breathe until he was certain she was breathing, too. Her racking coughs should have been evidence enough for him that she had survived, but his mind was still too raw with fear to think with much logic.

It took him long minutes to regain some semblance of control. Gavin knelt next to him.

"Alec, let her have some air," he whispered, barely recognizing his own weak voice.

Jamie opened her eyes to find her husband's worried face above her. She tried to smile at him through her tears. His eyes were misty, too, she noticed when her thoughts stopped trying to skip away from her. The smoke must have affected his vision, she decided.

She reached up to touch his forehead and only then realized she was still clutching one of the wilted flowers. She let go of the flower and began to stroke his brow.

He touched her forehead at the very same moment.

"I promised you I wouldn't leave you." Her voice sounded like a gruff old man's.

"I'll never let you." His voice sounded like dried leaves being stomped on.

They shared a smile. "You're all right now, Jamie? You weren't hurt?"

The caring in his eyes stunned her. "I knew you'd save me."

"How would you be knowing that?" he asked.

"Because you care, Alec Kincaid."

She had imitated his burr perfectly. Alec nodded, pleased with her answer. He stood up, keeping her head tucked under his chin. He noticed the crowd of soldiers when he turned to walk down the hill. "She's none the worse for her mishap," he called out.

Jamie tried to pull away just a little so she could nod to his men, but Alec slammed her back against his chest in a hug as fierce as a bear's.

He inadvertently squeezed another cough out of her, too. The man simply didn't know his own strength, she thought happily. He didn't know his actions were so telling, either. She could feel the tremors in his arms. And when she'd been waiting for him to save her, it was her name she'd heard him bellowing. He was beginning to love her, if only just a little, whether he was willing to admit it or not.

That realization made her forget all about her brush with death. "You took your sweet time coming after me, Kincaid," she reminded him.

"The hell I did," he countered with a grin. "I ran like Satan."

"I'm not so insignificant to you after all, am I?"

He didn't answer her until they'd reached the castle doors. "No, you're not."

She realized after a long minute that he wasn't going to give her any more than that. But all the same, she was enormously happy with him. One bite at a time, she reminded herself. That was how she'd boasted to Father Murdock she could eat a giant bear, and that was how she was going to conquer Alec Kincaid. She laughed again, though this time over her own foolishness. Why had it taken her so long to realize she needed his love as much as he needed hers?

"How can you be laughing now, Lady Kincaid?" Gavin asked. He saw the doors opened for them, then followed the pair inside. "I'm still shaking with anger."

"I was laughing because I've just realized something quite important," Jamie answered. "It's not going to be one bite at a time, you see, but one kiss at a time. There is a marked difference. And that's the only explanation you'll be getting out of me."

"The smoke has obviously affected her mind," Alec interjected, shaking his head.

"Why are you so angry, Gavin?" Jamie asked. She glanced over Alec's shoulder to see the soldier's face. "You can't be thinking this is all my fault, can you?"

Before Gavin could respond, Jamie turned back to Alec. "The wind caused my mishap, husband. It was so strong, it pushed the door right into my backside. It was high, all right," she continued when both men looked as if they didn't believe her. "The howling noise was eerie, too. Do you know it sounded as though someone was laughing at me? Alec, why are you looking so doubtful? Don't you believe me?"

"I believe you," Alec told her.

"We know it wasn't your fault, milady," Gavin interjected. "The door was . . ." He didn't finish his explanation when he caught Alec's signal.

"The door was what, Gavin?"

"Stuck. It was stuck," he blurted out.

"Aye, it surely was," Jamie agreed.

"Gavin, go and order a bath for Jamie. Then return to the hill and begin questioning the servants. Surely one of them will have a few important answers for us."

Alec carried Jamie behind the screen and gently placed her on his bed.

"After your bath, you'll stay in bed the rest of the day," he ordered.

"Why?"

"Why, Jamie? Because you need to recover," Alec explained.

"I've already recovered," Jamie argued.

Alec had to shake his head over her attitude. "You should be weeping now, lass, not smiling so sweetly up at me. Don't you know how soft you are?"

"I must stay in bed because I'm . . . soft? Alec, that doesn't make a bit of sense."

She sat there on the side of the bed, her face streaked with dirt, her hair tangled, her soot-marred hands folded demurely in her lap; she sat there looking absolutely beautiful to him. The servants marched in with buckets of water. Jamie gave each one a cheerful greeting. She not only remembered their names but also the names of their husbands and children. Alec was impressed. Her memory was really quite remarkable. When she asked each woman about her kin, she was letting her know how much she valued her.

The women, he noticed, gave Jamie just as much affection in their greetings.

Why, even dour-faced old Hessie, the main cook, was smiling at her mistress. "Will you be up to directing the men with the . . . kitchen work?" she asked, after giving her laird a timid look.

Jamie held her smile. "He noticed the hole, Hessie," she whispered. "And I have no intention of putting off the work. I'll—"

"I'll take over that duty," Alec announced.

"You will?"

She looked extremely pleased with him. He wondered then if that wasn't her goal all the while. "Angus can direct the soldiers," Alec stated, "after I've explained what I want done." He'd stressed the word "I" in his announcement, but he could tell by Jamie's smile that she still thought she was getting her own way. "The hole will be boarded up until the hall is finished."

"Hall? I don't understand," Jamie confessed.

"I don't want the kitchen directly attached," Alec countered. "The smoke from the cooking will fill the hall by noon. We'll make a covered hallway to connect the two buildings. Does that satisfy you?"

He guessed it didn't satisfy her when she gave him a suspicious look. "How long will this hallway be?"

"Not long," he heard himself promise.

She nodded, pleased now. "There, Hessie," she announced. "I told you Alec would see the rightness in this change." She noticed her husband's frown and hurried to add, "All of his clan is important to him." She turned back to Alec and added, "I've told Hessie that your soldiers and your servants deserve equal status in your mind."

He did surprise her then. "That is true," he said. "You needn't have told Hessie," he added with a nod toward the servant. "She understands her value."

The servant immediately straightened her shoulders with pride. Then she bowed to her laird and hurried to leave.

"Have your bath now, wife, before the wind turns your water to ice," he announced.

Alec had kept his smile firmly in place, yet when he was again on the other side of the screen, he quit his pretense. He started pacing in front of the hearth while he tried to reason through this atrocity. Someone had actually tried to kill his precious Jamie. If he hadn't gotten there in time . . . If he'd stayed inside the stables just a few minutes more . . .

"Alec? No one saw a damn thing."

Alec stopped pacing when Gavin called out to him. "Lower your voice," he ordered. "I don't want Jamie overhearing any of this talk."

"She's already overhearing," Jamie called out from behind the screen.

Alec let his exasperation show, then beckoned Gavin closer. "Jamie, don't listen," he called out.

"I can't help listening," she called back. "Have you noticed, Alec, the horrible lack of privacy? I asked Father Murdock if he thought I could move our things up to one of the bedrooms above the stairs, husband. Did he mention that request to you yet?"

"You should have asked me."

"You were busy," she shouted.

"She sure as hell doesn't sound as if she just went through a fire, does she, Gavin?"

"She's a lot stronger than we think she is," he told his lord quietly. "Father Murdock might be right, after all." Gavin had kept his voice low so his mistress wouldn't overhear him. His bid to exclude her didn't work, however.

"Of course Father Murdock is right, Gavin," Jamie sang out. "He's a man of God, if you'll remember."

"Jamie!"

"Alec, I'll close my ears to your conversation just as soon as you give me your answer. Surely you can see the wisdom in my request. We could be moved upstairs before—"

"We?"

"What? Well, yes, of course," she called out.

Alec grinned. She hadn't meant to move upstairs by herself after all. He told himself he never actually believed she'd entertained such a vile thought of having her own quarters. Still, she hadn't properly explained her plan, either.

"We'll move upstairs tomorrow," he called out.

"Thank you, Alec."

"A wife doesn't thank her husband. Now, have your bath without interrupting me again."

Alec had made his tone as harsh as he could manage. Jamie's laughter indicated it hadn't been harsh enough, however. His shoulders slumped with disappointment. "Tell me what you learned," he ordered Gavin as he leaned back against the mantel.

256

"Henry had a long conversation with Jamie, then went back to his duties. As you know, our blacksmith's hearing is anything but sound. He said he was bent over his worktable and didn't notice anyone coming or going. I questioned all the others, Alec."

"And . . . ?"

Gavin shook his head. "They'd gone for their nooning meal."

"Someone must have seen—"

"Alec, the hill was all but deserted," Gavin interrupted. "Why don't you want to tell Jamie?"

"I don't want her to worry," Alec admitted.

"She needs to be on her guard."

"No, we'll be on our guard for her. Once we've found out who it was, then I'll tell her. She isn't going to be left alone again. When I can't be by her side, either you or Marcus will be."

Gavin nodded. "I don't want her frightened, either," he whispered. "She has come to mean a great deal to me," he admitted. "I cannot believe this treachery."

"It's one of our own," Alec stated. "And when I find him . . ."

Jamie's voice reached the men then. She was singing to herself while she had her bath, a rather bawdy English ballad it was, which drew smiles and raised eyebrows from her appreciative audience. "She acts as though nothing out of the ordinary has taken place," Alec remarked, shaking his head over that odd fact.

"I understand why she wants her bedroom upstairs," Gavin said. "'Tis the truth, milord, you can hear every little sound."

Alec nodded. "Keep everyone outside the hall," he ordered. He moved away from the hearth.

"Where are you going, Alec?"

"To bed."

"To bed?" Gavin repeated, looking incredulous. "It isn't even noon yet."

Alec turned around and gave his second-in-command a most exasperated look.

"See that I'm not disturbed," Alec stated.

Gavin finally understood. The soldier grinned as he walked toward the entrance. His intent was to stand guard in front of the double doors. "Have a fair rest, Alec," he called out, the laughter in his voice quite obvious.

Jamie had finished her bath and had just stood up in the tub when Alec came strolling around the screen. As soon as she saw him, she let out a loud gasp and sat back down. She tried to cover her breasts by bringing her knees up and leaning forward.

"I don't have any clothes on," she informed him, stating the obvious.

He never paused in his stride. Jamie suddenly found herself hauled up against his chest. He turned with her in his arms. Before she could even think to ask him what in heaven's name he was doing, he had her flat on the bed. She didn't have time to blush. Alec trapped her hands above her head and covered her with his body.

He didn't kiss her but seemed content to grin down at her with that rascal's look on his face.

Her breasts were warmed by his bare chest, her thighs heated by his own heavy ones, and she couldn't seem to stop rubbing her toes against his bare legs.

He'd taken his boots off. That thought registered in her befuddled mind just as the realization he might want to make love to her hit. "Alec, are you thinking what I think you're thinking?"

"You're wearing my plaid now," he countered. "That's what I'm thinking."

"I'm not wearing anything," she whispered.

"Aye, you are. Your back is covered by the plaid blanket and I'm covering your front with my plaid. Yes, you're wearing my plaid all right."

She couldn't fault that reasoning. "Is this how you think to get me to rest, husband?" she asked, a teasing lilt in her voice.

He nodded. Her disappointment couldn't have been more obvious.

"You will rest," he told her.

"I'm not at all tired."

"You will be." He nudged her legs apart and settled himself between her thighs. "You'll be very tired when I've finished with you. I promise."

He was looking a little too arrogant, to her way of thinking. She pulled her hands away from his easy grip and put them around his neck. "You'll be just as tired, husband, when I've finished with you. I promise."

He might have managed a smile, but the passion in her was already affecting him. Her eyes had turned a deep violet. Her legs were moving restlessly against him. When she moved so she could keep him pressed more intimately against her, he let out a low growl of desire.

He nibbled at her lips, just to make her frustrated, then slowly drew her full lower lip inside his mouth. She sighed, telling him without words how much she liked what he was doing to her. His hands moved to cup the sides of her face to keep her just where he wanted her while he took his sweet time ravishing her. He was going to make slow love to her, no matter how much she provoked him.

Her lips were so soft, so pliant, and when his tongue finally sank deep inside her warm mouth, she started to make those sexy little whimpers in the back of her throat. He stroked, plundered, gave, and took, until Jamie was pulling on his hair with her demand for more.

The sounds she gave him made him forget his good intentions. The sleek thrusts of his tongue made her bolder. He placed wet, hot kisses along her neck, drawing shivers from her. She caressed his shoulders, his back, his buttocks, drawing tremors from him.

They both took his clothes off. Then Jamie pushed him onto his back and stretched out on top of him. He trapped her legs between his own as soon as she started rubbing against him. She leaned up on her elbows, shivering again when she saw the hot look of desire in his eyes. "I want to touch you the way you touch me," she whispered. "Please, Alec? Your body belongs to me as much as my body belongs to you, doesn't it?"

He was in wholehearted agreement. Yet he couldn't find

his voice to tell her she was right, his body did belong to her. She must have decided she had his permission, however, for she got a most mischievous look in her eyes.

He understood her intent when she lowered her head and began to rain hot kisses down his chest. He made a hissing sound when her tongue circled his right nipple. Her fingers were magical, scorching. And her mouth . . . dear God, her mouth made him forget to breathe. She kept edging down, lower, lower still, until she had reached the object of her quest. She bit the inside of his thigh when he tried to stop her. His hands fell to his sides then in total, blissful surrender.

She was awkward at first, but her enthusiasm made her innocence all the more arousing. And when she finally took him into her mouth, Alec closed his eyes and let her fire consume him. It was agony. It was heaven. Only when he knew he was about to spill his seed did he finally take control of her. He knew he wasn't being very gentle. Yet his need to fill her completely, to try to give her fulfillment before he found his own made him all the rougher.

She didn't seem to mind. In truth, she was as rough as he was in her own demands. Her nails dug into his backside, and she arched up against him so forcefully that he was fully imbedded inside her before they'd rolled all the way over. They lay on their sides facing each other, each watching the passion in the other's gaze. Their breathing was shallow, their skin slick with sweat. The wonderful scent of their lovemaking filled the air between them.

"I love the taste of you," she whispered. "Did you like—"

"Oh, God, yes, I liked . . ." He let out a low groan when she draped her leg over his hip. "Don't move, not just . . . don't . . ."

She wanted to tell him she was trying not to move, but it felt so incredibly good when she did move that she couldn't seem to stop herself. His hand moved down between their joined bodies, and he touched her just where her body needed his touch so desperately.

They both started moving together then. Their mating was wild, primitive, overwhelming.

And filled with love.

Alec didn't have the strength to wait any longer. He felt her tighten around him, felt the first spasms of her surrender, and immediately poured his seed into her.

It took him a long while before he could move. Then he rolled onto his back again, keeping her against him.

He sure as hell hoped he hadn't just killed her with his passion. He smiled over that rather arrogant notion, admitting to himself that his lusty wife had very nearly killed him.

He wanted to tell her how very pleased he was with her, wanted to hear her words of praise, too. No, he decided. He wanted more than that, more than pretty words of praise.

It was high time the little woman realized just what her real duty was. He shouldn't have to explain it to her, however. He wanted her to understand without being instructed.

It was her duty to love him.

The full realization of why he wanted her love hit him like a blow: he was already in love with her.

How in God's name had it happened? She was the most opinionated, ill-tempered, illogical, stubborn-to-the-bone woman he'd ever encountered. No one else would have her, he told himself. He smiled then, recognizing his own lie. Oh, they'd have her, all right, but she belonged to him.

With a resigned sigh, Alec closed his eyes and gave Jamie a fierce hug. He could hear her ragged breathing still, could feel her heart pounding in rhythm with his own. Her passion belonged to him, too, he thought to himself.

And his heart belonged to her. Alec let out a loud yawn. He guessed he was never going to get over this strange affliction.

His gentle little wife needed her rest, he decided with another yawn. He would stay with her for just another minute or two, until he was certain she'd fallen asleep.

It was his last thought before he started snoring.

He knows now that someone tried to kill his wife. By nightfall everyone will have heard of the sin. She'll be guarded well. He won't want to take any chances with her safety.

He doesn't understand that she wasn't meant to die yet. I'm much more cunning than he is, but I wish I could boast to someone of my prowess. I dare not, of course, and must therefore let them all believe they intervened in time. Oh, I knew she would be saved. The fire wouldn't have gone undetected. I knew.

It is his torment I want to see now, not his anguish. I'll not finish the kill until tomorrow . . . perhaps even the day after if I can control my greed.

I can still hear his scream. He was calling her name. I think he has begun to love her. This lesson will be all the sweeter if he does. . . .

I want to touch her when she's dying.

Chapter Fourteen

Jamie gave Gavin quite a start when she came up behind him and gently tapped him on his shoulder. He had not heard her approach. He whirled around to meet the challenge, then eased his stance when he saw it was his mistress standing before him. She was carrying a pair of shoes. He stared at them, feeling foolish, then admitted the obvious. "I never heard you approaching."

"I didn't mean to startle you," Jamie replied. "And do lower your voice, Gavin. Alec's having a little nap."

"The Kincaid?"

"Please, Gavin, don't shout so," Jamie said. "You needn't look so incredulous, either. Alec is human, after all. He wouldn't be sleeping so soundly if he didn't need the rest, now, would he?"

Gavin shook his head. He was trying desperately not to shout with laughter. The Kincaid hadn't looked the least bit fatigued the last time he'd seen him. Of course, he been on his way to bed, but Gavin knew he hadn't planned on doing any sleeping.

God, he couldn't wait to bait him.

Jamie took hold of Gavin's arm to balance herself while she put her shoes on. "I believe I'll ask Hessie to help me clean the bedroom upstairs now." She let go of his arm, smoothed her skirts, and tried to walk around him.

Gavin quickly moved to block her path. "I'll send one of the men to get her for you," he announced.

"The walk will do me good."

"Save your strength for your chore," Gavin advised.

"All right, Gavin," Jamie agreed, thinking to placate the soldier. He looked worried. She gave him a perplexed look. "Are you feeling well? You're acting very strange, you are."

He let her put the back of her hand to his brow before he answered her. "I'm feeling quite well, Jamie. Now, why don't you get started on your chore?"

She gave him another long look before she turned and started up the steps. Gavin was right behind her. She didn't make mention of that oddity until she reached the third door. Then she turned around to him again.

He blurted out his explanation before she could ask. "I thought if there was something you needed moved about, I could lend you a hand."

She offered him a pretty smile. "How very thoughtful of you, Gavin. Father Murdock already helped me move a chest, though, and there's now plenty of space for my things when they arrive."

"Your things did arrive, milady," Gavin suddenly remembered. "Early this morning. Should I have the men bring the baggage up from the lower bailey?"

"If you would, Gavin," Jamie answered. "Did you see . . . Was there a chair among the items in the wagon?"

"There wasn't a wagon's worth," Gavin explained. "It isn't possible for a wagon to make the narrow climb. There were four packhorses," he continued when he saw how disappointed she was looking. "Packed to the sky, milady, and yes, I did notice a rather odd-looking—"

"My very own chair," she interrupted, clasping her hands together. "'Tis odd because of the legs, you're thinking, but it rocks back and forth, Gavin. It belonged to my mama's family. Papa liked to sit in it every night and it was most thoughtful of him to send it on to me."

"A chair that rocks, milady?"

"I know," she said with a sigh. "The novelty will never catch on I fear. Still, it was my mother's and I will of course keep it until I die. It shall be handed down from generation to generation."

Gavin wondered what daft man had fashioned such an illogical chair but wisely kept his thoughts to himself.

He left Jamie to her dusting. He accompanied her up the stairs just to make certain no one was waiting to catch her unaware. Marcus was just coming inside when Gavin started down the steps. "Marcus, I need have a word with you," he called out.

"Aye, Gavin?"

The second-in-command didn't explain himself until he had Marcus well inside the great hall. From where they stood, Gavin could keep his eye on the door above the stairs. No one could go in or out without him noticing. "I want two soldiers below the window."

"What window?"

"Jamie's working in the first room above the stairs," Gavin explained. "Put two soldiers outside the door and two others below her window."

"Do I give them a reason?" Marcus asked, frowning intently.

"Of course. They protect their mistress," Gavin snapped out.

"Gavin, what are you trying to tell me?" Marcus asked, his patience wearing thin.

"You haven't heard?"

"Heard what?"

Gavin let out a sigh, then explained the near tragedy. "Someone trapped her inside, Marcus. I'm the one who lifted the beam of wood away from the door," he couldn't help but boast. "And still I could barely believe it."

"Who could have done such a thing?"

"No one saw anyone near the ridge," Gavin explained. "And Alec wants you and me to keep our guard up."

"He mentioned me specifically?" Marcus asked, looking as though he didn't believe that.

"He did. He values your loyalty, Marcus. Do you doubt it?"

Marcus shook his head. "I've not given him reason to doubt my loyalty," he said. "Still, I made it obvious I wasn't pleased with his marriage, forced or not."

"You insult your laird if you believe—"

"Nay," he returned, his voice emphatic. "I'm doing just the opposite. He shows he values me, Gavin, and I'm . . . humbled by his faith in me."

Gavin shouted with laughter. "You've never spoken so passionately before, and here I am laughing at you. Don't take offense, good friend, it's just that your face has heated up to a full blush."

Marcus lost his scowl when Gavin whacked him on his shoulder. He even managed a rare smile.

Both soldiers quit their smiling when their laird joined them. The look on Alec's face didn't suggest lighthearted conversation.

"Where's my wife?"

His bellow was so loud Gavin thought the soldiers training in the lower bailey surely heard him.

"She's above the stairs, cleaning the far room," Gavin explained.

"She's alone?"

"I checked the room before she entered," Gavin rushed out. "No one can go in or out without my watching," he added.

Alec nodded. "I want the two of you to stay with her until I return," he ordered. "She doesn't take a step without one of you in front of her and the other in back. Do you understand?"

Gavin and Marcus nodded. "She's going to wonder why," Marcus said then. "She's English, Alec, not stupid."

Gavin was more amazed by Marcus's jesting tone of voice than Alec appeared to be. "Yes, she will wonder," he agreed.

"Then let the woman wonder," Alec snapped. "Just tell

her it is by my order. The woman shouldn't be doing common chores, damn it all," he added.

"She wanted to, Alec," Gavin said. "And I could see she needed to work off some of her energy. Perhaps she borrowed some of your strength. You look plain tuckered out to me, if I may say so. Do you need a longer nap, milord?"

"He had a nap?" Marcus interjected, looking quite incredulous.

"Your amusement displeases me," Alec stated. "And if you two keep smiling at me like that, I swear to God I'll flatten both of you. When I'm done, I promise you'll sleep a hell of a lot longer than I did."

That threat gained him just the amount of respect he wanted. "I'm going to speak to Angus," he called over his shoulder. "I'll be back in a few minutes."

Alec's mood was as fierce as the rising wind when he made his way to Angus's cottage. The shouting he heard when he reached his faithful soldier's home told him Angus wasn't having a much better time of it.

Elizabeth opened the door. She gave her laird a wide smile, indicating she wasn't the least bit upset by her husband's bellowing. "You look none the worse for wear, Elizabeth, living with a wildman," Alec told her as he entered their home.

"Your wife warned me it wouldn't be easy trying to keep Angus resting. She was right, too, for Angus really has turned into a bear. He's a most difficult man to love right now," she added in a raised voice so that her husband would be sure to hear, "but I'm certain that once the threads are pulled out of his chest, he'll ease up with his constant complaining."

"Will you quit talking about me in such a disrespectful manner?" Angus shouted from his bed. "The laird has come to see me, wife. He doesn't want to listen to a woman's complaining."

Elizabeth gave Alec an exasperated look before she rounded on her husband. "May I offer him a drink of wine?" she asked.

Angus gave her a disgruntled look, then nodded. "I could use a spot myself."

Elizabeth ignored that hint. She poured Alec a fair portion of dark red wine and gave her husband a cup of water. Alec would not have been surprised if Angus had started growling. "I'll leave you two to your visit," Elizabeth said. She bowed to Alec and started out the doorway.

"Elizabeth? Come here before you leave," Angus instructed.

Alec leaned against the window ledge and watched Angus's pretty little wife hurry over to her husband's side. He'd caught Elizabeth's blush and understood the reason for her embarrassment when Angus reached up with his good hand, wrapped it around the back of her neck, and dragged her forward. He kissed her long and passionately.

He whispered something to her when she straightened back up, then patted her backside. Elizabeth fairly flew out the doorway.

"She's a good woman," Angus said with a long sigh. He tossed the water from his cup on the earthen floor, then got out of his bed to search for the jug of wine.

"She took it with her," Alec announced with a laugh. "The woman knows you better than you think she does."

Angus looked pleased with that statement. He motioned for Alec to share a portion of his drink with him, and when his laird had complied, he took a long swallow. "Lord, that tastes good. Your wife has told Elizabeth I can't have any wine until the threads come out. Only God knows why she would say such a monstrous thing. Elizabeth obeys every order though. I'm damned to misery with the two of them pecking at me like hens, Alec. You should have let me die, man, and saved me from such—"

"Angels?"

Angus nodded. "Did you have something in particular you wanted to discuss with me, or did you just want to see my sorry state?"

"Close the door, Angus," Alec directed. "I don't want anyone to overhear our talk. I need some information, friend, and advice."

Angus kicked the door shut. "I can tell it's serious, Alec. Your expression is grim."

Alec explained what had happened to Jamie. He ended the narrative by telling Angus that Jamie didn't know someone had tried to kill her.

The two men discussed the added protection that would be needed until the culprit was found. Though Angus wasn't an old man by any measure, he was still three summers senior to his laird, and in Alec's mind, three summers the wiser.

Angus sat down in a chair and propped his feet up on the bed. His scowl was as deep as Alec's by the time they'd finished making their plans.

When Alec started pacing the length of the room, Angus knew there was more to be discussed. He patiently waited for his laird to continue.

Long, silent minutes passed before Alec turned back to Angus. "Angus, I want you to tell me everything you remember about Helena. You were here, with Marcus and Gavin, during the short time I was married to her. Since I was away—"

"Aye, you were doing the king's business most of that time," Angus agreed. "Do you realize, Alec, this is the first time you've said her name since the burying day?"

"I wanted to put it behind me," Alec announced. "Yet I've always . . ." He stopped mid-sentence, shook his head, and then commanded once again that Angus tell him what he knew about Helena.

The Kincaid spent a good half-hour questioning his trusted friend. His mood wasn't much improved when he left Angus. Elizabeth had been hovering outside the door. Alec winked at her before leaving, causing yet another blush.

Alec had just reached the top of the hill when he saw Jamie in the window above the first story. If she'd just turned a little to the left, she would have seen him. Jamie's attention, however, was centered on the two soldiers lounging against the stone wall below her.

She was smiling. His mood immediately lightened. Lord, she was enchanting. He thought she was a bonny lass indeed with her hair tied up on top of her head. Long curly strands had already worked their way down the sides of her face. There were smudges of dirt on her nose and forehead. She would need yet another bath before nightfall, he decided with a grin.

Something one of the soldiers was saying to the other drew her full attention.

While Alec watched, Jamie braced her elbows on the ledge and leaned farther out. He could tell she was vastly amused by the story one soldier was relating to his friend.

Alec moved closer, then came to a sudden stop when he realized his men were speaking in Gaelic.

And she understood every damn word.

He was too surprised to be angry with her. Then he heard the last of an old jest the soldier was telling his friend, about a Scottish warrior finding an unclothed woman stretched out on the roadside. As was the man's natural inclination, the warrior immediately fell upon her and had his way with her.

The younger soldier let out a good snort of appreciation before his friend continued the telling. He explained then that another Scottish warrior came upon the scene and immediately shamed his friend by telling him the woman was obviously dead, for God Almighty's sake, and only a vile infidel would want to mate with a dead woman.

Jamie's hands had covered her mouth, probably to keep her laughter contained. Her eyes were sparkling with pleasure, too. She waited in anticipation for the punch line of the jest.

Alec waited to see her reaction.

"Dead?" the soldier shouted. "I thought she was English."

Jamie lost her smile then. She disappeared from the window while the two unsuspecting soldiers continued to laugh with merriment. She was back in his vision quickly, though, balancing a large bucket of water in her hands. Alec held his laughter as he watched her struggle with the awkward weight. He didn't bother to warn his men. Jamie took careful aim, then smiled with the joy of victory when the soapy water poured over her victims.

"Pray, do forgive me," she called down when they'd finished their litany of curses and turned to look up at her. "I had no idea you were standing there," she lied, ever so sweetly.

"It's Lady Kincaid," the one soldier gasped out to the other.

Both men were immediately contrite for having yelled. They apologized profusely. As they rushed past Alec, he heard one remark that it was a blessing their mistress didn't understand Gaelic, else she surely would have been offended by their crude remarks.

But she had understood. Alec did laugh then, a full booming sound that drew his wife's attention.

She smiled down at him. "You're in a fine mood, husband," she called out. "Are you feeling rested, then?"

She would have to bring up his nap. Alec quit his laughing. He decided two could play this foolish game of deception, and his mind was already thinking of the remarks he was going to make—all in Gaelic, of course—just to goad her temper. She wouldn't be able to retaliate, for to do so would prove she understood what he'd said.

He would beat her at her own game. Alec looked forward to the insults he planned to hurl at her. She was such a little temptress when she was riled. And he was just the man to rile her.

She was filled with surprises, pretending ignorance whenever Gaelic was spoken in her presence. Hell, he'd ordered his men to strengthen their skills in her language just to make her adjustment easier. Why, she'd have them all strutting around in English garb by winter if he wasn't more careful, Alec decided. That thought gave him a chill.

"Well, Alec? Why were you laughing?" Jamie asked again, leaning farther out on the ledge.

"Will you watch what you're doing?" he shouted up at her. "You're going to fall on your head, you daft woman."

She moved back a pace. "Thank you for being so concerned, husband. Now will you tell me why you were laughing?"

Alec recounted the tale he'd overheard, just to goad her.

Jamie didn't let him finish the jest, though. "I've heard that old jest, Alec," she called out. "The woman wasn't dead," she added. "She was Scottish, and that's that."

She left the window before Alec could argue with her.

She met him at the bottom of the steps. "What's all this clutter?" he asked in a growl. The distance between them was filled with bundles. A rather odd-looking chair, the seat as wide as two good-sized men, topped the pile.

"My possessions," Jamie announced. "Some will go into our bedroom, Alec, and the rest belong in the hall."

"I don't like clutter," Alec stated. He reached down, grabbed a tapestry, and held it up so that he could see the design. Jamie skirted her way around her things and snatched the tapestry out of Alec's hands.

"Don't frown so, husband," she whispered, for both Gavin and Marcus were observing the scene. "I thought we'd place this tapestry above your mantel," she continued.

"What the hell is it?" he growled. "I can't make . . ."

"You were looking at the wrong side," Jamie returned. She hurried over to Gavin, handed the tapestry to him. "Please hang this—as straight as a lance, if you please. And try not to look at it while you're hanging it, Gavin. I want you to be surprised."

"Did you do this with your own hands, milady?" Gavin asked, smiling over her enthusiasm.

"Oh, heavens, no," Jamie told him. "Agnes and Alice did all the work. It was their birthday surprise for me." She gave both Gavin and Marcus a long look then, and turned back to Alec. "Do you know, we must conspire to have my twin sisters meet Gavin and Marcus. I do believe they'd—"

"You aren't going to arrange any marriages, Jamie," Alec interjected.

"Are the twins like you, Jamie?" Gavin asked.

"No, no, both are much prettier."

Gavin's eyes widened. "Then I must meet these ladies," he announced.

"Their personalities are just like Mary's," Alec murmured.

"Never mind," Gavin rushed out. He turned and hurried

to the fireplace to hang the tapestry. Alec's laughter trailed behind him. "Gavin, if you ever tell anyone your laird slept during the day, I'll make certain you meet both sisters."

"What nap?" Gavin called out.

Even Marcus joined in their laughter. Jamie had never seen the dark-haired soldier smile before. She instinctively smiled back. "Why are you all so amused?" she asked.

"Never mind, Jamie," Alec said.

She gave her husband a suspicious look. "Were you just suggesting to your men that my sisters might not be worthy of them?" Her hands settled on her hips and she took a step toward him in obvious challenge.

"I wouldn't saddle a goat with the pair of them."

She let out a loud gasp. He couldn't resist. He took a step forward, then added in a lazy voice, "I don't believe in being cruel to animals, wife. Surely you've noticed that fact by now. I don't use a crop on my steed and I—"

"Are you insulting my family?"

He didn't answer her, just gave her that irresistible lopsided grin she liked so much. She couldn't help but laugh. The man was completely hopeless. "You're as shameful as they come, Kincaid. I now realize you simply don't know my family well enough to make a correct evaluation. I shall, of course, take care of that matter as soon as possible."

His grin faltered. She sweetened her smile. "I shall ask them to pay us a visit, husband. A nice, long visit."

"What's this supposed to be?" Gavin called out, drawing her attention. The soldier was climbing down from the stool on which he had stood to hang the tapestry.

"Stand back and you can surely see who it is," Jamie called out.

"Is it . . . good Lord, Alec, I just hung—"

"It's William, our beloved Conquerer, Gavin. A fair depiction I'm told. He was quite a handsome man, don't you think?"

No one said a word for a long minute. Gavin and Marcus were both staring at Alec to judge his reaction.

Their laird was staring at his wife, a most incredulous look on his face.

Marcus was the first to recover. "He was fat."

"He was solid, Marcus, not fat," Jamie corrected.

"What in God's name is that thing above his head?" Gavin asked, backing up yet another step. "That yellow thing."

"It's a halo," Jamie explained.

"You sainted the man?" Marcus asked.

"It isn't official just yet," Jamie said. "But it's only a matter of time before the church does acknowledge his sainthood."

"Why?" It was Marcus who asked what all three men were thinking.

Jamie was pleased that her husband and his soldiers were showing such interest in her history. She took her time explaining to them how William had single-handedly changed the way of life in England. In great detail she instructed them in the ways of the liege lord, the duties of a vassal, the bond each formed with the other. When she was finished, she was sure they had many questions to ask her.

No one, however, seemed inclined to ask her anything. "Do you think such a system would work here?"

"It already has, Jamie, for several hundred years," Alec snapped.

"You've just described the Scottish clan, lass," Gavin said, trying to soften her disappointment in her husband's reaction.

"Tear it down."

"Alec, you cannot mean it," Jamie cried. "My sisters spent long hours working on that tapestry. It was a present for my birthday. I want to look at it whenever the mood strikes me."

Father Murdock strolled into the hall in time to overhear Jamie's remark. One good look above the hearth told him the reason for his laird's scowl.

He could see an argument was brewing. He didn't want the little lass's feelings injured and hurried to intervene in her behalf. "Now, now, Alec, she isn't meaning to insult you by putting your enemy's likeness in your home."

"Oh, no, of course I didn't mean to insult him," Jamie

said. "He, on the other hand, is certainly testing my patience, I can tell you that much."

"I'm testing your patience?" Alec all but strangled on his urge to shout. Her delicate nature was the only reason he held back.

"You certainly are, Alec Kincaid," Jamie continued. "This is my home, too, isn't it? I should be allowed to hang any tapestry I want to."

"No."

Jamie and Father Murdock frowned at Alec. Gavin and Marcus were smiling. Jamie gave Alec her back. "Father, will you help me carry this chair into the hall? Or is this against your rules too, Alec?"

Father Murdock gave the piece of furniture a thorough inspection. "There are warped blades of wood stuck to the bottom," he noted aloud. "Something's wrong here, lass."

"The chair's supposed to rock back and forth," Jamie patiently explained.

The priest wobbled his eyebrows in reaction to her statement. "I know," she said then. "It will never catch on. Still, it's a most comfortable chair. You must try it, Father."

"Perhaps another time," the priest said, taking a step away from the strange-looking contraption.

Alec let his exasperation show. He lifted the chair and carried it down the three steps, then crossed the room with long strides and placed the chair adjacent to the hearth. He tried not to look up at William's ugly face smiling down at him.

"There. Are you happy now, wife?"

He sounded surly enough for Father Murdock to intervene once again. "Why, the seat's big enough to swallow me whole."

"My sisters would sit on Papa's lap after supper, and he would tell the most wonderful stories," she confessed, a soft smile on her face over that remembrance.

Her voice held a wistful quality Alec hadn't heard before. He was puzzled by her comment, too, for she'd inadvertently failed to include herself. Or had it been inadvertent? Alec beckoned her forward with a crook of his finger.

When she stood directly in front of him and no one could overhear their conversation, he asked her to explain. "Where did you sit, Jamie? Were you squeezed up next to Mary on one knee or next to one of the twins on the other?"

The picture of four little girls sitting on their father's lap for their bedtime story made Alec smile. The twins were probably crying, Mary was probably complaining, and Jamie was probably trying to soothe everyone.

"Eleanor and Mary usually sat on one knee and the twins took up the other side."

"Eleanor?"

"The eldest daughter," Jamie explained. "She died when I was seven summers. Alec, why are you frowning now? Did I say something to upset you?"

"As usual, you haven't given me a direct answer," Alec pointed out. He was already beginning to understand, yet he wanted to make certain his guess was correct. "I asked you where you sat."

"I didn't. I usually stood by Papa's chair," she answered. "Or across the way. Why is it so important to you where I sat?"

It wasn't important to him, but he believed it had been very important to her. "Did you never have a turn?"

"There wasn't room."

That simple statement, given so matter-of-factly, all but shattered his composure. She had been the outsider. Alec suddenly wanted to beat her unfeeling stepfather to a bloody pulp. The man damn well should have made room for her.

She'd just revealed to him exactly how her mind worked, too. She'd made her father notice her. The duties . . . yes, it was clear to him now. By making herself indispensable to her papa, she'd forced him to value her. Jamie had confused love with need. He thought that perhaps, in her mind, she really didn't know the difference.

And now she was trying to get him to treat her the same way. The more duties he piled on top of her, the more importance he would be giving her.

He was damned if he did and damned if he didn't. The woman was daft, but she was his woman, and he wanted her to be happy. Still, he wasn't about to shorten her life by watching her work herself into an early grave.

There was much to consider now. Alec decided not to discuss the issue further until he'd found a way to give her proper instruction in loving and needing. He instinctively knew that simply telling her how much he cared for her wouldn't be enough. He was going to have to find a way to show her.

"No one's every going to sit in that ill-designed chair, wife," Alec announced.

"You're afraid to try it?" she challenged.

He let her see his exasperation with her before giving in to her. The chair squeaked under his weight. It fit his back quite nicely too, even when he deliberately pushed the chair to make it rock. He was sure he was going to go flying backwards. He didn't topple over, though, and he had to smile over that fact.

"I fear you're right, wife," Alec stated. "It will never catch on. Still, if you're up to the jesting you'll be getting when the soldiers see this contraption, I'll allow you to keep your chair."

"Well, of course you'll allow me to," Jamie snapped. She had her hands on her hips again.

Alec bounded out of the chair so he could tower over her when he deliberately intimidated her. "You may keep this by the hearth," he announced. "And now I'll have your appreciation."

"And William?" she asked, ignoring his suggestion that she give him proper thanks.

"William can go to—"

"The bedroom?" Father Murdock blurted out as he bounded down the steps.

"He isn't the last face I want to see before I fall asleep," Alec snapped. "Put him in the wine cellar if you're bent on hanging him someplace, Jamie, but I don't want to see his face again."

Jamie looked as if she wanted to argue with her husband. Father Murdock clasped her hand in both of his. "One bite at a time, sweet lass," he whispered to her.

Alec gave the priest a hard look, then went over to the table and poured himself a goblet of ale. The priest chased after him, pulling Jamie in his wake.

"I'll have me a goblet of water," he told Alec. A sudden thought made the priest's eyebrows wobble again. "Do you know, Alec, what you get when you mix water with ale?"

Alec nodded. "Watered-down ale," he announced.

"And once you've mixed the two, you can't separate them, can you?"

"Of course not," Alec returned. "What are you trying to tell me, Father?"

"You're wanting her to settle in," Murdock answered. "I've heard you say so many times."

"I don't deny it," Alec answered. "She will settle in."

"Do you want her to change? Do you want her to become someone else?"

"No, she pleases me the way she is," Alec admitted.

Jamie knew he'd just complimented her, but his gruff voice and frown certainly soured his praise.

"Then you don't want her to become a Scottish lass?"

"Of course not."

His voice was so emphatic that Father Murdock guessed he was as surprised as Jamie was by his own strong conviction. "She's English. She can't change that fact. But she will settle in."

"And so will you."

The priest's remark fell between them. A long minute later, Alec responded. "Explain yourself. My patience wears as thin as watered-down ale."

"Jamie's rich in her own special way of doing things. Her traditions are part of her," Father Murdock said. "Just as you have your own traditions. Can you not blend the two in a peaceful manner? A fine tapestry of our King Edgar would look handsome hanging right next to William. What think you of that idea?"

Alec didn't much like the idea, but he could tell by his wife's smile she thought it had merit. Her tender feelings got in the way of his true opinions, however, and he found himself reluctantly agreeing.

"Very well," he stated. "But the dimensions will be larger than William."

Jamie was too happy with his compliance to argue over the size of the tapestry. She personally thought Edgar's likeness should be fashioned in half the size, but she guessed she'd have to make them equal. Alec would be bound to notice. Yes, she'd make them equal. She wasn't going to put a halo atop Edgar's head, though, and that was that.

"Thank you, Alec," she murmured.

The smile she gave him told him she thought he'd just done the bending. He was determined, however, to have the last word. "Marcus, remove that tapestry until Edgar's is completed. The soldiers will be coming inside for their meal soon. They'll be too sick to train this afternoon if they have to look at *him* while they eat."

Father Murdock waited until his laird had left the hall before he let his amusement show. The old man gave Jamie a slow wink, then strolled out of the hall, whistling a snappy Scottish tune between his chuckles. The priest couldn't wait for the next storm to start brewing.

In the Highlands, when it rained, it hailed. Jamie had just asked Marcus and Gavin if they didn't have something they needed to do. She'd just started back up the stairs and noticed the two of them chasing after her.

Both soldiers shook their heads. She put them to work then, carrying her baggage up to the clean bedroom. She thought it strange the important soldiers would want to do servants' work.

When her tasks were finished, she came back downstairs to repair her appearance. She noticed Annie and Edith standing together near the hearth. They'd been staring at her chair, but both turned when she called out a greeting to them.

Annie was smiling until she caught Edith's dark scowl. Then she joined in and scowled, too.

Jamie didn't pay any attention to Annie. The child couldn't help the way she was. Edith was another kettle of fish altogether.

Jamie thought Edith had to be the most unbending

woman in all of Scotland. There was a rigidness in her bearing and appearance that wasn't at all appealing. The woman always had her hair plaited into a crown atop her head. There was never a single strand left unattended. Her plaid gown was always spotless, too. Jamie had never seen her disheveled. Yes, Edith was as thorough in her grooming as she was in her hatred for her mistress.

And her mistress had had enough.

"What happened to you?" Edith called out, a snarl in her voice. "Did you fall into a bucket of suds?"

Marcus had been standing behind Jamie. He took a step forward, all but blocking her view with his broad back, and shouted at his sister. "Don't you dare use that tone of voice with your laird's wife."

Jamie felt as though she were in the middle of thunderclouds. Marcus's roar made her head start pounding. She prodded Marcus's shoulder, and when he'd turned around, she asked him for permission to handle his sister.

He immediately nodded agreement.

Jamie walked to the center of the hall. "Annie, go outside, child. Edith, you'll stay right where you are."

Her voice must have lacked authority, she guessed, when Edith completely ignored her command and started for the doorway.

Marcus intervened once again. His harsh command made Edith come to an abrupt stop.

Jamie turned to thank him, then asked if she could have a few minutes alone with Edith. In truth, she didn't want any witnesses to her conversation.

Gavin answered her. He stood on the bottom step, scowling fiercely at Edith. "Neither one of us is leaving."

She decided not to argue with the soldier. He did look quite determined. She walked back over to Marcus. When she was standing directly in front of him, she brushed her hair out of her eyes and motioned him closer to her.

Her whisper was so soft that only he could hear what she was saying. Marcus's expression didn't change, but when she was finished, he gave her a quick nod.

She thanked the soldier, then turned to confront his sister.

"Since the moment I arrived here, you've treated me like a leper," she told Edith. "I'm quite tired of your attitude."

Edith snickered right in her mistress's face.

"You're unwilling to try to get along, then?" she asked, her voice harder.

"I see no reason to get along with the likes of you," Edith muttered.

"Marcus?" Jamie called out. She hated having to ask his assistance, but she wanted to push through Edith's anger.

"Yes, milady?"

"If I ask Alec to have Edith removed from Kincaid land by nightfall, will he agree?"

Edith let out a loud gasp.

"He will."

"Where will I go?" Edith asked. "Marcus, you cannot let—"

"Silence!"

Neither Marcus nor Gavin had ever heard Jamie use that tone of voice. Gavin smiled in reaction. The look of outrage on Edith's face made him want to laugh.

Edith's hands were clenched at her sides. She was obviously furious. That wasn't good enough. Jamie wanted to push her beyond reason. She hoped that once her anger was completely out of control, she wouldn't guard her words. Then Jamie would be able to find out why her hatred was so fierce.

"I'm mistress here, Edith," she said in a low, arrogant voice. "If I wish you to become an outcast, I will get my way."

"Marcus would never let you."

"He would," Jamie boasted. Lord, she hated the horrible lies she was telling. "He's your brother, and your guardian, too, but Alec is his laird. Marcus is loyal to my husband," she added. "Unlike you. You aren't loyal to anyone, are you?"

"I am," Edith shouted.

"Perhaps once you were," Jamie countered, affecting a

shrug. "Yes, you were probably loyal to Alec when he was wed to Helena. Father Murdock told me you were very close to Alec's first wife."

"You can't replace her. I won't let you."

"I already have."

Those last taunting words snapped the shreds of control to which Edith was clinging. Before she could stop herself, she lashed out at her mistress. All she wanted to do was take the smug look off Jamie's face. She wanted to hurt her mistress as much as Jamie was hurting her.

Jamie had been waiting for the attack. She was smaller than Edith in stature, but much stronger. She'd captured Edith's wrist and had the woman kneeling on the floor before she'd finished her first scream.

Both Marcus and Gavin had rushed forward to intervene. They stopped when they reached Jamie's side.

"Stay out of this," she told the men while she kept her stare on her prey. She wasn't holding Edith's wrist now, but clasping her hand against her waist. She was gently stroking Edith's shoulder, too, and trying to maintain her balance at the same time. Edith was sobbing against Jamie's skirts.

No one said a word until Edith had gained a bit of control. "Oh, my God, I was going to strike you! I'm so sorry," Edith whispered. "When I saw you and Father Murdock moving Helena's chest out of the bedroom, I was so incensed. I didn't want you to throw her things away. I've been so filled with—"

"I wasn't going to throw Helena's things away," Jamie explained. "I just moved the chest to the other bedroom, Edith."

"Her baby's clothes were in the chest," Edith continued, as if she hadn't heard Jamie's explanation. "She'd worked so diligently on the little gowns."

"She wanted to have Alec's child, then?" Jamie asked, her voice a gentle caress.

"Please say you forgive me, milady," Edith sobbed, returning to her other worry. "I didn't mean to hurt you."

"You didn't hurt me, Edith. And I'm sorry, too."

"You're sorry?" Edith asked. She still knelt on the floor

and turned her face up to Jamie. Tears were streaming down her cheeks. Jamie used the hem of her bliaut to mop the wetness away. "I'm sorry for all the hurtful lies I just told you. Edith, you were so set against me; I did have to use a little trickery to get your attention."

"You aren't going to send me away?"

Jamie shook her head. She helped Edith stand up. "You're a very important member of this clan, Edith. I would never send you away. I lied about Helena, too. I haven't taken her place."

Edith shook her head. "But you're Alec's wife now."

"That doesn't mean we all pretend Helena never existed."

"He does."

"Alec?"

When Edith nodded, Jamie whispered, "It's painful for him."

"I don't know," Edith whispered. "I was sure he didn't care. They weren't married long, milady. There wasn't even time to bring her daughter—"

"Her what?"

She hadn't meant to shout, but Edith's casually spoken words so startled her that she could barely keep her expression contained. "Father Murdock said Alec and Helena were married only two months."

Edith nodded. "Alec was pledged to Annie," she said. "King Edgar changed his mind. Annie . . . well, she wasn't growing up quick enough, and Helena had just lost her husband. His name was Kevin. He died protecting his king. Helena was swollen with Kevin's child."

Jamie almost fell down. Marcus grabbed hold of her arm to steady her. "Are you ill, milady?" he asked.

"I'm not ill," Jamie countered. "I'm bloody furious. Edith, how long was Helena wed to Kevin?"

"Six years."

"Now, tell me about this child," she demanded.

"She had a daughter," Edith announced. "Helena was waiting for Alec's return to go and get her. The little girl was being cared for by Kevin's mother."

Edith led Jamie over to the table when her mistress

announced she needed to sit down. "You are ill," Edith stammered out. "I've caused you to—"

"Well, hell, no one tells me anything," Jamie shouted. "My mother was carrying me when she wed my stepfather. And if you think I'll let that—"

Jamie finally got hold of her emotions. She noticed the soldiers worried expressions. She took a deep, calming breath, then managed a smile. "Edith and I have settled this little dispute. We're both sorry you had to witness our unladylike conduct. Now, then, I don't want either of you to mention this to Alec. You'd only embarrass us and irritate him. Isn't that right, Edith?"

She waited for Edith's quick nod, then said, "Edith, you will continue to see to the household matters. I would like to help you every now and again. Do you think we might have something other than mutton for dinner tonight? I do hate mutton."

Edith smiled. Her eyes filled with tears again. "What is this daughter's name?" Jamie asked her.

"Mary Kathleen," Edith answered. "Kevin's family has some Irish blood."

"Mary is also my sister's name," Jamie said, smiling. "And how old is this child now?"

"Three years," Edith answered. "I haven't seen my niece since the birthing. I heard Kevin's mother died three months past. A distant relation takes care of Mary now."

It took all of Jamie's determination not to let her anger show. Edith looked as if she wanted to cry again, and Jamie didn't have time to soothe her. Her mind was busy racing with her plans. "There is much for the two of us to discuss, cousin, but later, after you've repaired your hair, will be soon enough."

That remark accomplished Jamie's goal. Edith immediately bounded to her feet. "My hair has come undone?" she asked, clearly appalled. She patted the sides of her crown while she waited for an answer.

"Just a little," Jamie told her, trying not to smile.

Edith made a curtsy, then rushed out of the room.

Jamie let out a long sigh. "You've had quite a day, Jamie,"

Gavin remarked. "First you battle a fire and then you battle a determined woman."

"Actually, I battled a fat boar, then Alec, then the fire, and last, Edith," she corrected with a smile.

"A boar? You battled with a boar?" Gavin shouted.

"I'm just jesting with you," she admitted. As soon as Gavin lost some of his angry expression, she told him what happened.

When she'd finished, she couldn't help but notice how incredulous the warriors looked. "So you see, I didn't actually battle the boar. I just got in his way. Do you know this child? His name is Lindsay."

Gavin had to sit down before giving her answer. "We know of his clan."

"My God, Jamie," Marcus began, "his father is a powerful—"

"Ruthless," Gavin interjected.

"Laird," Marcus finished.

"You could have gotten yourself killed," Gavin shouted as he bounded back to his feet.

"Don't censure her, Gavin," Marcus countered. "I'm sure Alec must have—"

"I didn't exactly tell him," Jamie interrupted.

The men let her know what they thought of that sin. "Quit your scowls," Jamie ordered. "I promised that child I wouldn't be telling on him. I see no reason to tell Alec what happened. He'll only worry. I'll have your word on this, Gavin. Yours, too, Marcus."

Both warriors immediately agreed. Neither, of course, meant to honor her request, but they wanted to appease her now.

"Did anything else happen that you've forgotten to mention?" Gavin drawled out.

"Give me time," Jamie countered. "The day's not half done, if you'll remember."

Gavin smiled, and miracle of miracles, Marcus smiled again, too. "It has been quite a morning," she said with a sigh. "Marcus, do you know where Mary Kathleen is?"

He nodded. "Is it a fair distance away from here?"

"Three hours' ride," he stated with a shrug.

"Then we'd best get started right away."

"I beg your pardon, milady?" Marcus asked. He turned to give Gavin a puzzled look, wondering if he'd understood their mistress's announcement. Jamie had already disappeared behind the screen.

"We'll leave at once," she called out. She peeked around the corner. "You wouldn't mind taking me, would you, Marcus? 'Tis the truth, even with proper directions, I would probably get lost."

"Where are we going?" Marcus asked.

"To see my daughter."

It was a lie, of course, for Jamie had no intention of merely seeing her daughter. She couldn't very well tell the soldiers the full truth, however, not if she wanted to gain their cooperation.

Besides, she guessed they'd find out soon enough.

Mary Kathleen was coming home where she belonged.

And that was that.

Chapter Fifteen

Alec's patience was nearing the shouting point. He blamed his ill temper on the fact that the early afternoon training session wasn't going at all well. It was teeth-grinding, frustrating work, for he was now instructing the younger, unseasoned warriors.

Young David, Laird Timothy's second son, bore the brunt of Alec's frustration. The boy didn't seem to get any better, no matter how long he trained. Alec knocked David and his sword to the ground for the third time, using the back of his bare hand to add humiliation to his lesson in defense. David's weapon went flying. It would have found a target in another soldier's leg if the older warrior hadn't sidestepped just in time.

"I should kill you now and be done with it," Alec roared at the boy. "David, you won't last five minutes in true battle unless you learn to pay attention to what you're doing. And hold on to your weapon, for God's sake."

Before the yellow-haired warrior could respond to that criticism, Alec hauled him to his feet. He had David by the throat now, thinking he might just strangle a bit of good sense into his head one way or another. When David's freckled face turned blotchy, Alec knew he had his full attention.

"Alec?" one of the soldiers called out.

Alec tossed David to the ground before turning to the soldier. He noticed the silence then. His soldiers had all quit their tasks without gaining his permission. That fact settled in his mind a scant second before he realized they were all staring at the top of the hill.

He knew before he turned around that Jamie was somehow responsible for this interruption. She was the only one who could cause such astonishment in his usually disciplined older soldiers, the only one to incite such chaos.

He had to brace himself, then thought he was prepared for just about anything, yet the sight of his wife riding down the hill on Wildfire's back did take his breath away. She was riding bareback, her hair flying out behind her, and Alec was afraid to move lest he startle her. She'd surely fall to the ground then and break her stubborn neck.

She rode like a queen. Even from the distance separating them, Alec could see her soft, beguiling smile.

Wildfire trotted down toward the slope where Alec and his men waited. Gavin and Marcus rode their mounts behind her.

Alec motioned Jamie over to his side with an arrogant wave of his hand. Though he was determined to hold on to his anger over her rude interruption of his duties, he was finding it a difficult endeavor. Pride kept getting in the way of his goal, his pride in his wife's horsemanship.

He lost his anger altogether when he spotted the bow and quiver of arrows slung over her shoulder.

He tried not to laugh.

Jamie obeyed her husband's command without any visible movement on the reins. She stopped Wildfire by using the pressure of her knees to give her command.

Alec suddenly wanted to feel the pressure of her knees around him again.

"Where do you think you're going?"

"Riding."

"With bow and arrow?"

"Yes," Jamie answered, wondering over the irritation in her husband's voice. "One must always be prepared for any eventuality," she added. "I might also do a spot of hunting."

"I see."

His moods were as unpredictable as the wind, she decided, for now he looked as if he wanted to laugh at her. There was a definite sparkle in his eyes. She heard several loud chuckles from the crowd of soldiers gathered in front of her, glared at the offenders for being so rude, and then turned back to Alec.

"You're serious, aren't you, wife?"

"I am."

"You couldn't hit the side of our stables," Alec announced. "Yet you think to kill a moving target?"

"You think not?"

"I know not."

"You should have more faith in your wife," Jamie muttered as she slowly slipped the curved bow from her shoulder and reached for one of her arrows.

It was high time she set the man straight, she decided. Jamie had noticed a brown hide anchored to the large bale of hay farther down the slope. There were a good fifteen arrows clustered around the center of the hide. She motioned to the target, then said, "Will you let me hunt if I prove my skill to you?"

Marcus coughed, obviously trying to disguise his laughter. Jamie turned to frown at him while she waited for her husband to answer.

"I would not let you disgrace yourself so in front of my men," Alec announced. He wanted to goad her temper with his insolent remark, knew he'd accomplished that goal when she turned back to him. She looked as if she wanted to strangle him.

"I won't disgrace myself."

He had the audacity to grin at her. "Kindly get out of my

way, husband," she ordered. "You may laugh later," she snapped when she saw how much trouble he was having restraining himself. "If you feel so inclined."

Alec nodded, then backed several feet away.

As soon as Jamie fit her arrow to her bow, the soldiers started running for safety. Jamie guessed they didn't have much faith in her ability, either.

Wildfire's head kept getting in her way. Jamie let out a sigh. She slipped off her shoes, then stood up on the mare's back, balancing herself as gracefully as a dancer. She took aim and shot her arrow a second before Alec reached her side. Jamie sat back down on Wildfire's back, patted her horse soundly for standing so still, and then smiled at Alec.

"Now why are you angry?" she demanded.

"You will never take such chances again, wife."

His shout nearly ripped Wildfire's mane apart. The horse immediately tried to bolt, but Alec grabbed the reins and had Wildfire docile in little time.

He couldn't help but notice that Jamie never lost her balance or showed the least amount of fear.

"What are you ranting about?" Jamie asked. "What chance did I take?"

He could tell from her expression she really didn't know why he was upset with her. He took a deep breath, trying to regain his control. When she'd stood up, his heart had stopped beating.

"You could have killed yourself," he muttered between clenched teeth. "If anyone's going to kill you, it's going to be me. Don't ever stand on your mount's back again. Not ever."

"I'm used to riding that way when the mood strikes me, Alec. While she gallops through a meadow I do sometimes stand up."

"Oh, God."

"'Tis the truth," she said. "Would you like me to show—"

"No."

"Don't yell at me, Alec. It's upsetting Wildfire."

"It's you I want upset, wife," Alec returned. "Give me your word."

"Oh, all right, then," Jamie said. "I give you my word. Are you happy now?"

"I am."

"Then please remove your hand from my leg. Your grip is painful."

"Wife, do you know how close you are to real jeopardy?"

She didn't look at all worried by that threat. "Alec?"

"What?"

"How long have you had that tic in your cheek?"

He didn't answer her.

"Her arrow ain't near the others," the young soldier named David called out. The eager boy picked up Jamie's shoes and offered them to her. Jamie thanked him and quickly put them on.

"Of course my arrow isn't near the others," she told the soldier.

"You knew you'd miss?" he asked.

"I didn't miss," she countered. "You'll find my arrow in the very center. Go and fetch it for me please."

David ran back down the hill to the target. He let out a whoop of laughter. "She's right," he shouted. "Her arrow is in the center."

Jamie was watching Alec when that statement was shouted. She ignored the men's cheers. Her husband's reaction was a little disappointing. He merely raised an eyebrow.

"Gavin? I want ten more men riding with you," he shouted.

The soldier immediately turned his mount back toward the stables.

"Jamie, you've forgotten something," he said when she tried to take the reins back in her hands.

"Oh . . ." She immediately started to blush, then motioned him closer and leaned down to kiss his brow.

He couldn't hide his exasperation. "I meant you forgot your saddle," he told her.

"I don't like it," Jamie argued. "It's too new. It makes me stiff, Alec."

"Marcus, get my wife one of my old saddles. Why didn't you tell me you could ride bareback? I thought you unskilled. You did fall off your mount today."

"I didn't tell you because you would have thought me unladylike," she answered.

He had to smile over that foolish statement. "I could never think you were unladylike."

She smiled. "You're forever reminding me," he added. "I should have realized you were skilled," he admitted then. "Beak told me you were the only one who could seat the mare. Still, he added that you didn't ride often."

"He was protecting me," Jamie explained. "He thought you'd be more considerate if you thought I wasn't properly trained."

Alec grinned. "Jamie? Don't ever kiss me the way you just did."

She thought he meant not to show any affection in front of his men. He motioned her toward him with the crook of his finger again and when they were almost nose to nose, he whispered, "Kiss me like this."

He didn't even give her time to smile. His mouth settled on hers in hard, hungry demand. She didn't open her mouth quickly enough to please him, but his low growl gained her full cooperation. His tongue drove inside just in time to taste her sigh.

She didn't hear the men yelling their pleasure at being witnesses to such a blatant display of passion. Alec heard them, however, and reluctantly eased his mouth away.

Jamie looked totally confused. He was arrogantly pleased that he could so easily rob her of all her thoughts, then realized he was holding her in his arms. He didn't recall taking her off Wildfire's back.

They both smiled. "You've wasted enough of my valuable time," he told her.

Jamie laughed. The sound of soldiers riding down the hill turned her attention then. "Why must I have so many soldiers accompanying me?"

"They also like to hunt," Alec replied. He let her slide to the ground when a soldier tossed him the saddle he'd requested. Jamie held the reins while Alec adjusted the straps around the mare's belly. He lifted her onto Wildfire's back. "Have a good ride, Jamie," he told her.

"I won't be coming back empty-handed," she announced.

"I know you won't," Alec told her.

She really didn't like skirting the truth this way, but she deliberately let Alec believe she was hunting food. Besides, she thought to herself, he'd settle in once he'd gotten over his initial bluster. He'd make a proper father, too.

Jamie turned back to Marcus when they'd reached the drawbridge. "Which way, Marcus?" she called out.

"The west, milady."

Wildfire was in a full gallop when Marcus gained her side. He motioned her to follow his lead, then made a half-circle, backtracking from the way they'd started.

Marcus was polite enough not to mention her poor sense of direction. Gavin, however, took great delight in reminding her.

Jamie was too pleased with both men to take exception. They hadn't told Alec what her true destination was, after all, and she was most thankful for their silence. She didn't care if it had been deliberate or not.

Alec kept telling himself he wasn't worried, but he found himself pacing in front of the hearth after dinner was finished and his wife still wasn't home. No, he wasn't worried. Marcus and Gavin would keep her safe. She'd be home any minute now. When the sun was completely gone, then he'd worry, he told himself for the tenth time.

He had used the time of separation well. As soon as Jamie left, he had called for his mount and gone directly to Helena's clan. He'd spent several hours talking with the cousins who remembered Helena, and had learned some rather interesting facts about the woman who'd found marriage to him so foul she'd ended her life in desperation.

He found Father Murdock as soon as he returned and spent a good long while listening to his opinions. The priest was clearly amazed that his laird was now speaking of his dead wife. He hadn't even mentioned Helena's name since the day of the burial. The laird's questions were perplexing to him, but he knew better than to try to find out exactly what Alec was looking for. It wasn't his place to question.

Now Alec paced a path in the great hall while he sorted through the information.

Jamie, having just returned to the castle, stood at the top of the steps, waiting for Alec to notice her. She was just about to call out to him when he suddenly turned around.

He was so relieved to see her that he gave her a good frown.

She retaliated by smiling.

He noticed her skirt was swaying back and forth, then saw the dusty little face peeking out at him.

Gavin and Marcus flanked Jamie. They were both staring down at the child.

Jamie took a deep breath and reached for Mary Kathleen's hand. "Come and meet your father," she whispered to the little girl.

Mary Kathleen didn't want to cooperate. Alec's size obviously intimidated her. Her golden brown eyes were as wide as round trenchers. "He's going to love you with all his heart," she promised.

Before the little girl could shake her head, Jamie clasped her hand and led her down the steps.

Alec didn't have any idea what was going on. The barefoot cherub was wearing his plaid, though, indicating she belonged to a Kincaid. The ill-fitted piece of blanket was wrapped around her and tied in a knot below her chin. Alec couldn't remember ever having seen her before.

She was an appealing little girl with a mop of honey-colored curls that hung lower on one side of her face than on the other.

"Who is this?" Alec asked.

"Your daughter."

"My what?"

Jamie ignored her husband's astonishment. "Well, actually she's our daughter now," she explained. "Say hello to your papa, Mary Kathleen."

The little girl was still frightened. She continued to stare up at Alec while she twisted a lock of her hair into a knot on top of her head.

Jamie leaned down and whispered to the child. She was trying to soothe the little girl and also trying to give Alec a little more time to get used to the idea.

When Jamie straightened up again, she could tell from her husband's expression that he was going to need a lot more time.

"She's Helena's daughter," Gavin called out just to break the staring contest.

"She's my daughter now," Jamie countered. She let Mary Kathleen hide behind her back again. "It's really quite simple to understand, Alec. When you married Helena, you became Mary's papa. You were going to bring her here to live with you, weren't you? And when I wed you," she continued before Alec could answer her, "well, I then became Mary's new mother. We have both been errant in our duties to this child, husband."

"The Kincaid provided well for Helena's child," Marcus interjected.

"Her grandmother died three months past. Did you know Mary was given over to a distant relation who wanted only your grain? It pains me to admit the woman was English, Alec. And do you know there are bruises up and down your daughter's back and on her legs, too? She would have been dead in another month's time if I'd left her in such care."

He hadn't known. He looked furious, too. Jamie nodded. Then everyone started talking at once. Alec just stood there, his hands clasped behind his back, staring down at the little innocent peeking out at him from behind Jamie's skirts.

"Come here, Mary," he ordered the child.

She shook her head at him while she tried to put a good portion of Jamie's gown into her mouth.

Alec started laughing. "God help me, she's been with you less than a day and she's already taking on your stubbornness," he told Jamie.

He scooped the little girl up into his arms and held her so that they were face to face.

"Be careful of her back, Alec. She's tender."

Alec whispered something to the child, then smiled when she nodded.

"Can you get her to speak to you? She hasn't said a word to me," Jamie whispered. "You don't think something's wrong with her voice, do you?"

"Quit your worrying," Alec ordered. "She'll talk when she wants to. Won't you, Mary?"

The little girl nodded again. "She was wearing Kevin's colors," Gavin stated. "He'd roll in his grave if he could see how filthy the garment was."

"Who changed her clothes?" Alec asked.

"I did," Jamie answered. "That's when I saw all the bruises. I knew I had to bring her to you then," she added.

"Nay, wife. You'd already made that decision when you put my plaid on her."

The man was too cunning for her. "Yes, Alec," she admitted.

"You knew you were going to bring her back when you left today," he continued. "That's what you meant by not coming back from your hunt empty-handed, now, isn't it?"

He didn't sound angry, but Jamie still wasn't sure what he was thinking. "Yes," she answered. "I had already made the decision."

Alec gently tucked the little girl under his arm, treating her much like a burlap bag of feed. "That isn't how you hold a baby," Jamie blurted out. "She's only three summers, Alec."

Mary Kathleen didn't seem to mind, however. She let out a giggle.

"What happened after you saw the bruises?" Alec asked her.

"I became . . . angry."

"How angry?"

"I threw the plaid on the ground," Jamie blurted out. "It was a deliberate insult. I did it on purpose. I restrained myself though. I wanted to give that horrible woman a few good bruises to remember me by."

"I spit on it."

Marcus had made that announcement. "In front of witnesses, Alec."

"Good."

Marcus lost his frown when he'd gained his lord's approval. "It means war," he reminded Alec.

"Two wars," Gavin interjected. "You're forgetting Helena's family. They'll also get involved."

"No," Alec countered. "They won't care. Why do you think Annie came with Helena when she wed me? The two sisters had been sorely mistreated by their family. The king was aware of this, of course."

"And that's why you were married to her so soon after her first husband's death? To protect her?" Jamie asked.

Alec nodded. When he finally looked at his wife, he was smiling. "Thank you."

"Why do you thank me, Alec?"

"For bringing our daughter home," he answered.

She was nearly overwhelmed by his compassion. Her eyes filled with tears and she would have burst into sobs if Alec hadn't pretended to drop Mary Kathleen just then. Jamie shouted instead.

Both father and daughter laughed. Alec all but flipped the child over his arms, then held her up to face him again. "Wife? This babe smells as rank as Murdock. Bathe her," he ordered. "Marcus, have someone go find Edith and Annie. They'll want to meet their niece."

"Then you truly claim Mary Kathleen as your daughter," she asked, her worry still obvious.

He stared at her a long moment before answering. "How could I not?"

She was too overcome with emotion to give him answer. When Alec handed the child to her, Jamie settled her on her hip.

Angus and Elizabeth walked into the hall just as Jamie started for the tub behind the screen. She quickly explained all about her new daughter. Mary Kathleen turned quite shy and hid her face against the crook of Jamie's neck. Elizabeth offered to help bathe the little girl. Jamie agreed, then caught Angus's remark about arrangements being made for their king's visit.

"Your king is coming to see you?" she asked Alec. She looked appalled.

Alec raised an eyebrow over such a bizarre reaction. "He is."

"Edgar?"

"'Tis the only Scottish king we have," he answered.

"When does he arrive?"

"Tomorrow. Does this news displease you, Jamie? You look upset."

"He's known for his cruelty," she blurted out.

Everyone in the hall gave her incredulous looks. "Edgar?" Alec asked. "Jamie, he's known for his kindness."

The grumbles of agreement made her feel much better. She smiled down at Mary Kathleen and then said, "I shouldn't have believed those stories. No, he couldn't have done what I heard he'd done if he's as kind as everyone says."

"What story?" Marcus asked.

"Tell us the worst," Gavin suggested. "And we'll tell you if it be true or not."

"I heard that when Edgar took over the throne, he had to unseat another and he . . . well, he blinded him so he wouldn't cause him any trouble."

No one said anything about that statement. They all looked at one another.

"I know," Jamie rushed out. "You all think me shameful for believing such gossip."

"Now, Jamie, lass, that story happens to be true," Gavin finally admitted when he realized no one else was willing to explain. "But he didn't kill his predecessor. He only blinded him."

"Aye, the man's still alive," Marcus interjected.

Alec watched the way his soldiers tried to allay Jamie's fears. He realized they wanted to protect her feelings as much as he did.

"How can you be smiling, Alec, over such a sin done by your own king?"

"England's king is far more ruthless," Alec stated.

"You shouldn't speak ill of Henry," she countered.

"Speak ill? Jamie, I just praised him."

He looked as if he meant what he'd just said. She gave him a good frown to let him know what she thought of his praise.

"What's your real worry, wife?"

"What if he won't let Mary stay with us?"

"He will."

"You're certain, Alec?"

Alec nodded. "Will I kneel before him, do you suppose?" she asked.

"If you want to."

"Will it make me disloyal to Henry?"

His smile was gentle. The woman was certainly lacking in her history lessons. "I doubt you'd be disloyal, Jamie. Edgar is Henry's brother-in-law."

She was so relieved by this news that her shoulders slumped. "Well, why didn't you tell me? I've been fretting like a child over this loyalty issue, Alec, and all for naught. You could have mentioned that Edgar and Henry were good friends, husband."

Jamie carried Mary behind the screen before Alec could tell her he thought she was daft.

"Why did you let her think Edgar and Henry were good friends?" Gavin asked.

"For the same reason you softened your answers about Edgar to her," Alec answered dryly. "None of us want her to worry. We're all bent on making her happy, now, aren't we?"

Gavin grinned. "Aye, we are."

They shared a laugh, but the sound was drowned out by all the noise the women were making. Jamie, Elizabeth, Edith, and Annie were taking turns bathing Mary Kathleen.

"She's a beautiful child," Elizabeth remarked.

"We must tell her so," Jamie advised. "Often. She mustn't ever feel she doesn't belong."

The bath was finally finished. Jamie stood Mary on the chest and gave her hair a proper trim.

The little girl didn't seem the least bit shy with the women, but it was still obvious she preferred Jamie's attention most of all. Once she was dressed in a clean white sleeping gown Edith had provided, she reached up for Jamie to hold her.

While Mary ate her dinner, Edith went upstairs with Annie to make her bedroom ready for her. It had been decided that Mary would sleep in the chamber next to Alec and Jamie. If the child cried out in the night, Jamie was certain she'd hear her.

"All mothers are light sleepers," she stated. "We instinctively know when our daughters need us. You'll understand what I'm saying, Elizabeth, after your baby is born."

Jamie's voice was so enthuasiastic, Elizabeth didn't have the heart to remind her she'd only been a mother for half a day. She agreed instead.

"Angus grows impatient to have the threads taken out of his chest wound," she reminded Jamie. "He's waiting at the table for you."

"You sit next to him," Jamie replied. "He won't shout as much if you're near."

"It will pain him?"

"Don't be fretting," Jamie soothed. "It won't hurt him at all. He'll be shouting over the inconvenience of it all, though."

Elizabeth hurried over to the table to do as Jamie suggested. Alec had just started a fire in the hearth. His back was turned to Jamie, but once he'd stood and noticed her, he only had enough time to accept the daughter she thrust into his arms.

Alec didn't have any idea what was expected of him now. Still, he wanted to please Jamie. He stared down at Mary, holding her awkwardly under her arms.

"You're not afraid of me, are you, Mary?" he asked in Gaelic. "I'm your papa now."

She shook her head, then gave him a smile.

Alec smiled back.

He was ready to put her down, but when he tried, Mary let him know she wasn't ready to leave him. She grabbed hold of his tunic and stiffened against him.

Alec perched her on his shoulders instead. The child liked that well enough. She let out a shriek of laughter and wiggled her toes with obvious delight.

Jamie nearly dropped the supplies she'd gone to fetch, when she rounded the corner of the screen and saw what Alec was doing. "You don't hold a child like that," she called out. "And for God's sake, Alec, don't shrug at me again. You'll send Mary flying through the air."

"I'm new to this, Jamie," Alec muttered. "She's the first child I've ever held." He pulled Mary back into his arms while he continued to frown at his wife.

"You'll get used to her," Jamie announced.

Alec had to glare at Marcus and Gavin then so they'd quit their disrespectful smiles.

Then he carried Mary over to the rocking chair, settled her on his lap, and ordered her to go to sleep. Mary tried to climb up his chest instead. She was just as suspicious of the moving chair as he'd been, and he had to soothe her back down into his lap.

Jamie had turned her back on the two of them and was giving Angus her undivided attention. Alec drummed his fingers on the arm of the chair, wondering what in God's name he was supposed to do now. He decided he might as well try telling a bedtime story. It took him a minute to pick his favorite, and then he related, in full, the tale of one of his finest battles.

In short minutes, he had Mary Kathleen enthralled. Her eyes had widened to saucers again and she seemed to be hanging on his every word.

Gavin and Marcus also became interested in the bloody tale. They pulled up stools near the hearth and took turns offering grunts of approval during the telling.

Jamie could hear Alec's soft burr in the background, but she wasn't paying any attention to what he was saying. Angus was letting her know how unhappy he was because she wouldn't let him remove the slats from his arm. "Your fingers are moving now, Angus, but that doesn't mean the healing's done. No, you have a good month, mayhap more, wearing this contraption, and that's that. Elizabeth, his chest has healed nicely, hasn't it?"

"It has," Elizabeth replied. "We are both very thankful to you, Jamie. Aren't we, Angus?"

"Aye, we are," Angus agreed.

It looked as though it pained him to make that confession. Jamie tried not to laugh. She'd already learned that Angus's gruff manner hid a soft heart.

She smiled at Elizabeth, then hurried to put her supplies away. It was time to take Mary Kathleen upstairs. The little girl was surely exhausted from her long day.

Yet when she turned the corner again and saw Alec holding Mary in his lap, she didn't have the heart to interrupt. Lord, she really must be exhausted, too. Why, her eyes filled up with tears over the wonderful sight.

He was telling his daughter a bedtime story. No, she qualified with a smile. He was telling Mary, Marcus, Gavin, and Angus a bedtime story. God's truth, the men looked just as engrossed in the tale as the three-year-old.

She loved Alec with all her heart. He was such a gentle, compassionate man. She felt like laughing now. Alec would certainly take great exception if he guessed she thought him kind, and she wondered how he was going to react when she finally confessed her love to him.

It didn't matter if he accepted her love or not, she thought with a sudden frown. In time, she was sure he'd see the rightness in it. Why, with proper prodding, he might even begin to love her, too.

How could she have ever thought the Scots were inferior? She had to shake her head over that shameful sin, then started forward to hear this story that held everyone so captivated.

Not everyone was captivated, she noticed when she saw Elizabeth's expression. Angus's wife looked positively horrified.

And then she caught one of Alec's remarks. "The mighty blow severed his arm . . ."

"What *are* you telling that child?" she demanded in a near shout.

"Just a story," Alec answered. "Why?"

"What specific story?" Jamie asked. She rushed forward to snatch Mary out of Alec's lap.

"The battle with the Northumbrians," he answered.

"In vivid detail," Elizabeth informed her.

Jamie's irritation vanished in the face of her husband's obvious confusion over her reaction. "Alec, you'll give this baby nightmares with such talk."

"She liked the story," Alec argued. "Give her back to me, Jamie. I've still to tell the ending."

"Aye, he has to finish the tale," Gavin interjected.

"She's going to bed." Jamie laughed then, in spite of her better intentions. "I cannot believe you'd tell a sweet child a battle story."

It soon became apparent to her that Alec and his soldiers couldn't believe she'd take exception to the tale.

"Give Mary a good night kiss," Jamie instructed. She handed the child back to her father and watched him place a gentle kiss on her brow.

"Go to your bed now, Mary," Alec told the child in a soft whisper. "I'll finish your story tomorrow."

When he put the little girl down, she hurried over to the hearth and stretched out on the rushes. "Does she think that's where she's supposed to sleep?" Alec asked.

Jamie chased after Mary and picked her up before answering. "I suppose she does," she said. "Her grandmother must have been very good to her, though. Mary has such a sweet disposition. 'Tis proof she hasn't been mistreated long."

"Why is that proof?" Alec asked.

"When a child is treated cruelly, sometimes the mind becomes twisted, Alec, or so I've been told. Why are you looking at me like that?" she added in a worried tone. "You look . . . stunned. We needn't worry about our Mary, Alec."

Alec forced a grin. "I never worry," he said. "You do enough for the both of us."

She decided to ignore that ridiculous statement. "May we

sleep upstairs tonight, Alec? I want to be near Mary. She might need me during the night."

He was the one who needed her during the night. That thought popped into his mind all at once, causing a fierce frown. Hell, she was supposed to need him.

He looked at little Mary. The child's face rested against Jamie's shoulder. Her eyes were closed, her expression bordering on blissful. It was very apparent she liked being held by Jamie.

The bruises would fade away from the child's back and legs, and Alec knew that Jamie would soon be able to soothe away any hurt lingering inside the child's mind. Aye, his wife would make Mary Kathleen content . . . as content as her magical love had made him.

She did love him. The way she looked at him told him so. She might not have reckoned with the truth yet, but Alec was certain that, in time, and with enough prodding, she'd settle in to accepting her fate. He had. God must have had a hand in sending Jamie to him, he decided, because if anyone had told him a year ago that he'd love an opinionated, bad-tempered, contrary English woman, he would have laughed first and then flattened the man for suggesting such a notion.

He guessed he'd have to tell her he loved her. Alec quit his scowl. He'd tell her tonight, he decided. In Gaelic. Just to be contrary.

"Alec? Will you be needing to speak to me again tonight?" Angus asked, interrupting his laird's thoughts.

"No, Angus. Take Elizabeth home. We'll discuss our plans again tomorrow."

Gavin waited until Angus had taken Elizabeth outside before questioning Alec. Though he was sure Elizabeth wouldn't repeat anything she overheard, he didn't want to upset her. "What plan are you thinking of, Alec? Do you know who tried to kill Jamie?"

"You're not including us in your discussion?" Marcus asked.

"Quit your frown, Marcus," Alec ordered. "I haven't had

time to include the two of you yet. You did check the bedrooms, didn't you, Gavin?"

The soldier nodded. "And I've been watching the doors ever since. Edith is waiting in Mary's room. She wants permission from Jamie to sleep with Mary tonight in case the child awakens."

"The soldiers are still stationed below your window, milord," Marcus added.

"Put two more at the bottom of the steps, Marcus. No one goes up those stairs."

"Do you know who it is?" Gavin asked again.

"I'm almost certain," Alec returned. His expression turned grim. "Tomorrow we set the trap. I've been looking in the wrong direction. And if I'm right, once this is over, Father Murdock will have to bless Helena's grave."

"I don't understand," Marcus whispered.

"If I'm right," Alec repeated, "Helena didn't kill herself. She was murdered."

He guards her like a precious treasure. The fool! Does he actually think he can stop me?

I'm too cunning for the Kincaid. The time has come to challenge him once again. I'll kill the bitch tomorrow.

The child will have to wait. . . . It can only be one pleasure at a time.

God give me the strength to hide my joy.

Chapter Sixteen

Jamie was sound asleep when Alec finally came to bed. She looked beautiful to him, peaceful, too. He really shouldn't wake her up, he thought, even as he moved the blanket away and pulled her into his arms.

She grumbled in her sleep, then threw one slender leg over his thigh. The woman was giving him hell even in her sleep, for when he trailed his fingers down her back, she mumbled something he didn't understand but guessed was shameful, then slapped his hand away when she rolled over on her back.

He wasn't at all deterred. Her nightgown was bunched up around her thighs, and in the soft candlelight, her skin was dappled gold. Her legs were tangled in the covers. Alec kicked the covers out of the way before trapping her with one thigh. He made short work of removing her gown, smiling over the muttering that action caused. She could even look disgruntled when she was sleeping.

He moved her hair out of his way, trailing the silky

rose-scented strands through his fingers as he nuzzled the side of her neck.

She sighed with pleasure. Alec raised his head to look at her. He smiled when he saw that she didn't look at all irritated now. He kissed her softly parted lips, the center of her chin, her neck again, then moved lower to kiss the gooseflesh on her chest.

Her shivers woke her up. She wasn't at all cold, though. No, she was getting warmer with each moment . . . with each kiss. Alec was caressing her breasts with his hands, his mouth, his tongue.

He was such a gentle lover with her, she thought in wonder. He could make her melt in his arms. His hand moved down to circle her navel, then lower still, until his fingers were stroking the soft curls between her thighs.

Her body was ready for him. She was hot, wet, and as her sweet moans told him, almost as wild with need as he was. He teased her stomach with his tongue. She clung to him and finally pulled on his hair when she'd had enough of that torment.

"You make me ache to have you, Jamie," he whispered.

"Have me now, Alec," she whispered. "Don't make me wait any longer. I want . . ."

Her moan of pleasure when his fingers stretched inside her ended her plea. She arched against him even as she tried to pull his hand away. "Stop this torment, husband. Come to me now."

Her hands moved down to capture him. "Two can play this game," she whispered, her voice a husky promise.

Alec groaned deep in his throat, then pulled her hand away. "Not tonight, she can't," he whispered. "I can't hold back much longer, Jamie."

He moved between her legs, cupped her thighs, and thrust inside her with one powerful surge.

She cried out in ecstasy.

Alec immediately stilled inside her. "Did I hurt you, love?" he asked, his worry evident in his gaze.

"No," she told him with a low moan. "You didn't hurt me."

"I'm being too rough," he whispered, still unconvinced he hadn't harmed her. He tried to pull back, to ease himself away from her, but her legs held him in a grip that wouldn't allow retreat.

"Don't you dare stop now," she whispered. "I'll die if you do."

"So will I, Jamie," he admitted on a ragged breath. "So will I." He might have managed a smile, but he couldn't be certain. His body was demanding release, yet he was determined to give her fulfillment first.

He captured her mouth in a searing kiss as he thrust deep, deeper still. Her body accommodated him so completely, so tightly, so wonderfully. He wanted her fire to consume him, amazed she would so easily make him burn for more, more, always more.

Jamie felt as though he was taking her to the stars. She gave herself over to the wonder then, clinging to the man she loved to share the splendor only he could give her.

As soon as he felt the first tremors of her release, he gave a final thrust and spilled his hot seed inside her.

He didn't know how long they stayed together. He thought he never wanted to leave her, though, and it wasn't until his heart and his breathing had calmed that he remembered he wanted to tell her he loved her.

"You get better each time, wife," he whispered as he rolled to his side.

Jamie rolled with him, tucked the top of her head under his chin, smiling over the teasing lilt in his soft burr. "You said practice would make me better," she reminded him. "I had no idea we'd practice so often," she admitted.

He could tell she was arrogantly pleased with herself. Alec smiled against the top of her head, then whispered in Gaelic, "I know you don't understand what I'm saying to you, Jamie, but I've need to tell you in my own language. I love you, lass, with all my being."

He felt her stiffen against him during his recitation, but when she tried to pull away from him, he held her secure. "I love you because you're so gentle and loving, caring, too. Ye have a heart of gold, lass."

She all but melted against him then. "But most of all, Jamie, I love you because you're such a truthful woman. Aye," he added when she stiffened against him again, "I could never love a woman who'd try to deceive me, but I have complete faith in you."

He thought she might have turned into stone. It took all Alec's determination not to laugh. "Good night, Jamie," he whispered, in her language.

"What did you just say to me?" Jamie asked.

She was trying to sound blasé. "I said good night," Alec drawled.

"Before that," Jamie whispered, a tremor in her voice.

"'Tis not important," he countered,

She pushed away from him so he'd be able to see her frustration. "Did you mean whatever it was you said?"

He shrugged. Jamie almost lost her temper then and there, but she'd already determined to give Alec quite a surprise tomorrow: she was going to kneel before Edgar and recite her pledge in Gaelic.

She wasn't going to let Alec ruin her surprise. There was that, yes, but there was also the fact he'd just told her he loved her because she was so truthful.

She was good and trapped by her own hand. And why did she suddenly sense that Alec knew it?

It was the sparkle that came into his eyes, she decided. "Why are you looking at me like that?" she asked.

"Because you look as though you're trying to solve all of England's considerable problems," he answered.

"I have thought of a small problem that needs solving," Jamie admitted.

"Tell me what it is."

She shook her head. "I will solve it tomorrow, Alec. It's my problem, after all. I will take care of it. Trust me on this."

"Oh, I do trust you, wife."

"You do?" she asked, looking very pleased with him.

"Of course. Honesty and trust are like the right and left hands. They're both important. . . . Now what's the matter?" he asked, trying not to laugh. "You're frowning again."

He decided he'd baited her enough for one evening. "It's

late, Jamie," he said as he pulled her back into his arms. "You must be exhausted after your long day. You shouldn't be trying to solve your problems now. You should be——"

"Sleeping," she interjected with a sigh.

"No," he countered. "You should be pleasing your husband."

"I just did please you, didn't I?"

"You've still to get it right, lass." He rolled her onto her back. "But you're most fortunate to have a patient husband."

"I have an insatiable husband, Kincaid. Do you know how many times we've——"

"Am I to keep count of our lovemaking, too?"

Jamie only had enough time to wrap her arms around her husband before he captured her laughter with a long kiss.

They made slow, sweet love. And all the while, Jamie kept hearing his pledge of love. Tomorrow, she promised, tomorrow I will give him my pledge in Gaelic.

She fell asleep before he'd rolled away. Alec covered both of them with his plaid and was sound asleep moments later.

He only awakened once during the short night, when the door was opened. He was reaching for his sword when Mary Kathleen came running toward the bed.

She ran to Jamie's side of the bed first. "Don't bother your mother," Alec whispered. "Tell me what's the matter, Mary."

When he added to his order by motioning to her, Mary finally obeyed. Her expression was solemn, and when she'd reached his side, he could see the fear in her eyes.

"What is it?" he asked her.

Mary held out the bottom of her nightgown. "I'm wet," she whispered. Tears welled in her eyes, then spilled down her cheeks.

Alec pulled her gown over her head and tossed the garment on the floor. "Now you're not wet," he announced.

Jamie had awakened to Mary's voice. She pretended to be asleep, though, for she knew her husband disliked women who wept. No, she didn't want him to see how misty her

THE BRIDE

eyes were. He wouldn't understand the overwhelming love she felt for him when he picked up his daughter and rocked her in his arms.

She closed her eyes when he stood up and carried the sleeping child to the door and handed her to one of the soldiers.

She almost called out that it should be the father putting his daughter back in her bed and not one of his soldiers, then remembered that her husband was stark naked, after all, and Edith would certainly die of embarrassment if she woke up and found him in her room.

That picture was so amusing she had to roll over on her stomach to stifle her giggles.

Alec came back to bed, hauled her up against his side, and was snoring before she'd even gotten herself properly settled.

Her soft sigh of contentment filled the air. She could barely wait for morning. Tomorrow was going to be a glorious day.

It was the worst day of her life.

Oh, it started out well enough. Jamie and Edith had the great hall looking as grand as a palace in less than two hours' time. Fresh flowers decorated the tables, new rushes covered the floor, and the tall box-shaped chair King Edgar would sit upon was scrubbed spotless.

Gavin and Marcus did try Jamie's patience, however. Every time she turned around, one of the big men was blocking her path. "Isn't there something you need to be doing?" she asked.

The soldiers didn't take her subtle hint. "It's our day away from our duties," Gavin explained.

She didn't look as if she believed him. Neither did Marcus, for that matter.

"But why are you following me around?" Jamie persisted.

The soldiers were saved from having to come up with a lie to that question when Mary Kathleen grabbed hold of Jamie's skirt. The little girl was dressed in a Kincaid gown.

311

The garment had come from the blacksmith's family and fit Mary well. Jamie lifted her daughter into her arms, gave her a quick kiss, and whispered a few words of praise in Gaelic.

"May I take Mary with me to Frances's cottage?" Edith called out.

"Frances?"

"The blacksmith's wife," Edith explained. "She has several pairs of shoes we can try on Mary."

"Be sure to tell Frances how much I appreciate her help," Jamie said.

Edith shook her head. "She'd be insulted. It's her duty to help."

Jamie didn't know what to make of that statement. She handed Mary to Edith, a difficult task, that, since Mary wanted to stay right where she was. Edith explained to her niece what their errand was and finally gained her cooperation.

"I'll tell Frances you're pleased with her," Edith called over her shoulder.

She bumped into Marcus when she turned around. "I cannot help but wonder why you're following me around," she said. She let him see her exasperation. "And why are those soldiers lounging above the stairs? Don't they have some duties to see to?"

Marcus shook his head. "It's their day off from other duties," he explained.

Alec walked into the hall in time to hear Marcus's outrageous explanation. He noticed his wife's incredulous expression, too. "Jamie? The clan is coming up the last hills. They'll be here in a few minutes. Some of Harold's clan is with them. I want you—"

"We're receiving guests now?" she cried out.

"We are," Alec stated.

He didn't realize his wife could move so quickly. Alec reached out to grab her when she tried to fly past him. He pulled her into his arms and forced her to look up at him.

She looked terribly worried. Alec couldn't resist. He leaned down and kissed her wrinkled brow. This spontaneous show of affection was still new to him, but he found he liked it well enough. He kissed her again.

"I don't like to see you frown," he whispered. "Are you worrying again?"

She shook her head. "I need to change my gown," she announced.

"Why? Whether your English garb be clean or not, it still won't matter. They're bound to hate it as much as I do."

She didn't give him an answer to that remark. He could tell, though, that she was more amused than irritated. Her reaction puzzled him. He kissed her again, a long, wet kiss on her sweet mouth, and when she wrapped her arms around his waist, his tongue moved inside and began to stroke the roof of her mouth.

She looked thoroughly bemused with him when he finally ended the kiss. He whispered in Gaelic that he loved her, pulled her hands away from him, and walked down the three steps into the hall.

He motioned Gavin and Marcus over to the table. Jamie, he noticed, was slumped against the arch, staring at him. "Didn't you want to change your clothes?" he called out.

She straightened away from the wall and hurried up the steps. Alec could hear her mutterings all the way across the hall. He smiled in reaction.

The man could make her forget her duties with such ease, Jamie thought. When he kissed her, all she could think about was kissing him back.

She had to force herself to put Alec out of her mind. There was his surprise to be seen to, after all, and she wouldn't let him ruin it by robbing her of her determination.

She straightened the covers on their bed, then changed into a cream-colored ankle-length chemise. Those two chores took her just a few minutes, but the wrapping of the plaid was another matter altogether.

The piece of material was approximately twelve feet long after she'd cut a third away. It was narrow, which should have made it easier for her to pleat, but no matter how she tried, she couldn't get it right.

In desperation, she opened the door and ordered one of the soldiers to fetch Father Murdock for her.

The priest arrived a short while later. She opened the door to his timid knock, then all but pulled him into the bedroom and slammed the door shut.

Alec had heard the priest wheeze his way up the stairs. He did raise an eyebrow when he was given entrance to the bedroom. He wondered what in God's name she'd need Murdock for, then put the matter out of his mind.

Still, he kept watching the door. When it was finally opened and Murdock came outside, Alec saw the wide smile on the priest's face.

"Father Murdock? What were you doing in my chamber?" he shouted.

The priest didn't answer until he'd reached Alec's side. "I was assisting your wife," he said then.

"Assisting her in what?"

"I cannot tell you," Father Murdock stated. He held his smile, even in the face of Alec's dark expression, then added, "She's wanting to give you a little surprise, Alec. Let her have her way. You don't want to be hurting her feelings by knowing ahead of time."

"So you also worry about her feelings," Alec answered dryly. "'Tis an affliction we all seem to share." He glanced over at Marcus and then turned to include Gavin in his gaze.

The bedroom door opened then, drawing his full attention.

Alec wasn't aware he'd stood up. He stared at the vision making her way around the smiling soldiers, feeling such incredible pride he could barely breathe.

She was wearing his plaid. And he was so pleased, he couldn't even speak. It was high time, he kept telling himself, high time indeed.

"She couldn't make the pleats. The lass had even folded the garment on the floor and tried to stretch herself out atop it. Aye, she'd tried ways I'd never heard of until she confessed them to me."

"And so you assisted her," Gavin interjected with a nod.

"She praised me for my quick hands," the priest whispered as he, too, watched Jamie come down the stairs. "My, she's a bonny lass."

Jamie knew she had the men's full attention. She kept her shoulders straight and her hands at her sides so she wouldn't accidentally pull one of the pleats away from her belt. When she reached the steps leading down into the hall, she gave her husband a formal curtsy.

He wanted to kiss her again. He might even tell her how proud he was to have her for his own.

When Alec motioned to her, Jamie gently lifted the hem of her gown and walked over to him. He reached for her then, but she shook her head and backed up a space. "Don't touch me, Alec."

"What?"

"Don't raise your voice either," Jamie returned, frowning. "You can tell me how pleased you are standing right where you are. I'll not have my pleats disturbed before the king arrives, and that's that."

He didn't look at all happy with her now. "You are pleased with me, aren't you, husband?"

"I'm very pleased."

"And?" she prodded, hoping for a little more praise.

"And what?"

She laughed then. Alec certainly wasn't one to hand out compliments. He didn't even know he was supposed to, she guessed.

"Never mind," she replied. She shrugged before she remembered her pleats. One quick look told her she hadn't done any damage, though. "I'm never going to get these folds just so," she remarked.

"We'll practice that, too," Alec promised.

She didn't start to blush until Father Murdock asked what else they were practicing. "Perhaps I could lend my expertise," he suggested eagerly.

"A private matter," Jamie blurted out. "We can't use your assistance, Father, but we both thank you for offering."

Alec's devilish smile widened. "Come along with me, Jamie. The guests are waiting outside to meet you."

"One of your guests is already inside," a stranger called out from the entrance.

Jamie turned to acknowledge their guest, then decided she should be standing by her husband when she was given introduction. She moved to his side and immediately gained his nod of approval.

Alec put his arm around her shoulders. The spontaneous show of possessiveness surprised her almost as much as his hard grip.

"Have a care with my pleats," she whispered.

Alec wasn't paying her any attention, though. His dark gaze was directed on the man approaching them. His scowl suggested he didn't much care for the man he was about to introduce.

"I was eager to meet your wife, Alec, and took it upon myself to come inside."

Alec's arm tightened around Jamie. "This is Harold's son, Justin."

"I'm pleased to meet you," Jamie said, smiling so he'd think she meant what she'd said. In truth, she wasn't pleased at all. The blond man was appraising her in an earthy way. Only a married man should be able to give his wife that kind of look.

If he'd been a fully grown man, she probably would have given him a proper set down, but the lack of marks on his arms and face indicated he hadn't seen any battles yet. His manners certainly needed improvement, too.

"Not nearly as pleased as I am to meet you, milady," Justin replied.

She gave him an abrupt nod, then suggested in a firm voice that he return to the others. "Alec and I will join you soon," she promised.

Her suggestion was rudely ignored. Justin continued to stand there gaping at her. "Was there something else you wished to say?"

Justin looked embarrassed. "Nay, milady. I—I just enjoy listening to your unusual accent," he stammered out.

"It's an English accent, Justin," she reminded him. "And

as appealing to most Scots as the sound of a nail being scraped across a pane of glass."

Marcus let out a loud cough to cover his amusement. Gavin had to turn his back so Justin wouldn't see his reaction.

Justin still didn't want to give up. "I understand your name is Jamie," he said.

"It is."

"It's a fine name," he announced.

"It's a man's name, and that's that," Jamie snapped. She was through trying to contain her temper. Justin was staring at her chest. She wanted to kick him.

She couldn't wait to get away from the insolent creature. She wondered why Alec hadn't noticed the boy's shameful conduct and glanced up to look at him.

Alec was smiling. She didn't know what to make of that oddity. Gavin interrupted then with the reminder that the tables had been set up in the courtyard.

Alec nodded. "Direct the servants to begin serving the food. Jamie and I will be along in a few minutes. Marcus, take Justin with you. He doesn't look capable of making it on his own."

The last of Alec's orders was given in a hard voice. Jamie thought her husband had finally noticed the lustful way their guest was staring at her.

As soon as Alec let go of her, she started toward the screen. She'd left her dagger on the chest the day before and wanted to put it back in her belt before she forgot about it.

Justin tried to follow her. Jamie had to give the boy a good frown when he dared to touch her. Justin proved determined, though. It was an embarrassment, for the other men were watching, but Jamie had to slap his hand away from her.

"You aren't perchance related to Laird McPherson, are you, Justin?" she asked.

"Nay, Lady Kincaid," Justin answered, looking puzzled. "I'm not related. Why would you ask such a question?"

"Your manners remind me of the laird," she answered.

She could tell Justin didn't know how to take that remark. Alec understood the insult she'd just given the boy, however. His laughter followed her behind the screen.

The dagger wasn't where she thought she'd left it. Jamie spent several minutes looking for her weapon, then gave up on the task.

She was given quite a fright when she turned around and saw Alec watching her. "You gave me a start."

Alec pulled her into his arms, ignoring her plea not to ruin her skirt's folds. He lifted her up, until she was at eye level. His mouth was a convenient breath away from hers. "I'll fix your pleats," he promised in a husky growl.

Jamie threaded her fingers through his hair and slowly leaned forward.

He met her halfway. His mouth settled on hers with blatant ownership. His tongue drove inside. He wanted to ravish her, to force any resistance away, but when she rubbed her tongue against his, he realized she didn't need to be convinced. She wanted to be appeased.

A shudder coursed through him; Jamie moaned in response. Alec lifted his mouth away from hers. He wanted to see the passion in her eyes.

"You're hot for me, aren't you, love?" he whispered.

She pulled on his hair to bring him back to her. He heard her sexy little whimper and gave her a growl in reply. He silenced her noise with another deep, tongue-thrusting kiss, then planted wet kisses along the column of her neck.

He took great delight in telling her what he wanted her to do to him with her soft, wet mouth, how he wanted her to take him inside her again, how he wanted to feel her squeezing him tight. He spoke in Gaelic, of course, just to confuse her.

His game trapped him, though, for he wanted her too much now to stop. He carried her over to the bed. His mouth slanted over hers again and again, allowing her no protest of his obvious intentions. He braced their fall into the center of the covers with his arm. With one forceful motion, he'd spread her legs and positioned himself between her thighs. He trapped the sides of her face with his big hands as he thrust his arousal against her.

He was nearly out of control now. Jamie's nails dug into his back. She drew her knees up so she could feel more of him against her. Alec drove his tongue all the way to the back of her throat and started pulling her clothes off.

Jamie suddenly tensed against him. She began to struggle, too, pushing against his shoulders with surprising strength as she tore her mouth away from his.

He heard the noise then, yet it still took him painful minutes before he could remember the time of day, his duties, their guests.

With an angry expletive, Alec lifted his head away. He braced himself on his elbows and looked down at the enticing woman sprawled under him.

She looked thoroughly ravished. He nodded with satisfaction. Her lips were a bit swollen, rosy, and too appealing for his peace of mind. He kissed her again, a hard, quick kiss.

"Do you know why I just kissed you, Jamie?"

She shook her head.

"To remind you whom you belong to."

Her eyes widened over that announcement. Alec pulled her to her feet, then refashioned her plaid with incredible speed.

He was walking away from her when she called out, "Do you know why I kissed you back, husband?"

She was prepared to remind him that he also belonged to her, but the arrogant man wouldn't let her. "Because you liked it."

His pleats were perfect, she'd give him that. She patted her hair, straightened her shoulders, and went back into the hall.

"Jamie?"

"Yes, husband?"

"Father Murdock will escort you outside. I'll join you soon."

Alec waited until his wife had left the hall, then motioned to the two soldiers still standing guard above the stairs.

"Don't let her out of your sight," he ordered. "Stay within ten paces of your mistress."

The two soldiers hurried to do his bidding. "Send Colin to me," Alec called out.

"Harold's second-in-command is here, too?" Gavin asked.

Alec nodded. "He has news he wants to share with us," he explained.

"Your wife wasn't very impressed with Justin's handsome looks, was she?" Gavin asked.

"I never thought she'd find him handsome," Alec lied.

Colin must have been waiting right outside the doors, Alec decided, for he was already rushing down the steps to the great hall. The gray-haired man was obviously in quite a hurry to relay his messages to the Kincaid.

The time got away from Alec. He became embroiled in a heated debate about the possible union of the Highland clans. He insisted it wasn't possible. Colin was just as vehement in his opinion that it was very possible.

Alec was damned if he would let Colin leave the hall before agreeing with him. Colin, if the set of his jaw was a true indication, was just as determined to sway Alec's judgment.

Jamie came rushing into the hall. Alec gave his wife only a quick glance before turning back to his guest.

He looked up again when she stood at his side. Alec thought she looked angry enough to spit fire. After giving her a frown to let her know he didn't want to be interrupted, he turned back to Colin.

She wasn't about to be ignored. Jamie prodded his upper arm. She managed a weak smile for the soldier speaking to Alec, then said, "Pray forgive me, sir, for interrupting this discussion."

Alec, believing her anger was due to her impatient nature, was quick with his reply. "You'll have to wait, wife."

"Alec, this can't wait."

"Aren't you capable of handling this problem?"

"I didn't say I wasn't capable," she argued.

"Then handle it."

His tone of voice infuriated her, though not nearly as much as his rude dismissal. He turned his back on her and calmly asked the soldier to continue.

Both Gavin and Marcus gave her sympathetic looks. She nodded to them as she walked back to the entrance.

Alec glanced up when Jamie stopped near the archway. She was staring up at the display of weapons hanging from their hooks. Alec tried to give Colin his undivided attention, but that determination was forgotten when Jamie reached up and tried to lift a long club into her arms.

The weight of the weapon must have been too much for her. Her grip lessened and the club bounced to the floor with a resounding thud.

She was determined, however. She'd gained everyone's full attention, too. No one said a word as they watched Jamie drag the club up the stairs and out the doorway.

Alec could hear her muttering over the clatter the club was making on the stone floor.

He continued to stare at the entrance a long while after she'd gone, wondering what in God's name his gentle little wife needed a club for.

The answer came to him in a blinding flash. Justin!

Alec bounded out of his chair with a roar of fury. The sound nearly drowned out the screams coming from the courtyard.

Alec ran outside, trailed by the three soldiers. The scene he witnessed so astonished him, he stopped in his tracks.

The priest was standing next to Jamie. The look on Father Murdock's face was one of stunned disbelief. Jamie wasn't looking at the priest, though. No, she was staring at the ground, frowning intently at Harold's son. The future laird was sprawled on his stomach and trying without much success to regain his feet.

"If you ever try to touch me again, I'll hit you twice as hard," Jamie shouted. "I'll have your word, Justin, before I let you up."

"Milady," Father Murdock interrupted, all but strangling on his words. "He doesn't understand—"

Jamie didn't let the priest finish his sentence. She assumed he meant to tell her Justin didn't understand her language. "Oh, he knows why I hit him, all right," she stated, speaking in Gaelic now. "He understands."

"But, Jamie, lass," Father Murdock said, trying to explain once again.

The man on the ground dared to look furious instead of contrite. He was slow to learn his lesson, Jamie decided. "How dare you touch me?" she asked in a furious voice. "I'm Alec Kincaid's wife, you fool. And I happen to love the man with a passion you'll probably never even imagine."

"Milady?" Gavin interrupted.

"Stay out of this, Gavin," Jamie commanded. She didn't dare take her gaze away from the soldier on the ground, or let up her hold on her weapon. "Alec has instructed me to take care of this problem and I won't have your interference. I told Justin I'd come back with something to make his knees weak and I did."

"He isn't Justin."

Alec made that statement. He stood so close to Jamie's back that she could feel his heat. "This isn't the time for jests, Alec," she stated before turning around. "That shameful, ill-disciplined boy grabbed hold of me and dared to kiss me. Just look what he did to my pleats," she added as she whirled around to show him the evidence.

"You hit Philip," Alec told her. "Not Justin."

"I didn't. He's—"

"Justin's brother."

"Philip, you say?"

He slowly nodded. He didn't look as if he was jesting. A knot immediately formed in Jamie's stomach. "I don't understand, Alec," she whispered. "He looks like—"

"They are twins."

"Oh, God, not twins."

He nodded again. "Identical."

She was horrified. A crowd had gathered, too, making her humiliation all the more stinging. "Well, spit," she muttered, low enough for only Alec to hear. "Why didn't you tell me? I've injured the wrong man."

Jamie immediately dropped her weapon and tried to help

her victim to his feet so she wouldn't have to look at her husband's dark expression any longer. Philip, however, refused to accept her assistance.

The poor man obviously thought she was daft. "I'm sorry I hit you, Philip. No one bothered to tell me you had a twin brother, you see," she added with a meaningful glance in her husband's direction. "I'm buying you another indulgence for that sin, Alec."

"You didn't mean to strike me down?" Philip asked as he continued to back away from her.

She was getting weary of chasing after him. "If you'll stand still long enough, I'll try to explain what happened," she promised.

Philip continued to look suspicious, but he did finally stop his retreat.

"I certainly didn't mean to strike you down," she repeated again. "I don't even know you, sir. Why would I want to harm you?"

Her speech seemed to placate Philip, but he reversed his decision to forgive her when she added in a casual voice, "I meant to fell your brother, of course."

"Of course? You were going to hit Justin?" Philip was back to shouting.

Actually, she'd meant to give Justin several good hits. She decided it wouldn't do her cause a bit of good if she told his brother that, though. Philip looked as if he'd take exception to such honesty. He obviously didn't know what a spoiled boy Justin was. He was protective, too. Jamie couldn't fault that admirable trait, though she believed it was misplaced.

She decided to use diplomacy. "Yes, I was going to hit your brother. Philip, surely you've realized by now that Justin has the manners of a pig."

"Bring Justin to me."

Alec's roar turned her attention back to him. "You told me to take care of this matter, Alec, and I would—"

"I'll take care of it," Alec told her.

"How?" she asked, worried about the look in his eyes now. "You won't truly hurt the boy, will you, husband?"

"Did he touch you, Jamie?"

"Well, yes," Jamie replied before she saw how furious he was. "But just a little touch, Alec. It was only a quick grab and a small kiss—"

"I'm going to kill the bastard," Alec interrupted. He hadn't shouted, but his cold tone of voice sent shivers down her spine.

Jamie started wringing the rest of the pleats out of her plaid.

A few minutes later, she found herself in the most ludicrous position. She was actually standing in front of Justin, defending his life. "Now, Alec, he's just a boy. The Kincaids don't kill children. Do be quiet, Justin," she ordered when he tried to protest her choice of words. "You *are* a boy or you would have known better than to challenge Alec. Please, Alec? Let him live long enough to learn some manners."

She looked as if she was about to burst into tears. That fact swayed Alec's intentions. He finally nodded agreement.

Jamie became weak with relief. That feeling didn't last long, however. The second she moved away from Justin, Alec moved forward. He had the young man off the ground and flying through the air like an arrow before she could stop him. Justin landed on his backside in a cloud of dust.

"Alec, you promised me."

"I won't kill him, love," Alec answered. "I'm just going to beat some manners into him."

There were several grunts of approval over that horrid statement. Colin, Jamie noticed, had also nodded his agreement.

"If you beat him into a bloody pulp, I'll have to spend the rest of the day patching him up, Alec. Would you completely ruin my day by making me stand so close to Justin?"

Alec had Justin by the nape of his neck now. He held him high off the ground but turned his gaze to her and asked, "Did you mean it, Jamie?"

"Mean what?" she replied, wondering why in God's name he could be smiling now.

"That you loved me."

She suddenly realized they'd both been speaking Gaelic.

324

"You ruined my surprise," she told Justin, ignoring the fact that the boy could barely breathe, let alone give her a proper apology.

"You shouted your love in front of everyone, wife. Don't deny it now," Alec demanded.

"You'll put that boy down first," she countered.

"You'll answer me first."

"Yes, I love you. There, are you happy?"

He tossed Justin to the ground with a quick flick of his wrist. His casual strength didn't upset her, she realized. The opposite was really the truth. She not only liked his strength, she depended upon it. Jamie gave Alec a smile, just because she'd finally sorted it all out in her mind.

"I'm very happy," Alec told her.

"I'm saying Justin didn't touch her," Philip shouted, drawing everyone's attention.

Jamie let out a loud gasp, then reached for the club.

Alec hauled her up against his side. The rest of her pleats gave up the battle. The plaid would have fallen to the ground if she hadn't grabbed hold of it.

"Did anyone else see this attack?" Alec asked the crowd.

The two soldiers who'd been ordered to follow Jamie stepped forward.

"We both were witnesses," one of the soldiers stated.

"Yet neither of you interfered?" Alec asked, scowling intently.

"We were about to intervene," the younger soldier stated. "But you told us to stay ten paces away from your wife so she wouldn't know we were following her, and by the time we'd rushed forward, it was too late."

"Alec, why would you have your men follow . . ."

Jamie quit her question when her husband squeezed her shoulders. She guessed he didn't want to go into his reasons now.

"I saw Justin grab her when she came around the corner," the first soldier continued.

"And?"

Alec's jaw was clenched tight with suppressed fury. "Justin proclaimed his admiration for your wife," the soldier related. "I heard him tell Lady Kincaid that her violet eyes had the power to make his knees weak. Since Harold's our ally, I thought one of us should go get you, but—"

"Was your ally," Philip shouted.

"Philip, you needn't get so upset," Jamie interjected. "I was only going to bring Alec outside to have a firm talk with your brother." She glanced up at her husband and said, "You were too busy."

"And so you used a club."

She thought she detected a spark of amusement in his eyes, but she couldn't be sure. "Alec, the only way I could get Justin to unhand me was to promise to give him something that would really make his knees weak. It was plain trickery. The foolish boy thought I meant to return his advances, but I really meant to have you shout at him. 'Tis the truth your voice can make anyone's knees go weak."

"You've disgraced me and humiliated my brother," Philip stated, once again demanding their attention.

"Nay," Jamie countered. "You've both done that all by yourselves."

If Philip's face turned any darker, his skin would surely ignite. "My father will hear about these insults, Kincaid. I promise you."

The laird's two sons turned and ran toward the stables. The crowd made a wide path for them.

Colin, Harold's trusted soldier, didn't follow the young men. He stopped by Alec's side. "Your conditions, Kincaid?"

"He has one week."

Colin nodded.

Jamie waited until the soldier had left, then asked Alec, "Who has one week?"

"Justin's father."

"What is he supposed to do during this week?" she asked, trying to understand.

"He'll try to allay my anger."

"And if he fails?"

"War."

She knew he was going to say that God-awful word, but

she was still stunned. This was all somehow, some way, her fault. It had to be. Father Murdock wasn't a lying man, and he'd told her just the day before that he thought the Highlands were a very peaceful place to live. Until I came along, Jamie qualified. Now the Kincaids were fighting with the McPhersons, thanks to her interference with the sick babe, and the Kincaids were only an insult away from taking up arms against the Fergusons because Daniel was being as cold as sleet since she'd given Mary sanctuary. Added to those worries were Mary Kathleen's relatives. They were probably marching toward Kincaid land now.

And now Justin's father would join the list of enemies. If things continued along this broken path, there wouldn't be a Kincaid warrior left alive in another week's time.

It all suddenly overwhelmed her. For the first time in her life, Jamie needed a good, long, loud cry. "I'm going to find Mary Kathleen," she whispered.

"She's with Elizabeth. She's going to stay with Angus and his wife until tonight, Jamie."

"Why?"

"Don't question me."

"You needn't snap at me, Alec," Jamie whispered. "Why can't I go and get our daughter? I want to hold her."

Alec reacted to the worry in her voice. "You'll ruin my surprise," he told her.

He thought he'd placate her and was therefore unprepared for her reaction. Her eyes filled with tears. "I had a wonderful surprise for you," she wailed. "It's ruined now."

Father Murdock rushed forward and awkwardly patted Jamie's shoulder. "Now, now, lass. The day isn't over yet. There's still the king—"

"He must not be coming after all," Gavin interjected. He thought that announcement would please his mistress, for he'd witnessed her initial reaction when she'd been told Edgar was going to pay a visit.

"Well, spit," Jamie cried out. "Now it's all ruined."

Alec meant to correct that misassumption when Jamie turned back to him. "Where's Edith? I want to ask her—"

"She and Annie are packing their things. Marcus?" Alec called out. "You'd better go and ready your things as well."

"Why is everyone packing?" Jamie asked.

"They're leaving," Alec stated.

"Where are they going?"

"Marcus is taking Edith and Annie over to Brack's holding. They are distant cousins," Gavin explained.

"For a nice visit?" Jamie asked, mopping at the corners of her eyes with her plaid.

"No," Alec replied. "They're going to live with Brack's family."

"Why? I don't understand, Alec. Edith and I are sure to become good friends," she said. "And Annie is Helena's sister, Alec. You cannot turn your back on her. Will you not reconsider this decision?"

"No."

His expression was set in stone. Jamie turned to Marcus. "You'll be coming back, won't you?"

Marcus gave her a quick nod. Jamie turned to Alec again. "I'm going back inside now. If you order anyone to follow me, I'll use another club on him. I wish to be alone for a few minutes."

Alec knew it was safe and therefore nodded approval. He needn't have bothered, he realized, as Jamie had already started up the steps to the castle. "There are guests waiting in the hall," he called out to her.

The door slammed shut on his words. Alec let out a sigh. He turned to his soldiers and gave them new instructions. He wanted to hurry through his orders so that he could go after Jamie. She'd look so dejected. The tears in her eyes had upset him, too. Perhaps if he fixed her pleats, she'd feel better. Then he could goad her into telling him she loved him again.

Jamie noticed four big soldiers dawdling in the entrance as soon as she shut the door behind her. The colors in their checkered plaid indicated they were from yet another clan. She noticed a fifth soldier standing near the hearth when he called out to his friends to let her pass. She turned to the man and gave a quick curtsy. The soldier immediately motioned her forward with a rather arrogant wave of his hand.

She didn't want to have to engage in conversation now. Still, good manners required that she at least introduce herself.

Jamie hurried down the steps, clutching her plaid to her waist. She was determined to get the sorry chore over and done with as soon as possible. Then she was going to go up to her bedroom and have her cry.

The elderly gray-haired soldier had already made himself at home. He held a goblet of wine in one hand and a fat wedge of cheese in the other.

When she stood a foot or two away from him, the soldier straightened away from the mantel. Jamie managed a smile. Her plaid fell to the floor when she affected a second proper curtsy. And that was simply the last upset she could take. Tears started streaming down her cheeks; she picked up the cloth. She might have been able to regain control of herself, though, if the soldier hadn't had such a kind, sympathetic expression.

"Dear lady, what has caused you this distress?"

Well, spit, the man had a kind voice, too. His eyes seemed to radiate compassion. His age reminded her a little of her papa too, which only made matters worse, of course. Now she wasn't just miserable; she was homesick, too.

"Surely it can't be as terrible as all that," the soldier added.

"If you knew what shame I've caused the Kincaids, why, you'd probably be weeping, too," Jamie blurted out. "I've started so many wars I can barely keep count."

The soldier's eyes widened over that pronouncement. Jamie nodded. "It's the truth I'm telling you. I might as well admit it all, for you're sure to hear of this mess by the end of your visit. If I were a coward, I'd take to my bed for the rest of my days."

"Perhaps I can help."

"No one can help, save the king, of course, and when he gets wind of this trouble, he'll probably have me flogged."

Her words were fairly tripping over themselves in her

hurry to explain. "I was trying to do the right thing, you see, only everything that's right in England is wrong up here. You can't say thank you because they take it as an insult. You can't save a baby's life because they think you've kidnapped him. You can't—"

"Slowly, dear lady," the soldier advised. "Start at the beginning. You'll feel all the better after sharing your worries, and I really would like to help. I have considerable influence here."

The man sounded sincere. "I don't know where to start this pitiful confession," Jamie admitted.

"Start with the first war," he suggested.

She nodded. "I started a war with the McPhersons because I tended the laird's dying son. When the babe was better, the laird came to fetch him and accused me of kidnapping the child."

The soldier gave her a sympathetic expression. "I didn't kidnap the baby, of course, but I did save him from sure death. You would think his papa would be appreciative."

"I would think so," he replied.

"He wasn't. I called him a pig."

"The laird?"

"No, I do believe I called him a goat." Jamie shrugged. "It doesn't matter now. He went home in a pout and now the Kincaids can't go near his land. We can't go to Ferguson's holding either, because I gave Daniel's wife sanctuary."

"I see."

"Daniel was furious, of course."

"Of course," the soldier agreed. "Did Daniel threaten war, too?"

"No, but he's thinking about it. I'm going to tell the king what a prickly temper Daniel has if he doesn't treat my sister better."

"What do you think the king will do?"

"He'll have a firm talk with Daniel, most likely. He'll set him straight about his duties to his wife."

"You have complete faith in King Edgar, then?"

"Oh, yes," Jamie rushed out. "I haven't met the man, of

course, but Alec would only be loyal to a good king." She ended her statement with a delicate shrug.

The soldier smiled. "Still, you must have heard wonderful stories about Edgar," he prodded.

"Oh, heaven's no," Jamie returned. She mopped the wetness from her cheeks with her plaid while she added, "I heard he was a monster."

The stranger's reaction indicated his displeasure. "When I was in England, of course," she went on. "Now I know the stories aren't true. Alec wouldn't pledge himself to a monster."

"And so you are loyal to the Kincaid, is that it?"

"To both Alec and Edgar," Jamie qualified, wondering why the soldier seemed so determined to continue this topic. "I can even understand why Edgar will want to throttle me when he hears about the problems I've caused."

"I'm sure he'll be most understanding."

"Sir, no one is that understanding. I've started a war with Mary Kathleen's family, too. Did I mention that? They say I kidnapped the child away from them."

"But you didn't."

"Oh, yes, I certainly did. I threw their plaid on the ground, too. Marcus spit on it. The child had been beaten. She belongs to Alec and me now. My husband is certain Edgar will stand by us."

"Who is this Mary Kathleen?"

"Helena's daughter."

"And she was mistreated?"

"She bloody well was," Jamie stated. "She's just a baby, too," she continued. "And certainly couldn't defend herself. Gavin said Kevin, her blood father, would turn in his grave."

"The king would stand by your side," the soldier announced then. "Now tell me about the commotion going on outside when I arrived, if you please."

"Justin grabbed me and kissed me. I had to retaliate, of course, and so I hit him in the back of his legs with one of Alec's clubs."

The soldier's eyes widened over that confession. "I'm certain your wife would have done the very same thing," Jamie continued. "No lady wishes to be pawed by any man but her husband."

"I'm not married," he countered.

"But if you were?"

"I'm certain that if I were, my wife would have done the same."

"You are most kind, sir, for agreeing with me."

"Did Alec know you hit Justin?"

"Yes—I mean, no. You see, it wasn't Justin I felled. It was Philip. It was an easy mistake to make, sir, because I didn't know Harold's sons were identical twins, until Alec told me."

"After you hit Philip?"

"Sir, this isn't the time to laugh. Nay, this is a serious matter."

"I do apologize, my lady," the soldier returned. "And then what happened?"

"Alec picked up the laird's son and sent him flying, just like a caber."

"He threw Philip?"

"No, no," Jamie countered. "Do pay attention," she suggested. "It was Justin he threw. He shouldn't have done it, but I can't really be angry with him."

"Justin?"

"Alec," she countered again. She gave him a look that showed her displeasure over his short attention span, then said, "Alec shouldn't have tossed Justin, and he ruined my surprise."

She suddenly started crying again. "How did Alec ruin your—"

"Alec didn't ruin anything," she wailed. "If you want to hear this story, I beg you to try to concentrate on what I'm saying. Do you know what the worst of it is? I wanted to kneel before Edgar and recite my pledge of loyalty in Gaelic. Alec didn't know I could speak his language, you see. Then he heard me shouting at Justin in Gaelic, and of course he knew. I dressed in his plaid, but I can't fashion these pleats to save my soul. I wanted everything to be perfect when I knelt before my king. I was going to tell him I loved him, too."

"Your king?"

"No, my Alec," Jamie answered. "I honor my king, sir, but I love my husband. Surely you can see the rightness in that, can't you?"

"Alec will right the damage you believe you've done," the soldier stated. "Why don't you show me how you were going to give your king this pledge?"

Jamie thought that was a rather odd suggestion. She didn't want to offend the kind gentleman, though. He'd patiently listened to her trouble. "I do suppose I could use the practice," she admitted aloud. "He might want me to recite my pledge before he has me flogged."

She knelt down and bowed her head. "I wasn't certain if I should put my hand over my heart or not," she admitted.

"He wouldn't have a preference," the soldier stated.

Jamie closed her eyes and recited the words of loyalty. The soldier helped her stand again. He looked very pleased with her effort.

"And now I shall help you adjust your plaid," the soldier announced.

Jamie smiled her appreciation and turned around so he could get to the task.

Alec leaned against the arch of the entrance, a soft smile on his face as he watched the king of Scotland adjust his wife's plaid.

Chapter Seventeen

He knew he really should tell her who the man she'd wept all over was, yet he didn't have the heart to upset her again.

Jamie was in much better spirits once her plaid had been adjusted for her. She sounded happy, too, when she again offered her appreciation. When she spotted her husband lounging against the entrance, she gave him a wide smile. Alec was so pleased she wasn't crying that he smiled back.

No, he wouldn't upset her now. He'd wait until they were alone and no one else could witness her embarrassment.

Jamie walked up the steps, her hands folded demurely in front of her pleats, drawing her husband's full attention. She stopped in front of him, bowed her head, and whispered in Gaelic, "I love you, Alec."

"I love you too, Jamie."

He tried to take her into his arms but she backed up a step and shook her head. "We have a guest," she reminded him.

"So I must wait until later to . . . paw you?"

"You heard it all, didn't you?"

"I did," he admitted. "You don't look too distressed with me, though."

"Your king is a very kind man."

His mouth dropped open in astonishment. "Then you knew, all the while?"

"Do you honestly believe I would have instructed the man to pay attention to what I was saying if I'd known all the while?" she whispered. "I'm a little slow, Alec, but I'm not completely ignorant. I realized who he was when I was kneeling."

Alec started laughing. "You mustn't tell him I know," she whispered.

"Why?"

"It would hurt his feelings."

"It would?"

Jamie nodded. "He thinks he's protecting my feelings, Alec. We mustn't disappoint him."

She'd bowed and left the hall before he could make a comment to that ridiculous remark. His king called out to him then, drawing his full attention.

Alec said, "Do you think I'll try to challenge you, Edgar, or thank you for forcing me to marry her?"

"You'll thank me, of course," Edgar returned. "And we'll both be challenged by Henry if he realizes what a gem he's given us."

Both Alec and Edgar laughed over their own cunning. "We won't have long to wait," Alec predicted. "My wife will probably start a war with England in another week or two. There was a moment when I thought she was Henry's secret weapon," he admitted.

Jamie could hear the howls of laughter coming through the doors. She wondered what jest Alec had just told the king, then decided it was probably that foul story about the dead Englishwoman.

She'd nearly collapsed to her knees the minute the doors had closed behind her. All the horrible comments she'd made to Edgar were screaming inside her head. Heaven help her, she'd actually cried in front of the man.

And he'd given her his understanding. That sudden thought made her heart warm with gratitude. He really was a kind man.

"Jamie, what are you doing out here by yourself?" Gavin asked.

"Why do you ask such a question, Gavin? Am I to have an escort all the time?"

"You are," the soldier admitted before he could stop himself.

"By Alec's order?"

He turned the topic rather than answering her. "One of our cooks has burned her hand, Jamie. She'd like you to look at it."

Jamie's attention was immediately swayed. "Oh, the poor woman," she said. "Take me to her at once, Gavin, and I shall see what I can do."

The next two hours were spent ministering to the sick woman. The woman's burn really wasn't too severe, but Jamie ended up having a nice visit with the cook's large family.

Gavin stayed by her side all the while. When they started back toward the main house, Jamie said, "I'd like to put fresh flowers on Helena's grave, Gavin. Will you walk with me?"

"I will," he agreed. He called out their errand to Marcus when they passed the stables and saw him readying his mount.

Jamie and Gavin maintained a tranquil silence as she picked wildflowers. When her arms were brimming with her collection, they started up the hill to Helena's grave. They passed the consecrated cemetery, squared off by old pine slats, and continued on.

"Gavin? Were you here when Helena died?"

"I was," he replied.

"I was told she killed herself," Jamie went on. "Father Murdock said she jumped off one of the cliffs."

Gavin nodded. He motioned to the rise to the left of Helena's grave. "It happened over there."

"Did anyone see her jump?"

Gavin nodded. "Yes, Jamie."

"Where were you? Did you see—"

"Jamie, must we speak of this?"

Jamie knelt down beside Helena's grave and brushed the old flowers away. "I'm just trying to understand, Gavin," she whispered. "Would you think me daft if I admitted that I think Helena wants me to understand?"

"I probably would," Gavin replied, trying to make his tone light. "Someone has already put flowers on her grave," he remarked in an attempt to change the subject.

"I did," Jamie explained. "The day before yesterday."

She didn't speak again until she'd finished blanketing the grave with the colorful flowers.

Gavin waited until she turned back to him before questioning her. "Jamie? Will you explain what you meant about Helena wanting you to understand?" He knelt on one knee and began to twirl one of the flowers between his fingers while he waited for her to answer. He noticed then that Jamie was patting the grave.

"It doesn't make sense," Jamie suddenly blurted out. "How can I make Mary Kathleen understand when the time comes for her to be told? I have to understand first."

"What is there to understand? Helena was in despair. She—"

"But did you see this despair, Gavin?"

He shook his head. "I didn't know the woman well enough to make such a judgment. I admit I was . . . surprised when she . . ."

"Then you didn't see this terrible unhappiness. Father Murdock was just as surprised as you were. She seemed content to him. She was anxious to bring her baby here. If she was afraid of Alec, or if she hated him, she wouldn't have wanted to bring her daughter here."

"Perhaps she didn't think she had a choice," Gavin remarked.

Jamie stood up and started toward the ridge where Helena had jumped. "She could have fallen. Yes, it could have been an accident. Why was she damned by everyone?"

She stopped when she neared the edge. A shiver passed

down her arms. She rubbed them to take the sudden chill away. "When I first met Alec, I was a little afraid of him. It took me less than a day to realize what a good man he was, and I knew, from the very beginning, that he'd take care of me, Gavin. Helena would have felt the same, I'm sure of it."

Gavin nodded. "You must remember, Jamie, that Helena didn't know Alec well. He was called away——"

"Did she die quickly?" Jamie whispered.

"No," Gavin returned. "She landed on that ledge down there," he told her, pointing toward the jagged stone. "When Alec arrived home, they'd already dragged her back up. You couldn't have saved her. No one could. Her back was broken."

"She wasn't dead?"

"She died two days later," Gavin answered. "She never opened her eyes, and I don't think she was in pain, Jamie."

"She lost her footing," Jamie insisted, trying to believe that possibility.

"We should go back now, Jamie," Gavin announced, trying to change the subject. "Alec will be looking for you. Now that the king has left——"

"He's gone?" Jamie interrupted. "When, Gavin? He only just arrived."

"He was taking his leave while you were collecting your flowers, Jamie."

"Well, spit," Jamie muttered. "I didn't get to say good-bye."

"He'll come back soon," Gavin promised her. "Alec is like a son to him. He visits regularly."

A sudden sound drew Gavin's attention. Just as he turned around, he was struck on the side of the head by a large rock. Gavin saw only blinding light before he staggered backward.

Jamie turned just as Gavin began to fall. A stone hit her forehead, gouging a deep cut. She cried out as she grabbed Gavin from behind. She was desperately trying to keep the soldier from falling over the ledge.

Something sharp hit her shoulder. Jamie screamed in pain. Gavin's weight was too much for her. She knew they were going to fall, but she remembered that the ridge sloped sharply to the left . . . or was it the right? "Please, God, help us," she whimpered as she tightened her hold around the warrior's waist. She used every ounce of strength to push the two of them toward the low overhang.

The eerie sound of laughter followed them over the ledge. Jamie tried to protect Gavin's head by pushing his face into the crook of her shoulder. Sharp pain radiated throughout her body from the stones they rolled over, and when they finally reached the ledge, Gavin's body took most of the impact.

The laughter was getting closer. Blood poured over Jamie's left eye, blocking her vision. She wiped the blood away with the back of her hand and then pulled Gavin back against the rock wall. She was desperately trying to hide them from their enemy. Gavin groaned when she was tucking him under the overhang. She slapped her hand over his mouth and then flattened herself on top of him.

Long minutes passed before she realized the hideous laughter had stopped. Her shoulder and upper arm were throbbing. Jamie reached up to try to rub the ache away. She whimpered when she felt the hilt of the dagger protruding from her arm, and let her hand drop back to her side. She realized that the sharp object had been her dagger— someone had thrown her own dagger at her!

She heard someone calling to her, but did not answer until she recognized the voice. "Marcus! We're here, on the ledge," Jamie shouted then, though her relief was so great it weakened her voice.

"My God, Jamie, what—" Marcus asked when he leaned over the edge of the cliff and saw Jamie's bloody face peering up at him. "Give me your hand, lass."

"Be careful, Marcus. Don't kneel so close to the edge. Someone tried to hurt Gavin and me. Look behind you to make certain it's safe."

Marcus did as she ordered, and when he turned back to her, the look on his face began to frighten her. "Gavin's injured," she rushed out, ignoring his outstretched hand again. "If I leave him, he might roll off the ledge."

Marcus nodded. When he started to withdraw his hand,

Jamie suddenly reached up and grabbed hold. "I want Alec," she cried. "But I don't want you to leave us here, Marcus. Please don't leave us."

The warrior gave her hand a good squeeze. "Hold on to Gavin, Jamie. I won't leave you. I'll shout for help."

She thought that was the most wonderful idea she'd ever heard and told him so in long, rambling sentences. Her mind was so filled with pain now, she could barely make any sense. "Jamie, let go of my hand. I know you trust me."

"You do?"

He gave her a tender smile. "'Tis the reason you grabbed hold of me," he told her. "Now you must let go of me. Hold Gavin."

He'd kept his voice soft, soothing. "Yes," she agreed, trying to keep her concentration on what he'd told her. "Hold Gavin. I will, Marcus. I'll protect him."

She finally let go of his hand. "That's a good lass," she heard him say as she scooted back to Gavin. She put Gavin's head in her lap. "Alec will be here in just a few minutes, Gavin. Marcus will keep us safe until he arrives."

Marcus's deep bellow sent several pebbles cascading down the slope. Jamie closed her eyes against the noise. The ledge suddenly started spinning around and around until all her thoughts began to whirl together.

And then she couldn't think at all.

Jamie didn't wake up until she felt someone pulling on her hands. She opened her eyes and saw Alec bending over her. "Alec," she whispered in wonder. She tried to reach out to him, but the pain in her upper arm stopped her. She managed a weak smile instead, as she noticed she was still on the ledge.

His expression was grim. When she noticed that, she began to frown. "Don't build me a box. Promise me, Alec. Don't build me a box."

She could tell by his puzzled look that he didn't know what she was talking about. "You were going to build Angus a box," she reminded him. "Please . . ."

"I won't build you a box, love," Alec whispered.

She smiled again. "I'm so happy to see you."

His hands shook. "I'm happy to see you, too," he told her in a gruff voice.

"I lost my dagger."

She looked as though she was having as much difficulty as he was believing that statement. She frowned up at him while he gently brushed her hair away from her face, trying to remember the other question she wanted to ask him.

She gave up after a minute. "Alec, the dagger—"

"Don't worry about your dagger, love," Alec soothed. "Can you move your legs, Jamie? I want to take you into my arms and lift you up to my men. Sweetheart, let go of Gavin now. Let me—"

"Gavin?"

"Yes, love, Gavin," he explained.

Jamie looked down when Alec started prying her hands away from Gavin's chest. She remembered everything then. "He was hit by a rock," she said. "The blow knocked him backwards, Alec. He was going to fall over the steep edge. I got behind him," she rushed on. "He was so heavy. I couldn't keep him from falling, so I put my arms around his waist and pushed us both down toward the slope."

She smiled at her husband, ignoring his worried grimace. "I couldn't remember which direction, but I guessed the right way, didn't I?"

"You did," he told her in a hoarse whisper.

"You have to take him up first," she ordered. Her voice was surprisingly clear now; she was so blissfully relieved to have Alec taking charge she wanted to weep.

Alec decided not to argue with her. He eased Gavin up, over his shoulders in much the same way a woman would wear a shawl, and then stood up. His legs were braced apart for balance as he slowly lifted the sleeping soldier high above his head.

"We've got his hands," Marcus shouted down.

Alec moved Gavin's legs away from the rock once the weight was taken away. He knelt down beside Jamie again. His eyes looked suspiciously misty to her. She realized then that she must have caused him considerable worry. "I'm going to be fine, Alec. I told you I wouldn't leave you."

He couldn't believe she was trying to comfort him. "No, you're not going to leave me," he muttered affectionately. "I can see the blood on your face is all bluster," he added, remembering those words from her remarks about Angus's chest wound.

"My dagger's in my shoulder," she blurted out.

He didn't show any reaction to that statement. Jamie immediately decided the injury wasn't as horrible as she imagined. Still, she needed to have him tell her so before she quit her worrying. "Is it awful, Alec?"

"No," he answered. "It isn't in your shoulder, either, Jamie."

"I can feel it," she argued. She tried to turn her head to look for herself, but Alec grabbed hold of her chin. "It's in your upper arm," he explained. "You're most fortunate. It went through the fat."

"I don't have any fat," Jamie argued. She watched him tear a strip from his plaid, yet still didn't guess what his intent was. "Clear through, Alec? Oh, God, it's going to hurt something fierce when it's—"

She never finished her sentence. Alec had the dagger out of her flesh as quick as lightning and was wrapping the strip of cloth around her arm before she could get enough strength back to scream.

"There! That didn't hurt, did it?" he asked.

"It did!"

"Hush, love," he soothed. "You would have worried about the dagger coming out until you'd made yourself sick."

He was right and they both knew it. "If you had to get yourself stabbed, I imagine you picked the best spot. The dagger didn't hit bone."

She let out a gasp. "I knew you'd think this was all my fault," she told him. Her mind concentrated on his contrary remark and she barely noticed Alec had lifted her into his arms and was slowly standing up. "I didn't get myself stabbed and you damn well know it."

"I know, love, but it's good of you to remind me," he told

her. He was lifting her above his head now. Jamie started to look down. He felt her tense in his grasp. He thought to warn her not to look down, then decided against it. His caution would only remind her of her precarious position. "At least you found your dagger," he announced, sounding outrageously cheerful.

"There is that," she snapped. "Alec, you're hurting me," she cried out when his hand accidentally brushed against her arm. She closed her eyes against the excruciating pain.

"I'm sorry, Jamie. I didn't mean to hurt you, lass."

The agony in his voice tugged at her heart. "It didn't hurt overly much," she said quickly. She felt someone lifting her away from Alec and opened her eyes again. Marcus had her in his arms an instant or two later, and then Alec was over the rise again and she was gently given back to him.

It barely bothered her injuries at all when Alec gained his stallion. He kept her well cushioned in his arms. His strength was such a comfort to her. She sighed against his shoulder.

"Why haven't you asked me if I saw the attacker?" she asked him.

"I know who it was," he answered.

"I think I know, too," Jamie whispered. "But you'll have to give me the name first."

She knew that didn't make any sense, and Alec's grim expression suggested he'd rather not discuss the topic now. She ignored the suggestion, of course, and asked, "Who was the witness?"

"What witness?" he asked. His concentration centered on keeping his stallion at an easy gait, and he barely took the time to look down at his wife's face.

"The witness to Helena's death," she whispered.

"Annie."

Two hours later, Jamie was propped up in her bed in the great hall. Alec had kicked the screen to the floor in his hurry to get her settled. The screen had been carried outside and the hall was now crowded with her clan.

THE BRIDE

Alec tended to her injuries. She'd given him instructions about the proper powders to use, and made him refashion the bandage on her arm twice before she was satisfied.

Gavin was awake, too. He had a fierce headache. Jamie wouldn't let anyone give him any ale, though. She ordered cold cloths on his head and water to drink. He'd have to suffer through his headache, she dictated from her bed, and that was that.

Jamie never made a sound or showed a grimace while she was being patched up. In truth, vanity was her real motive, not courage. She wasn't about to act cowardly in front of her relatives.

Father Murdock had made that task easy for her. The dear priest sat on the edge of the bed and held her hand all during Alec's work. Little Mary Kathleen was carried in and settled next to her mother when Alec was finished. The three-year-old started crying when she saw the bandage on Jamie's forehead. Alec soothed the child by telling her to give her mother a kiss.

Mary immediately did as Alec suggested and was rewarded by her mama's surprised announcement that she was feeling ever so much better now. The little girl fell asleep a few minutes later, cuddled up against Jamie's side.

Jamie saw Marcus motion to Alec. "You've found her, then?" she called out.

No one answered her. Alec started toward the door. "Alec, bring Annie inside," she said. "I want to ask her why."

Alec shook his head. "I'll listen to what she has to say outside."

"And then?"

"I'll decide."

Father Murdock squeezed Jamie's hand when she started to call out to her husband again. "Leave it in his hands, lass. He's a compassionate man."

Jamie nodded. "He doesn't like admitting it, but he is compassionate. Annie's mind is twisted," she whispered. "Alec will remember that."

And then the sound of that horrid, inhuman laughter

filled the hall and she found herself clutching the priest's hand for comfort. Annie's words lashed out with the sting of a whip. The venom she screeched was made worse by her singsong tone of voice. "I'll be your wife, I will. No matter how long it takes me, Kincaid. It's my right. My right. Helena took you away from me. I challenged you then, Alec, and I'll challenge you again."

Jamie heard another loud burst of laughter, and then Annie started chanting again. "I'll kill again and again and again until you've learned your lesson. It's my right to stand beside you. It's—"

The sudden silence, after such demoniacal sounds, was startling to Jamie. She tried to get out of the bed.

"Stay where you are, Jamie," Gavin ordered from the foot of the bed. He loomed over her like an angry avenger. His command was ruined when he put his hands to his head and groaned. "I shouldn't have yelled at you, milady, but Alec wants you to stay put."

"You shouldn't have yelled at me because it made your head pound," Jamie countered.

"That, too," Gavin admitted.

Jamie moved her feet out of the way just in the nick of time. Gavin collapsed on the foot of her bed and let out another pitiful groan as he fell back. She guessed he was trying to turn her attention away from the happenings outside by demanding her sympathy.

"I have complete faith in my husband," she told Gavin. "You needn't carry on so to turn my concentration."

"Then I can have a drink of ale?" Gavin asked.

"You can't."

"The bed is getting damn crowded," Alec announced from the top of the steps.

Jamie smiled. She waited until he'd kissed her properly before asking, "It's finished?"

He nodded. "Alec? You were supposed to marry her, weren't you?"

"Edgar had planned to unite the Kincaids with their clan to gain peace. I was pledged to Annie, aye."

"But she's so much younger than you . . ."

"She's only one year younger than you, Jamie."

"She seems so much a child still," she whispered. "Edgar changed his mind after Helena's husband died?"

Alec nodded. "He did. Helena was carrying her babe, and the king wanted to give her a good home."

Jamie nodded, understanding. And then she gave him a magnificent smile. He had to shake his head over her strange reaction. "She didn't want to leave you either, Alec."

He still didn't comprehend her joy until she turned to Father Murdock and said, "Tomorrow you'll have to bless Helena's grave. She must have a requiem mass, too. The entire clan must be there, Alec."

"Do you want her to be reburied in consecrated ground, Jamie?" Father Murdock asked.

She shook her head. "We'll extend the consecrated cemetery to include that whole section. Alec and I will, of course, be buried next to Helena. It is fitting, isn't it, husband?"

"It's fitting," Alec announced, his voice husky with emotion.

"Don't sound so pleased," Jamie teased. "I'm leaving instructions for you to be placed in the center, Kincaid. You'll have a wife on either side to keep you 'settled in' for all eternity."

"God help me," Alec muttered.

"He already has," Father Murdock announced. "He's given you two good women in your lifetime, Alec, and that's a fact. Our Maker has a sense of humor, too."

"How's that?" Gavin asked between his groans.

"The sweet lass Alec happens to love comes from England, if you'll all remember, and if that isn't a trick on God's part, I sure as spit don't know what is."

"Oh, God, he's starting to sound like her," Gavin said with a laugh he immediately regretted, for his head started aching again.

Jamie noticed Edith across the room then. She could see how upset the woman was. "You aren't really meaning to send Edith away, are you, Alec?" she asked.

When Alec shook his head, Jamie motioned Edith closer.

"Edith, you aren't leaving us. It was just a plan to get Annie to try to kill me again."

"Again, wife? Then you knew the fire——"

"No," Jamie interrupted. "I didn't know until I heard Annie laughing just now. I recognized the sound. It was the same I'd heard when I was trapped inside the hut."

She paused to give Alec a good frown. "It was most unkind of you to use me as your bait, Alec."

"It wasn't supposed to happen that way," Alec replied, his tone hard. "Gavin was supposed to stay with you and Marcus was supposed to keep Annie in his sight at all times."

"It's my fault," Edith blurted out. "I didn't know you were planning a trap. I thought Annie was ill. She took to her bed after we were told we were being sent away. I was so upset, I didn't notice when she left."

"No, sister," Marcus interjected. He walked over to stand at Edith's side. "It's my fault. I take full responsibility."

"But I told you to ready the horses," Edith argued.

"It wasn't anyone's fault," Jamie said. "Edith, you do want to stay with us, don't you? I can't get along without you . . . until you decide on a proper husband," she added.

"You were never meant to leave," Alec told Edith. "But I wanted Annie to believe I was sending you both away because of your relation to Helena. You'll remember when I ordered you to leave, I said I didn't want any reminders of my first wife."

Edith nodded. "I do remember."

Alec smiled. "You never questioned me. Didn't you wonder why Mary Kathleen wasn't included?"

Edith shook her head. "I was too upset to think it through," she admitted.

"I thought of it," Alec returned. "Though only after I'd left your cottage."

"Forgive your laird for causing you such distress," Jamie advised Edith.

Edith quickly nodded. "Oh, I understand now."

"Would you mind taking Mary up to her room now?"

Jamie asked, guessing Edith was close to losing her composure.

Jamie waited until Edith was carrying Mary up the stairs before she asked Alec the question most worrying her. "What will you do with Annie?"

He wouldn't answer her.

Alec was being impossible. He wouldn't let Jamie out of their bed for almost a week. He expected her to nap the days away and then sleep soundly through the nights. She thought it rather odd she was able to accommodate him.

Her convalescence was made easier by her sister's daily visits. Mary helped her sew the tapestry of Edgar's likeness, finally taking over the task in full when she realized Jamie didn't have the patience or the skill for the job.

During Mary's first visit, she whispered the news that Daniel had still not bedded her. Jamie was more upset over this announcement than Mary was, but once she'd explained how truly wonderful this intimacy was—in carefully chosen, general terms, of course—Mary's interest was piqued.

"He keeps a mistress," Mary confessed. "But he sleeps in my bed each night."

"It's time to clean your house, Mary," Jamie advised. "Throw the woman out."

"He'd get angry with me, Jamie," her sister whispered. "I've grown to like his smiles too much to prick his temper. He's being very kind to me, too, now that I've quit crying. The man can't stand tears. I am beginning to care for him."

Jamie was thrilled with that admission. "Then ask him to bed you," she suggested.

"I have my pride," Mary countered. "I have thought of a plan, though."

"What is it?"

"I thought to tell him he could keep his mistress and have me, too."

"You cannot mean to share the man," Jamie argued.

Mary lifted her shoulders in a helpless gesture. "I want Daniel to like me, Jamie," she admitted.

She started crying then, just as Alec strolled into the great hall. Jamie held her smile for Mary's benefit, but she did have to struggle. As soon as Alec saw Mary's condition, he turned around and walked back outside. "Men do hate tears," she said in agreement with her sister's earlier statement.

"Tell Daniel he must keep his mistress," Jamie advised. "Now don't look at me like that, Mary. Then you're to tell him you think he must need the practice and when he's gotten it just right, he can come to you."

Alec returned to the hall when he heard Jamie and her sister laughing.

Mary didn't come to see her sister for two long days. Jamie was in a fretful state, worrying about her sister, but when Mary finally did pay her call three days' later, she could tell by her happy smile that all was well.

Mary wanted to give Jamie the details. Jamie didn't want to hear them. Mary was insistent, and right in the middle of her whispers about how wonderful Daniel was, Alec, Gavin, Marcus, and Daniel came into the hall. They wanted to be included in the conversation. The topic immediately changed.

Alec kept Jamie up most of the night, making love to her. He wouldn't let her be as aggressive as she wanted to be, fearing her strength wasn't fully restored. In the end, he admitted to her the sorry fact that although he was stronger, she certainly had more stamina.

He left the following morning on duties King Edgar required, and wasn't due back home for a full week. Jamie used his time away to make another little change in his household.

She had the bed and its platform moved out of the great hall. The screen now enclosed a buttery. It was yet another English tradition, but once the soldiers realized it would make the ale easier to get to, they went along with her orders without voicing too many complaints.

Alec came home three days later. The soldiers took their place in line again, ready to defend her.

Alec sat at the head of the table. His jaw was clenched

shut while she explained the necessity of a buttery to him.

He did have trouble accepting change. Jamie was pleased with him, though, for he hadn't raised his voice at all. She knew the effort cost him dearly. His face became flushed and the muscle was flexing in his cheek again. She was full of sympathy for him, too. For that reason, she didn't even bat an eyelash when he asked her in a low, controlled voice to leave him in peace for a few minutes.

Alec knew she wasn't upset with his request when she didn't pause to take a coin from the box atop the mantel. He'd caught on early to her subtle way of letting him know whenever he'd made her angry. She'd never say a word, just give him a good glare and then grab one of her shillings. She didn't know Father Murdock replaced the coins in the box each night.

She was still having trouble settling in. Some nights, Father Murdock had as many as nine shillings in his hand.

Jamie's sister was just dismounting when Jamie came outside with Mary Kathleen on her hip.

"I've the most horrible news," Mary rushed out. "Andrew's on his way here."

"Andrew?"

"The man you were pledged to," Mary reminded her. "Honestly, Jamie, how could you have forgotten him already?"

"I haven't forgotten," Jamie answered. She handed Mary Kathleen to Mary when her sister reached for the child. While Mary hugged the little girl, Jamie tried to stay calm. "Mary, why would Andrew be coming here? And how did you find out?"

"I heard Daniel talking to one of his men. All the Highland clans know he's coming, Jamie. He and his army had to pass through their lands."

"Oh, my God, he's coming here with an army?"

"He is."

"But why, Mary?"

"The loan," Mary whispered after she'd put her niece

down. "Remember the coins Papa borrowed from Andrew?"

"How could I forget? Papa all but sold me to Andrew," she wailed. "Oh, Mary, I can't be humiliated in front of my clan. I can't let Andrew shame me this way. Good God, Mary, Alec is bound to kill Andrew."

Mary nodded. "Those were Daniel's very words."

"Then he knows the reason Andrew is coming here?" Jamie asked, clearly appalled.

"Yes. Andrew has had to explain his reason for being in the Highlands. He wouldn't have gotten very far without being killed already if he hadn't explained. Sister, haven't you noticed the Scots don't like the English very much?"

"Well, spit, Mary, who doesn't know?"

"Jamie, you shouldn't be talking so unladylike."

"I can't help it," Jamie cried. "I'm always the last one to know anything around here. Do you think Alec knows Andrew is coming?"

Mary lifted her shoulders in a helpless gesture. "Daniel says all Scots know when someone comes near their holding. I would guess—"

"I can't let this happen. I won't be responsible for starting a war with England, too."

"England? Alec will probably only kill Andrew and his followers."

"You think King Henry won't notice one of his barons is missing, Mary? He's bound to think it odd when he calls up his army and no one comes. . . ."

She didn't bother to finish her explanation, but snatched the reins out of her sister's hands and quickly mounted Mary's horse.

"What are you planning, Jamie?"

"I'm going to find Andrew and reason with him. I'll promise to send the coins to him."

"Jamie, it's going to be dark soon. 'Tis the reason Daniel wouldn't let me come to visit you."

Jamie smiled. "Yet you came anyway, didn't you, Mary?"

"I had to warn you, sister. I thought you might want to hide for a while."

"It was a most unselfish, courageous thing you did, warning me, but you know very well I'd never hide."

"I hoped you would. I certainly didn't think you'd go chasing Andrew down. Was I truly courageous, Jamie?"

Jamie nodded. "Now listen well, Mary. I want your promise you won't tell anyone where I've gone. Please?"

"I promise."

"Watch over Mary Kathleen until I get back."

"What will I tell Alec?"

"Don't tell him anything."

"But—"

"Cry," Jamie blurted out. "Yes, cry, Mary. Alec won't ask you any questions if you're weeping. I'll be back before he even notices I've left. Now point me in the right direction, Mary."

"You just head down the hills, Jamie."

Mary made a quick sign of the cross while she watched her sister race down the hill. Father Murdock strolled over to Mary, bade her good day, and then remarked that Lady Kincaid had certainly taken off in a hurry and did Lady Ferguson happen to know where the lass was going?

Lady Ferguson immediately burst into tears.

She kept her promise to her sister, too. She didn't tell Alec where Jamie had gone. She didn't have to. Mary Kathleen told him everything.

The little girl went back inside as soon as her mother left. She ran over to Alec, climbed up on his lap, and drank a big gulp of ale before he realized what she was doing. Alec snatched the goblet away and then gave her a cup of water. When she'd finished her drink, he asked her almost absentmindedly where her mama was.

Mary Kathleen leaned back against her papa's chest and played with her toes and his belt while she repeated almost word for word the entire conversation she'd overheard.

For his daughter's sake, Alec didn't start shouting until he was outside. Once Jamie's sister saw Alec's face, she didn't have to put real effort into her sobs. She went into immediate hysterics.

Father Murdock did his best to try to console the poor, loud woman, but his efforts were all for naught. By the time Alec had left with his contingent of soldiers, Mary was screeching like a trapped hen. The priest went inside the chapel to pray for peace. More specifically, he prayed Daniel would come and fetch his wife.

Alec followed Jamie's trail. When it curved to the east, he began to relax. She was now headed for Ferguson land.

"Did she change her mind, then?" Marcus shouted.

"She's lost," Alec called over his shoulder. "And thank God for that," he muttered to himself.

He caught up with Jamie fifteen minutes later. He forced her to stop by motioning for his soldiers to encircle her.

Husband and wife faced each other. Neither said a word for a long minute. She was desperately trying to come up with a plausible explanation. He was wondering what outrageous lie she'd give him.

"You asked me to leave you in peace for a little while," she said.

"I did."

She nudged her mount forward. When she reached Alec's side, she whispered, "I was just going to try to reason with Andrew. My sister told you all about my errand, didn't she?"

"Your daughter told me."

Her eyes widened in reaction to that announcement. "I must remember in future not to speak so openly."

"You'll remember not to attempt anything this foolish in future."

"Please don't be angry with me, Alec," she pleaded.

Alec grabbed her by the nape of her neck and gave her a long, hard kiss.

"Why didn't you come to me when you heard that Andrew—"

"I was ashamed," she whispered before he could finish his question. "Papa took coins for me. I didn't want you to think my father had actually sold me to Andrew, but even I was beginning to think—"

Alec shook his head. "What your father did has nothing to do with how I feel about you. I'll repay the bastard. Come along, wife. We might as well get this over and done with."

She knew better than to argue with him, yet she did wonder how he was going to repay Baron Andrew. He was riding bareback and didn't have a pouch on his belt. He had carried his sword along, though. "Alec, are we expecting trouble?"

He didn't answer her. Jamie was left with her worries as she followed behind her husband. He was right, she decided after thinking about it a long while, she really should have gone directly to him. Husbands and wives should share their problems. It felt good, too, to have someone help with the burdens. No, she admitted. It didn't just feel good. It felt wonderful to have him to lean on every now and again.

They didn't speak again until they'd reached Andrew's camp. Jamie tried to move in front of Alec, but he grabbed the reins of her mount and forced her next to him. He raised his hand. His soldiers immediately lined up on either side of their laird and his mistress.

"Oh, Alec, did you have to bring so many soldiers?"

When he didn't answer her, she let out a loud sigh. "At least they'll keep my shame to themselves," she muttered.

Alec smiled, drawing her attention. Then he motioned again.

The other clans came forward then. While Jamie watched in astonishment, the lairds and their clansmen took their positions. A wide, yawning circle formed, with Andrew and his men trapped inside.

The English soldiers drew their weapons. Alec signaled again. The circle began to tighten as the horses moved forward.

When the English soldiers saw the numbers they faced, they threw their weapons to the ground.

Andrew separated himself from his men and started toward Jamie.

She'd forgotten what a little man Andrew was. Had she ever thought him handsome? She couldn't remember. He was certainly unappealing to her now though, and his short-cropped hair reminded her of a little boy. No, she thought to herself, she couldn't have found him the least bit attractive.

The man didn't even walk properly. He strutted. A shiver went through her when she realized she might have ended up with him. Jamie suddenly wanted to turn to her husband and thank him for saving her from certain misery.

Alec raised his hand again when Andrew was still some thirty feet away. The baron understood the silent command. He came to a quick stop.

"We cut off a man's feet when he trespasses on our land."

Alec's threat seemed to take the wind out of Andrew. The baron backed up several spaces before regaining his composure. His expression showed fear and disdain when he looked from Alec to Jamie.

"You wouldn't let him do it, would you, Jamie?"

Jamie's expression was very serene. She stared at Andrew when she spoke to her husband. "With your permission, I would like to answer him."

"You have it," Alec replied.

"Andrew," she called out in a voice as cold and clear as a frigid winter morning, "my husband does whatever he wishes to do. I am sometimes allowed to help, though. If he decides to cut off your feet, I will, of course, offer him my assistance."

Jamie heard Marcus's low grunt of approval but kept her gaze on Andrew and her smile contained.

The baron looked furious. "You've become a savage," he shouted, obviously forgetting in his anger his precarious position. He pointed to Alec and added, "He's turned you into a . . . Scot."

She knew he thought he'd insulted her. Jamie couldn't keep her amusement contained a minute longer. Her lusty laughter echoed through the hills. "Andrew, I do believe your compliment has just saved your feet."

"State your business," Alec roared. He wanted to finish this as soon as possible so he could take Jamie into his arms.

He ached with the need to tell her again how much he loved her, cherished her . . . and how very proud he was to have her for his own.

His roar accomplished his goal. Andrew fairly tripped over his explanation. Jamie, humiliated to the very core of her being, kept her gaze downcast as the baron explained the dowry he'd given her father.

When he finished his explanation, Alec pulled his sword from its sheath.

"Are you going to kill him, then, husband?" she asked in a whisper.

Alec smiled. "You know damn well I'm not going to kill him. It would displease you, and I'm forever wanting to make you happy, wife. I'm going to give him the sword. Its value—"

"You'll not give the likes of him your magnificent sword, Kincaid," Jamie returned, staring straight ahead. "I'll forget my dignity and make a scene you'll never live down. They'll be talking about it for years to come, I promise you."

She heard him sigh and knew she'd won. "Aye, you probably would, you contrary woman. Give me your dagger, then."

Jamie did as he ordered. She watched as Alec used the dagger to pry one of the large rubies from the hilt of his sword. When the task was done, he gave her back her weapon.

She watched Andrew when Alec threw the stone. The ruby landed at the baron's feet. "Repayment, Baron, from Lady Kincaid."

Another fat stone hit Andrew in the shoulder. Jamie turned in the direction the stone had come from and saw Laird McPherson replacing his sword. "Repayment from Lady Kincaid," the old man bellowed before turning to look at her.

A third stone hit Andrew on the side of his face. "Repayment," came the shout from Daniel Ferguson.

"Repayment," echoed once again. Jamie didn't recognize the laird who'd thrown that jewel.

"Alec? Why are—"

"McPherson repays because you saved his son's life. Daniel repays because you placed yourself in front of his wife to protect her. Harold threw the emerald. You took his son's insult and then pleaded for his life."

A fifth stone cut the skin on Andrew's forehead. "Repayment," another man roared.

"Who is he?"

"Lindsay's father," Alec answered. "You didn't think I knew about the boar, did you?"

She was too stunned to answer him. Yet another stone fell in front of Andrew's boots. A young warrior had thrown it. "Repayment," he shouted.

Alec explained before she could ask. "Laird Duncan. His wife wishes you to attend her birthing. He's paying for future aid."

"I am overwhelmed," Jamie whispered. "Do I thank them, Alec?"

"They're thanking you, Jamie. Each would give his life to keep you safe. You've done the impossible, love. You've actually united our clans."

She closed her eyes to keep herself from crying. Her voice shook with emotion when she said, "You've made Andrew a very rich man."

"No, Jamie. I'm much richer. I have you."

His voice had been so soft, so filled with love. A tear slipped down her cheek. Alec saw it. He immediately turned back to Andrew. "Go home, Baron. The next time you step on Highland ground, we'll all take a turn putting our swords through you."

A resounding cheer echoed around the circle. Andrew was kneeling on the ground, collecting his treasure. Alec pulled Jamie into his arms. She immediately wrapped her arms around his waist.

Baron Andrew stared at the fortune he held in his hands. When he looked up again, not a Scot was in sight.

Jamie closed her eyes and hugged her husband. She still didn't understand most of the odd habits of the Highlanders, guessed it would take her a good twenty or thirty years before she truly did comprehend them.

There was joy in the learning, though, such incredible joy and love. Perhaps, she thought with a secret smile, when she and Alec had grown old together, perhaps then she might just settle in.

**Pocket Books celebrates
Julie Garwood's new hardcover with
a $2.00 rebate—and invites you to**

OFFICIAL MAIL-IN OFFER FORM

To receive your $2.00 REBATE CHECK by mail,
just follow these simple rules:

• Purchase the hardcover edition of Julie Garwood's
THE WEDDING by December 31, 1996.

• Mail this official form (no photocopies accepted), proof of
purchase (the clipped corner from the inside front jacket flap that
shows the product price and title), and the original store cash
register receipt, dated on or before December 31, 1996, with the
purchase price of THE WEDDING circled.

All requests must be received by January 7, 1997. This offer is valid in the United
States only. Limit one (1) rebate request per address or household. You must
purchase a hardcover copy of Julie Garwood's THE WEDDING in order to qualify
for a rebate, and cash register receipt must show the purchase price and date of
purchase. Requests for rebates from groups, clubs or organizations will not be
honored. Void where prohibited, taxed, or restricted. Allow 8 weeks for delivery
of rebate check. Not responsible for lost, late, or misdirected responses. Requests
not complying with all offer requirements will not be honored. Any fraudulent
submission will be prosecuted to the fullest extent permitted by law.

Print your full address clearly for proper delivery of your rebate:

Name_____

Address_____Apt #_____

City_____ State_____ Zip_____

Mail this completed form to:
Julie Garwood's THE WEDDING $2.00 Rebate
P.O. Box 9037
Bridgeport, NJ 08014-9037

1241

Dear Reader,

When I finished writing _The Bride_ several years ago, I was reluctant to say good-bye to the Kincaid clan. I have always held a special affection for Alec and Jamie Kincaid, and in the back of my mind I think I've always known I'd write another story that would include them.

I've finally done just that, and I've called it _The Wedding._ The story takes place seventeen years after _The Bride_ ends. The hero is Connor MacAlister. He's been raised in Alec Kincaid's image, so, of course, he has a fair amount of arrogance. He's a warrior who thinks he's invincible until he meets Brenna, a lady who knows he isn't. They're totally unsuited for each other, have absolutely nothing in common, and if ever two characters needed to find each other, it would have to be these two.

The Wedding will be in bookstores soon, and I hope you'll have as much fun reading Connor and Brenna's story as I did writing it.

Your letters have been both heartwarming and encouraging, and I thank you for every one. I will be sending out a newsletter soon in response to those of you who have asked for one. If you would like to receive the first issue, please send a self-addressed, stamped envelope. My address remains the same: P.O. Box 7574, Leawood, KS 66211. If you would like to drop me a line, I would love to hear from you.

Sincerely,

Julie Garwood

Julie Garwood

The Wedding

England, 1108

It wasn't love at first sight.

Lady Brenna didn't want to be presented to company. She had far more important things to do with her day. Her nursemaid, a dour-faced woman with God-fearing ways and with clumped together, protruding front teeth, wouldn't listen to her arguments, however. She cornered Brenna in the back of the stables and lunged forward. Never one to let an opportunity or a little girl slip past her, the nursemaid lectured her charge all the way up the hill and across the muddy courtyard.

"Quit your squirming, Brenna. I'm stronger than you are, and I'm not about to let go. You've lost your shoes again, haven't you? And don't dare lie to me. I can see your stockings peeking out. Why are you dragging that bridle behind you?"

Brenna lifted her shoulders in a shrug. "I forgot to put it back."

"Drop it this minute. You're always forgetting, and do you know why?"

"I don't pay attention to what I'm doing, like you tell me to, Elspeth."

"You don't pay attention to anything I tell you, and that's a fact. You're more trouble than all the others put together. Your older brothers and sisters have never given me a moment's worry. Even your baby sister knows how to behave herself, and she's still sucking on her fingers and wetting herself. I'm warning you, Brenna, if you don't change your ways and give your parents a little peace, God himself will have to stop His important work and come down here to talk to you. Just how are you going to feel about that? You don't like it much when your papa has to sit you down on his knee and talk to you about your shameful behavior, now do you?"

"No, Elspeth. I surely don't like it. I try to behave. I really do."

She peeked up to see if the nursemaid believed she was contrite. She wasn't, of course, because she really didn't believe she'd done anything wrong, but Elspeth wouldn't understand.

"Don't you bat those big blue eyes at me, young lady. I don't believe you're the least bit sincere. Lord, but you smell. What have you gotten into?"

Brenna lowered her head and kept quiet. She'd

been chasing after the piglets just an hour before, until the tanner put their mama back in the pen, and her peculiar stench was just a small price to pay for all the fun she'd had.

Her torture had only just begun. Even though she had had a bath two days before, she was bathed again, and in the middle of the day, of all times. She was scrubbed from head to toe, and so thoroughly, she had to cry about it. Elspeth wasn't at all sympathetic to her wails, and Brenna eventually got tired of crying. She barely struggled at all while Elspeth dressed her in a blue gown and too-tight matching slippers. Her cheeks were pinched hard for color; her white blond tangles were brushed into curls, and she was then dragged back down to the hall. She would have to pass her mother's inspection before she could be left alone.

Her oldest sister, Matilda, was already seated at the table with her mother. Cook was there, too, going over supper arrangements with her mistress.

"I don't want to meet no company today, Mama. It's sorely wearisome for me."

Elspeth came up behind her and poked her in the shoulder. "Hush now. You mustn't complain. God doesn't like women who complain."

"Papa complains all the time and God likes him just fine," Brenna announced. "That's why Papa's so big. Only God is bigger than he is."

"Where did you hear such nonsense?"

"Papa told me so. I want to go outside now. I won't run after the piglets again. I promise."

"You're staying right where I can keep my eye on you. You're going to behave yourself today. If you don't, you know what will happen to you, don't you?"

Brenna pointed to the ground. "I'll have to go down there." She dutifully repeated the threat she'd heard over and over again.

The little girl didn't have any idea what was 'down there,' she only knew it was awful and she didn't want to go there. According to Elspeth, if Brenna didn't change her sorry ways, she was never going to get into heaven, and just about everyone, including her family, wanted to go there.

She knew exactly where heaven was, because her papa had given her exact directions. It was right on the other side of the sky.

She thought she might like it, but really didn't care. Only one thing was important to her now. She wasn't about to be left behind again. She still had nightmares at least once a week over what her mama referred to as "the unfortunate incidents," because the terrifying memories were still lurking in the back of her mind, where everyone knew all little girls tucked away their worries, just waiting for the right opportunity to jump out in the dark and scare her. Her screams would wake her sister, of course. While Elspeth was busy soothing baby Faith, Brenna would drag her blanket to her parents' chamber. When her papa was away from home doing important work the king could give only to someone as trustworthy and loyal as he was, she'd sneak into the big bed and cuddle up next to her mama, and when her papa was home, she'd sleep on the cold floor right next to Courage, his beautiful silver-handled sword, which Mama swore he loved almost as much as his children. She felt safest when her papa was there, because his loud snores always lulled her back to sleep. Demons didn't try to crawl in through the window, and nightmares about being left behind didn't visit her when she was with her parents. They wouldn't dare.

"Please tell Brenna to keep her mouth shut when company arrives, Mother." Matilda requested. "She shouts every word. She does it on purpose. When will she stop?"

"Soon, dear, soon," her mother replied almost absentmindedly.

Brenna moved away from her sister. Matilda was bossy by nature, but now that their brothers were away learning how to be as important as their papa for their king, her condition had worsened. She was becoming as bothersome as Elspeth.

Brenna's shoulders slumped. "Mama, I'm weary of everybody telling me what to do all the time. Doesn't anybody like me?"

Her mother wasn't in the mood to placate her daughter.

"Brenna, do not say another word until you are given permission to speak."

Elspeth moved forward to offer her opinion. " 'Tis my fear you'll never catch a husband for that one, milady."

Brenna put her hands over her ears and ran across the room. She hated it when the nursemaid referred to her as "that one." She wasn't one of the piglets, after all.

"I'll catch a husband by myself!" Brenna shouted.

Joan walked into the hall in time to hear her sister's boast.

"What have you done this time, Brenna?"

"Nothing."

"Tell me what you've done. I promise I won't lecture you."

"I sassed Mama. Did Papa catch your husband for you, Joan?"

"Catch a husband?" she asked. She didn't laugh, because she knew she'd injure Brenna's tender feelings, but she couldn't stop herself from smiling.

"I suppose he did," Joan admitted.

"Did you help?

"No. I'll meet my husband on the day I marry him."

"Aren't you scared he's ugly?"

"What he looks like won't matter. Papa assures me it's a strong alliance."

"Is that good?"

"Oh, yes. Our King has given his approval."

"Rachel says you have to love your husband with your whole heart."

"That's only a foolish wish."

"Elspeth says Papa won't ever find anyone for me. She says Papa's too busy for the likes of me. I have to catch one by myself. Will you help me?"

Joan smiled. "I can see this is worrying you. I'll be happy to help."

"How do I get one?" Brenna whispered.

Joan pretended to consider the matter for a long minute before she answered.

"I imagine you select the man you want and then

you ask him to marry you. If he lives far away, you must send a messenger to him. Yes, that would be how you would do it. Why are we whispering?"

"Mama told me not to talk."

Joan burst into laughter. The noise alerted Elspeth, who immediately rushed over.

"Please don't encourage her, Lady Joan. Brenna, you were told to keep quiet. Doesn't that mouth of yours ever rest?"

"I'm sorry, Elspeth."

The nursemaid snorted in disbelief. "No, you're not sorry." She moved closer, wagged her finger in front of Brenna's face, and said, "One of these days God's going to march in here and lecture you sound, young lady. Mark my words. You'll be sorry then. He doesn't like little girls who sass."

Elspeth finally left her alone. Brenna fell asleep waiting for company to arrive. Her sister Rachel shook her awake and pulled her along to stand with her older sisters.

Brenna hid behind Rachel until her name was called and she was dragged out for display. She was suddenly feeling too shy to look up at the company, and as soon as her papa finished bragging about her, she moved behind her sister again.

None of the strangers paid any attention to her, so she decided to sneak out of the hall while she could. She turned around, took one step towards the entrance, and then came to a quick stop.

Three giants strode into the hall. She was too stunned to move and couldn't stop staring at them. The one in the middle was taller than the other two, and held her interest the longest. She watched him closely, and when her parents crossed the hall to greet the newcomers, she realized he was bigger even than her own papa.

She grabbed hold of Rachel's hand and started tugging. Her sister took a long time to look down.

"What is it?" she whispered.

"He isn't God, is he?" she asked, pointing to the dark-haired guest.

Rachel rolled her eyes heavenward. "No, he most certainly isn't God."

"Did Papa lie to me? He told me only God is bigger than he is, Rachel."

"No, Papa didn't lie. He was just teasing you. That's all. You don't need to be afraid."

Brenna was thoroughly relieved. Papa hadn't deceived her after all, and God hadn't bothered to come down from heaven to lecture her. There was still time for her to change what Elspeth told her was her sinful life.

Her papa's shout of laughter drew her attention. She smiled, because he was having such a fine time, and then turned to look at the middle one again. She'd been told time and again that it was rude to stare, but she didn't obey her mother's rule now. The giant mesmerized her and she wanted to remember everything she could about him.

He must have felt her staring at him, though, because he suddenly turned and looked directly at her.

Brenna decided to make her papa proud of her and

behave like a proper young lady. She grabbed a fistful of her skirt, hiked it up to her knees, and bent down to curtsy. She promptly lost her balance and almost hit her head against the floor, but she was quick enough to lean back so she could land on her bottom.

She stood back up, remembered to let go of her skirts, and peeked up at the stranger to see what he thought about her newly acquired skill.

The giant smiled at her.

As soon as he looked away, she squeezed herself up against Rachel's backside again.

"I'm going to marry him," she whispered.

Rachel smiled. "That's nice."

Brenna solemnly nodded. Yes, it was nice.

Now all she had to do was ask.

Papa let his daughters leave the hall a few minutes later. Brenna waited until everyone else had gone upstairs, then ran back outside. She was determined to catch one of the piglets today so she would finally have a pet of her very own. She would have preferred a pup, but papa had let her older brothers and sisters all have them, leaving none for her, and she meant to right his terrible wrong by taking one of the piglets.

Luck was on her side. The piglets' mama had once again left the pen and was now sleeping in a mud pool on the far side of the stables halfway down the hill. Brenna tried not to make any noise, but she slipped in the mud and made a loud splatter anyway. The babies must have worn their mama out. She didn't even lift her head or open her eyes. Brenna heard the loud squeak of the front doors being opened next. Because no one shouted at her, she was certain she hadn't been seen.

The piglets made her task easy, for they had rolled themselves into little balls and were sleeping on top of each other. Brenna scooped one up in the hem of her skirts, wrapped it up tight, and clutched it against her chest. She thought to run to the kitchens and hide her prize there, and she was sure she would have succeeded with her plan, if her new pet hadn't made such a fuss about it all.

Brenna didn't realize her jeopardy until she was outside the pen and heard the horrible noise coming towards her. Pigs weren't supposed to fly, but the enraged mama seemed to be doing just that. Her head went down when she reached the yard, and she charged forward.

Brenna started screaming. Suddenly too terrified to think, she ran in circles, around and around the pen, clutching her piglet in her arms as she bellowed for her papa to come and save her.

Papa didn't rescue her; the giant who'd smiled at her did. And just in the nick of time. The mama's snout tripped her, and as she was being pitched to the ground, she felt herself being lifted high into the air. She squeezed her eyes shut, stopped screaming, and looked around again. She was still in his arms, yet on the opposite side of the fence a fair distance away from the pen. How had he ever gotten over the fence?

Chaos surrounded her. Everyone was running

toward her and the giant. Her papa was the last one to reach the fence.

She didn't even want to think about her punishment if he discovered what she had hidden in her skirts. She fervently hoped he never found out.

She knew her savior could feel her pet wiggling between them. She finally gathered enough courage to look up at him to see what he was going to do about it.

He looked surprised, and when the piglet let out another squeal, he smiled.

She was so happy he wasn't angry, she smiled back before she could remember to be shy.

One of his friends stepped closer to the fence. "Connor, is everything all right?"

He turned to answer. Brenna stopped him by putting her hand on the side of his face and nudging him back to her again.

She whispered her plea then. He must not have heard her, because he leaned down closer until their foreheads were almost touching.

"Don't tell."

The giant suddenly threw his head back and let out a bellow of laughter. She told him to hush, but that only made him laugh all the more.

He didn't tell on her, though, and once he'd put her back down, she was able to run past her papa before he could grab hold of her.

"Come back here, Brenna."

She pretended she didn't hear him and continued on.

It wasn't until she was safely hidden under the

kitchen table with her new baby sleeping in her lap that she realized she'd forgotten to ask the man to marry her. She wasn't discouraged. She would ask him tomorrow, and if he told her no, she would come up with another plan. One way or another, she meant to catch him and save her papa the trouble.